The Moonglow Sisters

Center Point
Large Print

Also by Lori Wilde and available from
Center Point Large Print:

A Wedding on Bluebird Way

The Moonglow Sisters

A Novel

LORI WILDE

CENTER POINT LARGE PRINT
THORNDIKE, MAINE

This Center Point Large Print edition
is published in the year 2020 by arrangement with
William Morrow, an imprint of HarperCollins Publishers.

The text of this Large Print edition is unabridged.
In other aspects, this book may vary
from the original edition.
Printed in the United States of America
on permanent paper.
Set in 16-point Times New Roman type.

ISBN: 978-1-64358-655-7

The Library of Congress has cataloged this record
under Library of Congress Control Number: 2020934756

To Traci Marsh Burnam, who knows why

CHAPTER ONE

Helen

MEMORY QUILT: Quilt made to remember people and/or an event significant in their lives.

May 17

My Dearest Darling Gia,

As I write this, I sit on the back veranda in my favorite Adirondack chair. Draped across my lap is the triple wedding ring quilt we started for Madison's marriage. Pyewacket lazes at my feet, occasionally batting the seat cushion's dangling tie. I watch the waves break against our stretch of shoreline and recall, in the misty way of old people, how everything fell apart.

It is a familiar spot. I've sat here countless times, inhaling the salt air, listening to the immutable lull of the rising tide, and fingering the raw edges of the unfinished quilt.

But today is different.

I remember too much, and yet, oddly, not enough. How we spent months collecting just the right fabric scraps from bits and pieces of clothing that meant something special to us. But then I forget where the pink seersucker came from. Is it from Shelley's Easter dress, or your mother's apron? Or is it a piece of the table runner from your sixth birthday? A tea party theme, I believe, but it could have been Holly Hobbie. You so adored that doll.

At my age, memory is unreliable, but in the files of my mind, I excavate a few treasures.

I see you flying your kite on the beach for the first time with Mike guiding you, your head thrown back, laughing so hard you shivered. Shelley giggling over her cold bottom as she sat on the old-fashioned ice cream freezer, so it wouldn't walk off the porch as we took turns cranking the handle. Madison getting up early on Easter morning to hide the eggs she'd colored the night before for you and Shelley to hunt. The three of you in harvest season, picking lush, ripe Moonglow pears from our trees, then later, in the kitchen blasting music from the windowsill boom box and singing "Who Let the Dogs Out" at the top of your lungs while we canned pear preserves.

These are the things I miss. Laughter.

Giggles. Singing. You girls lying on a quilt in the backyard underneath the stars, sharing your hopes and dreams. It seemed those lovely summer days would never end.

Sadness fills me now as I look back on what we've lost. Our sense of family. Our closeness. Evaporated like morning sea mist burned off by the sun.

You girls were my salvation in those dark days after your mother's death, but in the end, I lost you three as surely as I lost Beth.

My hand caresses the edges of the unfinished quilt made for a wedding that never took place and my eyes well with tears, but I'm not writing for pity. I made my choices, some smart, some dumb, and I've found peace with how things turned out.

But I do regret what ruined your relationship with your sisters and I hope you will honor my wishes.

This quilt is important. Family is important. You are the heart of us, Gia. When I think of you girls and your personalities, I'm reminded of your beautiful kites. Madison is the solid anchor on the ground, Shelley is the high-flying kite itself, and you, my dear, are the string that keeps the two connected.

I hate to put this burden on your shoulders, but you are the peacemaker and the only one who can mend things. Please, come together. Finish the quilt. Repair the rift. Sew. Heal. Bloom. Grow. This is my last request. All I want in this world is to see the Moonglow sisters happy and whole again.

—With all my abiding love, Grammy

Helen Chapman finished writing the letter, set down her pen, and turned to the white-haired woman sitting beside her.

Darynda Fox had once been a stunning beauty. Even now, in her midseventies, she was still striking. Tall. Fit from daily jogs on the beach and nightly yoga stretches. She possessed patrician cheekbones and piercing blue eyes that took Helen's breath.

Silently, Darynda read the letter and when she looked up, a single tear slid down her cheek. "You should let me call them. You should tell them in person. They have a right to know."

"It's better this way." Restlessly Helen folded the edge of the quilt inward.

"Better for whom? You are putting a lot on Gia's shoulders."

"She's the only one who can do it and you know that."

"I'd accuse you of taking the coward's way out,

but you are the bravest person I've ever known." Darynda reached for Helen's hand and squeezed it tightly.

"They must figure things out for themselves. I can't spoon-feed them. If I could fix what went wrong, I would have done it already."

Darynda held up the letter. "You think a letter is enough to change minds?"

"I'm hoping." Helen crossed her fingers.

"Those girls can be stubborn."

"I know. It's why I'm doing things this way."

"They'd want to be with you during the surgery. They'll feel guilty that they weren't there."

"Maybe a little guilt is what they need to shake them awake. I hate to resort to manipulation, but I've stayed out of it for too long. It seems they can't or won't fix this unless I give them a push."

"What if"—Darynda paused, gulped, lowered her voice—"you don't come out of surgery?"

Helen smiled gently at the woman she'd known for fifty years. "At the very least they must deal with one another to handle my estate."

"And if you make it?"

"Then perhaps the four of us can finish the quilt together."

Darynda was full-on crying now, tears slipping down her face in a steady stream. "I hate cancer."

"C'mon." Helen patted her arm. "Don't cry. You'll stain the letter."

Darynda heaved a heavy sigh. "Oh you, practical as always."

Helen leaned over the quilt to hug her friend, the effort taking all her strength. "Call them when I go into surgery. Not a minute before."

"They'll be so mad at me."

"Tell them it's my wishes."

They'd been going around and around about this since her family physician had given Helen the bad news. Darynda had wanted to call the girls immediately, but Helen knew her granddaughters.

"What if Madison doesn't come?" Darynda fretted.

"She will."

"What if we can't find Shelley?"

"You will."

"Are you sure?"

Helen met Darynda's eyes. "You've never let me down. Not once."

"I wish I had your faith."

"Those girls are all so different, but they have one thing in common."

"What's that?"

"Chapman blood runs through their veins and Moonglow Cove is home. They'll return."

Darynda looked dubious, but said, "I've chosen to believe that you'll pull through and assume you'll be here to whip them into shape."

"I like your optimism." Helen cupped her

friend's cheek. "But just in case it all goes south, you know what to do."

Then she sank back against the Adirondack chair, pulled the quilt to her chin, closed her eyes to the sound of the ocean, and dreamed of three little girls building sandcastles on the beach.

CHAPTER TWO

Gia

STRAIGHT GRAIN: In quilting, the threads running parallel to the selvage in a woven fabric. Straight grain is the most stable with the least amount of stretch.

Townsfolk called them the Moonglow sisters. In part because they'd come to live at the Moonglow Inn, in Moonglow Cove, Texas, at the end of Moonglow Boulevard when Madison was nine; Shelley, six; and little Gia, just three years old.

But there was more to the nickname than locale.

They bore the noble heritage of the town's founding family, Chapman by blood, if not by label. Descending from the town's original forbearers lent them prestige, heft, and mythological clout.

And they were orphans, having lost both mother and father, banding together in a tight little unit, watching after and taking up for one another. Despite the six-year age difference between oldest and youngest, they went everywhere together.

Climbing on that odd bicycle built for three

Grammy Chapman bought for them, they pedaled up and down the seawall for hours. Blond hair blew in the Gulf breezes as their legs pumped in unison. They'd stop for frozen Italian ices at Mario's, waving and smiling to tourists, and feed the seagulls who snatched bread tidbits from their hands and followed them, cawing for more.

They linked arms and skipped along the beach. Shelley, the more adventuresome sister, was always nearest the ocean. Gia, the smallest, stayed in the middle, and Madison, the fierce protector, on the outer side. They fished off Paradise Pier, legs dangling, humming tunes of the day, and bringing their catch home to Grammy, who cooked it up for guests at the old Victorian manor. They flew kites, in three unique colors and designs, swooping and diving, soaring and dancing against the prevailing wind rolling off the Gulf of Mexico.

When they got older, they took beach jobs. Madison, responsible and bossy, was a lifeguard. Gia, easygoing and generous, taught kiteflying lessons. Shelley, fun-loving and harum-scarum, bounced from waitress to souvenir vendor to tour guide at the Seafaring Museum. All three helped at the Moonglow Inn, serving in the B&B as housekeepers, bellhops, and concierges.

They *looked* like moonglow—shimmering, golden-haired, luminous. There was magic to them. A softness. A shining. A warm, gentle light.

They brought smiles to faces, and the town embraced them. Loved them. Grieved when they broke apart on Madison's wedding day.

It was almost like a death in the family. Something constant and enduring suddenly vanished forever.

People whispered, "If it could happen to the Moonglow sisters, what hope is there for the rest of us?"

Indeed, hope seemed quite lost.

After the rift occurred between the sisters, they scattered to the winds. Madison to New York City. Shelley to Costa Rica. Gia to college in San Diego, and then later for a time to Japan to study under an artisan kitemaker, before finally coming home and opening a kite shop kiosk on the Paradise Pier boardwalk.

Now Gia had been back in Moonglow Cove for five months; the time had passed in a blur as she consulted with lawyers, accountants, and real estate agents to get her tiny shop, Tako Kichi, up and running. Tako Kichi was Japanese for "kite crazy" and described Gia's passion perfectly. She loved what she did for a living, but she didn't have a natural head for business and it took all her concentration to get her shop up and flying.

She looked in on Grammy as often as she could, but in all honesty, she'd been too distracted to pay close attention to what was going on in her grandmother's life. On the surface, things seemed much the same. Grammy was maybe a little slower, and the inn looked a bit shabby around the edges, but not enough to raise alarm bells.

Not enough to contact her sisters.

Gia and Madison were on speaking terms, although they didn't talk often. They exchanged an occasional text, but they were both so busy and there *was* that underlying tension. Neither one of them had heard from, or seen, Shelley in five years. She could be dead for all they knew.

With Grammy, Gia had established a weekly routine. Since Mondays were blackout days for the inn, and all the guests left on Sunday, Gia would drop by for breakfast on Grammy's one day off before she opened her kite shop at ten when the boardwalk came to life.

This Monday morning in the middle of May, she strolled up from the beach in her pink bikini and gauzy purple cover-up, climbing the back porch steps and swaying into the kitchen calling, "Hollow, hollow, hollow."

The family greeting was a leftover from when the Moonglow sisters first came to live at the inn and were impressed with the way the wooden floors of the old Victorian vibrated an echo throughout the house; they had repeated *hollow, hollow, hollow* endlessly to one another, and then collapsed into hysterical giggles at the waves of rippling sound.

Silence.

The only sound came from the ticking grandfather clock at the end of the hall.

"Gram?"

Gia moved farther into the kitchen. On the table, wedged between the rooster and hen salt and pepper shakers, she spied a white envelope with her name on it in Grammy's broad handwriting.

Just then the house phone rang, and Gia ambled to the phone docking station on the counter. Saw Darynda's name on the caller ID and answered.

"Gia?" Darynda sounded hesitant and scared. "I'm afraid I have unsettling news."

She caught her breath at the urgency in her grandmother's best friend's voice, and she just *knew* it was serious. "Where is Grammy?"

"Moonglow Cove Memorial."

"What?"

"Brain tumor."

"When?"

"Surgery. Now."

"Did you call—"

"Not yet. I thought I'd leave that to you since I'm not family."

"Okay, I'll handle it. How are you, Darynda?"

"Holding it together," she said, then added in a whisper, "barely."

"On my way."

"No need to rush up here," Darynda said. "It

will be a long surgery. Could you please feed Pyewacket her breakfast? We forgot."

Shocked, clutching the letter to her chest, Gia stumbled to the pantry, found the cat food, and measured out a scoop for the Siamese. She went outside to dump the kibble into the food dish, scoop and all, and dropped onto the steps.

Pyewacket came out from underneath the porch and stretched, before leisurely strolling, tail held high, toward her breakfast.

Gia called Madison, who said she'd be on her way as soon as she wrapped up filming her morning show. Gia tried not to judge her for not dropping everything immediately. Maddie's life was complicated.

Then she wrestled down Shelley. Neither she nor Madison had been in contact with Shelley since *The Incident with Raoul*. And Grammy, although she knew their sister had accepted a barista position at a yoga retreat called Cobalt Soul in a remote part of Costa Rica, hadn't heard from her since.

A Google search and a phone call hooked Gia up to the front desk of Cobalt Soul, where the serene-voiced receptionist told Gia that she would give "Sanpreet" her message when she emerged from her healing session.

Apparently, Shelley had reinvented herself, a new name and all. *Good for her,* Gia thought. Check it off the list. Job done. Sisters notified.

Gia shifted her gaze to the Gulf of Mexico.

The envelope, dampening from the humid sea air, softened in her hands. Raking her bare toe against the weathered, sandy boards of the back steps, Gia blew out her breath through puffed cheeks and turned the envelope over. Her finger twitched to tear open the flap and find out what was inside, but her mind said, *Whoa, hold up.*

What if it was a living will?

Oof. Gia grimaced. She did not want to find *that* on her own. Then again, how could she ignore the letter? There was something in here Grammy wanted her to know.

Her hand trembled. The urge to bury her head in the sand was so strong she could taste it. She couldn't help feeling something irrevocable was about to happen.

Memories spiraled through her head in a string of snapshots. She saw Grammy at the back door, waving them in from the beach on a bright summer day. Her long hair braided and curled on the top of her hair in a bun, wearing a painting smock over her housedress and stocky Doc Marten boots. Sunscreen in her hand. Warning them of sunburns. Darynda standing behind her with a tray of lemonade and iced glasses, a bribe to coax them off the sand.

There was the time Grammy and Darynda took them hiking in the nearby nature preserve. Grammy passing the binoculars over, so they could watch the birds flying in. Blindsided by the spotting of a rare whooping crane. The joyous dance they did, the five of them, arms locked to each other's shoulders, feet kicking sand in a jig.

Movie night in Moonglow Park, lawn chairs placed side by side for Grammy and Darynda, a quilt spread out for the girls. Giggling and sighing over *Fifty First Dates* and dreaming of when they'd get to fall in love.

There was a glorious innocence in those days in the way they thought the future was bright and attainable, so sure of themselves and possibilities. Family, they'd believed, could save you from anything.

"Pyewacket," Gia whispered to the Siamese. "What are we going to do without her?"

The cat, who'd finished her meal, let out a soft meow.

"Got it. Be brave. Just do what needs doing." She tore open the letter and read it, the words pummeling her hard. Hot tears slipped down her face at the sacred mission her beloved grandmother tasked her with. Pyewacket curled into her lap and she scratched the Siamese behind the ears, taking comfort in the cat's small, warm body.

"Oh no," she whispered. "Oh no. This is impossible. Grammy must have been out of her mind when she wrote this. It's got to be the brain tumor. She's not thinking straight. I can't get those two to stay in the same room together, much less finish that cursed quilt."

Pyewacket dug her claws into Gia's bare thigh and kneaded.

"Ouch. Hey there, missy, that hurts." She deposited the cat on the porch and dusted her palms.

The Siamese tossed her haughty head and stalked off.

Breathing so fast she was almost hyper-ventilating, Gia closed her eyes and leaned her back against the porch rail in the same way she'd done as a child, imagining herself growing smaller and smaller until she was the size of a mouse and no one could see her. She could slip between the floorboards, munching on crumbs the B&B guests dropped when they breakfasted on the veranda, and live there happily forever.

Nah, if she were a mouse, Pyewacket would catch and kill her. The cutthroat Siamese hated mice.

The spring ocean breeze chilled her skin. Without opening her eyes, she wrapped her arms more tightly around her chest and told herself to stay small and out of the way. *Don't be a bother to anyone.* If she stayed quiet, then everything would be okay. Grammy would come out of surgery with flying colors. She'd have radiation or chemo or whatever she needed to do, and she'd kick cancer's ass. She'd get well and sort out her sisters and Gia wouldn't have to do any of the heavy lifting.

Gia would move into the inn and take care of her. Gia's roommate, who was also her part-time employee, wouldn't like it, but some things couldn't be helped.

She'd juice vegetables for Grammy and they'd go for long walks on the beach and in the evenings, they would sit on the porch swing, quilting and watching the sunset. Grammy would heal and grow robust and live to see Gia get married and have kids of her own, offering her sage child-rearing advice. She'd die quietly in her sleep at a hundred and one. Everything would work out.

It *had* to.

"Hey, stranger." A jovial male voice broke through her trance.

Gia's eyes flew open to see Grammy's next-door neighbor, Mike Straus, standing on the stone wall separating his property from the Moonglow Inn. In the 1920s, the well-to-do Chapman family had built the Craftsman-style bungalow as caretaker quarters for their grand Victorian manor, but during World War II, the family downsized, sectioning off half an acre of beachfront property and selling the bungalow along with it.

Mike's family had owned the bungalow long before Gia and her sisters came to live in

Moonglow Cove. After his parents retired and moved to Arizona for his father's health, Mike bought the place from them.

Mike was seven years older than Gia, and at thirty was a year older than Madison. He was a master carpenter who built magnificent handcrafted furniture. He'd made the inn's four sturdy white rocking chairs, and the two Adirondack chairs, along with the three-person porch swing. Mike was also the one who'd gotten Gia into kiteflying and he'd been the first one to encourage her to follow her heart and do what she loved for a living, even as others pooh-poohed her interest.

They kept up with each other on social media. However, she hadn't seen him in months. Although Gia came home to visit Grammy every week, since the first of the year, Mike had been out of the country with Habitat for Humanity's Disaster Response program, helping to rebuild houses on a hurricane-devastated Caribbean island.

He was a square-jawed man with ocean-blue eyes and molasses-dark hair that swirled at the crown with an intractable cowlick. His tanned skin contrasted with the rolled-up sleeves of his crisp white shirt, and his heartfelt smile stunned bright in the morning sun.

She caught her breath for a beat, surprised by the quick kick of sexual attraction. What was wrong with her? This was *Mike*. She'd known him for as long as she could remember. Why was she suddenly seeing him in a different light?

"You're back from the Caribbean," she murmured, flabbergasted by the quickening of her pulse.

"Just this minute got home." He suppressed a yawn, then held his arms wide. "Get over here, Short Stack, and give me a hug or I'm gonna pout."

"You don't have to ask me twice. I can't stand pouting."

"I know. That's why I threatened it. You haven't changed. Same little peacemaker." He wriggled his fingers. "Now, bring it in."

She tucked the envelope in the pocket of her purple cover-up and launched herself into his embrace.

Mike wrapped her in a bear hug and swung her around in a circle as if they were still kids. She felt giddy and girlish and warm all over.

He put her down, stepped back, and shook his head. Beamed at her with his big old Texas-sized grin. "How have *you* been?"

"Great. Well . . . except for . . ." She waved a hand, tears pushing against the back of her eyes again at the thought of Grammy. "You?"

"Except for what?" He frowned in concern. "Is something wrong?"

"I don't . . . I can't . . ." Aww damn, here came the waterworks again.

"What's wrong?" His hand went to her forearm, comforting and solid. "What's happened?"

Dabbing at her eyes, she told him about Grammy.

He shoved his hair back with a palm. "Damn, Gia, that sucks hard. I'm so sorry. If there is anything I can do, anything at all, you say the word."

"Thanks." She tried for a smile, failed.

"Do you need another hug?"

"Please." She fell against him and he gathered her close. His shirt smelled like fresh laundry, his skin like sunshine, and beneath that, a rich, more masculine scent.

He smelled good. Too good. It was weird how good he smelled and how much she liked it.

"Hey, how's your girlfriend?"

He winced. "We broke up."

"I'm sorry." Except she wasn't. Did that make her a bad person? And why did the thought of Mike being girlfriendless send a tingle through her body?

"Don't be. It wasn't right. We mixed like ketchup and caviar."

"Oof."

"She was the caviar, by the way."

"I suspected." Gia grinned at him. "Salty as fish eggs?"

"Now that you put it that way . . ." His grin widened. "Kinda. A little salt goes a long way."

"You need a potato woman. Nothing goes better with ketchup than french fries. Sweet and tangy. The perfect condiment."

"I'll put that at the top of my dating profile. Desperately seeking potato woman."

"Don't you dare tell your dates *that*. Every woman wants to be treated like she's caviar, even if she is a spud at heart."

"What about you?" Was it her imagination or did his voice lower? And why was he staring at her mouth? "Do *you* like to be treated as if you were caviar?"

Gia gulped, licked her lips, felt her pulse notch up. Was he flirting with her? Or just trying to take her mind off Grammy? "Well, not *me,* of course. I'm no caviar. French fries are my favorite food."

"With *lots* of ketchup as I recall."

Holy smokes, he *was* flirting. She wasn't sure how she felt about that. It was a huge paradigm shift. "You're out of touch, Straus. Lately, I've taken to dunking my fries in wasabi."

"You've gone rogue," he said. "I blame Japan. Stick around. We'll soon get you back in a Moonglow state of mind."

"I'm not going anywhere."

They stared at each other and goose bumps zipped up Gia's arms.

"Your sisters?" he asked. "Are they coming home?"

"Madison's on her way. Shelley . . ." Gia shrugged. "Who knows?"

"How are you holding up?" His gentle tone and tender eyes unraveled her.

To keep from tearing up again, she started chattering. "I'm good. Things were going really well for me until this. The kite store is up and running. I have an apartment downtown but took on a roommate to afford it . . . but this changes everything. I should move back home and help Grammy recover."

"Your grammy wouldn't want you to give up your life for her. Not even to keep peace between your sisters. Besides, she's got Darynda."

"Darynda's not family."

"She and your grandmother have been best friends for fifty years." Mike put a palm over his mouth to stifle another yawn. "Kinda the same."

"I've spent so many years trying to smooth things over, I don't know if I can stop."

He put both hands on her shoulders, looked her square in the eyes. "You can't please everyone, Gia. At some point you have to please yourself or your life will never be your own."

Uncomfortable with his chiding look and the idea of putting her needs before her family, Gia slapped her palm against her forehead. "Look at me prattling on. You're exhausted. I'm so rude."

"You? Rude? Never. That's Madison's territory." He chuckled.

"Maddie's not rude, she's just—"

"Controlling?"

"She has high standards." Uneasy at talking about Maddie behind her back, Gia shifted her weight.

"I guess it works for her. High standards got Madison on TV. Nothing gets past your big sister."

"Except the past."

"So what will happen when she and Shelley—"

"Who knows?" Gia shrugged. "I try not to think about them if I can help it. Hurts too much."

"About your grandmother . . ." His eyes overflowed with sympathy. "This is serious stuff."

"She *will* make it."

"If you have anything to say about it, I'm sure she will." He nodded, but the expression on his face said he thought Gia was fooling herself. "I meant what I said, Short Stack. Not to sound like a *Toy Story* theme song or anything, but you've got a friend in me. If you need anything, anything at all, just call and I'll be there."

CHAPTER THREE

Madison

BIAS: The bias grain runs on a forty-five-degree angle to the selvages and has ample amounts of stretch, so it is less stable than the lengthwise and crosswise grain.

Get to Grammy, fix this thing. Madison Clark massaged her throbbing temple. *Don't get a migraine, dammit. Don't get a migraine.*

She sat in the back of the town car staring out the window as they oozed down the newly repaved highway heading southwest from Houston to Moonglow Cove and trying not to spin worst-case scenarios. People underwent brain surgery every day and survived. Grammy was a tough old bird, she'd pull through.

But Madison couldn't shake the forbidding sense that her life was about to change in a fundamental way.

The gloominess had been creeping up on her for months. Lately, it had even invaded her job as she introduced guests, faked smiles, injected her voice with false enthusiasm; pasting and gluing and stapling, creating crafts, making beautiful spaces, coaching viewers on how to pretty up their lives.

As if she had all the answers. Despite having achieved the lofty dream she'd fought so hard to win. Despite having built an orderly, controlled, and glamorous life. It seemed she was standing outside herself from a great distance and looking down at her world, absolutely numb.

Absentmindedly, she fingered the crystal star necklace at her throat. Sighed a bone-deep sigh of loss and longing.

More sorrow was in store. No escaping.

Madison unzipped her purse and reached inside for her cell phone to text Gia for an update on Grammy. Her fingers brushed against *the* piece of paper and her heart skipped a beat. Quickly, she stuffed it to the bottom of her purse. She should have destroyed the paper, but she couldn't bring herself to let go.

Not yet.

Her fingers kept searching for the phone, but she found instead the bottle of Xanax her doctor prescribed after her first panic attack.

She opened the bottle; shook out one pill, stared at it, then for good measure, shook out another. The last thing she needed was another panic attack. She uncapped her water bottle and popped the pills into her mouth.

Madison caught sight of herself in the rearview mirror. Eyes, hollowed and stark, stared back at her.

"Don't judge," she muttered and swallowed the Xanax. "I gotta deal with Shelley."

"You say something, miss?" The bulky middle-aged driver met her gaze in the mirror. He smelled of cheap cologne and expensive salami, and he had a loose, lived-in face and a foreign accent she couldn't quite place.

Ukrainian maybe?

"No." She shook her head and posted up her automatic, camera-ready smile. *Ta-da.*

"This is Moonglow Bridge." He motioned as the tires hit the metal bridge.

"I grew up here."

"You lucky. Prettiest town on Texas coast."

"Yes," she murmured, "it is."

Down the hill and around the first curve and they hit Moonglow Boulevard. Stately houses built during the early 1900s graced the right side of the road; the beach and seawall, alive with tourists, shops, and restaurants, were on the left.

Madison sipped water and watched the ocean gliding past like a ponderous dream, too much blue, long and endless. She'd forgotten how bright it was here. The beach stretched full of umbrellas, kites, and bodies. Light and casual and seriously, much too happy.

She didn't trust happiness.

It faded.

Always.

The beautiful old Victorian where she and her sisters once lived with Grammy Chapman lay straight ahead. Built by their two-times-great-grandfather, Josiah Chapman, it stood out among the other buildings lining the beach. It was one of the few historical homes along the waterfront that had survived Hurricane Allen in 1980.

The three-story B&B looked like something from a fairy tale—all gingerbread trim, towers, turrets, dormers, and wraparound porches. Over the decades, five generations of Chapmans had painted it many shades and hues. Today, the color was a gentle aqua with violet shutters and white porch rails and columns. She and her sisters had picked out those colors, painted the house together.

Back when things were good.

A small orchard of Moonglow pear trees bloomed white in the side yard. Butter-yellow daffodils proliferated around the base of the pear trees. And in the tidy flower beds, irises and hydrangeas thrived, scenting the air with their sweet perfume.

Grammy adored those pear trees, and every fall she made preserves in her commercial kitchen. To supplement her B&B income, she packaged and sold the preserves online and through local vendors.

Madison hadn't been home since Christmas. Almost half a year since Grammy, smelling of cinnamon and Shalimar, had wrapped Madison in her arms and told her how much she loved her. An erratic five months of giddy ups and sharp downs. Until now, she hadn't realized the depth of her homesickness and she ached to go inside the house.

"Wait, stop!"

Startled, the chauffeur trod the brakes. "What's the problem?"

A topless, doors-off Jeep blasted the horn behind them. The angry frat boy driver whipped around the town car, thrusting a proud middle finger skyward as he sped by.

The chauffeur eased the car over. "You sick?"

"No, no." Madison waved away his concern. What was wrong with her? She had a mission. *Get to Grammy. Fix this thing.* No reason to stop, except . . . "Never mind. Just go. Please keep going."

He made a chuffing noise and merged back into the flow of traffic.

She peered over her shoulder at the Moonglow Inn. Nostalgia took Madison's hand and led her down memory lane.

In her mind's eye, she saw the hopscotch squares they'd drawn on the sidewalk outside the white picket fence that surrounded the house. Shelley had been the hopscotch queen, athletic and leggy, but Madison kept an eye on her. Shelley cheated. Which, Shelley claimed, was Madison's fault because she made too many impossible-to-keep rules.

From the corner of her eye, she glimpsed plump

Pyewacket, curled on the front porch, swishing her tail. She remembered when Gia brought the skinny, bedraggled kitten home from the animal shelter, thirteen and full of angst for all creatures in trouble.

"Grammy," Gia declared. "We *hafta* keep her."

Madison pressed her fingertips to the window and watched until the house was out of sight.

At four P.M. on the dot, the town car deposited her and her luggage at the emergency room entrance outside Moonglow Cove Memorial Hospital.

She was here. Goal in sight. At least the get-to-Grammy part. The fix-this-thing part was more complicated.

Head throbbing, heart sinking, Madison stared at the red neon Emergency sign over the door. She felt the flutter of panic stir at the bottom of her spine and inch up vertebra by vertebra.

C'mon, Xanax, kick in.

She curled her fingernails into her palms and forced herself to slow her breathing, pulled in a lungful of hospital antiseptic mingled with fragrant ocean air.

The pneumatic doors opened and Darynda walked out, arms wrapped tightly around her chest as if she were chilled. Her snow-white hair was pulled back into her signature low chignon, elegant as the woman herself. She wore pleated gray slacks, a soft purple blouse and matching sweater, and silver kitten heels. No one would ever guess where she'd come from originally.

Darynda Fox was a self-described sand hill tacky, a Texas term for a girl who'd grown up poor in the sand hills of West Texas. She was the daughter of a cowhand, raised riding and roping and punching cattle. She was a crack shot with a rifle, and sometimes, Grammy affectionately called her Annie Oakley. Her vivid blue eyes shone like beacons in her wrinkled face, and her gaze latched tight to Madison's. Without a word, she held her arms wide for an embrace.

Madison hesitated.

She and Darynda had never been buddy-buddy, but she was Grammy's best friend in the entire world and she had taken up the slack after . . . well, after everything zoomed to hell in a wicker handbasket.

Madison steeled herself and moved in for the hug, catching the light honeysuckle scent of Darynda's perfume. Quick squeeze and she was out of the greeting, stepping back, fetching another made-for-TV smile.

Willowy, graceful, Darynda dropped her arms. "It's so wonderful to have you home, Maddie."

"Thanks," Madison mumbled, not knowing what else to say, and hitched her purse up on her shoulder. She was out of place on the hospital sidewalk of the coastal beach town in her white

Ralph Lauren silk suit and Manolo Blahniks, her Louis Vuitton carry-on beside her. She'd come straight from the set of *Madison's Mark* without going home to change, instead sending her assistant to her apartment to pack her bag while she wrapped up shooting.

Luckily, the morning show would go on summer hiatus in two weeks, and until then, her producer had coaxed a popular, retired talk-show host to fill in for her. But if things went well with Grammy's surgery, Madison hoped to return to New York by next week at the latest.

And if things don't go well?

Madison moistened her lips. She'd cross that bridge when she came to it. She met Darynda's gaze. "Grammy?"

"Still in surgery."

Alarm sent fresh pounding through her head. "It's been hours!"

"Eight and counting. It could go even longer." Darynda's voice turned husky and tears shimmered in her sharp blue eyes.

"What happened?"

"About three weeks ago, Helen started having dizzy spells, and she fell a few times. I insisted she go to the doctor. She's got brain cancer. Grade IV glioblastoma."

Fear spread heat throughout Madison's body. She didn't know what that meant, but it sounded bad. "What's her prognosis?"

Darynda briefly closed her eyes, wobbled her head. "Not good."

"She'll make it."

Darynda didn't respond.

"She *will* make it." Madison injected steel into her tone.

"I don't pussyfoot around," Darynda said, in a let's-get-something-straight voice. "The cancer will kill her, but the surgery and radiation will give her time."

Madison gasped. The truth, and Darynda's blunt delivery, was a stake through her heart. Too much to process, even with Xanax. "But she's *fine*. She jogs three miles a day. She runs a B&B at seventy-six. She's iron woman."

"Madison"—Darynda pulled no punches—"those days are over."

She did not run from responsibility, or the truth. If Grammy was dying, then she was dying. That's what her mind said, anyway. Her heart rolled over, kicked and screamed, *She's wrong, Grammy's strong, she's not going anywhere*.

"How long does she have?"

"Fifteen months, give or take."

Horrified, Madison palmed her mouth. "Why didn't she call us before now?"

"She didn't want you to worry. There were tests and consultations."

"We've lost time with her." Madison glared at Darynda. "Why didn't *you* call us?"

"I had to honor her wishes. This is Helen's life. She's in control. Not you."

Not you. A judgment. Criticism. Who was Darynda to issue edicts?

Get to Grammy. Fix this. The words were part of the pounding in her brain, merging with the throb of the migraine.

"Dammit, Darynda." Madison smacked her fist into her open palm. "You know this isn't right."

"No, it's not." Her eyes and tone softened, and Darynda looked as if she wanted to touch her.

Madison stepped back, bottom lip trembling. She bit down hard to keep from crying. She would *not* break down. "Where's Gia?"

"In the waiting room."

"Shelley?"

Darynda shook her head.

"Shelley's not coming?" Madison blew out her breath, relieved, yet feeling strangely like a boxer who'd geared up for a much-touted grudge match only to learn her opponent was a no-show.

"We don't know. Gia didn't speak to her directly. She left a message at the last place where your grandmother knew Shelley was staying, but she hasn't called back."

Madison snapped her mouth closed before she said something regrettable. *Don't stir that pot.*

"What if Shelley doesn't come?" Madison's head hammered so hard it was all she could do to keep her eyes open.

"Give her time, Madison."

"She's had five years."

Darynda angled her head toward the emergency room doors. "Let's go inside."

"I can't believe this." Madison brought an index finger to her mouth and almost chewed her fingernail.

When she and her sisters first came to live in Moonglow Cove with Grammy, she'd chewed all ten fingernails to the quick. Even though the sunlight fueled her migraine, she wasn't ready to go into the hospital. Not just yet. She needed time to collect herself before she saw Gia. Maddie was the oldest. The pacesetter.

"Are you all right?" Darynda put a hand to Madison's forearm. "You're shaking."

"Just a headache." Madison itched to pull away but didn't.

"Little wonder. Have you eaten?"

Food was the last thing on her mind and she didn't need Darynda turning maternal. "I'm fine."

"You need to eat something."

Past the black drumming in her head, she stared at Darynda. "When did *you* last eat?" Her words came out too harsh, but apologizing would draw attention to her rudeness.

Darynda dropped her hand to her side and tucked her lips around her teeth. "I see your point."

A man shuffled outside, lounged against the building, and lit up a cigarette. He blew a cloud of smoke.

Madison wrinkled her nose, stifled a cough.

"We should go inside." Darynda stuck out a hand as if to usher her. But Madison hardened her scowl and Darynda quickly dropped her hand.

Why was she being so touchy? *It's the headache,* her mind offered as an excuse. But honestly, was it? She could lay her irritability at the feet of what caused the migraines.

Family tension.

Secrets.

Lies.

Self-deception.

"I'm scared," Madison blurted, startling herself with the truth.

"It'll be okay," Darynda soothed.

"Will it?"

"It *can* be okay," Darynda corrected, but underneath the steel of her conviction, Madison heard a catch in her voice. "*If* you can forgive."

Darynda made it sound so simple. As if there wasn't a stone wall entombing Madison's heart, as if everyone she'd ever loved hadn't betrayed her. Madison put a hand to her belly. She thought of the paper in her purse and let out a soft sigh. Sometimes, no matter how badly you wanted to let go, you simply couldn't.

The wheels of her suitcase clattered as she

followed Darynda through the hospital to the elevators. People turned to stare and whisper as she went past. Madison didn't know if it was because of the noisy luggage wheels or if people recognized her from TV. In New York, where celebrity sightings were an everyday occurrence, she didn't worry much about being approached by fans.

But this was Moonglow Cove. As they waited for the elevator, two thirtysomethings, giggling like teenagers, sidled over, pen and notebook in hand.

"May we get your autograph?" drawled the boldest one, dressed in hospital scrubs. She wore an ID badge twisted backward so Madison couldn't see her name. "We watch your show every morning and we're your number one fans!"

"Number one fans," the other woman repeated.

Ahh, the price of fame. Madison heard Grammy's laughter in her head. *Suck it up, buttercup. You wanted this.*

Soldiering past the migraine, Madison turned "on." Shifting into her celebrity persona, she took the pen and notepad they offered. "Thank you so much for watching. I appreciate you more than you can know. Who should I make it out to?"

"May June," the woman said, turning her badge around so she could read it. May June Barton, certified nursing assistant. She was tall and stocky and had a tattoo on her wrist that said

House Boss, the name of Madison's old YouTube show.

Holy crap. In her head, she flashed to Kathy Bates in *Misery*, spouting *I am your number one fan* as she crippled James Caan with a sledgehammer.

Then she heard Shelley's witty voice in her mind whisper, *Stalker adjacent*. Did Shelley still love the word *adjacent?*

May June chattered like a spider monkey. "The hospital said I was born at eleven fifty-nine P.M. on May thirty-first, but my daddy's watch said it was midnight, June first, and my daddy, who never admits he's wrong, insisted his watch was right and the hospital screwed up. Hence the double name." May June lowered her voice to a whisper. "My mama always gives me a secret present on May thirty-first, before my June first birthday party."

"How creative of your parents," Madison said. "And you'll be having a birthday soon. Congrats."

"Creativity runs in our family. That's why we love the Create It Yourself Network," she said. "And we love your show most of all."

"I love the network too," said the second woman, dressed in various shades of pink from head to toe, including a mauve beret, a blush-colored blouse, a Barbie DreamHouse–pink miniskirt, and bubble-gum-colored pumps. "Especially your show. The program on year-round door wreaths literally changed my life." Pinky clasped her hands together in front of her heart. "I mean totally changed . . . My. Life."

"Um . . . you're so welcome. I'm glad you enjoyed it."

Pinky twirled her finger at the notebook May June had given Madison. "Could you just tear a page out of her book and sign it for me, too?"

Madison almost wrote to "Pinky" but stopped herself in the nick of time. "What's your name?"

"Blenda."

"My goodness. What another brilliantly creative name. It's no wonder you two are such good friends," Madison flattered.

"Blenda's not as creative as May June. My dad's named Brent and my mom is Glenda. Mash 'em together and you get Blenda. Like in a blender." She giggled.

"Imagine if your dad's name had been Spike," Madison said.

May June's eyes got wide, and she poked Blenda in the ribs with her elbow with a loud laugh. "Oh, oh, you'd be Splenda!"

"Aren't you just the wittiest thing!" Pinky . . . Blenda . . . enthused, clutching the autographed paper to her chest.

"I'm glad you ladies got to meet Madison," Darynda intervened. "But we have a family member upstairs we need to check on. If you'll excuse us . . ."

"Are you her manager?" May June stepped across the threshold of the elevator to keep the door from closing as Madison and Darynda got in.

"No," Darynda said. "Just a family friend. I'm sure you ladies understand that Madison needs her—"

"Who's sick?" Blenda asked. "Is it one of your sisters?"

May June splayed her hand over her chest. "Is it Shelley? Is she back? Did you guys make up? Does she have some terrible disease?"

"Don't tell me it's Gia!" Blenda did the prayer hands again. "I'd planned to hire her to teach kiteflying for my son's fifth birthday party next month."

Startled, Madison tossed Darynda a how-do-they-know-this-stuff expression.

Darynda shrugged. "Small-town gossip."

"*We're* not gossips," May June said, as the elevator door bumped her in the butt and then retracted. "We won't tell a soul. Promise."

"It's my grandmother," Madison said. "She's got brain cancer, and she's dying. Happy now?"

That wiped the salacious look right off their faces; they mumbled apologies and words of sympathy and May June got out of the way fast, and Blenda did prayer hands and bowed as the elevator door shut tight.

Madison sank against the wall, closed her eyes.

"I don't think the snark earned you any brownie points with your number one fans." Darynda punched the elevator button for the third floor.

"Not even sympathy points for a dying grandmother?" Madison pried one eye open.

"You embarrassed them."

"If the shoe fits . . ."

Darynda shook her head and murmured in a disappointed voice, "You know, Madison, sometimes you remind me exactly of your mother."

CHAPTER FOUR

Gia

UNBALANCED BORDERS: Borders of different widths resulting in an asymmetrical look.

In the packed waiting room, Gia sat in a corner chair mindlessly playing Candy Crush on her cell phone. Her vision blurred by tears and memories, she didn't really see the vivid candies dropping in columns.

After sitting in silence for hours like some noble monk, Darynda had gone to stretch her legs, leaving Gia alone to fret.

Grammy's letter, spelling out Gia's monumental task, was still tucked into the cover-up that she'd tossed over the loose, sleeveless, white cotton shift dress printed with flower bouquets she'd changed into at the inn. Not having enough room in her small apartment, she still kept the clothes she had before college stuffed into the dresser in the bedroom that she and her sisters had once shared.

Finish the quilt. Repair the rift.

Gia scratched her cheek as she one-handed the on-screen jelly beans. *Dear Grammy, thanks so much for Mission: Impossible.* Immediately, she felt ashamed for thinking that way.

Her fingers flew over the tiny keyboard, manipulating the falling candies and feeling like a female David facing two Goliaths. *Flying pigs.* How would she get her sisters to finish the quilt, much less mend the family?

"I'm not Wonder Woman," she mumbled, wishing she had some candy right now. Pure junk. Laffy Taffy or Skittles or Starburst. She needed a sugar rush.

Gia lost the game, tossed her phone in her tote, and looked up.

Madison, with Darynda trailing behind her like a ghost, looked chic and smart in her white designer suit and contrasting black silk blouse. She marched right across the waiting room. As always, tough, smart, and in control; her spine touch-me-not straight.

Joy eclipsed fear. Forgiveness brushed aside hurt. Love crowded out anger.

"Maddie!" Gia squealed, launching herself off the chair and running to her big sister with her arms outstretched.

Madison's hug was perfunctory, an obligation, like Memorial Day visits to the cemetery of long-dead relatives whose faces you couldn't recall. She took a moment to melt into Gia's embrace. But the stubborn little sister she was, Gia held on, until she felt Maddie's stiff limbs loosen and heard her sigh against Gia's hair.

"Maddie."

“Shh, s’okay.”

She squeezed her sister like the scared three-year-old she’d been their first night at Moonglow Inn when she crawled into Maddie’s bed for comfort.

“I can’t believe—”

“I’m here. I’ll fix this.”

Those words that had once reassured her now sounded arthritic and impotent. Madison was not stronger than cancer.

Gia pulled back and peered into her sister’s face. “You look wiped out.”

Madison kneaded her temple. “And you’re wearing my dress.”

“Oops, sorry; I didn’t know it was yours. I’d dropped by the inn for my Monday morning breakfast with Grammy when Darynda called and told me what was happening. I was wearing a bikini and grabbed the first thing in the dresser. Should I go home and change?”

“No, of course not.”

“But you brought it up, so it must be eating at you.”

“I shouldn’t have brought it up. Petty of me, I know, but you and Shelley were always ransacking my closet.”

“That’s because you had the best stuff.” Gia fished out her most cajoling grin. “You have such good taste.”

Madison snorted.

Flattery would not work.

Her sister moved her hand from her temple to her chin, the gold bracelet at her wrist catching the sunlight filtering through the blinds. Twenty-four karat, no doubt. No more gold-plated for Madison. Not since she hit the big time.

Can you blame her? She worked her butt off to get to the top.

Gia pulled the corner of her bottom lip up between her teeth and fingered the woven bracelet at her wrist. It was made from strands of colored strings braided together. Years ago, she and Madison and Shelley had made matching bracelets from a kit—a celebration of their sisterhood—and they'd vowed never to take them off.

Only Gia had kept her promise. Madison had symbolically burned her bracelet after *The Incident with Raoul* while Shelley had flung hers into the ocean.

Their sisterhood irrevocably broken.

Except on Gia's wrist.

Gia gulped. Regret tasted like burnt pennies in her mouth, and her throat clotted thick with the salty taste of grief. Was she the lone idiot for holding on to her bracelet? Or was she, like Grammy claimed in her letter, the only one who could rebuild what they'd lost?

Peacemaker.

Guilty as charged, but not happy about it.

She'd much rather be a warrior like Madison or a swashbuckler like Shelley. Peacemaker. Boring as white cotton panties.

Madison's gaze tracked Gia's movements to her wrist, but her expression didn't change. Did she remember the significance of the bracelet? "Have you heard from Shelley?"

Shelley.

The name fell from Madison's lips like hailstones pinging the earth.

That pissed Gia off. She wasn't quick to anger, but dammit, Grammy was in surgery for brain cancer and Maddie still clung to that stupid grudge.

Get out the slingshot, Davida. Find some rocks. Time to shine.

"We need to talk—"

Madison held up a palm. "Not here. Not now."

Gia gritted her teeth. Her sister's anger was justified. Shelley *had* screwed her over. But five freaking years had passed. Maddie lived an amazing life *because* of what Shelley had done. It was time she got over herself.

But telling off her big sister wasn't easy. "I haven't heard from Shell," Gia murmured.

"Typical," Maddie muttered.

"You've got to stop—"

Again, with the damn stop sign palm, Madison silenced Gia before she got started. Gia curled her hands into fists.

Maddie closed her eyes, rubbed her temple. Her skin blanched white.

"Do you have a migraine?" Gia asked.

Madison opened her eyes and nodded. "Travel . . . stress . . ."

"C'mon, sit down." Sympathetic, she took Madison's hand and guided her to the chair Gia had vacated. "I'll fetch coffee and aspirin."

For the first time since coming into the waiting room, Madison smiled. Worn and wan, but the smile counted. "How did you know?"

"You carry all your tension in your head. You always have. Me? I'm a gut girl. Tummy aches." Like the one she had now. Gia rummaged in her purse, found the packet of aspirins she carried with her—never knew when she'd find someone in need—and passed the pills to her sister. "You think too much."

"Curse of the oldest."

Gia turned to Darynda. "Would you like coffee?"

"If I drink coffee this late, I can't sleep a wink." Darynda shook her head and sank down on the couch where she'd been sitting before she'd gone outside to stretch her legs. "Not that I imagine I'll get much sleep tonight." She took material from her tote bag and started hand sewing a quilt square.

Gia went to the coffee station in the corner of the waiting room and poured coffee for them both. Black for Maddie, creamy and sweet for herself.

"Thanks." Madison took the coffee and Gia sat beside her and for a moment, things were nice.

Sighing out loud, Madison cradled the paper cup in her hands, leaned her head against the wall, and shut her eyes.

Maddie was such a force of nature when she was in motion, but resting, she looked utterly worn out. Her face was far too pale and there were long-standing dark shadows beneath her eyes.

This was more than just Grammy. Something else ate at her oldest sister and had for some time.

Gia's heart lurched. She hadn't seen Madison since Christmas. They had exchanged polite chitchat and token gifts but shared nothing deep. Nothing meaningful. And they had said absolutely nothing about Shelley. Their middle sister's absence was the invisible elephant in the room, unseen but there all the same.

When they were children, she and Madison often teamed up against Shelley. Gia had adored her oldest sister. Not that she didn't adore Shelley as well, but Shelley was closer in age. That closeness created squabbles and sibling rivalry.

Madison and Gia never had a fight. That is until *The Incident with Raoul* and the wedding gone awry.

RIP, sisterhood.

Gia fiddled with her bracelet and wished for a fidget spinner.

A door leading to the surgical suite opened. Every head in the waiting area swiveled in that direction and people sat up straighter in their chairs.

A weary-looking woman in scrubs, lab coat, surgical cap, and mask dangling around her neck shambled into the waiting area, paper shoe covers on her feet. “Chapman family?”

Simultaneously, Madison, Gia, and Darynda jumped to their feet. Madison squared her shoulders. Darynda dropped the quilt square into her tote bag. Gia interlaced her fingers and clasped her hands over her heart.

“Please, follow me into the conference room.” The woman nodded.

Darynda plunked back down.

“What are you doing?” Madison asked.

“You girls go on. I’m not fami—”

Gia reached for her hand. “C’mon, Darynda, you *are* family.”

A hopeful smile twitched at Darynda’s mouth. Her lips were lined in mauve pencil, but she’d chewed off the top layer of her lipstick. She shot an uncertain glance at Madison.

With a half-hearted lift of one shoulder and a brief nod, Madison turned and followed the doctor into a small room with two couches, a coffee table, and several boxes of tissues.

Darynda picked up her tote, clutching it with both hands as if it were her lifeline. Gia settled an arm around Darynda's shoulder and guided her after Madison.

"Please have a seat." Looking somber, the woman directed them to the couches.

They settled in.

Madison was on the corner closest to the coffee table where the doctor perched, her knees cocked as if ready to run for an emergency at a moment's notice. Gia sat beside her sister. Hesitating, Darynda slid down next to Gia.

"I'm Dr. Hollingway. Your grandmother's neurosurgeon." She shook their hands, and they all murmured hellos and nice-to-meet-yous, which seemed both silly and inadequate in the context—civil, polite, and utterly worthless. Then the doctor launched into the details of the nine-hour surgery.

Gia fixated on Dr. Hollingway's feet, noticed specks of blood on her shoe covers and the hem of her scrubs. Grammy's blood? Her gut reeled, and she wished she hadn't drunk that coffee without something in her stomach.

The doctor crossed her legs. "Your grandmother is a fighter. Her resilience will go a long way in her recovery."

Darynda made a small sound, a tiny, tight *eep* like a hiccup. Gia reached over to take her hand and Darynda clung to her like a tether.

Dr. Hollingway cleared her throat. She directed her gaze straight at Madison.

"Yes?" Maddie's voice sounded strong, but Gia could detect a faint tremor. Madison fiddled with the crystal necklace at her throat, rubbing it like a talisman.

"I was able to resect the entire tumor."

"That's good news, right?"

"It is excellent news. But—"

"But what?"

Gia wanted to yell at Madison and tell her if she'd just shut up for half a second, and let the doctor finish, they'd find out faster.

"With complex brain surgery we expect complications—"

"Such as?" Madison leaned forward as if getting closer would pull the information from the doctor faster.

The doctor ticked off the points on her fingers as she spoke. "Swelling of the brain."

"Oh dear," Darynda exclaimed and sagged against Gia.

"Brain swelling is . . ." Dr. Hollingway held her hands parallel in front of her, palms cupped as if cradling a human brain. "Part and parcel of brain surgery. So please, don't get overly alarmed."

Gia rubbed her hand up and down Darynda's back to soothe herself as much as the older woman. Darynda was trembling. So was Gia.

"Continue." Madison's gaze never left the doctor's face.

"Because of the swelling, we've put her in a

medically induced coma. Brain surgery is a lot for the human body to cope with and recovery takes time. When she regains consciousness, we need to watch out for complications—"

"Such as?" Madison tapped a fingernail on the couch arm.

"Weakness, dizzy spells, poor balance, seizures."

"She had those symptoms before the surgery," Darynda said.

Madison shot Darynda the side eye. "She had seizures?"

"Once. A big one. At Walmart. There was this flashing sign—"

"Why didn't you tell us? Why didn't you call *me?*" Madison's voice sounded like gravel dragged across concrete.

Darynda seemed to shrink into the couch. "Helen asked me not to."

Madison pursed her lips, narrowed her eyes. She looked as if she had gone Marie Kondo on her closet, sorting things into a "keep" or "discard" pile based on how much joy the items brought her and Darynda had fallen solidly in the discard pile. Gia kept quiet for fear of joining Darynda in the reject heap.

Madison whipped her gaze back to the doctor. "Survival rates?"

"From the surgery itself or the cancer?" The doctor steepled her fingertips, studying Madison with cool eyes. She was not afraid of ending up in any discard pile.

"Both."

"Her heart is in excellent shape, and she has a ninety percent chance of recovering from the surgery."

"And the cancer?"

"Talk to her oncologist about that," Dr. Hollingway deferred. "But I can share that resecting the tumor has bought her extra time."

"She could live for years, right?" Gia's knee bumped up and down in a nervous jerking of its own accord. "If we got her on a healthy diet and juiced vegetables and gave her supplements and fed her probiotics. There was a woman on YouTube who—"

"Anecdotal."

"What does that mean?" Gia asked.

"There's no proof that juicing cures cancer."

"But we could try, right? It's something." Gia's knee bounced higher, the muscles in her leg drawn tight.

"It won't hurt," the doctor conceded. "But I caution you against getting your hopes up."

"That's what hopes are for, right? To give you strength when all seems lost—"

"There's hope . . ." Dr. Hollingway's voice softened, but the look in her eyes said it all. She was a surgeon. She cut. Bedside manners weren't her jam. "And there is delusion."

"So the cancer will kill her." Madison's face was flint.

Dr. Hollingway's lips pulled taut. "Talk to her oncologist." She took three business cards from her lab coat, passed them out. "If anything comes up concerning her surgery, please call my office."

"When can we see her?" Darynda asked.

"She's in the postanesthesia recovery unit and she'll be there overnight. The nurses are at her bedside constantly. You'd only be in the way. You can visit her in the morning when they take her up to the neuro intensive care unit. There's nothing more you can do tonight except go home and take care of yourselves. I know she'd want that." The doctor got to her feet.

They did too.

Madison shook the doctor's extended hand. "We appreciate what you've done for our grandmother."

"Thank you," Darynda said.

"We're so glad you're in our corner." Gia made a mental note to send the doctor and her staff a thank-you fruit basket.

"You're most welcome." The doctor nodded and swept out a side exit, leaving them to go out the way they'd come in.

Madison opened the door and ushered them ahead of her; Gia went first but stopped dead in her tracks.

There, in the middle of the waiting room,

dressed head to toe in gossamer white, shouldering a raggedy backpack, and sporting beat-up Birkenstocks, stood a woman Gia barely recognized.

Waist-length blond hair frizzed around her face, her cheeks hollowed, her limbs way too thin, her eyes glazed and spaced out, as if she'd just jolted wide awake from a long, dreamless sleep.

She looked lost in a fundamental way. As if she no longer had an internal compass and no way to get her bearings.

It was Shelley.

CHAPTER FIVE

Shelley

TRIAD: Any three colors equally spaced on the color wheel, one of which usually takes precedence in a color scheme.

Does anyone have two hundred dollars?" Shelley mumbled, the bedrock of her shame as hard and unyielding as marble. This was not the triumphant return she'd dreamed of for five long years. "I need to pay the taxi."

Gia's gaze jumped from Shelley to Madison.

"Seriously?" Madison sneered.

Donning emotional armor, Shelley drew herself up tall underneath Madison's withering gaze. Height. The one advantage she had over her older sister. Even if it *was* only an inch. "The driver is waiting."

"Why didn't you take an Uber?" Maddie scolded. "It'd have been cheaper."

"Complicated story." Yeah, like she didn't even have a cell phone or credit card, much less an Uber account.

Maddie rolled her eyes hard. "With you, isn't it always?"

"Are you going to give me the money or not?"

"I've got fifty dollars." Gia dug in her purse. "Can you chip in, Darynda?"

"I'll handle it." Madison gritted her teeth. "Where's the driver?"

Shelley hung her head. "He's at the emergency room entrance."

Shouldering her purse, Madison marched off.

Shelley felt like shit and longed for the days before their rivalry started back in high school. Back then, it was a subtle thing, the middle child's insecurity, as Shelley attempted to find her place in the limelight that shone continuously on Madison.

She'd tried the proper channels but repeatedly fell short. She'd run for class president and lost, whereas Madison won class president four years in a row. Shelley enrolled in AP courses like her older sister, but her grades plummeted, and the principal moved her back to regular classes. She snagged second chair clarinet in the band, but Madison sat first chair.

By her junior year, Shelley surrendered. Waved the white flag. Took up with the rebels. Skipped school. Smoked. Drank. Wore short skirts and too much makeup. Frolicked with the summer tourists. Earned a reputation as the "fun" Moonglow sister, although she'd never caused any real trouble . . .

Until *The Incident with Raoul*.

"You made it," Gia exclaimed, rushing over to wrap Shelley in a big bear hug.

Ahh, this was more like it.

Tears welled in Shelley's eyes. She bit down on the inside of her cheek to keep from crying. What the fudge? Shelley wasn't a crier, but after what she'd been through to get here, her emotions were razor sharp.

"I was worried about you," Gia said. "My goodness, you're as thin as a rail."

"I was a vegan."

"Was?"

"I ate bacon for breakfast this morning."

"Well, good for you . . ." Gia gave an anxious laugh. "I guess."

Shelley didn't blame her. She was nervous too.

"It's good to see you again, Shelley." Darynda came over for a hug.

"Thanks for hanging with Gia during all this," Shelley said.

"And Madison," Gia added.

Shelley ignored that.

Darynda nodded, a mist of tears in her eyes.

"So . . ." Shelley sank her hands on her hips. "Grammy? What's up with that?"

Gia shook her head and made a sad little noise. Told Shelley about the cancer diagnosis, the nine-hour brain surgery, and the medically induced coma.

Shelley's heart dropped to the bottom of her Birkenstocks. Grammy had been their lifeline. Ever since the Child Protective Services worker dropped three little orphaned girls off on her front porch twenty years ago.

A grandmother they'd never met. A grandmother they believed long dead. A grandmother who loved them instantly, and soon they loved her right back.

Guilt curled up against Shelley's heart. She hadn't spoken to her grandmother in five years. Why had she waited? She'd allowed feelings of remorse and betrayal to keep her isolated. Well, that and Cobalt Soul.

"Is she . . . ?" Shelley couldn't bring herself to ask more than that.

"She'll survive the surgery." The tone in Gia's voice and the sorrow in her eyes said that cancer was a whole other topic.

"How have *you* been?" Shelley's gaze fixed on Gia's bracelet. She still had the silly thing? Involuntarily, Shelley fingered her own bare wrist.

"Hanging by a thread." Gia's voice trembled. "If it hadn't been for Darynda . . ." She shot the older woman a grateful look and reached over to pat her arm.

That drew Shelley up short. Gia hated to admit her own needs. Or at least that's how she used to be. So much time had passed, Shelley felt as if she didn't know her sister anymore. "I'm sorry I wasn't here."

"Me too," whispered Gia. "I missed you so much."

Shelley couldn't hold on to the tears. A big fat one trickled down her cheek. She swiped it away with the back of her hand. Sniffled. Hiccuped. "I've missed you, too."

"You're here now. That's what matters." Gia touched the tip of her tongue to her upper lip. "But where have you been?"

"Costa Rica," Shelley said, offering as little as possible. She did not want to get into *that*. She still hadn't processed it herself. At least not the part about . . . well . . . She shook her head.

"Where is your luggage?"

Shelley patted her backpack.

"That's all you've got?"

"I travel light." Because she had no choice. Everything she owned was in that backpack.

"How did you get home if you're so broke?"

Gak! Shelley didn't answer; instead she asked, "How is Madison holding up?"

Gia looked as if she might push her to elaborate, but let it go. "You saw her. She's not taking this well."

"Grammy's illness? Or me?"

"Both, I guess."

"I'd hoped she'd mellowed in five years."

"I think something else is bothering her," Gia said. "But she's not talking. It's been tense ever since she arrived."

"I'll say," Darynda muttered.

"But she'd rather die than admit she's hurting." Shelley sighed. "Typical."

"Never mind Maddie right now." Gia kept twisting the bracelet at her wrist.

"Back to you." Shelley placed both hands on Gia's shoulders. "What's going on in your world?"

"I'm okay." Quickly, she filled Shelley in. The art degree, Japan, opening a kite shop.

"Wow, little sister, you've blossomed. That's amazing. Congratulations." Shelley was truly happy for her.

"It's been an adventure."

"When can we see Grammy?"

"The doctor said we can't see her until they move her to neuro ICU tomorrow morning. We were headed home when you showed up. You can ride with me."

"Maybe I should stay elsewhere." Shelley wasn't sure why she'd said that. She had nowhere else to go and no money for a motel.

"Don't be silly. It'll be fine. Maddie can get over herself."

Define "fine."

Madison returned, and they took off for the inn. Shelley rode with Gia, Madison with Darynda. On the drive, Gia told Shelley about Madison's shooting-star success. Her TV show and glamorous life in Manhattan. Well, bully for Maddie, fairy dusted as always.

Petty much, Sanpreet? Shelley clenched her teeth. No. No more Sanpreet. That dog and pony show was over.

At the Moonglow Inn, Darynda didn't get out of her car.

"Aren't you coming inside?" Shelley went around to the driver's window as Madison got out of Darynda's forest-green Mini Cooper.

"I'm exhausted," Darynda said. "I need to feed my dogs. Besides, you three should catch up. *Alone.*"

Yes, the thing Shelley dreaded most. Being alone with her sisters.

Darynda waved and drove away.

Without looking back, Madison grabbed her wheeled luggage and walked up the porch steps to unlock the front door.

Gia and Shelley followed her inside. Madison flicked on lights as she went. It was almost six P.M., but sunset was still over an hour away.

"Are there guests at the inn?" Shelley asked.

"I don't think so but let me check her calendar." Gia went to the check-in desk and flipped open the monthly calendar to May. Grammy still kept a physical reservation book as well as computer booking software. No reservations for the entire month. "Nope, I'm assuming since Gram knew about the surgery, she proactively shut things down."

Without speaking, Madison lurched stiff-legged out onto the porch. Shelley exchanged glances with Gia, who shrugged and trailed after Madison.

Shelley went too. What else could she do?

Madison plunked down on the right side of the porch swing, her usual spot, and Gia took the middle, settling in beside her.

Shelley did not sit with them as she once would have.

Instead, she shrugged off her backpack, dropped it to the porch, and settled into Grammy's Adirondack chair several feet from her sisters. So many times, Grammy had sat in this chair, hand sewing quilt squares or snapping black-eyed peas or peeling Moonglow pears, watching over them while they rocked on the porch swing.

No one said anything.

Finally, Gia cleared her throat. "There's something you guys need to see."

"What is it?" Madison asked.

Gia reached into the pocket of her lightweight cover-up and pulled out a letter. She passed it to Madison, who opened it with a well-manicured fingernail.

Shelley stared down at her own fingernails, broken and jagged from physical labor. Her hair was messy as well. Dry and frizzy with split ends. Where she'd been, there wasn't a beauty salon within fifty miles, and her hair hadn't seen scissors in five years. Mindlessly, she dragged a strand of hair up through her fingers to stare at the split ends in the dappled sunlight.

Silently, Madison read the letter, and then looked up, her face impassive, before handing it to Shelley.

As Shelley read, her heartbeat jumped in her chest.

The letter was a plea to Gia. Grammy's last request. *Finish the quilt. Repair the rift. Sew. Heal. Bloom. Grow.*

The words seemed to swell, expanding until they floated off the page above the rest of the text, flooding Shelley with emotional waves so big she could hardly breathe. The letter was clear. Grammy was dying, and she knew it.

"This isn't right," Madison said. "She should have addressed the letter to *me*. I'm the oldest."

"Says here . . ." Shelley held up the letter and tried her best not to smirk. "That only Gia can mend things."

Madison glowered and toyed with the crystal pendant she wore, dragging it back and forth across the chain.

It was all Shelley could do not to stick out her tongue. What was it about being home that made her feel so childish?

"We've got to finish the quilt," Gia said. "To honor Grammy and straighten things out between us."

"Good grief." Madison shot Shelley a scathing

glance. “As if sewing a quilt together could solve anything.”

“So you won’t do it?” Gia shifted on the swing, angling her body away from Madison.

“I don’t see the point.” Maddie drummed her glossy pink fingernails on the arm of the swing slow and controlled—*thump, thump, thumpity, thump*.

The repetitive noise set Shelley’s teeth on edge.

“But it’s Grammy’s last request.” Gia looked distressed and speared her fingers through her hair.

“You can’t force people to do things, Gia,” Shelley said. “If Madison doesn’t want to finish the quilt, she doesn’t want to finish the quilt. You and I can finish it.”

“I don’t need you defending me, Shelley,” Madison snapped.

“Stop it.” Gia hopped to her feet. At five three, she was the shortest, but with her shadow growing long in the gathering dusk, she looked bigger than them both. “I ask very little from you two. I believe in live and let live. I don’t get mixed up in your business. But Grammy is dying. She might never wake from the coma.”

“If Grammy dies, then there’s *no* point to finishing the quilt. She wouldn’t know whether we completed it or not.” Shelley chuffed.

“*I’d* know.” Gia narrowed her eyes and folded her arms over her chest.

"Grammy *will* pull through." Madison smacked a fist against her thigh and glared lasers at Shelley.

"We have to finish the quilt," Gia said. "For Grammy."

"Look." Madison hooked one hand around the porch swing chain. "The world doesn't rest on your shoulders. It'll keep turning without you taking on everyone else's burdens."

"What are you saying?" Gia paced in a tight circle around the Adirondack chairs, stepping over Shelley's feet each time she passed.

Shelley crossed her ankles, tucked her feet underneath the chair.

"Grammy can't expect us to drop our lives to sew a quilt. I have responsibilities. I'm on TV."

Oh yeah, rub our noses in it. Shelley rolled her eyes.

Gia stopped directly in front of Madison, arms akimbo, face fierce. "So, you *refuse* to finish the quilt."

"I'm saying I won't work with her." Madison threw a stony stare in Shelley's direction. "If you want to finish the quilt, I'll be happy to do it with you, but *only* you."

"Reconsider, please," Gia begged.

"I can't even . . ." Madison stood up, stalked off down the steps, and headed toward the beach.

Shelley had had enough. She leaped to her feet, chased after her. Got in front of Madison and stopped her in her tracks. "I'm sorry, okay?

I don't know what else I can do. I'm sorry. I'm prepared to make amends. I'll do whatever it takes, but you've *got* to forgive me."

Pain haunted Madison's eyes. "I don't . . . I can't."

"You're the one hanging on to the grudge. It was five damn years ago. Raoul is long gone. And from what Gia told me, you have a great life in New York because you *didn't* marry him. So really, you should thank me. Besides, I'm a different person now."

Madison's eyes narrowed to slits. "Are you really, Shelley? Who showed up here broke ass and expecting *me* to pay her two-hundred-dollar taxi bill?"

"There were extenuating circumstances you know nothing about and I *will* pay you back."

"With you, there are always extenuating circumstances."

"Nothing is *always,* Maddie. That's an exaggeration and you're using it to get a rise out of me." Shelley's nostrils flared.

They toed off, hands on their hips, eyes locked on each other.

Shelley heard Gia storm off. The screen door slammed. Guilt played up her spine, but embroiled, she couldn't reel in her anger.

Breathe.

Shelley forced a long inhale, drawing air down into the base of her lungs to the count of four the way Guru Meyer had coached her. Held her breath for seven seconds. Exhaled to the mental count of eight.

Madison's face was a mask, her mouth set in a harsh line.

"What's it gonna take?" Shelley asked. "How do I earn your forgiveness?"

"You really want to know?" Madison snorted.

"I do."

"Go back to Costa Rica. It's where you belong."

The screen door slammed again. Gia stalked from the house, the offending quilt tucked underneath her arm. The weight of the queen-size quilt threw her off balance, causing her to list to the right as she thundered across the lawn toward them.

Nostrils flaring and sweat pearling along the neck of her cover-up, Gia reached the middle of the yard where Shelley and Madison stood arguing. Baring her teeth like a mad little puppy, she unfurled the quilt with a quick, hard snap of her wrists and spread it out on the grass.

"Listen here, you two." Gia growled. "We *will* finish this quilt. All three of us. *Together.*"

"I'm happy to do it," Shelley said. "But Madison is so unforgiving. Like she's Miss Perfect."

"Shelley can say she's sorry all she wants, but actions speak louder than words. Until I see it, I don't believe her." Madison snorted.

"What will get you both on board?" Gia asked.

"Face it. You're not magical. You can't fix everything." Madison shook her head. "No matter what Grammy says in that letter. Some things are beyond your control."

"Look at this quilt." Gia crouched to run a finger along the border of the material. "We were so close to having it finished—"

"And then Shelley made out with *my* fiancé in the butler's pantry," Madison snarled. "On *my* wedding day!"

"Only because you wouldn't listen when I told you Raoul was a sleazebag." Shelley raised her palms.

"If I wanted to marry a cheater, that was my business."

"If you wanted to marry a cheater, why didn't you go right ahead and marry him?" Shelley shouted.

"Why didn't *you* bang his brains out while you had the chance?"

"I didn't want him, Maddie."

"No, that's right, you just wanted to humiliate me. You were always taking what didn't belong to you," Madison accused. "You took my clothes, my shoes, and my fiancé. All you ever cared about was yourself."

"Me?" Shelley splayed a hand to her chest. "Who—"

"Stop it!" Gia yelled, jumping between them. "Stop it right now!"

Simultaneously, they stared at her.

"Look at this quilt." Gia's voice quivered. "And remember when we worked on it together. How happy we were. Back when we were the Moonglow sisters."

"Before Shelley ruined everything." Madison tossed her head.

"Maddie," Gia pleaded. "You've *got* to forgive her."

"I do not." The wind whipped Madison's cool blond hair over her shoulder, making her look like Helen of Troy launching ships.

Madison was easily the prettiest of them with her elegant beauty. A throwback to sleek, chic Grace Kelly. Blue eyes and pale blond hair, willowy and well put together.

Although Shelley did look the most like their late mother, next to Madison, Shelley felt like a mud hen. Her hair was neither cool platinum like Madison's, who'd taken after the Chapmans, nor rich gold like Gia's, who resembled the Clarks, but rather a muddled shade somewhere between blond and light brown. Hairdressers called it dishwater blond or sandy brown or brond. It meant she didn't fit in any camp. It was the same with her eyes. They were a sort of brown and a sort of green combining in an odd mosaic of hazel.

Declaring that Shelley kissed Raoul because she felt insecure about her looks and she was trying to prove she was sexier than Madison was one of the meaner accusations that she'd ever flung at Shelley.

Maybe she was insecure, but that wasn't why she'd kissed Raoul. She'd wanted to wake Madison up and get her to see the huge mistake she was making. Shelley had zero interest in a slick social climber like Raoul, no matter how handsome he might have been.

Oh God, why *had* she kissed him? She should've just let Maddie marry the guy. They would have divorced by now and she and Madison wouldn't be eyeing each other like cage fighters.

"But Grammy . . ." Gia whimpered.

"What about Grammy?" Madison hardened her jaw, not budging an inch.

"The quilt means *everything* to her," Gia said. "We have to finish it and we have to do it *together*."

"You're acting like finishing the quilt will save Grammy from cancer. It won't," Madison said, contradicting what she'd said earlier. Face flushing bright red, Madison stalked up the yard to the barbecue grill, grabbed it by the handle, and dragged it clanging down the lawn toward the beach.

"What are you doing?" Gia ran after her.

Feeling gobsmacked, Shelley just stared.

Madison parked the grill at the edge of the

water and returned to snatch the quilt from the lawn.

"Maddie!" Gia ran in circles like a panicked puppy. Pyewacket sprinted across the yard and climbed a pear tree.

Their older sister's expression was determined and angry. Passersby strolling the beach stopped to watch the drama.

Madison flipped open the barbecue lid and stuffed the quilt onto the grill. "It's my damn wedding quilt. I get to destroy it. The way Shelley destroyed my wedding."

"Help me, Shelley!" Gia cried.

"Madison, stop." Shelley ran over to the grill.

"Get away from me." Madison shouldered her aside.

"Don't do this. Please, it's upsetting Gia," Shelley begged. "Stop and I'll leave."

Fury-driven, Madison reached into the cabinet at the bottom of the grill and pulled out a bottle of lighter fluid. Flipping the cap up, she soaked the quilt with it.

"Stop, Maddie, stop!" Gia grabbed hold of Madison's arm.

"Let go." Madison howled and yanked away from her. She fumbled for the lighter. Flicked it. A small blue flame shot from the end.

"No!" Gia yanked for the quilt, dragging it off the grill.

But Madison's rage had momentum and bulk.

She body-checked Gia with her hip and sent her tumbling to the sand.

Gia lay on her back gasping for air, the lighter-fluid-soaked quilt locked in her arms.

"Madison!" Shelley said, horrified. "Stop, stop, stop. I'm the one you're angry at, not Gia. Take it out on me. Not her."

Madison sank to her knees in front of Gia, tears tracking down her face. "I'm so sorry, I'm so sorry, I'm so sorry."

"Are you okay?" Shelley knelt beside her sisters on the sand.

Gia nodded, the smell of lighter fluid pungent around them. She looked like the kid she used to be when she carried her baby quilt around with her everywhere. She would suck her thumb and hang on to that quilt for dear life. On wash days, she and Grammy got into a tug-of-war. Grammy always won, but Gia would sit on the laundry room floor and not move a muscle until she got her quilt back.

Beachgoers gave them curious looks. Joggers. Couples holding hands. People reeling in kites. Mothers folding beach blankets and gathering up children. The tide was rising. Along the shoreline lights flickered on against the gathering dusk. Toe-tapping music filled the air. Water lapped at the legs of the barbecue grill.

If someone captured this moment in a Pinterest snapshot people would ask, *What's the deal with the barbecue grill?* It was out of context. Like Shelley herself.

"Can you sit up?" Shelley asked.

"I'm so sorry." Madison stroked Gia's hair. "I didn't mean to knock you down."

"What the hell is wrong with you?" Shelley glowered. "She's tiny. It's a wonder she doesn't blow away when she flies her kites."

"Oh, that's rich." Madison snorted. "You're jumping on me?"

"Stop it," Gia said. "Both of you. If you're really sorry, you'll help me finish the quilt."

"That's a big ask," Madison said.

"Look at us fighting." The wind tossed Shelley's unfettered hair into her face and she battled it back, stabbing her fingers through the mess. "How do you expect us to sit across from each other quilting for hours on end, Gia?"

"Why does this mean so much to you and Grammy?" Madison asked.

"Because the quilt is a symbol of when we were together. When things were good," Gia murmured, sadness in her eyes.

"Gia, I don't mean to be contrary, but we'd be sewing a quilt for a ruined wedding. To finish it would rub salt in my wounds." Maddie bit her bottom lip. "Is that what you want? To hurt me?"

Fear lit up Gia's eyes. Why? If Madison didn't want to finish the damn quilt, even for their dying grandmother, then fine.

"There is a reason for us to finish the quilt beyond Grammy's request. More than just getting us back together."

"What's that?" Madison rocked on her butt in the sand. "Why?"

"Why?" Gia said. "Because *I'm* getting married."

CHAPTER SIX

Gia

EMBELLISHMENT: Adding decorative items or stitches to a quilt top.

"You're engaged?" Shelley's gaze flew to Gia's bare ring finger. All three sat cross-legged on the sand in an unintentional circle.

"Uh-huh."

"Who's the groom?" Maddie asked.

Finally, Gia had their full attention, and they weren't at each other's throat. She could yank the plug on her lie and tell the truth, put a stop to this before it got out of hand, but both her larger-than-life older sisters—who'd tucked her in the sweet-girl-family-cheerleader-don't-rock-the-boat box years ago—were suddenly watching her with surprise and respect. It went to Gia's head like the dandelion wine she'd first gotten drunk on when she was eighteen.

Still, the deception went against her code of conduct and the rules she lived by. *Treat others the way you want them to treat you. Don't lie if you don't want to be lied to.*

"You didn't just make this up to stop us from fighting?" Shelley's mouth slanted in suspicion.

"Um . . ." Gia gnawed her bottom lip, and she anchored her gaze on the quilt. A fresh lie came to her fully formed. Not a small white lie, but a great big fat golden one. Shining like the Holy Grail. A solution. "Mike. He's the one. He's my fiancé."

"Mike Straus from next door?" Madison's mouth dropped open and her eyes lit up. "You're kidding."

"Why? What's so weird about that? Yep, it's Mike. Mike's the one. But it's new. Really, really new. We-haven't-told-anyone-else-yet new." Her lie shifted like quicksand dragging her into boggy depths with nothing to latch on to but more sand.

"How new?" Madison asked. "A day? A week? A month?"

"Um . . . a few days."

"How did he propose?"

"With a ring."

Shelley tapped her chin with a sand-dusted finger. "Where's the ring?"

"Oh, that." Gia waved her left hand as if she'd forgotten her ring wasn't there. "It's being sized."

"That's not what I meant," Madison said. "*How* did he propose? Did he get down on one knee? Where did it happen? Were you completely surprised? Deets. I need deets."

Damn Madison's dogged persistence and her attention to details.

Gia barely shook her head. She let her gaze settle on the pattern of three intersecting rings in the quilt. Just as those rings sewn into the squares composed within them the promise of comfortable union, so, too, her lie, if elaborated upon, composed . . .

What?

The mending of their family?

Or the end of it?

Her sisters stared at her expectantly.

"Um . . . right here on the beach. At sunset. He got on one knee. I was surprised, but not entirely shocked."

Madison eyed her as if she did not believe Gia's story. "When were you going to tell us?"

"Now. So, you can see why finishing the quilt means so very much to me . . ." She inhaled audibly, then pushed the lie further. "And Grammy. It's *more* than just her dying request. Finishing the wedding quilt also means the world to me. I'll bring the last quilt Grammy ever sewed into my marriage."

"Why didn't you say so?" Madison scratched her shin where the leg of her pants had risen, leaving faint pink scratch marks from her long, manicured nails.

Gia raised her shoulders and dropped them hard and quick. "I guess I was waiting for the right moment. There's been so much going on with Gram getting sick."

Shelley glanced at the grill and the tide creeping toward them. "And this is it?"

"So . . . Mike Straus, huh?" Madison swiveled to stare at Mike's bungalow.

"I buried the headline, didn't I?" Gia chuckled, but the sound came out as shaky as she felt. "I'm sorry."

"This is wonderful news!" Shelley applauded.

"The best news," Madison enthused. At least they agreed on something. "We all love Mike so much."

"I always thought you guys would make a cute couple." Shelley sighed dreamily. "I'm thrilled for you."

"How did you two get together?" Madison asked. "Was it before Grammy got sick? Does Grammy know? When is the wedding? Where are you having the ceremony? Who's officiating?"

Gia felt like a mouse in a trap. She had no answers for Madison's questions.

"Stop giving her the third degree." Shelley stood up. "And you, Gia, stop apologizing. Everything is not your fault."

"Who died and made you the boss?" Madison snapped.

Shelley stilled, curled her hands into fists at her sides. For one dangerous moment Gia feared her sisters would go at each other again.

There was something about Shelley, dressed in ethereal white, spindly legs dug into the sand, bony elbows and knees, scraggly untamed hair whipping wild in the breeze, that scared Gia. Shelley looked both hungry and empty like the vacant lighthouse on the far end of Moonglow Cove. And more unpredictable than ever.

"Who's hungry?" Gia asked. "I'm starving. Takeout from Mario's? Or something else. You guys choose. I'm buying."

Shelley and Madison exchanged glances as if deciding on whether to call a truce for the sake of Mario's famous lasagna and to celebrate Gia's engagement. If only it wasn't fake.

Gia's mind went back five years to *The Incident with Raoul,* when she'd helplessly watched her family unspool, drifting further and further away from her like kites snapping loose from their tethers, and wondering how long it would take before they disappeared from her forever.

They ordered from Mario's and, as the sun set, lounged on the back porch eating from the containers, feeding Pyewacket tidbits of garlic bread, the cat's small pink tongue rough against their fingers. They didn't talk, and Gia was afraid to ask if they could work together to finish the quilt. Some things took time to simmer, like Mario's Bolognese gravy.

Shelley finished her food, got up, and headed for the door.

"Where are you going?" Gia asked.

"Upstairs to find something to wear." Her gaze met Gia's. "If my old clothes are still here."

"Yeah, I've been meaning to ask you . . . what's with that getup?" Madison asked.

Shelley didn't answer.

"Your old clothes are right where you left them." Gia rushed to fill in the gap. "In the dresser."

"Will we sleep in the same room?" Shelley asked. "Like before?"

"God no. Since there're no guests, I'll take the blue room," Madison said, claiming the best room at the inn.

Shelley's gaze shifted to Gia, and she raised her eyebrows, sending her a look that asked, *Are we going to let her have her way?*

"You can have our old room, Shell," Gia said. "I'll sleep in Grammy's bed."

Shelley simply nodded, picked her backpack up off the floor, shouldered it, and sauntered inside. The screen door bumped closed behind her.

"Whatever that's about . . ." Madison muttered from the porch swing, "is one strange mystery."

Sleep eluded her.

In the long hours stretching toward dawn, Gia fretted.

She fretted about Grammy. She fretted about Madison and Shelley. And she fretted about herself.

About the lie.

What else could she have done? What other choice did she have? The potential consequences of her lie were so weighty Gia felt smothered, carrying a burden far too heavy for her small shoulders.

Obviously, she would have to tell Mike, but he was a straight arrow, honest as the livelong day. He was the guy who gave back change when he'd gotten too much. The guy who'd return someone's lost wallet. The guy who'd tell you the truth even though it hurt. Something like this . . . it could end their friendship.

That terrified her.

Mike was a staple in their lives. The constant, enduring neighbor they could always count on. She would have to clue him in and quick, before one of her sisters ran over to congratulate him on the engagement.

And if he gets upset?

Well, she'd worry about that bridge when it needed crossing. She drifted off but woke with a jolt just before sunrise, one thought on her mind. Get to Mike and get him on board so she could finish the quilt with her sisters and mend her family.

Gia crept from the bed, got dressed in shorts and a T-shirt, slipped out the front door, and scurried in the dewy grass toward the bungalow. She worried about waking Mike, but she needed to get ahead of this. Plus, she wanted it finished in time for the eight A.M. ICU visiting hours.

Gingerly, she stepped over the small stone wall separating the inn from Mike's house. His four-door pickup truck was parked out front.

At the door, she paused with her fist held aloft, ready to knock.

Hesitated.

What if he got mad at her? Mike had never gotten angry with her and the thought sent a shiver down her spine. Uncertain, she turned to leave. Maybe it was for the best that she come clean to her sisters.

Flying pigs. Without even starting work on the quilt? What about Grammy's letter?

Okay, okay, okay. She could do this. Gia smoothed down the hem of her shirt that had hiked up on her belly when she'd raised her hand to knock.

The door opened.

"Hey, Short Stack, why are you hanging around my porch?"

"I . . . I . . ."

Mike grinned as if overjoyed to see her and he motioned her inside. "Come on in."

Heart thumping quick, Gia followed him.

He wore faded blue jeans and a red T-shirt that said MOONGLOW DRAGONS, the name of their high school football team he'd once quarterbacked. He was barefoot, and his damp hair was combed back off his forehead as if he'd just gotten out of the shower. With his dark complexion, dark hair, and surprisingly out-of-context Scandinavian blue eyes, he looked like a movie star who'd taken on the role of a carpenter, liked it so much that he'd thrown over acting for his hobby. Harrison Ford in reverse. He smelled of sandalwood soap and basil-scented shampoo. Gia just wanted to take a big deep breath and sniff him.

"Are you hungry? I was about to cook eggs."

"Sure." She shrugged.

He seemed to want to feed her and since her breakfast was usually a protein bar, or an apple, why not? Although she wasn't sure she could eat after she told him the shenanigans she'd involved him in.

"Scrambled?"

"That's fine."

"I could make an omelet."

"Don't go to any trouble for me."

"Why not? You're always doing things for other people. I still remember when you made me chicken soup because I had the flu."

"You were all by yourself," she said. "Your parents had just moved, and your sister and her family were out of town. You were so miserable. I felt sorry for you."

"Ahh, pity soup." He winked. "Nothing tastes quite like it."

That wink unraveled her in a bizarre way. Why? "I owed you. You looked out for me plenty of times. Remember that guy who got handsy with me at that Labor Day beach party a few years ago? You knocked him flat on his ass."

"No one messes with one of the Moonglow sisters when I'm around." He went to the fridge. "Just made a pot of coffee," he called over his shoulder. "Help yourself."

She poured a cup of coffee and perched on a barstool, watching as he assembled the ingredients for an omelet on the kitchen counter.

"How's your grandmother?" Adeptly, he cracked the eggs and whisked them in a bowl.

"I don't know. They sent us home last night and told us to come back this morning at visiting hours."

"I'm sorry for what you're going through." His eyes met hers, latching on to her gaze for a beat too long, then he shifted his attention back to his work, and melted a pat of butter in an omelet pan.

Heat simmered in her belly, but she had no rational excuse for it. "Thanks."

"What was happening with you three on the beach yesterday?"

Gia took a long sip of coffee and avoided meeting his eyes again. "You saw that spectacle?"

"I was varnishing a table on the back porch."

Gia ducked her head. This was it. Her opening.

"Wanna tell me why Maddie was pouring

lighter fluid on a quilt and trying to barbecue it?"

She explained.

Mike winced. "Ouch, that puts you in a tough spot."

"Exactly."

"Knowing you, Short Stack, you tried to make peace."

"Guilty as charged." She raised her hand halfway.

"Did you convince them?"

"Um, yes, but—"

"I had no doubt." He chuckled. "Trust you to negotiate a truce. You might have missed your calling. You should have been a diplomat."

"Don't do that," she whispered.

"Do what?" He cocked his head and watched her as he flipped the omelet.

"Don't praise me. I'm not a diplomat. I'm just a liar."

"What did you lie about?" His tone changed from amused to curious.

Guiltily, Gia set down her coffee. She looked for judgment in his face but saw none. She shivered and covered her eyes with her hand. "Ugh. I still feel slimy over it."

"Lying isn't optimal . . ." He paused, understanding in his voice. "But does the end justify the means?"

"I don't know." She peeked at him from behind her palm and studied his face.

"What did you lie about?"

Here it was. The reason she'd come over. "Um . . . well . . ." she hedged. "I told them the quilt was for my wedding."

He looked shocked. "You're getting married?"

"No, that's the lie." Gia covered her head with her arms. "I'm a horrible person, aren't I?"

"No," he murmured. "Not horrible. You just want everyone to get along and to honor your grandmother's wishes. But I am concerned."

Her stomach took a nosedive. "What about?"

"I know you. The lie will eat you up inside. Is finishing the quilt worth your peace of mind?"

"It's not about the quilt. The quilt's just a symbol. If we can finish the quilt, then maybe, just maybe, we can mend our family."

"They'll forgive you." He gave her a look so tender that it stole her breath away and made her wonder when things had changed between them. "No one can stay mad at you for long."

Wow. Her heart skipped. Was she reading more into his expression than was actually there? "Yes, but will *you?*"

"Me?" His eyebrows shot up in surprise. "Why do you need my forgiveness?"

"Because I kinda told them *you* were my fiancé."

Mike's eyes widened, his smile vanished, and his voice raised. "You did what?"

"I told Shelley and Maddie you were my fiancé."

"Huh." He looked shocked and paused as if mulling it over.

"I was desperate."

"Gia, I don't know what to say." He shook his head vigorously, mouth pressed into a grim line.

"I shouldn't have done it. I freaked out. It was stupid." Oh gosh, she'd upset him. Gia raised her shoulders to her ears, cringed.

"Not stupid. Not you. Not even." His voice gentled. "In fact, it seems natural."

"What do you mean?" she whispered, feeling all tingly.

"I'm right next door. We've been friends for as long as either of us can remember. Why not?" His smile was back, and he looked as if he might be warming to the idea of being her pretend fiancé. He was such an amenable guy.

Her heart swelled against her chest and she felt an odd pressure in her throat. "I'm sorry. Do you hate me?"

"I could never hate you, Short Stack."

"But I lied and roped you into this crazy drama."

"For a good cause." He raked his gaze over her. His eyes were kind, and his smile understanding. "The best cause, actually. Family."

"Still . . ." She scrunched her nose and bit her lip. "It's not right."

"Just out of curiosity . . ." He lowered his

voice, and his gaze never left her face. "Why *did* you pick me?"

"You said you'd do anything for me. Anything at all . . ."

"I meant like mow the yard, or cook dinner, or drive you to the hospital or sit with your grandmother . . ."

"I know. I know. I'm so sorry. It's way too much to ask for you to be my pretend fiancé. It's like something out of a goofy romantic comedy. I'm such an idiot." She dropped her forehead to the bar.

"Hey, I like goofy romantic comedies."

"I didn't mean to rope you in. I was desperate to stop Madison and Shelley from fighting and it just popped out." She banged her head on the counter. "Never mind. I'll tell the truth. Maybe just knowing I was willing to lie to make this happen will convince them to stay and finish the quilt."

"Gia?"

"Yes?" she mumbled.

"Look at me."

She raised her head. The glimmer in his eyes kicked the air from her lungs. "What is it?"

He cupped her chin in his palm and tilted her head to meet his beautiful blue-eyed gaze. "Will you marry me?"

"Wh-what?" Stunned, she gaped at him, her skin tingling from his touch.

"Say yes. Then it's not a lie. We'll be *officially* engaged."

She shook her head. “Nooo . . . Mike, you don’t have to do this.”

“I know.”

A dozen different emotions pelted her, most of them conflicting. “I—”

“Say yes and it’s not a lie,” he repeated.

This was too much to ask. He was so nice for trying to make her feel better.

“Say ‘Yes, Mike.’ ” He locked his gaze onto hers. “ ‘I’ll marry you.’ ”

Why was her pulse going nuts? Spiking hard and fast against her veins. “Yes, Mike,” she parroted. “I’ll marry you.”

“Good. I’m glad we got that out of the way.”

“Me too,” she said, feeling marginally better and yet slightly faint. “But this is a lot to ask.”

“We only have to be engaged until you guys finish the quilt, right?”

She nodded.

“So only a few weeks?”

“We could finish the quilt much faster if Shelley and Madison can get over themselves and work together instead of yanking in opposite directions.”

“I’m sure you’ll whip them into shape.”

“I wish I was as confident in me as you are.”

“What’s next?” he asked, plating the omelet and setting it in front of her. She wasn’t so sure she could eat.

“We’ll need an engagement ring. My sisters

were already asking about one. I fibbed and said it was being sized. Maybe I could find a cheap zirconia we could use." She picked up her fork.

"I have a ring," he said casually.

She put down her fork. "You have an engagement ring?"

"Yeah. It's not a big honker or anything. But it'll make me look better than a zirconia." He laughed.

"You bought someone an engagement ring?"

He shrugged, looked sheepish.

"Seriously? I didn't know you'd ever been engaged." Gia took a bite of the omelet. It was delicious, loaded with cheese, onions, and mushrooms, but she was too tense to enjoy it.

"I wasn't," he said. "Until now. Until you. I never got around to asking her."

"But you were close enough to marriage to buy a ring for a woman?"

"I was serious."

"And you never returned the ring?"

He shook his head, plated his own omelet, poured a cup of coffee, and came to sit beside her at the bar.

"Why not?"

His shrug was easy. "I dunno."

Mike was their neighbor and a close family friend. How had she not known he was on the verge of becoming engaged? This bugged her. She thought she knew him.

She snapped her fingers. “Let me guess, it was that woman you used to work with before you started your own business. What was her name? It started with a C.”

“Good memory. Her name was Cassandra.”

“So why didn’t you ask her?” Something weird punched Gia in the gut. An odd feeling she couldn’t identify.

“Cassandra scored a high-powered job in Houston. I couldn’t hold her back.”

“You could have gone with her.”

“Nah. I’m a Moonglow Cove man. Always have been. Always will be.”

“You love your town more than her?”

“Guess so.” He met her gaze. “That’s how I knew she wasn’t the One. If I wasn’t willing to leave Moonglow Cove for her—”

“Not a legitimate excuse. You travel often in your Habitat for Humanity thingy.”

“But I always come back home.”

“Where’s the ring?”

“Safe-deposit box at my bank.”

“Please don’t tell me you were planning on keeping the ring to give to the next woman you wanted to marry. That’s truly tacky.”

“No way,” Mike scoffed. “I’m frugal, but not an idiot. When the time came, I figured I’d trade it in and buy a much bigger ring. Now that I can afford it.”

“I see.” It still bugged her that Mike had

almost gotten engaged and she hadn't known about it.

"You know what this means, don't you?" he asked.

"What's that?" she whispered.

"One slip and the whole town will know our engagement is a fake. To pull this off, we've *got* to be convincing."

Her throat tightened. "Meaning?"

"Public displays of affection." He touched her elbow. "How do you feel about that?"

"Um . . ." She moistened her lips. "You mean like holding hands?"

"Yes . . . and more."

"Cuddling?"

"At times."

She gulped, felt her entire body heat. "K-ki-kissing?"

Mike leaned in so close she could feel his warm breath on her cheek. Gia's heart stilled and for one long heartbeat she thought he might kiss her right then and there.

"If the situation calls for it." His voice turned husky.

"I see."

"Still on board?"

Mutely, she nodded. "Are you?"

He eyed her up and down. Cracked a wide grin. "I wouldn't call it a hardship."

Her heartbeat thundered in her ears and she had

absolutely no idea why. My goodness, he was being so nice. How could she ever repay him? "So we're really doing this?"

"Looks like." He bobbed his head. "My bank opens at seven. Should we go get that ring?"

CHAPTER SEVEN

Shelley

RAW EDGE: An unfinished fabric edge.

The sound of the front door closing woke Shelley.

Unable to fall back to sleep, she got dressed and set off running on the empty beach, barefoot, just as she had every morning in Costa Rica.

Last night filled her mind. Had she and Madison made headway toward repairing their relationship? It was hard to tell. Could her older sister be closer to forgiving her? Hope pounded through her with each footstep.

Maybe. Maybe. Maybe.

Don't count on it, whispered a skeptical, naysaying voice.

Okay, perhaps she and Madison would never be close again. It was something she was prepared to accept. Life at Cobalt Soul had taught her a few things about acceptance and letting go. The trick was separating the beneficial lessons from the dogma and rhetoric.

Bigger question: Why had Shelley expected things to be different simply because five years had passed?

Magical thinking.

On the trip home, she'd indulged in magical thinking, the same way a child fervently believed in Santa Claus, expecting a miraculous family reunion. Ha! They were trapped in the same old crazy-making conversations and conflicts.

Madison wanted to control her.

Shelley resisted being controlled.

Would she ever learn? She was the odd one out. Always had been. Apparently always would be.

Accept what is. Guru Meyer's voice was in her head.

Dammit.

Shelley ran, flying down the beach, bare feet pounding the sand, heart slamming into her chest. Tears burned her eyes. The T-shirt she had on, relegated to a rag drawer, smelled like cedar and mothballs, but underneath that strong scent, a hint of lavender that reminded her of her mother.

Shelley might not remember what her mother looked like, or the sound of her voice, but she remembered her smell. When she was little, Shelley would crawl up in her parents' bed and bury her face in her mother's pillow and take a big whiff, filling her lungs with the fragrance of *Mom*.

After their parents, Beth and Liam Clark, died in an avalanche during a skiing trip, Madison put up a fight over the pillow. Since she was the oldest she claimed she should get it. But their foster mom, who'd looked after them immediately following their parents' deaths, said Shelley needed the pillow more than Madison did.

The message she'd taken from that conversation?

Needy. She was too needy.

In retrospect, a childish distortion. They were *all* needy, all of them crippled by their parents' sudden deaths. But the foster mom's words had seemed like an indictment. Shelley's needs were a burden.

Shelley kept the pillow long past the time it was threadbare. And Maddie claimed Shelley wasn't sentimental. Grammy, who'd come into the picture at that point, had thrown away the gunky pillow one day while Shelley was at school.

She recalled the stark hit of pain when she realized she'd lost the beloved pillow forever. Her last real connection with her mother severed. She'd acted out, howling like a she-wolf and trashing the bedroom she shared with Gia and Maddie.

Her feet sank into the sand as she ran, pushing herself harder. She ran until her lungs felt as if they might burst, leaving the Moonglow Inn and her sisters miles behind. The sun gleamed orange, bluing the sky and spreading it with pink and purple hues.

Dawning of a new day.

Up ahead lay a fishing pier with a charming little gazebo. A tuxedoed man stood beside a woman in a wedding dress. Well-wishers in nice clothes surrounded the couple.

Shelley stopped running, chest heaving, and bent over to catch her breath. She straightened, pressed her palms to her back, and stood on the beach near the pier, watching the ceremony unfold.

A dawn wedding. How beautiful.

Soon, her baby sister would get married to their next-door neighbor, Mike Straus. No, not *their* next-door neighbor. Not anymore. Shelley no longer belonged at the Moonglow Inn. Nor did she belong at Cobalt Soul. Not after she'd run away taking nothing with her but her knapsack and the clothes on her back.

Honestly, she belonged nowhere.

"I'm a woman without a home," she whispered under her breath and clenched her hands.

But you have a family.

Ah, but did she? Yesterday's welcome, especially from Madison, suggested otherwise. A fresh pain knifed her gut. Madison clung to her grudge with both hands. But Shelley deserved it. She had no right to expect sympathy, even though at the bottom of her actions, her motives had been pure.

Shelley shifted her thoughts back to Gia and Mike. So sweet. She was beyond happy for her baby sister. Mike was a stand-up guy. Salt of the earth. Honest and open. The sort of guy who'd never appealed to Shelley. She'd gone for the bad boys, the rebels, the fringe dwellers, the disenfranchised.

Which explained how she'd ended up in a place like Cobalt Soul.

Would she ever have a real home? A man of her own? Somewhere to belong? A deep yearning filled Shelley. She wanted those things, but that need terrified her. Family could go so wrong. Had gone wrong in so many ways for the Moonglow sisters.

You're not the Moonglow sisters anymore.

True confessions.

At twenty-six, while she'd had her share of lovers, she'd never had a serious relationship. Before going to Cobalt Soul, she'd been all about *fun, fun, fun*. In Costa Rica, they'd taught her to transmute her sexual desires into spiritual energy. She'd gone from promiscuous to celibate overnight. She hadn't had sex in five years and she'd been *happy* about that.

But watching the wedding unfold, she remembered what she'd been missing. Not just hot sex. But something deeper. Something like what Gia and Mike had.

Connection.

She realized with a start that marriage was no longer a turnoff. Even though she'd found no one who accepted *her* for her. No one who fully accepted her, warts and all. Not even her own family. Well, unless she counted Guru Meyer and the folks at Cobalt Soul.

Except, looking back on that experience, she realized they'd only accepted her as long as she adhered to the group's rules. Not that they'd overtly shunned her or anything. Their manipulation came through positive reinforcement. They lavished praise when you did what they wanted and when you didn't, they withheld their approval.

Why hadn't she noticed that before?

Guru Meyer had her salivating like Pavlov's dog at the ringing of a bell. During the group healing sessions, the pleasure centers of her brain lit up, and she'd dived right into the thick of their midst, hungry for recognition and reward. What was wrong with her that she'd been so easily manipulated?

The bride and groom kissed, and the crowd applauded. The ceremony was over.

Leaving the beach for the boardwalk, Shelley meandered along Paradise Pier, reluctant to let go of the sweet wedding scene. She ticked off the day's chores in her head. Visit Grammy in the hospital. Deal with Madison. Sew that cursed wedding quilt.

It was still early, barely after seven. None of the shops or restaurants were open. She wandered along but stopped when she saw a poster in the window of an art gallery that read: *Featuring Straus Handcrafted Furniture*.

On the poster was a photograph of Mike making the ornate baby crib that sat in the display case.

Aww.

Mike had hit his stride.

Her pulse quickened, and she felt impossibly sad. Five years were gone, and she'd missed out on so much. Turning away, Shelley glimpsed her image mirrored in the plate-glass window. Her face was gaunt, her eyes hollowed, her hair frizzing about her face. She looked like a stranger. Distant and lost.

But she had no one to blame. She'd brought this on herself.

As far back as she could remember people labeled her impetuous. The first time, she recalled, her parents had taken Shelley and her sisters for a picnic in a Denver park after a fresh summer rain. Shelley had been fiveish because Gia was a toddler. Mama and Daddy told Madison and Shelley to wait while they unloaded the minivan, but Shelley had seen the playground swings and took off. She ran so fast that by the time she spied the huge mud puddle underneath the swings, it was too late to stop. She smacked into the puddle, tripped, and went slipping face first like a clean-up batter sliding home to tie the World Series.

Covered head to toe in mud, she'd burst out bawling.

"Shelley ruined the picnic," Mama declared. "You can thank her for being impetuous."

Roughly, Mama dumped the picnic supplies from the big cardboard box, plunked a mud-covered Shelley inside, and stuck her in the back of the minivan. On the ride home, Madison pouted, Gia cried, Daddy frowned, Mama scolded, and Shelley shivered cold and dirty in cowering shame.

From the beginning, she'd leaped before she looked, never bothering with a safety net. Time after time she acted without thinking things through and she paid the consequences, never learning from her mistakes.

She'd done it with Raoul.

She'd done it when she joined up with Guru Meyer at Cobalt Soul.

She'd done it when she fled the compound.

Why was she so intractable? Could she ever change? Shelley longed for the person she'd never been. Controlled and responsible like Madison, or easygoing and accepting like Gia. Either was preferable to Shelley's slapdash approach to life.

Yoga and meditation helped, but now she wondered if her practices were just a bandage covering a festering wound, tricking her into thinking she'd healed. Shelley shook off her gloom. Sighed. One good thing about being impetuous? It didn't take her long to move on.

She left the boardwalk, returned to the sand, and jogged back to the Moonglow Inn. When she reached the beach in front of the B&B, she saw Madison perched on a ladder on the porch, struggling to hang Grammy's wooden quilting frame by herself.

Grandpa Chapman, who'd died of a stroke long before any of them had been born, had rigged eyebolts to the ceiling so Grammy could sit outside and enjoy the ocean while she quilted.

Madison was in full makeup. She wore a straw sunhat and a sleeveless white tiered sundress that tied at the neck and had small yellow flowers embroidered along the bottom tier. Yellow espadrilles with wedge heels graced her small feet. She looked cute as the dickens, but the espadrilles were not ladder-climbing footwear. Her sister could fall and bust her ass in those shoes, but Shelley would be damned if she'd warn her.

She hesitated, reluctant to approach the house when it was just her and Madison without Gia around as a buffer.

"Can you help me?" Madison called out.

What could she do? Say no?

"Sure." Shelley climbed the porch steps, softly chanting under her breath, *Keep things light, keep things light, keep things light*.

“Get the second stepladder from the pantry.” Madison was perched atop her ladder, four quilt frame chains clutched in her hands, the wooden frame dangling awkwardly beneath her. Madison didn’t smile, but she wasn’t frowning, either.

Um, was there a hidden meaning in that? The pantry was where everything had gone down with Raoul.

“Okay.” She should be safe with one-word sentences, right? Shelley fetched the stepladder and brought it back.

“Open it parallel to my ladder.”

On it, boss lady. Shelley placed the ladder underneath the second set of ceiling eyebolts and climbed atop it. Madison’s ladder was taller, and she towered over Shelley.

“Here.” Madison handed her two of the chains.

No *please*. No *thank you*. Just *obey me*.

Should she salute? Shelley accepted the chains, the wooden frame swinging between them. She stood on tiptoes to reach the eyebolts.

“Wait.”

Shelley paused for further instruction.

“Let’s do this together. On my count. One . . . two . . . three.”

Simultaneously, Madison and Shelley lifted the chains and attached the hooks to the eyebolts, the wooden frame dangling between their ladders.

Well, will you look at that? They’d worked

together for a common goal and neither one of them had killed the other.

Yet.

"Good job," Madison said.

Shelley just about fell off her ladder. "Thanks."

They stared at each other over the wooden quilting frame and for a moment a truce seemed a sweet possibility.

"Where's the quilt?" Shelley glanced around.

"I carried it over to the dry cleaners," Madison said. "I want to get the quilting frame up before we go see Grammy. I promised Gia I'd do this, and I *always* keep my word."

Was that a dig at her?

Shelley let it go and curled her bare toes around the edge of the ladder. Rubbed the end of her itchy nose with a knuckle. "Grammy says no one should own a quilt that has to be dry-cleaned."

"I know, but since the quilt is unfinished, I was afraid to wash it."

"But why are you so dressed up?"

"I left the house." Madison's tone turned condescending.

"And you can't run to the dry cleaners in shorts and a T-shirt without war paint on?"

Madison assessed Shelley's attire with a cool stare. Shelley wore shorts—baggy because she was fifteen pounds lighter than she'd been five years ago—and an even baggier blue T-shirt with a rip in the sleeve and a logo that said, regrettably, SORRY, NOT SORRY.

"I'm a public figure. I can't go out looking . . ." Madison roved another judgmental look over Shelley. "Shabby."

"Woo, a public figure." Shelley shook her palms, jazz hands–style.

"My show *is* number one on the CIY Network."

"How did *that* happen?"

"*House Boss* went viral following my disastrous wedding. I did a show on creative ways to repurpose your wedding dress." Madison's voice came out slivered with glass shards. "If you'd bothered to contact any of us and let us know if you were alive or dead, you'd know this."

"Good for you." Shelley hitched in her breath. "I mean that, Madison. I'm happy things turned out so well."

Madison did a diva head toss. "Yes, I took lemons and made lemonade."

"You're welcome," Shelley said.

"Excuse me?"

"If I hadn't kissed Raoul, you wouldn't be leading the life you have now. So yeah, you're welcome."

Madison's face turned to slate, and her skin blotched. Through clenched teeth she said, "*No one* has ever hurt me as badly as you did."

Here it came, the shame spiral, swirling over

Shelley like a black swarm of bees. "How many times do I have to say I'm sorry?"

"Your T-shirt says it all."

"Ignore the shirt. I *am* sorry."

"Sorry doesn't cut it."

"What do you want from me, Madison? A pound of flesh? You have everything, and I have . . ." She raised her arms, swept her hands. *"Nothing."*

Madison's mouth dropped open, and she looked at Shelley as if she'd lost her mind.

"Don't you think I've suffered the consequences?" Shelley asked. "I have no home, I have no family. The only clothes I have are the ones I found stuffed in a drawer. Clothes I wore when I was twenty-one. I'm broke as hell and I owe you two hundred dollars for the taxi. I can't even buy myself a breakfast burrito at McDonald's. You flipping win!"

Tears misted Madison's eyes, and that shocked the hell out of Shelley. Maddie wasn't a crier. This was more than their quarrel. Something had hurt Maddie.

Hurt her badly.

Again, Shelley opened her mouth to say she was sorry but feared she'd just fuel Madison's anger, so she kept her trap shut. She'd already blundered and punched a soft spot.

"You do *not* understand what you're talking about." Madison's voice quivered. "I am sorry you're in a bind, but you have no call to weigh in on my life."

"And you have no call to weigh in on mine. You just bragged that you're a hotshot TV personality, and you clearly have money falling out of your butt. What else could you want? So what that you don't have a husband. No biggie. You'll get one if you want one."

Madison blinked furiously. She clamped her lips so hard her chin trembled. "Stop talking right now or I won't be able to keep my promise to Gia and Grammy and finish that stupid quilt."

"Yeah, well, me either."

Madison put her hands on her hips. So much for the minitruce. But Shelley had to try. If she didn't, well, she had no idea what would happen to her.

"In the spirit of putting our differences aside"—Shelley cleared her throat—"I thought it might be nice to throw Gia and Mike a bridal shower."

"What?"

"A shower."

"That's a bit premature."

"Why?"

"We don't know a thing about what's going on."

Shelley frowned and scratched her head. "What *thing* are you talking about?"

"Their engagement. Something doesn't feel right. It's rushed."

"God, you are so skeptical," Shelley replied. "They've known each other for years. Friends turn into lovers all the time. All I'm saying is that a bridal shower would be a nice gesture."

"Like you could afford to throw a party." Madison looked smug.

Watching her sister, Shelley had a stunning moment of clarity and she understood the *real* reason she'd kissed Raoul. It hadn't been to protect Madison from marrying a douchebag cheater as she'd convinced herself. It was because she'd wanted to knock Madison off her high horse.

Was she that vindictive and petty?

Yes, dear, yes you are.

New shame blazed through her. That was why everyone had sided with Madison. Everyone except Gia, who'd refused to take sides.

Shelley opened her mouth to tell her sister her revelation, thinking if she admitted her dark motive that Madison would soften and finally accept her apology.

From out of nowhere, Pyewacket shot across the porch like a Flying Wallenda, leaping onto Madison's side of the quilting frame and sending the opposite side of the wooden plank rocking up into Shelley's shins.

Wham!

"Mother of blueberries!" Shelley yelped, and in her pain stumbled backward off the ladder and landed hard on her ass.

Irony.

That cold little bitch.

CHAPTER EIGHT

Gia

TENSION: The balancing forces exerted on the needle and bobbin threads by the sewing machine that affect the quality of its stitch.

Gia found her sisters on the back porch. Madison was dressed to the nines while Shelley looked like she'd just finished a kick-boxing competition . . . and lost.

"Shell, what happened to your legs?" Gia sucked in her breath through clenched teeth, sympathy curling tight against her chest.

"Pyewacket." Shelley shook her head. "Don't ask."

"I tried to get her to put ice on it." Madison held up a zippered plastic sandwich bag filled with melting ice cubes. "But she refused."

"I'm fine," Shelley insisted.

"You're just being contrary." Madison squeezed the ice pack in her fist.

"And you're trying to run the show, like always."

Madison looked hurt and pressed her lips together as if struggling to keep from making a smart comment. She tossed the ice pack onto the circular picnic table.

"That cat is still a scamp in her old age—" Gia started to smooth things over, but for the first time noticed the frame. "Oh, my gosh, you guys set up the quilting frame!" Surprised and delighted, Gia clamped her hands over her mouth. "This is amazing. Thank you!"

"You're welcome." Madison efficiently dusted her palms together.

"Where's the quilt?" Gia glanced around for the triple wedding ring quilt.

"Dry cleaners." Shelley inclined her head toward Madison. "Maddie took it in. That's why she's so gussied up."

"Really?" Pressing a palm to her heart, Gia sighed, endorphins flooding her body with happiness.

"Don't look so shocked," Madison said. "We promised to finish the quilt."

Gia rubbed her chin with the pad of her thumb. "I wasn't sure you meant it."

Hope planted roots, sprouted, grew. Maybe this would work. Even if she had to create a fake engagement to make it happen. Gia toyed with the unaccustomed weight of Mike's ring on her finger. They'd just picked it up from his safe-deposit box at his bank and she wasn't used to the pressure of it yet.

The ring fit perfectly. How coincidental was that?

Mike, the optimist, had simply said, "It's a sign that this story line is meant to be."

She wasn't sure if by story line he meant the fake engagement or the two of them as a couple, and she was afraid to ask him to clarify, uncertain if she wanted his remark to signify the former or the latter.

The porch steps creaked behind them and they all three turned simultaneously to see Mike wearing starched chinos and a crisp white shirt with the sleeves rolled up. The man had the sexiest forearms. He came over and slid one of those delectable arms around her waist, playing his part.

It was unfamiliar, his proprietary touch, but it felt nice, too, and that freaked her right out. *Settle down.*

"Ready to go to the hospital, Honeysuckle?" he asked.

Honeysuckle? A sweet shiver ran through her. He'd traded in Short Stack for Honeysuckle? He'd already given her a romantic nickname? She had to hand it to him, when the man played a role, he Tom Hanksed the hell out of it.

"You bet, Sugarplum," she shot back, grinning.

Madison raised an eyebrow at him. "You're coming with?"

Mike linked his arm through Gia's, enveloping her in his sandalwood-and-basil scent. "Wherever Gia goeth, I goeth."

Madison rolled her eyes and mumbled, "Sounds codependent to me."

"Blow her off." Shelley waved a dismissive hand at Madison. "You two are adorable as a couple."

"He's almost family." Gia leaned over to pat Mike's taut abdomen the way she imagined a fiancée might do. But she was unprepared for the jolt of awareness that blasted through her fingers. Her eyes rounded, and she did her best not to look astounded.

"Who's driving?" Madison asked.

"We can take my King Ranch, room for five," Mike volunteered. "Is Darynda coming?"

"I just came from the hospital."

Everyone turned to see Darynda climbing the steps, a large, brown paper H-E-B grocery bag in her arms.

"How?" Madison asked. "The visiting hours aren't until eight and it's just now seven forty-five."

"I was the nursing supervisor's high school English teacher." Darynda looked pleased with herself. "I have pull."

"What's with the groceries?" Shelley peeped into the bag.

"Let me carry that for you." Mike took the bag from Darynda.

"I'm making lunch for you all," Darynda said. "Mike, you're included."

"Thank you." He carried the groceries inside and they all followed.

"That's good that you included him," Madison said. "Because apparently wherever Gia goeth, Mike goeth."

Darynda tilted her head to study Madison. "What?"

"You didn't know they were engaged?" Madison's eyes narrowed as if she smelled a rat. "Grammy didn't tell you?"

"W-we . . . hadn't told Grammy yet," Gia said. Oof! She was such a terrible liar.

"Let's see the ring." Darynda held out her hand.

Feeling like Pinocchio, Gia flashed the sparkler on her left hand. Mike had been modest. The one-carat diamond was impressive enough for anyone.

"Nice." Darynda smiled. "Good job, Mike."

"What are we having?" Shelley dug through the bag Mike settled onto the kitchen table.

Silently, Gia blessed her sister for shifting the attention off the fake engagement.

"Fried chicken, your grandmother's recipe, mashed potatoes with real cream, and buttermilk biscuits," Darynda said.

"Omigod." Shelley splayed a hand on her belly. "I've died and gone to heaven. I could kiss you so hard right now, Darynda."

"I thought you were vegan," Gia said.

Shelley flapped a hand. "That's way over."

"When is the wedding?" Darynda's gaze drifted from Mike to Gia and back again.

"September," Mike said.

Gia gave him a bug-eyed stare. *Don't rush things*. "*Next* September."

"Why September? Why not June?" Madison unpacked the groceries. "Shelley, go put on some decent clothes. Let's get this show on the road before visiting hours end."

Shelley hesitated as if she might argue, but then she shrugged and left the room.

Madison rolled her eyes again. "I swear, that woman—"

"Don't," Gia said so sharply that Madison stopped with a carton of eggs in her hands.

"Don't what?"

"Pick on her. She's doing the best she can." Gia said.

Mike's hand went to Gia's neck, a gentle touch, a light massage, just letting her know that he was there, and that he had her back. It felt nice.

"Well, so am I." Madison's tone was flat as flint.

To smooth things over, Gia said, "Thank you for taking the quilt to the dry cleaners. I appreciate it."

Madison sighed and stowed the eggs in the fridge. "Okay, okay, I'll lighten up on her. But just for you."

Gia beamed at her. "You're the best."

Shelley came back downstairs in white cargo pants and a blue tank top that used to be Madison's.

Gia darted a quick glance at her oldest sister, who clamped her mouth shut. She pressed her palms together in front of her chest and mouthed, *Thank you.*

Madison's face softened and for a moment, Gia saw the woman her sister used to be before everything fell apart. Her heart squeezed, and she thought, *It's okay to lie about being engaged if it gets Madison back to herself.*

Justify it all you want. Still a lie.

Yes, but she was hip-deep in it now. No going back.

"Ladies"—Mike pulled a key fob from his pocket and started out the door—"your chariot awaits."

"I definitely see the appeal," Shelley murmured under her breath to Gia. "Nice ass."

"Hey, hussy, stay in your own lane," Madison grumbled, but in her voice, Gia heard a note of humor. Was Madison finally thawing?

She pressed her palms into prayer hands again, and this time Gia whispered a single word.

Please.

At the hospital, the neuro ICU nurse cornered them and gave a strict admonition. "Maximum two people at a time."

The sisters looked at each other.

"You two go first," Gia said. "Mike and I'll wait."

Madison looked as if she might argue at being saddled with Shelley, but she just pivoted and started through the double doors without looking back, leaving Shelley to hustle after her.

"You've got your work cut out for you," Mike muttered.

"Maddie seems tough, but you don't understand her like I do. Her heart is so tender, she's built up a tall wall. She can't bear getting hurt again."

Mike reached over, took her hand. "What about you?"

"What about me?"

"Maddie isn't the only one who lost her parents. You've been hurt too. Why didn't you build a tall wall?"

Gia shrugged. "I dunno."

"Well, tall wall or not, I'm here for you, Honeysuckle."

Unnerved, Gia eased her hand away from him, confused by the feelings his touch stirred. "You don't have to pretend when we're alone."

"I can't comfort my friend?"

"Is that what you were doing?"

His eyes met hers. "It was."

"Oh, well, then." She picked up his hand, and he held on tight.

An hour later, Madison and Shelley returned

to the waiting room. Shelley was pale and trembling, tears in her eyes. Madison's mouth was set in a grim line. They looked so wrecked that Gia wasn't sure she was ready for this.

"It's okay." Mike read her thoughts. "I'm with you all the way."

The sight of her vibrant grammy looking so pale and lifeless in that bed, plugged into machines, her head swaddled in bandages, was almost too much to handle.

Gia's knees buckled underneath her and if Mike hadn't been there to catch her before she hit the floor, she might well have cracked her head open.

Mike guided her to a chair, fetched crackers and orange juice from the nurses' station. Crouched in front of her while she ate them.

"Are you feeling any better?" he asked when she finished.

She nodded.

"The color is back in your cheeks."

She offered him the best smile she could muster, which was pretty feeble. "Could you give me some time alone with her?"

"Sure." He nodded. "Whatever you need."

"Thanks."

After he left, she sat beside the bed unmoving, the crumpled cracker wrapper clutched in her hand.

Grammy was the only mother she'd ever

known. She didn't remember her parents. Her earliest memory was of arriving on the steps of the Moonglow Inn, holding on to Maddie's and Shelley's hands as the CPS worker rang the doorbell, waiting to meet the grandmother they'd believed long dead.

The grandmother who had quickly become their entire world.

On her eighteenth birthday, Gia asked Grammy why their mother had told everyone that her mother was dead when she wasn't.

Staring out at the ocean with tear-filled eyes, Grammy had murmured, "It was a different time."

Gia wanted to ask what that meant but Grammy looked so sad, she'd let it go and vowed never to bring it up. When she'd asked her sisters about their theories, Madison said Grammy had given her a similar answer, and Shelley, the girl who preferred a superficial life, had said it was none of their business.

Heartbroken now, she studied her grandmother's slack features and saw nothing of the strong, vibrant woman she loved so fiercely. She reached for Grammy's hand.

Cold.

Her skin was so cold. Interlacing her fingers through her grandmother's, she slid their joined hands underneath the covers to warm her.

"Grammy," she whispered. "It's me, Gia."

Was it her imagination or did Grammy's eyelashes flutter? Hope lent her heart wings. Maybe, maybe she would pull through.

"Madison and Shelley came home. I let them read the letter you left me. Madison didn't want to finish the quilt. She's still so mad at Shelley that she doused the quilt with lighter fluid and tried to burn it. You should have seen her. She looked crazed. Not the family reunion I bet you were hoping for."

Gia glanced over her shoulder, making sure she was still alone in the room, and lowered her voice. "But I got Madison to agree to stay and finish the quilt. Unfortunately, I had to tell a whopper to make that happen." She confessed to her comatose grandmother about the fake engagement to Mike Straus. "He was really sweet about it. I don't think many guys would have agreed to play along. Mike even loaned me an engagement ring. He was almost engaged once. Did you know about that?"

A soft knock sounded at the doorway and she turned to see Dr. Hollingway enter the room.

Gia got up.

"Please, sit." The woman pressed a palm downward. Her face was grim.

But Gia didn't sit. Sitting felt like a disadvantage. Her stomach rolled, and her pulse slowed. The tips of her fingers turned icy and a sour taste filled her mouth. She wanted to plaster her palms against her ears, and hum, tra-la-la. Or dig out her cell phone and escape into Candy Crush.

Fighting her fear of unpleasantness, she popped on a bright smile. "How is she this morning? I thought I saw her eyelids flutter. After you stop the medication that's putting her in a coma, I think she'll be just fine."

The doctor shook her head. "Miss Clark, I—"

"Let me go get my sisters."

"I'm in a hurry. Can I just tell you what's been happening and let you relay the information to your family?"

Um, no. She needed her family. Madison should handle this. She moistened her lips. "Let me just—"

"We've already withdrawn the drugs we administered to keep her comatose."

Gia blinked and glanced from the doctor to Grammy lying lifeless in the bed. "What does that mean?"

"It's no longer a medically induced coma. She didn't regain consciousness when we took the drugs away."

Her breathing jacked from the slow lane to autobahn fast. Each breath slammed into the next with no space in between. She sat down in a hard chair, pulled her knees to her chest, clasped her arms around her knees, and swayed to and fro to calm herself.

"I know this is distressing news," Dr. Hollingway said. "But don't give up hope. This happens sometimes. It doesn't mean she won't eventually wake up."

Where was Madison? This was too much for Gia. "Wait, what . . ." She was having trouble pushing words through her constricted throat. "What *does* this mean?"

"We're here for the long haul. I suggest you and your family pace yourselves. Set up a schedule to take turns being with her. Get plenty of rest."

"Okay."

"Any other questions?"

She couldn't think. Her mind blanked. Numbly, she shook her head.

Dr. Hollingway stuffed her hands in the pockets of her lab coat. "We'll get you through this."

"Thanks," Gia whispered, but she was too scared to ask what "this" was.

After the doctor departed, Gia stumbled into the waiting room, her mission to finish the quilt more essential than ever. She needed it completed by the time Grammy woke up. She'd insist they get started right after lunch.

Not that she was great at insisting.

She must have looked wrecked because the second her sisters spotted her, they hopped to their feet. Dazed, Gia blinked at the people assembled in the waiting area. Many familiar faces. Grammy's friends from her quilting group, the Quilting Divas. Mike's sister, Anna Drury, who ran the Moonglow Bakery across the street from the inn. Their mailman. The beach cop who patrolled the beach in front of the Moonglow Inn.

Word had spread.

"What is it?" Madison took hold of Gia's arm and eased her into the seat she'd just vacated. "What's wrong?"

In as few words as she could, Gia relayed Dr. Hollingway's message.

For a brief second, panic crossed her older sister's face, but Madison quickly regained her composure. "All right then. I'll get us organized. We'll draw up a vigil chart and take shifts."

"But we need to finish the quilt together," Gia protested. "How will we juggle the hospital and quilting—"

"Sweetie," said one of Grammy's oldest friends, a petite little gnome of a woman named Erma. "That's why we're here. Darynda already called us in."

"That's a lot to ask of you ladies," Gia said.

"We're retired." Erma waved at Madison, who was already setting up a spreadsheet on a phone app. "Write my name down, Maddie; I'll take the first shift. I'll stay here right now while you girls go home and have that lunch Darynda's cooking up for you. I'll do a three-hour shift."

"I'll take a spot," Anna said.

"Put me on the list too," Mike added.

Within minutes, they filled the empty slots for the next three days. Then they all spent the next couple of hours telling lively stories of Grammy.

Gia couldn't believe the outpouring of generosity. Her heart overflowed, and it was all she could do not to cry as she thanked every volunteer.

Darynda texted that lunch was ready. Mike ushered them to his truck. They swung by the dry cleaners to pick up the quilt and arrived back at the inn just as Darynda took the last pieces of chicken from the fryer. They washed up and the five of them enjoyed the delicious meal on the back porch. To keep everyone's spirits up, Gia redirected the conversation whenever it started turning tense or gloomy.

When they finished eating, Darynda and Mike insisted the sisters relax while they did the dishes and cleaned the kitchen.

"We should begin quilting," Gia said.

"Now?" Shelley groaned and patted her belly. "I'm sooo full. I haven't eaten like that in five years."

"I think . . . um . . ." Gia stammered. "It would be a good idea to get started . . . I mean, since . . ."

"Yes," Madison said, getting up and going for the quilt Mike had left on the porch swing when he'd brought it in out of his truck. "Shelley, go in the sewing room and grab the quilting supplies."

Shelley made a noise like a tire going flat. "On it, General Patton." She scooted into the house while Gia and Maddie rolled the quilt into the frame.

"Is it too early for wine?" Madison muttered.

"Should we drink while we're quilting?" Gia asked.

"Shelley says she hasn't had a drink in five years."

"No kidding?" Gia pulled a rocking chair up to the frame.

"She says she stopped vaping, too." Madison grabbed a second rocker.

"She's changed." Gia positioned the third chair at the frame.

"I'm unconvinced."

They both turned. The fourth rocker loomed like a ghost. Grammy had sat in that rocking chair when they worked on the quilt five years earlier.

"She *will* pull through," Madison said.

"I know."

But the look they gave each other said otherwise.

"Here we are." The screen door slammed behind Shelley, who toted the wooden decoupaged sewing box.

They set everything up and took their places at the quilting frame. It was awkward at first. No one said much. Through the screen door they could hear Darynda and Mike talking in hushed whispers.

"Should we invite Darynda to quilt with us?" Gia glanced over her shoulder at the door.

"Grammy's letter said she wanted *us* to finish it," Madison said, taking tight, small stitches, and mumbled, "This'd be easier on a sewing machine."

"It's not the same." Shelley made stitches the same way she walked, with a loose-hipped, looping gait. "And you know it."

"Yes, forget modern efficiency. Let's take an eternity to sew a quilt. It's why we didn't get it finished in time for . . ." Madison trailed off, kneaded her shoulder with one hand. "I should book a massage after this."

"Still," Gia said. "Maybe we should ask Darynda, anyway? It's weird not having anyone on Grammy's side of the quilt. It feels unbalanced."

"Does being alone with us freak you out?" Shelley asked.

"Yeah." Gia shot her a sheepish grin. "Kind of."

The screen door creaked and Darynda came out onto the porch holding her cell phone. "Madison, Erma wants to know if you can print off copies of your spreadsheet in a big sans serif font, so that she can distribute it to the Quilting Divas. I'll take it back up to the hospital when I go."

"Sure thing." Madison looked relieved and darted for the door. "Grammy's computer password the same?"

"It's still you girls' names and birthdays all run together."

"Thanks." Madison disappeared inside the house and Darynda followed her.

"Do you think she's acting weird?" Gia asked Shelley.

"Who, Darynda?"

"No, Maddie."

"I dunno. I haven't seen her in five years. She seems bossier than ever if that's what you mean."

Mike came outside, smoothing his cowlick down with his palm. "I'm headed home, Honeysuckle."

"Thank you so much."

He walked over to Gia's rocker.

Oh dear. She supposed she should say or do something fiancée-ish. But what?

He leaned down to whisper in her ear. "Don't get up. I can see that you're elbow-deep in needles and thread." Then he kissed her lightly on the cheek.

As far as kisses went it was next to nothing. A soft brushing of his warm lips. No one on earth would call that kiss erotic.

But inside of Gia something weird, wild, and wonderful happened. A calm, pleasurable tingling started at the top of her head and slowly oozed down her spine, triggering a euphoric sensation inside her, much like the aftermath of a full-body orgasm.

Shocked, she felt her eyes widen, her jaw fall, and her pulse quicken.

What *was* this lovely sensation?

Mike smiled down at her as if he knew exactly what he'd done and strolled away, leaving Gia topsy-turvy.

Just then Madison burst from the inn, waving a piece of paper in her hand, distress painted on her face. "Stop quilting this instant. Family emergency. Grammy is about to lose the Moonglow Inn!"

CHAPTER NINE

Madison

INTENSITY: The amount of pure color or muted color present in a fabric.

Fix this.

Madison assembled her sisters and Darynda in the kitchen. In the middle of the table sat a letter from the bank, threatening foreclosure if three months of back payments weren't received within the next two weeks. Along with it, a stack of bank statements, unpaid invoices, and a calculator.

She'd done the math. Grammy was forty-six thousand dollars in debt.

"We've got trouble," Madison said. "Big trouble."

No one argued.

"How did this happen?" Madison stared pointedly at Darynda. "Did you know about this?"

Looking stricken, Darynda interlaced her fingers, rested her joined hands on the table, and slowly shook her head. "I knew the inn had gotten a few bad Yelp reviews and your grandmother planned on fixing up the place, but

I didn't know she'd taken out a mortgage against the house."

"I can't believe she put her livelihood, and our ancestral home, in jeopardy. This isn't like Grammy." Madison paced around the table where everyone else was sitting, palm to her forehead. "The house was one of the first homes ever built in Moonglow Cove. It's a local treasure."

No one said anything. They all knew that.

"Well?" Frustrated, Madison settled her hands on her hips.

"Do you think the brain tumor messed with her decision making?" Gia traced a groove in the wood grain of the table with her fingertip and didn't meet Madison's eyes.

She didn't have to look at her for Madison to know that tenderhearted Gia was struggling not to cry.

"If she borrowed the money to fix things up"—Shelley tilted her head back and waved her hand at the water stains on the ceiling—"where'd the money go?"

"Good questions," Madison said, feeling stronger now that she had something that was within her control to tackle. "I'll need to go through these bank statements. Try to track down what happened. If I could find where the money went—"

Darynda cleared her throat. "I can answer that."

All eyes swung her way.

"Helen paid a contractor who never showed."

Madison's mouth dropped. "She gave him all the money? Up front?"

"I don't how much she paid, I only know what she told me. That she paid a contractor and he disappeared on her." Darynda sat with her hands in her lap and her shoulders squared, a tight little unit unto herself.

"Why didn't you call me?" Madison glared at the elderly woman. "Why didn't you at least tell Gia since she lives in Moonglow Cove?"

"You're not holding me responsible for this, are you?" Worry and guilt saturated Gia's voice.

Madison shook her head. *No. Yes. Kind of.*

"Helen was embarrassed." Darynda brushed aside a lock of hair that had fallen across her forehead. "She didn't want you girls to know that she'd gotten taken. She asked me not to contact you. Besides, that was before we knew about the brain tumor. I didn't realize she wasn't firing on all cylinders. If I had known, I would have hidden her checkbook and I would have called you."

Sighing, Madison rubbed her eyes and willed away the migraine teasing at her temple. *Please, not two days in a row.* "Okay, so that's probably not money we're going to recoup, although I *am* making a police report and getting the advice of an attorney."

"How long has it been since Grammy's had

guests at the inn?" Shelley shot a glance from Gia to Darynda.

"She had guests last week," Gia said.

Darynda shook her head, contradicting her. "She hasn't had any bookings since New Year's. She told me she was clearing the decks for renovations . . ."

"What?" Gia looked hurt. "But she specifically told me she had guests. Why would she lie to me?"

"You didn't notice there were no guests? And why didn't you ask questions when the renovations didn't happen?" Madison asked Darynda.

"I did ask." Darynda stayed cool, unruffled. Madison liked that about the woman. "That's when she told me about the contractor."

Frustration whipped up Madison's spine and landed in her throat. Darynda should have called her. There'd been half a dozen red flags.

Yeah? And you should have checked on Grammy more often. You hadn't seen her in almost half a year. At most, you call her twice a month. Point the finger where it really belongs, Madison. On you.

But Gia and Darynda had been here. She'd expected them to pick up the slack. Remorse kicked irritation's ass to the curb. She couldn't hang this on just Darynda and Gia. They'd all played a part in the situation. They'd let Grammy, and one another, down.

No more finger-pointing. Time for solutions.

"I'm sorry if I sounded rude," Madison apologized. "But this is bad. We're at risk of losing the inn. We can't lose the house. It's been in the family for five generations. We've got to do something. We've reached a tipping point."

Everyone nodded. At last. Something they could all agree on. Pyewacket hopped onto the table, wandered over, and plopped down on top of the stack of bills, as if to say, *Pay attention to me*. Shelley reached over to scratch the cat under her chin.

"But what?" Gia toyed with the ends of her hair, coiling a strand around her finger, a nervous habit from childhood whenever she felt stressed.

"Do I always have to find the solutions?" Madison snapped, but Gia's hurt face sent instant regret shooting through her. She had to start tempering her irritation or she was going to isolate everyone.

Frowning, Shelley stood up and in a firm voice said, "Sit down, Maddie."

"Excuse me?" So much for quelling her anger. Why was it so hard for her to let things go? *Um, maybe because you've lost so much already?*

"Sit down. You're about to blow a gasket. That vein in your head is—"

"Don't tell me what to do."

"I don't know what your problem is . . ." Shelley's nostrils flared. "But you gotta stop taking it out on us. You bitch about always having to take the lead, but let's be honest, you don't give anyone else a chance to harness up. You plunge ahead, snorting and raring because no one else jumped in. Wanna know why we don't jump?"

Madison did not sit. Instead she folded her arms over her chest, feeling the raw edge of her anger scrape against the inside of her mouth. *Calm down, calm down.* But all the self-admonishment in the world couldn't tame her grief that cropped up under the guise of anger. "Please, enlighten me."

"Because you'll shoot down our ideas no matter what. You think you always know best," her younger sister said.

Her anger stumbled. Suddenly, she felt worn and weary. Shelley was right. She didn't trust others to get the job done right. She was a perfectionist. Guilty as charged. Finn had accused her of it as he'd walked out the door. *You never let anyone help you, Madison. Until you let someone help you, you'll always carry your burdens alone. If that's the way you want to live life, fine. But me? I want a* real *partner.*

Madison gulped, and unshed tears pushed against the back of her eyes. She tightened down on every muscle in her face, determined not to let them see the pain in her eyes. Hardened her jaw. Clenched her fists. "Let's hear it."

Shelley blinked. “Hear what?”

“Your ideas. I’m open to input. You have my full attention. What do you want to say?”

Mouth dropping open, Shelley sat down.

“Well?” To show she was accommodating, Madison sat down, too.

“I-I don’t know. I’m so used to you taking charge that I haven’t had time to think.”

“Go ahead. Think. I’ll wait.” Madison stretched her hands out on the table, palms down, and glanced at Gia. “How about you? Got any ideas on how we could raise money to save the inn?”

“I—um . . .” Gia moistened her lips.

Yeah, that’s what she thought, and they wondered why she made all the decisions.

Madison passed her gaze over to Darynda. “Do you?”

“My two cents?” For a moment, Darynda’s polished tone slipped into a lazy West Texas drawl. “Whatever the solution, you three girls should do it together.”

Madison ironed her mouth into a straight line. She wasn’t a girl. Hadn’t been one in a long time.

“Fundraiser. We need some kind of fundraiser.” Shelley snapped her fingers.

“Thanks so much, Captain Obvious.”

“Maddie,” Gia chided.

“Okay, sorry for the smartass quip,” Madison apologized to Shelley, who looked amused, not offended.

"How about Kickstarter like I did for the kite store? Or a GoFundMe campaign." Gia twisted another strand of hair around her finger.

Madison recalled one time when Gia was little she'd gotten her finger caught in a curl tunnel like a Chinese finger trap and she couldn't pull it out. Her high-pitched screams brought Madison running to the rescue.

"I don't like the idea of taking donations to save the place," Madison said. "It feels desperate."

"Well, aren't we?" Gia asked.

Shelley used her hands to simulate an airplane dropping a bomb, ending with clenching her fists, then opening them quick with her fingers splayed, indicating an explosion.

Madison cleared her throat and ignored Shelley. "All right, I'll try not to dismiss your ideas out of hand. How about we put Kickstarter as a possibility?"

Darynda got up and fetched a pen and paper from beside the house phone. "I'll make a list."

"Thank you." Madison nodded and lowered her shoulders, which had crept up to her ears. "Next?"

"How about a pop-up store?" Gia suggested. "We could shoot for the Fourth of July weekend. It's the biggest holiday weekend of tourist season."

"I'm liking . . ." Madison nodded, yet didn't finish her sentence.

"But?" Shelley propped her chin in her upturned palm.

"The Fourth is six weeks away. We need money *now*. I have some money put back that I can access to fend off the impending foreclosure, but we need to get the inn opened, ASAP. Grammy needs to get out from under that mortgage. And that's not even considering the medical bills that are piling up."

"Helen can't run this place on her own anymore." Darynda said it as if Grammy was going to pull through. "There are three of you. She shouldn't *have* to do this alone."

If her intention had been to shame them, it was working.

"I'll stay here and run the inn," Shelley said.

Madison snorted.

"What?" Shelley glowered.

"Don't pretend you're Miss Altruistic. Truth is, you don't have anywhere else to go, do you?"

"Madison," Shelley said, "do you have to work at being a jerk, or does it just come naturally?"

Madison gritted her teeth. No one here had any idea what she was going through. It was so easy for them to judge. They saw the external trappings—her own TV show, a glamorous life in New York City, enough money for a very comfortable life. But it came at a price and they had no idea of the personal cost, or how much she'd paid.

Because you're too proud to share that with them. It was Finn's voice in her head again.

"The upshot is that Shelley has graciously volunteered to run the Moonglow Inn." Darynda's tone was light, but her expression left Madison feeling scolded. "Don't dismiss your sister out of hand."

"If we're going to keep the inn open, we've got to renovate," Gia said. "Or we'll have the same problems with those Yelp reviews."

"How will we afford the renovations?" Madison asked.

"You're rich." Shelley drummed her fingers on the table. "Why don't you pony up the cash?"

"My money is tied up in investments." Heat burned up the back of Madison's neck. Did they expect her to sacrifice her future to save the inn?

"Madison shouldn't have to foot the bill for everything," Gia said. "I could ask Mike to donate his time. He's good with his hands. And the three of us could do the rest. Paint. Replace the kitchen tile . . ."

"Yes, yes. We're on a roll." Madison rubbed her palms together. She liked having a plan of action. She was at her best in motion. Brainstorming with her sisters was not the worst idea in the world. There was trouble at the Moonglow Inn, but there were also answers. Fingers crossed they could find them together. "Keep going."

"What do we sell in the pop-up store?" Shelley asked. "What services can we offer?"

"I can offer my kites," Gia said. "But my inventory is pretty small since they're hand-made."

"That's your livelihood." Madison shook her head. "We can't ask you to do that."

"You're putting in your own money to catch up on the back payments." Gia fingered the woven bracelet at her wrist. "I can do this. Let me do this."

"You're just getting your business started. It's not wise to deplete your inventory. You need something to live on."

"I can give up my new apartment," Gia said. "Move back in here. And I can let go my roommate who I hired to help run the kite shop part-time."

"Ouch." Madison winced.

"If you fire your assistant, then you'll have to spend all your time at the kite store," Shelley pointed out. "When would you have time for the renovations? Or your fiancé? Or finishing the quilt?"

"I'll do it," Darynda piped up. "I'll run the kite store and free up Gia's time."

Madison looked at the elderly woman and shook her head. Darynda might be in great shape, but at her age, things could go wrong at the drop of a coin. Grammy, a case in point. "Not a good idea."

"Madison," Darynda said. "Let me do this . . . for Helen."

"It's too much to ask."

"So only you get to make sacrifices?" Shelley launched in on her. "Only *you* get to martyr yourself for the cause?"

"I'm not . . ." Madison clamped her mouth shut. Shelley was just trying to get a rise out of her. "Fine. I accept your offers. Yes. We'll put kites in our pop-up store. Yes, Darynda, please help Gia with the kite shop. Yes, Shelley, you can run the inn."

Everyone stared at her.

Great. What had she done wrong this time? Madison resisted rolling her eyes. "That is, if it's okay with you all."

"It's more than okay, Maddie. It's nice that you're letting us shoulder some of the burden." Gia smiled, and it felt like a gift-wrapped package. "We feel useful."

"Wow, is this really happening?" Shelley pulled an incredulous face. "The Moonglow sisters becoming a democracy? Never thought I'd see the day."

"Watch it," Madison said, feeling weirdly lighthearted. They were joking about it. That was positive. "I reserve veto rights."

"I knew it was too good to be true," Shelley mumbled.

"Baby steps," Darynda said.

"Back to the pop-up store." Madison motioned for Darynda to write it down. "I can make door wreaths to sell. People go crazy for my wreaths. It's sort of a mystery to me why, but hey, if it works, it works. What about you, Shelley?"

"I suck at arts and crafts. The only reason I can quilt is because Grammy insisted I learn," Shelley said.

"So, we make quilts."

Gia looked alarmed. "How? There's no time for quilting. Not in the midst of renovations."

"If we got on it seriously, the three of us could crank out a quilt in a week," Madison said.

"That's assuming we work ten hours a day. A brutal pace." Shelley wriggled all ten fingers. "Especially for these fingers. Remember how stiff your finger joints get when you quilt for too long without a break?"

"And what about my wedding quilt? We have to finish that for my wedding," Gia said.

"The wedding quilt can wait." It would suit Madison just fine if they never finished *that* damn quilt. "You're not getting married until next September, right?"

Gia made a face.

"Right?" Madison repeated.

"We need to finish the wedding quilt for when Grammy wakes up." Gia reached in her purse and pulled out the letter Grammy had written her.

Just Gia. Why hadn't Grammy written a note

to Madison? A pang punched her in the heart. "*If* Grammy wakes up," Madison said.

"She *will* wake up." Gia stubbornly set her jaw. "She'll understand that saving the inn is more important than finishing the wedding quilt," Madison said firmly. "We'll cross that bridge when we come to it. Shelley, is there anything else you can offer for the pop-up?"

"Yoga classes."

Lame idea. There was no space for yoga classes in a pop-up store, but Madison held her tongue on that. "All right. I'll make wreaths, Gia will donate kites, we'll all work on quilting—"

"The Quilting Divas will help with the quilts," Darynda said. "So that it's not just the three of you building inventory. Many of our members have quilts they would donate. I have three at the house that I've never used. Presents for friends who passed away before I could gift them."

"You'd do that for us?" Shelley asked.

"You girls are like family," Darynda said. "The granddaughters I never had."

"I could ask Mike if he'd donate some of his furniture." Gia tapped her chin. "And build us a kiosk for the pop-up."

"We'll have to look into getting permission from the city," Madison mused. "If we get the permits, we could sell right here on the beach. You can hold classes on the beach, too, Shell."

"Politics are your bailiwick," Shelley said. "We'll leave that up to you."

"It's a good start," Gia said. "I feel better."

"Thank you." Shelley met Madison's gaze.

"For what?"

"Letting us have a voice."

Madison studied her sister. She knew that she tended to rush in and take control, but until this minute she hadn't realized that Shelley and Gia really wanted a voice. She'd taken control because no one else stepped forward.

Or she'd never let them before.

"We have a mission," Madison said. "This is good. But for now, it's my turn to sit vigil at the hospital. Darynda, can you give me a ride?"

"Indeed." Darynda took her car keys from her pocket.

Madison shooed Pyewacket to the floor, gathered up the bills, and carried them back to the desk where she'd found them, and for the first time since coming home, she felt like she could finally breathe.

Half an hour later, Madison was back at Moonglow Cove Memorial, standing in the doorway of Grammy's room, her hopeful mood eroding.

Nothing had changed. Same beeping machines. Same nurses moving quietly through the intensive care unit.

"You can go on in," said a voice behind her.

Madison turned to see the large nursing assistant who'd pestered her for an autograph the first day she'd arrived. May June, the woman of the folksy stories. "Oh, hello."

"Don't be scared of the machines—"

"I'm not scared."

"It's still your grammy underneath the whistles and bells."

"I know," Madison said, but her voice rose at the end making it sound like a question instead of a statement.

May June walked into the room, pulled up a chair at Grammy's bedside. Patted the seat. "Get close. Talk to her. They say that hearing is the last sense to go."

"Go?" Madison's throat tightened. "She's dying?"

May June smiled kindly. "We're all dying, honey."

"You don't think she'll make it."

"Only God can answer that question." May June fingered the gold cross on her necklace. "But either way, talk to her. What's it gonna hurt?"

Madison nodded, too close to tears to speak.

"Let me just turn her and I'll get out of your way."

"Can I help?"

May June looked surprised and pleased as punch. "Sure, that would be nice."

The nursing assistant showed Madison how to take hold of the folded support sheet underneath Grammy and use it to turn her on her side. "On the count of three . . . one . . . two . . . three."

Madison lifted her side of the sheet and Grammy smoothly sailed up in bed. It surprised Madison how light she was.

"Now, I'm going to take your side of the sheet and roll her over, while you stuff that pillow against her back. We don't want her getting pressure sores."

Once they finished positioning Grammy on her side, May June smiled again and reached over the bed to pat Madison's shoulder. "It's gonna be all right."

Easy for her to say. She had no idea of the chaos at the Moonglow Inn. "Thank you for saying so."

May June left, and Madison sat down in the chair next to the bed. Grammy looked so lifeless, as if she were already gone.

Stop thinking that way.

She scooted the chair closer to Grammy's bed, reached for her hand. "Gram? It's me, Maddie."

Grammy didn't move. Not that Madison expected her to.

"I found out about the inn. I wasn't snooping. The bills were right there by the computer. I'm so sorry I wasn't here to help. I'm so sorry you felt as if you had to handle things on your own."

She took a deep breath, paused. Peeked over

her shoulder to make sure May June hadn't lingered to eavesdrop. "Why didn't you tell me the inn was in trouble? Why didn't you call me when you found out about the brain tumor? I would have dropped everything. I would have been here in a heartbeat."

The minute the words were out of her mouth, irony hit her. Grammy had gone it alone, preferring not to bother her granddaughters or her friends with her burdens. Madison was exactly the same way. She hadn't told anyone about Finn, or the . . .

Swallowing hard, her fingers reached for her purse. She opened it and took out the piece of paper buried at the bottom.

The sonogram picture.

A snapshot in time of the baby she would never have.

"Guess I'm a fine one to talk, huh?" The tears she'd been holding at bay broke loose and slid down her cheek. "I've kept just as many secrets as you."

Pain twisted her stomach in a tight knot, wringing her out. "I never told you about Finn. I wanted to be sure of him and I didn't want a repeat of Raoul . . . but he left me anyway."

The tears came faster now. Madison laid her head on the mattress beside her grandmother and wept.

Finally, she sat up and dried her eyes. "What

is wrong with me? Why can't I find someone to love me?"

In her mind's eye, she saw her grandmother as she remembered her. Strong, but kind. Raising three little girls on her own while she was in her sixties. Even back then, Madison didn't cry easily, but sometimes at night, when her responsibilities got too great for her, Madison would sneak from the bedroom she shared with her sisters and find her way into Grammy's bed.

Grammy would scoot over, lift the covers, and pat the mattress beside her. She'd wrap her arms around Madison and hug her close. There, in the comfort of her grandmother's arms, she would sob her troubles away. Grammy would rock her and coo to her, give her a tissue and kiss her forehead, and tell her how courageous she was. How unfair life had been to her, but the challenges made her stronger, smarter, braver.

The memories spurred more tears.

"I thought I'd found the One with Finn. Of course, I thought that with Raoul, too. Finn was bright and ambitious. He *got* me. We finished each other's sentences the way you and Darynda do. I thought that meant we were compatible. But then I got pregnant and what I thought was a miracle turned into my worst nightmare."

She reached for Grammy's hand.

Clung to it.

Clung to her.

But there was no warm squeeze in return. Grammy's hand lay limp and cold.

"Finn said it was too soon to have a baby. He wasn't over the moon the way I was. He didn't suggest I not keep her, but I could tell that's what he was thinking. I resented him for not being one hundred percent on board and I think he knew that." God, she'd been such a fool. "I told him I was going to have the baby with or without him. He called my attitude selfish, Grammy! He said it was always my way or the highway. I know I can be controlling, but I was thrown for a loop. Was he right? Am I selfish?"

She paused, straightened, reached for another tissue. Dabbed her eyes. "Finn said losing the baby was for the best. That nature had a way of working things out. I was shocked to hear him say that. We broke up. Finn never really wanted her, and I wanted her more than anything in the world." Madison held up the sonogram as if Grammy could see it, hiccuped. "Best-laid plans, huh?"

The beeping of the machines was the only sound in the room.

"I started getting everything ready for her arrival. I turned the guest room into a nursery. I sailed right through the first trimester and just when I was starting to show, when I was about to tell my producers that I was pregnant . . ."

Fresh tears blazed down her cheeks. Damn,

she hated to cry, but losing that baby had just about killed her. "In my fourth month, I had a miscarriage."

The sob that wrenched from her throat was pure anguish. It took her several minutes to get control of herself. "The doctors say I have an incompetent cervix. I could have more miscarriages in the future. I don't think I can go through this again."

She raised her head, wiped her face. "Biggest irony? *Madison's Mark*, the nexus of my success, is about making a home warm and inviting. I'm a professional homemaker without a family to make a home for. How's that for a laugh?"

Outside it started to rain. Wind gusted at the window. Raindrops hit hard and fast against the glass.

Madison shivered. "You know, I almost told you when I came home for Christmas, but I couldn't bring myself to ruin our visit. I'm glad now that I didn't. It might have been our last Christmas together." She squeezed her grandmother's hand again.

The sonogram slid off the bed, floated to the floor.

Madison stared down at the image of her loss. The baby she'd been holding on to. She'd been carrying around this secret for six long months and it was eating her up inside. What had Grammy's secrets done to her?

Let go.

She heard Grammy's voice so loudly in her head that she startled and dropped her grandmother's hand.

"I can't let go of you. You're all I have left."

That's not true. You have Shelley and Gia. Hold on to what you've got. Let go of what's gone.

The sonogram was a symbol of her deepest pain. Of the relationships that had fallen apart. The baby she'd never hold in her arms. She'd been nursing her grief.

Feeding it.

She couldn't start healing as long as she carried the sonogram around with her. It *was* time to let go. Some things in life were beyond fixing, and this was one of them. A fresh tear warmed her cheek as she leaned over and picked up the sonogram and studied it for a long time.

Memorized it.

Tucked the picture far back into her mind.

Then slowly, deliberately, Madison tore the image of her loss into pieces and watched them flutter brokenly to the ground.

CHAPTER TEN

Gia

IN-THE-DITCH: Stitching next to the seams on the quilt surface; often used to define blocks or shapes.

"What happened in here?"

It was the next morning and Gia looked up from her store kiosk counter where she was dabbing the spinach-kale-kiwi-cucumber mess off the stingray-inspired delta kite that had taken her two weeks to make. Her pissed-off employee/roommate had thrown the drink against the wall when Gia told her she'd have to let her go and that she was moving out of their apartment.

Mike stood in the entrance of the small kiosk. He had a sprinkling of sawdust in his hair and a bemused smile on his face. He wore aviator sunglasses, khaki cargo shorts, a blue chambray work shirt with the sleeves rolled up, and deck shoes. He looked as cool and easy as the Gulf breeze.

"It was a thing. It's over." Gia rolled her eyes. "Don't ask."

"Are you okay?"

"Yes, sure. Why wouldn't I be okay?"

"You look . . ."

She raised a hand to her face and realized she hadn't applied any makeup this morning. Why bother? The ocean spray wiped it off anyway. And yet, she couldn't help wishing she looked her best for Mike. "What?"

"Gorgeous," he said. "But not your usual self."

"No?"

"You're not smiling. I'm used to the smile."

"Things are tense these days."

"I know." He paused. "That's why I came by."

"Oh?" She tried to sound casual but feared more trouble. It seemed that kind of week. Trouble around every corner. Inside every smoothie glass.

"Gimme that roll of paper towels."

"You don't have to do this."

"What are fiancés for?"

"You're not a real fiancé."

"I believe that *is* my ring on your finger. I believe you did say, 'Yes, Mike, I'll marry you.' "

"You know what I mean." She tossed him the paper towel roll.

Mike caught it one-handed, peeled off several sheets, and put the roll down on the counter. "Cleaning solution?"

"I'm using vinegar." She nodded at the gallon jug of white vinegar on the floor.

He moistened the paper towels with vinegar and selected a soiled kite to clean. They worked in companionable silence. The boardwalk sounds in the background—cawing seagulls, delighted screams from the amusement rides, the bump of Rollerblades on wood slats as a group of teens skated past. Just having him around, she felt calmer, more peaceful.

That is until Mike said, "I can tell something's bothering you. What's bothering you besides the angry roommate?"

She sighed.

"You don't have to tell me. Just know that I'm here if you need me."

"I don't mind talking about it." Gia set aside the kite she'd just cleaned. "Grammy is about to lose the inn." She turned to face Mike and told him everything that had happened after he'd left the inn the previous day. "I'm afraid I volunteered you for a few things. I hope you don't mind."

"Of course not, I'll help in any way I can. You know that."

"You're already doing so much." She held up the ring finger of her left hand. "I hate to ask more of you."

"It's my pleasure. Honestly, I mean that."

"Thank you." Gia put down her cleaning towel, wiped her palms against the seat of her yoga pants.

His smile was so reassuring that her heart skipped a beat. "To be honest, I don't know how I'm going to keep the kite store running during all this, even if Darynda does work for free. I'll have no time to create more inventory and I've promised my current inventory"—she flapped a hand at the smoothie-splattered kites—"to the pop-up store. I don't resent it, but I just got the business off the ground. I don't know if the store can survive me taking six weeks off to save the inn. I signed a year's lease on this kiosk and at this rate, I won't be able to make the monthly rent."

Mike moved to wrap an arm around her waist. His touch felt so nice, so reassuring. She longed to drop her head on his shoulders and let him make it all better.

"Things seem bleak now, but it'll dovetail. Give it time," he said.

"I'm being whiny, aren't I? I'm sorry. I don't mean to whine."

"You're not whining." His gentle smile sent her hopes flying. "You're going through some big rite-of-passage stuff."

"This adulting thing sucks."

"Sometimes, yeah it does."

"Hang on a minute," she said. "This is bugging me."

"Huh?"

She reached up and brushed the sawdust from his hair. Instantly, her body burned hot as if she'd been standing too close to a stove. She dropped her hand. Backed off.

He stared at her, his mouth partially opened as if he was stunned and wondering what had just happened.

Believe me, I feel the same way. It was weird and kind of wonderful, this curious new chemistry.

"You had . . ." She rubbed two fingers together. "Sawdust."

"Ah," he said, his smile as hot as August. "Casualty of being a carpenter. I just came from my workshop."

"What are you making?"

"A wedding arch for a beach wedding next month." His gaze found hers, held it for a moment too long.

Gia gulped. "Nice."

"About your problem. May I offer a solution?"

"Please do. I'm barely keeping my head above green goo here."

"Sublet your kiosk to me."

She shook her head. "I can't let you bail me out. You're already doing enough pretending to be my fiancé."

"It's not charity. I was already thinking about opening my own shop. I'm outgrowing my space at the art gallery."

"Good effort, but you're not fooling me." Gia shook her head. "There's not enough space in this kiosk, either."

"Hear me out." Mike held up a big palm thick

with calluses, nicks, and scars. "I'd keep the big pieces at the gallery and use the kiosk to display my smaller projects."

"Like what?"

"Shelves, scroll trim, wood boxes, stepstools, wall racks. If it hits, that'll be my cue to rent a bigger space when the time comes. If not . . ." He shrugged. "I'll square it up as a worthy experiment . . . and a nice tax deduction."

She wanted to say yes. Having Mike take over her kiosk lease would save her fanny, but was it fair to him? She'd already asked so much. "I don't know if that's such a hot idea."

He seemed puzzled. "Why not?"

"You don't owe me anything, Mike. In fact, I owe you."

"No, you don't."

She twirled his ring on her finger. "I do."

"Oops," he said.

"What?"

"More goo." He polished the underside of the counter with a paper towel, but she saw him cut his eyes at her butt.

Grinning, she turned slightly, giving him a better view of her backside, but casually, like she wasn't doing it on purpose. "I need to take down every kite, so we can make sure we get all the green stuff. It exploded everywhere."

"See? You gotta take the kites down anyway, might as well move out and let me assume your lease. I'll help you pack up and haul the kites back to the inn."

"So we're doing this?"

"If that's what you want."

Was it? She glanced around the kiosk. Gnawed her thumbnail. It had taken so much work to get the place up and running and now she was walking away. It felt like failure. *You're not doing it by choice.* Grammy needed her. Her sisters needed her. Family came first.

"I've got my van parked in the boardwalk lot if you want to go ahead and start moving now."

Wow, this was happening so fast. Her life was moving at a frantic clip, but yet at the same time, it also felt impossibly slow. Her time built around news from the hospital. Waiting to find out if Grammy would live or die.

"Okay," she said.

He came closer.

Lowered his head.

The look in his eye said he wanted to kiss her. Gia wondered if the expression on her face said that same thing. She moistened her lips with her tongue. Softening, wanting, waiting . . . so much damn waiting.

"You're awfully nice," she said. How come he wasn't already married?

"Not to everyone."

"I'm special?"

"As bird's-eye maple. Don't you already know the answer to that by now?"

Well, she knew nothing about bird's-eye maple, but she assumed it was something a woodcarver might cherish. Gia parted her lips, her pulse galloping. Mike thought she was special?

"You're trembling. Are you cold?"

Slowly, she shook her head, bounced on her rubber band knees.

"Scared?"

"No," she whispered.

"What is it?"

Sex starved. "I'm not used to Sir Galahad swooping in and rescuing me." She ran two fingers along her lower lip. "I'm not sure I like it."

"So you're what?" His eyebrows dipped in confusion. "Mad at me now?"

"No. Not mad."

"What then?" he whispered, his head dipping lower and lower.

"Well, *I'm* mad!"

Startled, they turned.

Mike's sister, Anna, stood at the doorway of the kiosk, a baby stroller parked in front of her.

Anna was three years older than her brother; tall, willowy, with a lush cap of auburn curls that Gia envied and a slender, swanlike neck that lent her a graceful air. She usually smelled like cinnamon and yeast from the bakery, and she had a smile that lit up the world, just like Mike. She'd married her high school sweetheart, Kevin, and they had two adorable kids.

Inside the stroller, Mike's sweet baby nephew, Logan, was sound asleep. The wind whipped Anna's calf-length floral dress around her legs, and she had her head cocked like a sharp-eyed judge ready to render a guilty verdict.

"Hi, sis." Mike raised a hand.

"Don't you 'hi, sis' me, little brother." Anna barged into the kiosk. "How come I have to find out from the UPS guy that you two are engaged?"

Yikes. More blowback. Twice in one day.

"Really? I felt sure you'd find out from the Beach Patrol cop first," Mike drawled.

"Don't be smart."

"Don't pull the big-sister card." Mike folded his arms over his chest.

"What card should I pull?"

"Go fish?"

Anna, a natural redhead, with intense brown eyes, didn't look a thing like her younger sibling. She glared at Mike but turned to Gia. "I'm disappointed. My brother is a knucklehead, but I thought surely you would have told me. Why didn't *you* tell me? I'm right across the street. It's not like it's a long walk."

Gia offered Anna her most apologetic smile. "I'm so sorry, I've been preoccupied with Grammy."

Anna's pique deflated. "I am so sorry about Helen. I told Darynda I wanted in on the vigil schedule."

"That means a lot, thank you."

"Your grandmother means a lot to me. She's the first one who ever bought anything from my bakery." Anna's face turned earnest. "I'm making the wedding cake, right? By the way, where and when is this wedding?"

"We haven't worked that out," Mike said smoothly.

"Let me know as soon as you do. I've got so many ideas to show you." Anna clapped her hands softly. "I'm so happy for you two! You are perfect together. Why didn't I see this before? Why didn't you?"

"We're asking ourselves the same question." Mike sent Gia a look that asked, *Am I handling this okay?*

Gia raised her shoulders slightly. How would she know?

"Don't I get a hug?" Anna held out her arms to her brother and embraced him. Then she moved on to hug Gia. "This is thrilling. Have you told Mom and Dad?"

"Not yet."

Anna stepped back, taking her cinnamon roll smell with her. "What's the holdup? I'd think you'd want to shout it to the world."

"Gia's grandmother comes first," Mike said.

"Plenty of time for celebrating after Helen gets out of the hospital."

"Yes, yes, you do have a knack for staying on point, Mikey. We'll discuss this later."

From the stroller, Logan broke into a wail.

"Oh Lord," Anna muttered. "Here we go again. He's been teething and barely sleeps for more than thirty minutes at a time. I'd forgotten since Allie how fussy teething babies can get. I'm frayed to the end of my rope with Kevin out of town," she said. Her insurance adjuster husband was frequently on the road. Anna leveled a look at Gia. "Word to the wise, don't wait seven years between babies. The gap is too big."

Babies.

With Mike.

The thought had never occurred to Gia, but now that it was out there . . .

Her gaze zapped straight to Mike's. The man *would* make the most gorgeous babies. She felt a strange and wonderous heat besiege her womb. Overwhelmed, she shook her head. This was too much.

Baby Logan tuned up quick, going from finicky whimper to full-on, I'm-not-happy wail in under sixty seconds. Sighing, Anna pushed up the three-quarter sleeves of her frock and headed for her son.

Mike put up a palm. "Let me. You need a break, sis."

Anna looked surprised but nodded. "Have at it."

Mike lifted the crying, squirming baby from the stroller. "Hey there, that's a pretty big noise for one little guy."

The small child cradled in the sexy carpenter's big, work-toned arms tugged at something deep inside Gia. A longing she'd never known was there.

Logan's small face was screwed up tight, tears springing from his eyes as he smacked his gums together.

"Let me find his teething ring." Anna rummaged through the stroller, pushing aside the baby blanket. When she didn't find what she was searching for there, she turned to the diaper bag strapped to the back of the stroller. Took out diapers, a bottle of milk, another blanket, her purse . . . "Oh no! He must have dropped his teething ring somewhere on the boardwalk."

Logan was crying so loudly that passersby paused to gawk.

Anna offered up a vague, harried smile as she continued to hunt for the missing teething ring.

"Shh, shh, boy-o." Mike bounced the baby in his arms and blew raspberries to get his attention. "It's okay, it's okay."

Instantly, Logan quieted, his eyes rounding as he stared at his uncle.

"Bet you don't even remember me, do you?"

Mike cooed, a tinge of wistfulness in his voice. "Since I was gone so long. But I missed you, boy-o. So, so much."

Aww. Gia melted. Slick butter in the hot sun.

Logan bumped his gums together harder and shivered, his face screwing up for a fresh round of tears. He sobbed and rubbed his little fists against his mouth.

"Your toothies hurting bad, huh?" Mike sounded completely besotted with his nephew.

Anna was still fumbling through the diaper bag, hands flying every which way as she muttered, "I can't believe I only brought one."

Unflustered by the racket, Mike offered up the knuckle of his index finger for baby Logan to gum and immediately the child soothed, giving a happy smile. "Is that better, tough guy?"

Logan clasped his small hands around Mike's wrist, holding on for dear life.

"He's got a strong bite. I feel like I hooked a catfish." Mike chuckled. "I can't wait until he's old enough to take fishing."

Awed, Gia stared at him. The guy had a way with babies. Who knew? But Mike could charm the birds from the sky without ever trying. Even babies fell hard for the guy.

Is that what I'm doing? Gia wondered. *Falling for him?* A fizzy thrill passed through her, as crazy as it was powerful.

"Found one!" Looking beleaguered, Anna

straightened, her hair falling messily back into place after she'd been almost upside down in her hunt for the teething ring. Triumphant, she held up the ring, saw it had a bit of blanket fuzz on it, and plucked that off. "I'll swap this out with your knuckle before he gnaws it to a stub."

Mike eased his knuckle from the baby's mouth and his mom stuck the teething ring between Logan's gums.

"Thanks," Anna said, combing a hand through her lush red curls. "You are going to make the best father ever."

For realz, Gia thought.

"Better than Kevin?" Mike teased.

"Kevin *is* a great dad," Anna said. "But you're far more patient. More patient than me even."

"That's only because I don't have to parent twenty-four, seven. You're a wonderful mother, Anna, and don't you forget it."

"Okay, flattery will get you everywhere. You're officially off the hook for not telling me about your engagement right away." Laughing, Anna reached to take her son.

Grinning, Mike handed her the baby.

"I can't wait for you to experience fatherhood for yourself." Anna winked at Gia.

"Fatherhood?" Mike gulped visibly.

"Not that I'm putting pressure on you or anything." Anna chuckled. "But Logan sure could use a playmate close to his age. While

Allie loves him to pieces, she gets bored with him pretty quickly."

"Cool it, big sister," Mike said. "We're a long way off from having kids."

Yes, especially since we aren't really engaged.

"It'll be the best thing that ever happens to you," Anna said. "I promise."

For the first time, it fully hit Gia how much her lie would affect other people. She'd told it for a noble reason, but standing here, in the face of Anna's overwhelming joy at her brother's engagement, her lie smacked her like a sucker punch.

There were consequences to her falsehood. Consequences she hadn't foreseen. It wasn't just an innocent lie. Other people were going to get hurt.

Ashamed of herself, she met Mike's eyes and his steadfast gaze of support was the only thing that kept her from coming clean.

CHAPTER ELEVEN

Shelley

SELF-BINDING: Using backing fabric as binding, rather than attaching a separate binding strip.

To pace themselves for the long haul, the three sisters divided their days into thirds. Or more accurately, Madison divided their days up into thirds and Shelley and Gia just fell in line like always.

Madison even made a spreadsheet and gave them all copies, just in case spontaneity broke out and it had to be wrangled into submission.

Excel, oh ye purview of the anal retentive, Shelley thought but did not say.

After leaving eight hours for sleeping, and one hour for transitions, Madison sliced up their schedule thusly. From seven A.M. to noon, they would rotate who sat at Grammy's bedside. The twenty-six members of the Quilting Divas would fill in on the afternoon and evening shifts. Darynda—who was only partially committed to Maddie's rigorous schedule because of her age—would take Wednesdays. Of the remaining six days, they each took two days apiece. Shelley ended up with Thursdays and Sundays. The two sisters who weren't sitting at Grammy's bedside would then run errands and cook breakfast and lunch for the sister who was on hospital duty.

The tight schedule was possible because none of them currently had jobs getting in the way. Madison's show was going on hiatus, and Gia had temporarily closed the kite shop and sublet her kiosk to Mike.

That meant the parlor—aka the TV room—was now kite central, with Gia's inventory hanging all around the room. Until they got the renovations finished there'd be no guests anyway and no time for TV watching. Shelley had been without a TV for five years, so that was no sacrifice. As far as a job? Shelley's employment prospects were bleaker than February in Alaska, but she couldn't worry about that now.

From noon until five P.M. they would work on renovating the Victorian. Each day, they'd take turns cooking dinner, one of them breaking off from the renovations at four for food prep. Then, from 5:30 to 10:30 P.M. they would all quilt.

Shelley added her own personal time to the schedule, sleeping only six hours and getting up at 4:30 A.M. as she had at Cobalt Soul for yoga, meditation, and a run on the beach. Maintaining her daily practice kept Shelley grounded and sane. Especially in the face of Madison's control-freakishness.

On Thursday, May 21, three days after she'd

come home, Shelley slipped into her grandmother's hospital room with ten different colors of fingernail polish tucked in her tote. When she was small, she loved playing beauty shop, and Grammy had good-naturedly been Shelley's guinea pig.

"Look what I brought, Gram-Gram," Shelley said, calling her by the nickname only she used.

She fished the bottles of nail polish from her tote and settled them on the blanket at Grammy's feet. Once upon a time she had rocked mani-pedis, going for interesting colors and intricate designs, back before *The Incident with Raoul* and that whole shit show.

Which was why she was in possession of so many bottles of polish. She'd found them where she'd left them, stored far back in the extra fridge Grammy kept in the garage.

"All the colors of the rainbow. Let's hope some of them are still good. I brought polish remover to thin them down, if need be, to get them flowing again."

She grabbed the chair, recently vacated by one of the Quilting Divas who'd spent the night—those Divas were the bomb-diggity—moving it from the side of the bed to the foot. Shelley plopped down and folded the covers back to expose Grammy's toes. Clicked her tongue, *tsk, tsk*.

"Girlfriend, you are in serious need of a pedi."

Shelley put a pillow under her grandmother's right foot to elevate it, then got out cotton balls to wedge between Grammy's stiff toes.

"Not that I can talk." Shelley stared down at her own bare fingernails. "But don't worry. I've got you covered." She picked up a bright red polish, Essie, *Forever Yummy*. "What an optimistic name. Me likey. Let's use that for your big toes."

Holding the bottle by the neck, she whacked it against her palm to mix the stagnant polish, then rotated it in her hands to warm it. Painstakingly, she leaned over the end of the bed and carefully painted the big toe of Grammy's right foot.

When she finished, she reached for a bottle of yellow polish. Grabbed OPI, *Sun, Sea, and Sand in My Pants*.

Laughing, Shelley said, "The name sums up my entire life."

Nothing from Grammy.

"Where are you?" Shelley raised her head, studied her inert grandmother's empty face below the bandages swaddling her head. "Where are you? Where did you go?"

Only the ventilator keeping her grandmother alive answered with a soft, rhythmic whooshing. The room clogged with the astringent smell of nail polish, mingling with the generalized hospital funk of citrusy disinfectant, mushy oatmeal, and stark mortality.

Tears threatened but Shelley sniffled them

back, not wanting to water down the pedicure. She finished up with the yellow polish, reached for a gentle purple-tinged blue color. Picked up the bottle but froze when she recognized the brand and saw the polish name.

Smith & Cult. *Exit the Void.*

Eep! Goose bumps popped up all over her arms.

"No, no, no, definitely not that one." She tossed the bottle over her shoulder and into the trash.

Shivered.

What could she say? She'd screwed up royally. In more than one way. Idiot adjacent. That was her. *Idiot adjacent? That's kind. Face it, you were just plain idiotic.*

Studying her grandmother's slack features, guilt swamped her. A hurricane of remorse and regret and sadness. She hadn't spoken to her grandmother in five years. Grammy had taken Madison's side in *The Incident with Raoul* and Shelley had been hurt to the quick.

But that was ego and pride. She should have stopped nursing her hurt sooner. It had been wrong. She'd been wrong. She should have forgiven her grandmother, even if Grammy couldn't forgive her.

The truth would have set her free, but telling the story of what had motivated her would cripple someone else, so Shelley had shouldered the blame in silence. It was okay. She'd go to her grave keeping that secret. In the meantime, she had to live up to her hussy persona. Embrace it even.

Misery tugged at her. Would she ever be able to make amends?

Shaking off the heebie-jeebies, she grabbed another polish and went to work. A few minutes later, she'd finished the second coat, each toe a different vivid color.

"Look, Grammy, coma toes!"

Staring at the cheerful, lively colors got to her. A rush of tears came then, sliding down her cheeks in a slick mess. She buried her face in an extra pillow, crinkly and stiff from the plastic protector.

"Oh, Grammy, I took it for granted that you would always be here. I thought we had all the time in the world."

A soft hand settled on her shoulder.

Shelley jumped, whipped her head around, convinced for a moment that it was Grammy who'd reached out and touched her.

Instead, she saw a sturdy-looking nursing assistant in scrubs and a badge identifying her as May June Barton.

"Are you okay?" May June had a whisper like a purring Pyewacket, rumbly, low, and lazy.

Shelley smiled, nodded, and swiped her tears away with two fingers.

"You did a great job on her toenails." May June

admired Shelley's handiwork. "When she wakes up, she'll see rainbows."

"That's what I thought," Shelley said.

"Good choice. Rainbows are a reminder of what awaits us after we've weathered a storm." May June dropped her hand. "Like God's promise to Noah after that forty days and forty nights flood."

Shelley crossed the fingers of both hands. "Here's hoping for many more rainbows in her future."

May June nodded but looked as if she didn't believe it even as she fingered the cross at her throat. "I just came in to check on her."

"Thanks."

May June leaned over the bed, readjusting the covers and plumping Grammy's pillow. As she stepped back, she glanced into the trash basket. "Dried-up bottle?"

"Huh, oh, the polish? No. It just wasn't the right color." She wasn't about to get into the knee-jerk reason she'd thrown out the polish.

"Smith & Cult is really chic . . . and expensive." May June fished the bottle from the trash. "May I have it?"

"Sure."

May June closed her hand around the polish, looking as if she'd just won the Powerball lottery. *Geeza Louisa, it's just nail polish.* The woman paused.

"Yes?" Shelley prompted, sensing there was something May June wanted to say.

"You Moonglow sisters"—May June slipped the polish into her pocket—"throw away some valuable things."

One of her sisters had thrown something important away? Shelley slanted her head and studied the nursing assistant. "What do you mean?"

"The other day. Your sister . . ."

"Gia?"

"Madison."

"What did Maddie throw away?"

"Maybe I shouldn't have said anything." May June buttoned up her lips.

Ah come on. Don't be coy, May June. "You gotta tell me now. My curiosity is begging on hind legs."

"Huh?"

Shelley waved a hand. "Never mind."

"Oh, I get it. Like a puppy. Cute." May June scratched her temple as if trying to work something out internally. "Maybe I shouldn't have taken it out of the trash, but Madison's a big wheel, and paparazzi are hound dogs and I wanted to protect her. One of the paparazzi already made it to the ICU nurses' station last night—although granted, it was just Jimmy Littlejohn from the *Cove Chronicle* and he's not exactly TMZ material. But the MCM security? Let's just say it's less than stellar."

Shelley had no idea her sister was so well

known there were people willing to go through their ailing grandmother's hospital trash to get gossip on Maddie. "Um, okay."

"Maybe you should give it back to her." May June scratched her elbow.

"What's that?"

"Hang on, BRB." May June raised a finger and bebopped out of the room.

TMZ, MCM, BRB? Shelley felt woefully out of step with the acronym culture the US had evolved into the five years she'd been out of the country. It seemed no one spoke in full words anymore, and forget complete sentences.

"Is she playing with a full deck?" Shelley asked Grammy. "You don't have to answer. It's rhetorical." Leaning over, she picked up the polish bottles and stowed them in her tote while she waited on May June's return.

The nursing assistant hurried back into the room holding a picture frame. She thrust it at Shelley.

Shelley stared down at the photograph of a sonogram. It had been torn in half four times and scrupulously taped back together so that all the edges lined up perfectly. The baby was a girl. Four months along. The date was the past November and the name at the top said *Madison Clark.*

Shelley's mouth dropped as she tried to absorb what she was seeing.

"I'm guessing she lost the baby because otherwise . . ." May June made a wide rounding motion over her belly. "She'd either be out to here by now or already have a baby."

Madison had lost a child? Apparently, she hadn't told a soul. Shelley's heart ached for her older sister. *Oh, Maddie, I am so sorry.*

She raised her head, met May June's gaze. Was that kind of snooping grounds for dismissal? Probably not since Grammy, not Madison, was the patient, so technically May June wasn't violating patient confidentiality. Still, it didn't seem aboveboard. Then again, they were talking small-town hospital here and May June had believed she was protecting Maddie from paparazzi.

"Are you the one who framed this?" Shelley asked.

May June gave an apologetic shrug. "I *am* Madison's number one fan."

"A little creepy . . ." Shelley chuckled nervously. "But okay."

"That's what my husband said." May June interlaced her fingers. "That's why I'm giving it to you. It's too personal for me to hang on to."

"Thank you for keeping the sonogram out of the hands of Jimmy Littlejohn and his sort. I know Madison appreciates it." Why had Madison thrown this into the trash at the hospital in the first place?

“You’re welcome.”

“I’ll get the frame back to you,” Shelley said, not really sure what she should do with the sonogram.

“No, no, keep it.” May June flapped her hands like a giant bird trying to take off.

“Um . . . thanks again.”

“Sure. Gotta get back to work.” May June popped out the door.

She left Shelley peering at the torn sonogram in a cheap plastic frame. Madison had gone to the trouble of tearing the sonogram up. Would she want it back? Most likely not. As proud and independent as her sister was, she probably didn’t even want anyone knowing she’d been pregnant.

“You should have burned it, Maddie, not left it in the hospital garbage for May June to dig through.” Shelley held the sonogram up for Grammy to see. “Did *you* know about it? Yeah, that was another rhetorical question. Don’t rush to answer.”

Feeling lost and more than a little lonely, Shelley stuck the picture in her tote bag and went back to admiring Grammy’s rainbow pedicure.

When Shelley returned to the inn a little after noon, she found her sisters having sandwiches from the Moonglow Bakery on the back porch. Plastic tarps covered the kitchen cabinets, double oven, and counters. Prep on the renovations had begun.

"We got you a veggie sandwich." Gia waved at the third box on the table. "We didn't know if you were still quasi-vegan or not."

"That's great. Thanks."

"Eat quick." Madison glanced at her cell phone. "Mike is picking up the tile for us and he'll be here any minute. We've got to get the kitchen demo started today. With Mike's help, we should have the floor torn up, cleaned out, and ready to start tiling by tomorrow. Fingers crossed."

Shelley wolfed down her sandwich—it was delicious—and finished just as Mike came up on the porch with a box of tile in his arms. They all jumped up to help unload his truck. Within thirty minutes, they had hammers, chisels, and scrapers whaling away at the old cracked kitchen tiles.

Pyewacket, disturbed by all the racket, took off upstairs to hide. Most likely her favorite hiding spot under Grammy's bed. Poor kitty was missing her mistress.

Physical labor was a great outlet. At Cobalt Soul, Shelley had learned that exhausting the body calmed the mind. Quickly, she fell into a routine knocking tiles with the hammer and felt herself mentally zoning out to the mindless work. Hummed "If I Had a Hammer." Which got on Maddie's nerves. Shelley could tell by her frown, but her sister didn't say anything, so she kept humming. Temporarily, she put aside thoughts of the baby sonogram in her tote bag. It was too noisy, and they were too busy, to talk about it anyway.

Besides, what would she say? How would she bring it up? Should she even bring it up? So many questions, but no decent answer.

Shelley glanced over at Madison.

Her older sister, dressed in beige capri pants, a black tank top, and leopard-print Roxy sneakers, made home renovations look stylish enough for TV, but of course, that was Madison's jam. She was in her element.

Sighing, Shelley glanced down at her own ratty T-shirt, holey jeans, and worn-out sneakers. Once upon a time she'd been such a clotheshorse. And then *The Incident with Raoul* happened and shoved her on a course of reluctant self-discovery.

Shelley finished demolishing the tile she was whacking on and duckwalked in a crouch to the next tile.

The tile in front of the pantry door.

Ugh.

The pantry where it all went down.

Guilt crawled up against Shelley's heart as her mind flew back to that fateful day five years ago. The day that ruined everything and changed the Moonglow sisters forever.

A sunny May day, much like this one. Maddie had been in their bedroom upstairs with Grammy,

Gia, and Maddie's two best friends helping her get ready for the wedding.

Shelley had never liked Raoul and after what happened at the Mardi Gras party two months earlier—well, that was something she didn't want to think about either. She hated that he stared at her when no one else was watching. Or how he'd wink at her and make flirtatious comments. Nothing too overt. Nothing blatantly sexual.

But he would smile that smug smile and rake his gaze over her as if he were imagining her naked. And she just knew that he knew that she knew what a douchebag he really was.

Maddie had sent Shelley to the kitchen for ginger ale to settle her nervous stomach. On her way to the pantry, Shelley had peeked out the kitchen window at the beautiful backyard with the Gulf of Mexico glimmering blue beyond.

Grammy had hired Mike to build an altar in the backyard for the wedding. Raoul was standing beside it with his best man. Satin covers and bows decorated the folding chairs. White rose petals lay strewn over the red carpet rolled out toward the altar. So beautiful.

Guests had started arriving. Ushers guided guests to their seats. Raoul's family, having just flown in from Paris, huddled together looking uncertain. Raoul had moved to the United States with his parents when he was a small child, because his father, a petroleum engineer, had gotten a job in the oil and gas industry in Houston. When his father retired, his parents had returned to France, but Raoul, a grown man by then, had stayed and gotten his US citizenship.

Raoul moved to speak to them. He murmured something, then looked up and caught Shelley watching him. His eyes narrowed, and his smile said, *I'd love to get you naked,* and soon he came up the porch stairs headed toward her.

Shelley stepped back from the door, heart pounding, and scurried to the pantry for the ginger ale. Busying herself with her search, she didn't turn around when she heard the back door open . . . and close.

It could be anyone after all.

Footsteps came closer.

Shelley went up on tiptoes telling herself she was looking for ginger ale, but she couldn't see a thing. Her entire body tensed as she recognized the sound of Raoul's arrogant walk. He was coming after her. She smelled his cloying cologne as he opened the pantry door and stepped inside with her.

"My last day as a free man." He paused.

Shelley couldn't look at him.

Her sister was marrying this creep, but Maddie couldn't seem to see how smarmy he was. Such a cliché with his slicked-back hair and gold nugget bracelet. Yes, he was handsome. Beyond handsome. And rich. He owned two car lots. One in Moonglow Cove, and the latest in Houston.

Was that what appealed to her sister? Good looks, money, power, status? Why couldn't Madison see through it to the jackhole beneath? Then again, Shelley had secret information about Raoul she didn't dare share with anyone because it would destroy someone she loved with all her heart and soul.

"This is your last chance." Raoul flashed those straight, whiter-than-white teeth. "To kiss me."

Shelley wanted to puke all over his polished Guccis. He closed the pantry door behind him, shutting them in together. They were alone, but people were outside on the lawn. She could scream, and they would come running, but it would be a case of "he said, she said" and she knew her sister. If Shelley claimed Raoul tried to kiss her, Maddie would say Shelley instigated it.

Shelley had to be honest. In the past, she'd done outrageous things to shift attention off her beautiful, successful older sister onto herself. The overlooked middle child.

Besides, there was the whole Mardi Gras thing and the secret Shelley must keep at all costs.

Raoul took the ginger ale from her hand and set it back on the shelf. Then he placed his hands on her shoulders and turned her to face him. Outside, she could hear conversations and the guitarist tuning up.

Inside, sweat pearled between her breasts and her heart raced and she thought, *I'm taking too long coming back with the ginger ale.* Maddie, in bridezilla mode, as she'd been the last few weeks, would certainly send someone after her.

That's what she was counting on. That was her on-the-fly plan.

Shelley's brain whirled. If she let Raoul kiss her, and they got caught, Maddie would have no choice but to call off the wedding and Shelley would never have to reveal the dark secret she carried.

Shelley would save her sister from making a terrible mistake. She'd be the hero for once. How appealing.

Raoul was the one who pulled her closer and lowered his head. He was the one who licked his lips and murmured her name.

But it was Shelley who went up on tiptoes and kissed him.

And she couldn't have planned it any better.

Just as Raoul grabbed her by the hair, pulled her head back, and shoved his tongue down Shelley's throat, Maddie threw open the pantry door, muttering, "If you want something done right, you've got to—"

Maddie let out a sharp cry.

Raoul jumped back, smoothing down his hair, and stammered, "Y-you-your sister kissed me."

At the same time Shelley crowed triumphantly

as if she'd done a good thing, as if she was expecting heaps of praise. "I told you Raoul was a lecherous asshole, now you have proof!"

But the only thing her impulsivity had done was break her sister's heart.

Madison collapsed, sobbing her heart out. That's when Shelley realized what a truly horrible thing she'd done, despite her best intentions. She'd never seen Maddie so defeated.

And she'd been running from herself ever since.

No more running. It was time to make full amends and put her family back together, no matter how much she had to grovel.

CHAPTER TWELVE

Gia

BLOCK: A quilt design unit generally composed of multiple squares that are repeated and formed together to make a quilt top.

By five, they'd completed the kitchen floor demolition and just as they finished, Darynda showed up with soft tacos, queso, tortilla chips, and salsa from El Mercado at the far end of Moonglow Boulevard.

Mike stayed for dinner and they devoured the food, while Pyewacket, whom they'd managed to coax back downstairs, snacked on kibble at their feet underneath the sturdy picnic table.

Gia and Mike sat next to each other, giving each other surreptitious glances and coy smiles, playing at being the happily engaged couple.

It was fun.

After the meal, Shelley cleaned up the dishes and insisted everyone else chill while she handled the chore. Darynda lowered the quilting frame from the porch ceiling with the pulley system and unfurled the quilt. While Madison went inside for the sewing box, Gia took Mike's hand and walked him home.

"Thanks so much for helping with the demo," she said.

"I'll be back tomorrow to lay tile."

"I'm sitting with Grammy from seven until noon, according to Madison's schedule." Gia angled just a little closer to him.

"Madison says 'jump' and you guys still say 'how high.' It's nice to see some things never change."

Playfully, Gia nudged him in the ribs. "Downside to living right next door? You know too much about us."

They stopped at the short stone wall that divided the two properties.

"Gia." His stare was a bit disconcerting.

"Yes?"

"How come it is that we've never considered taking our friendship to another level before?"

She'd asked herself that question a time or two over the years. Usually when they were hanging out on his couch watching football with pizza and beer and everyone else had left. Once, they'd even almost kissed. It was during a New Year's Eve party at the Moonglow Inn as the clock had struck midnight.

Mike was standing right next to her as everyone was shouting "Happy New Year!" and kissing people for good luck.

Mike had been twenty-five to Gia's eighteen, and for the first time she'd seen him as something more than their handsome neighbor.

He'd looked down at her, grinned, and lowered his head . . . and . . .

She'd panicked, grabbed a champagne flute from the tray Grammy was passing out to the guests, shoved the glass into his hand, took one for herself, clinked her glass to his, and hollered, "Cheers!"

Mike had the same look on his face now that he'd had back then, hungry, and hopeful.

Did he have feelings for her? Feelings that went beyond friendship? Or was it just the craziness of pretending to be engaged?

Her heart thumped at the notion. When she was fourteen, she'd had a terminal crush on him, but he'd been twenty-one, and much too old for her back then. Now, however, seven years did not seem like that big of an age gap.

What was going on here?

This was a man she'd known most of her life. Their families had spent holidays together. He'd taught her how to fly kites, and he'd given Gia her first taste of the pastime she'd turned into a career. He'd even carved the headboard of the bed she slept in at home with his own two hands.

That was some pretty intimate stuff right there. Was he feeling something shift between them as well? Or was she imagining things?

She stared at Mike's lips and he stared at hers, and a hard shiver shot straight down her spine. "I didn't want to mess up our friendship."

"Me either."

"Are we messing it up now?" She searched his face for answers.

"Not from where I'm standing."

Her knees quivered. "If this—"

"Gia," he whispered.

"How come you were never interested in Madison or Shelley?" she asked. "I mean, it would make sense if you were. They're closer to your age."

"I dunno. Madison was always so ambitious and focused. Shelley so carefree and unfocused. You, on the other hand . . ." He reached to brush a stray strand of hair from her face. "Are the perfect balance."

"Like the wobble boards you made for us when we were kids?"

"Exactly like that." He smiled. "Madison would stand on hers so rigid, afraid to move in case she got thrown off. Shelley rode the thing like it was a bronco, wildly overcorrecting and ending up getting pitched off every time. But you, Short Stack, you could gently wobble back and forth for hours without falling off."

"It's my low center of gravity," she said. "Madison and Shelley were just too tall."

"You don't give yourself enough credit. I say what kept you balanced was your flexibility. Neither too stiff, nor too loose."

"I better get back," she said. "We've got to get that quilt finished."

"Should we kiss?" he asked.

Kiss Mike? "What?"

"In case they're watching, I mean. We need to make this engagement look like the real deal."

"Oh, for sure." She nodded, eager for any chance to kiss him. "Let's put on a convincing show."

With a throaty groan, he wrapped an arm around her waist and pulled her close against him.

She raised her chin and he covered her mouth with his.

A soft little moan escaped her lips and he chuckled, the sound vibrating through her mouth. Gia wound her arms around his neck and wriggled nearer, letting him know he could certainly deepen the kiss if he wanted.

Oof, but he tasted so good. Hot and spicy with just the right amount of moisture.

The man knew his way around a kiss!

His lips were sweet, sweeter than she'd ever believed possible, and her giddy thoughts bounced all over the place. *I am kissing my friend. Oh gosh, oh gee, what have I done?*

Then, all at once, he stopped. "I'm sorry, I shouldn't have done that."

"No . . . no . . . it's fine." Oh, so much more than fine!

"Just part of the show?" His grin turned wry.

"Just part of the show," she echoed.

"Okay."

"All right. I'm just gonna . . ." She stood there staring into his gorgeous eyes.

"Go?" He arched his left eyebrow and the right side of his mouth.

"Yeah," she said. "That."

"Night."

"Good night."

As if in a dream, she turned, fingering her lips, and practically floated back across the lawn.

The breeze was soft and steady, bringing festive sounds and provocative smells from the restaurants farther down the beach. Music drifted from somewhere nearby. A solo guitar strumming "Sisters of the Moon."

The sun was still quite bright as spring barreled toward summer, and the longest day of the year. Dusk was still two hours away.

Drawing closer, she heard Madison mutter, "The girl's got it bad."

Was her sister talking about her?

"Jealous?" Shelley murmured.

"I can hear you," Gia said.

Madison was unpacking the sewing kit, putting the supplies within reach. Needles, thread, thimbles, a new pair of scissors sharp enough to slice through layers of material. She set the scissors on the small table situated between two of the chairs. The blades caught the sunlight, glinted.

Her oldest sister plunked down in a chair, reached for a needle, and threaded it with purple thread that matched the square she would be quilting.

Yay! At last. They were finally getting somewhere thanks to Madison's strict schedule. Her sister's overly orderly ways could tax a less structured person, but Gia had to admit, Maddie's organizational skills came in handy.

As always, Maddie was dressed camera-ready. Full makeup. Hair flat-iron smooth, the ends of the lob gently curled below her jawline. Stylish clothes. Tailored white slacks and a chic, button-down, navy-blue sleeveless blouse. Flawless mani-pedi. Gold sandals. A large gold cuff bracelet, diamond stud earrings, the crystal necklace she seemed never to take off. A Margot Robbie look-alike.

Shelley's hair frizzed about her face and she wore a long prairie skirt that looked like it had come from a thrift store and an oversize T-shirt. No makeup and she was barefoot. But she moved with such self-assured grace her outward appearance hardly mattered. Once upon a time she'd been so into fashion. What had happened to her in Costa Rica?

"Before we begin . . ." Gia touched the quilt as if it were a lifeline. "Should we explore some ground rules?"

"Ground rules?" Madison's eyebrows shot up.

"Explore?" Shelley looked amused.

They were making fun of her. Damn, sometimes it sucked being the youngest with two headstrong older sisters.

"Ground rules," Gia confirmed. "And yes, let's explore the off-limit topics to keep things running smoothly. Raoul is off the table. Don't mention his name."

"We get it," Madison said. "No mention of Shelley's transgression."

"Hey—"

"Shelley, please," Gia interrupted. "Let it *go*. And, Madison, I don't want you to bring that up around me again. That was five years ago. You're different. Shelley's different. Everyone is different. Got it?"

"Yes, ma'am." Madison saluted.

"Woo, look at you." Shelley batted her hair from her face. "All different and everything."

Gia blinked at them meaningfully. "May I continue?"

Shelley swept an expansive hand. "Go on."

"No talk of politics, money, sex, or religion. No talking about your show, Madison. Or—"

Shelley raised a hand. "Ahem, what *can* we talk about?"

"Grammy, quilting, Moonglow pears, the beach, flowers, kittens, puppies, sunshine and rainbows."

"We get the drift," Madison said. "Nothing

incendiary. Let's get this show on the road so we can finish the damn quilt and get on with our lives."

Gia's nose itched the way it did when she got irritated. Madison was not being a good sport, but at least she was here. *Take what you can get.*

With Gia's off-limit-topics ground rules in place, things started off well enough. But Madison seemed antsy. She pressed her mouth into a straight line and didn't glance up from her work. What was going on inside her oldest sister? There had to be a million emotions churning through Madison's head. To her the quilt must represent everything that had gone wrong with her life.

But Madison had survived. Not just survived but thrived.

Shelley, on the other hand . . . Gia cast a sidelong glance at her other sister.

What had happened to Shelley? She'd lost her spontaneous vibrancy. A hollowness lurked beneath her eyes that hadn't been there five years ago. She had been living with the guilt and shame over what she'd done. It couldn't have been easy.

"Shelley," Gia said, "would you like to tell us what you've been up to the past five years? We've been so busy with Grammy, we haven't had a chance to—"

"Off-limits," Shelley said. "If you can set up topic parameters, so can I."

“Okeydokey.” Gia focused on her sewing, her curiosity about Shelley’s whereabouts for the past five years growing.

They worked in silence for half an hour.

Gia pulled her needle through the cotton batting, making sure her stitches were tight and even. The square she worked was pink-and-white-striped seersucker fabric, gleaned from the dress she’d worn as a volunteer candy striper when she was sixteen. She gave as much attention to the quilt as she would give her kites. This project was for Grammy. It meant something monumental, whether her sisters appreciated that or not.

The evening weather was balmy, the sea light gray and calm. The sky was slightly overcast with puffy white clouds, the setting sun playing peekaboo.

On the beach in front of the house, a young mother formed sandcastles with her three children, all girls in sunbonnets and heart-shaped sunglasses.

In between stitches, Gia watched the laughing mom play with her children as they giggled and ran from the waves. Her heart gave a strange little bump. She barely remembered her own mother, and part of her still longed for the hugs and kisses she’d lost. Nothing could make up for that.

Madison had tried her best to fill the hole left by their mother’s death. Gia had appreciated the attempt and took comfort where she could find it. But Shelley went in the opposite direction. Gia remembered frequent fights between her two sisters, with Shelley yelling at Madison, "You can't tell me what to do! You are *not* my mother!"

Tonight, no one was talking about anything. Not even Darynda, who could usually find something nice to say. Gia thought maybe she'd been too strict with her rules.

Should she leave well enough alone and accept the silence? Or risk starting a conversation that could blow up? So many land mines lay between them. Resentment, hurt, guilt, shame. So much guilt.

The four of them were gathered around the quilt, Darynda taking Grammy's spot on the north end. It felt good, having the square balanced by a fourth person, but Gia still felt her grandmother's absence.

Hand sewing a quilt was a painstaking task, but Grammy advocated for the purity of hand quilting. Especially this wedding quilt, which was more of a piece of art than something intended for daily use. It was an heirloom, designed to be passed down.

The design was a triple wedding ring quilt. Three overlapping concentric circles. The pattern chosen by Maddie at the time of her wedding to represent the three Moonglow sisters. It seemed sad now, the history of the past weighing heavily on the quilt. Would they ever be connected like those three circles again?

"How was Grammy today?" Madison asked Shelley, her gaze on her sewing.

"Same." Shelley got her needle threaded and started quilting her section. "I painted her toenails."

"She would like that." Darynda's voice held a smile. "Helen did like to pamper herself when she had the time and money."

"No doctor visited?" Maddie's voice was light, but her jaw clenched.

"Not while I was there." Shelley quilted the way she lived her life, loosey-goosey, with imprecise, relaxed stitches.

Gia didn't mind Shelley's quilting style. Her personality showed on the palette. When you studied the quilt, you knew right away which section she'd sewn. Madison, however, was not a fan of her loping style. She watched Shelley's bendy wrist motions with pursed lips.

"So, nothing new at the hospital?" Madison asked. "No change at all? Nothing happened?"

Why did Maddie have to be so pushy? Gia noticed that Shelley glanced over at her tote bag sitting near the back door where she'd dropped it when she'd come in. Darynda was watching all three of them.

"Your number one fan was working today," Shelley said. "That happened."

"May June? She's quite nice."

"A little snoopy, don't you think?"

Maddie's head came up and she met Shelley's gaze. "What do you mean?"

"I threw away some nail polish and she took it out of the trash." Shelley watched Madison closely as if waiting for something.

Please, no fireworks, you two.

"Eww." Gia crinkled her nose in distaste. "I wouldn't fish *anything* out of the hospital trash."

"I know, right?" Shelley bobbed her head but didn't take her eyes off Maddie.

"She could disinfect it," Darynda said sensibly.

Madison stopped sewing, the needle clutched between her index finger and thumb, and sat still as a statue. "Was something wrong with the polish?"

"No."

"Then why did you throw it away?"

"It wasn't a flattering color on Grammy."

"So you just threw it away instead of bringing it home?"

Gia didn't know what was going on between those two, but she had a feeling it had nothing to do with nail polish.

"Yeah." Shelley locked Maddie into a staredown. "I did."

"That's wasteful."

"Yeah? Well, it was my polish to waste."

Anxious, Gia said, "Darynda, how was your day?"

"Things went well." Darynda's eyes shifted from Shelley to Madison and back again. "I—"

"Why do you care if May June took it out of the trash?" Madison asked. "If you threw away perfectly good nail polish?"

"I don't care about the damn polish." Shelley stabbed her needle through the square in front of her and raised both palms. "I'm saying May June likes to snoop through Grammy's *trash*."

There was a tone to Shelley's voice, innuendo that flew right over Gia's head. Something else was definitely unfolding between her older sisters, but she had no idea what it was.

"Oh." Suddenly, Madison blanched pale, then she said again in a completely different tone, a soft and surprisingly vulnerable tone, *"Oh."*

"Yeah." Shelley grimaced. *"Oh."*

Gia straightened. "What are you two talking about?"

"Nothing," Shelley and Madison said in unison.

Well, at least *they* were finally on the same side, but now Gia was feeling overlooked and incidental.

"You guys always leave me out," Gia grumbled. "Treat me like a mushroom, keep me in the dark and feed me—"

"This conversation has taken a strange turn," Darynda interrupted. "Why don't we change the subject? How are the wedding plans coming, Gia? Have you given the ceremony much thought?"

Grateful for Darynda, Gia said, "Anna Drury's making the wedding cake. We're having strawberry."

"A strawberry wedding cake?" Madison frowned. "Are you sure? Do that many people like strawberry cake?"

"Strawberry shortcake *is* a universal crowd-pleaser," Shelley said.

"I don't like how soggy the sponge cake gets with all the strawberry juice," Darynda said.

"Really?" Shelley stared at Darynda as if she were an oddity. "The sogginess is the best part."

"*True* strawberry shortcake is actually made with sweet biscuits." Madison shifted into full-blown hostess mode. Gia got it. Homemaking was both her passion and her job.

"Thanks for the strawberry shortcake history lesson, Martha Stewart," Shelley mumbled. "I feel so enlightened now."

Gia was getting irritated with them both. "We're having strawberry cake, *not* strawberry shortcake."

"You mean like a strawberry pound cake?" Shelley asked. "Or angel food? Dang, I'm getting hungry for cake now."

"You can't be serious, Gia. You're getting married in the fall . . . and it's a *wedding,*" Madison protested.

"So she should serve spice cake because it's

fall?" Shelley snorted. "How many people like spice cake?"

"I do." Darynda raised her hand. "I like all cake."

"Except soggy strawberry shortcake," Shelley pointed out.

"No. Gia should serve *white* cake," Madison said firmly. "It's tradition, and they should have a chocolate groom's cake on the side."

"We're not having a groom's cake." The ridiculousness of the conversation was indicative of their faltering relationships. There wasn't even going to be a wedding. It was all pretend. They were arguing over a pretend wedding cake.

"Why not?" Madison straightened her shoulders.

"Who needs so much cake?" Gia threw her hands in the air. "Who needs the extra expense?"

"What about the people who prefer chocolate?" Madison's sleek blond bob bounced in time to her vigorous head shake. "And if money is the issue, I'll make the groom's cake."

"What about the people who prefer strawberry, hmm?" Gia asked. "What about them?" Why was she being stubborn? It wasn't like her and it wasn't as if she was married to the idea of strawberry, but she couldn't seem to stop defending the flavor choice.

Shelley blew a raspberry. "Pfftt on tradition.

She can have strawberry cake and forget having a groom's cake if that's what she wants."

"A good host thinks of her guests' wants and needs, not her own." Madison looked so damned prim.

"But Gia is the one getting married and she didn't hire you as her wedding planner. Let her serve whatever she wants."

Okay, things were officially out of hand.

Desperate to get the quilting back on track, Gia pressed her palms together in front of her heart. "Could we not—"

"Traditions are traditions for a reason. Sacred rituals give—"

"Oh, save the *Madison's Mark* speech for your TV show." Shelley's eyes narrowed and her nostrils flared. "We're not your demographic."

"Girls," Darynda said. "Let's all—"

Madison stuck out her palm. "Hand me the scissors."

Gia added, "Please."

Shelley picked up the scissors from the table beside her, held them out of Madison's reach. "Tell Gia that strawberry cake is perfectly fine for her fall wedding."

"But it's *not*." Madison stood up.

Shelley jumped up, knocking over her chair in the process. It smacked to the floor with a loud bang.

Gia and Darynda cringed in unison.

"It's not your wedding. You already had your chance."

"Yes, I did, Shelley, and *you* blew it."

They glared at each other, arms akimbo.

"I'll have white cake, Maddie," Gia said. "I'll have white cake. Just please, sit back down. White cake it is. And I'll do the groom's cake, too."

"Don't cave in to her, Gia," Shelley said. "Bowing down just feeds the beast."

"Are you calling me a beast?" Madison's eyes were daggers.

"Girls!" Darynda's voice was sharp but no one was listening to her.

"If the shoe fits . . ." Shelley crossed her arms and glowered.

"Please, please, please, can we just get along?" Gia beseeched.

"Give me those scissors right now." Madison growled, her eyes dark and her body shaking all over as she glared at Shelley. "Or I *will* come over there and I *will* take them away from you."

Shelley dangled the scissors over her head. "C'mon, I dare you."

"Son of a bitch!" Madison exploded.

"Madison, stop it," Darynda said.

For one horrific second, Gia thought Madison was about to throat-punch Shelley. She swung her gaze to her older sister, ready to fling herself in front of Shelley to protect her, but Madison was staring out across the yard at the beach.

Something else besides Shelley had triggered her curse.

"What is it?" Gia swiveled her head.

Darynda stood up. "Mercy, what is going on here?"

Her sister stormed down the porch steps. On her way across the sloping lawn, Madison stopped long enough to snatch up one of Grammy's pink flamingos staked into the ground. "Hey, you. You there!"

Simultaneously, Shelley and Gia hurried down the steps after her as Madison waved the plastic pink flamingo at a male jogger who'd stopped to urinate in the shrubbery dividing the Moonglow Inn property from their neighbors to the west. Darynda stayed on the porch watching the altercation.

The guy startled and fell back into the sand on his butt, raising his arms to cover his face as Maddie charged him.

"Pervert!" she exclaimed.

Even from the middle of the lawn, Gia could hear the swoosh when Madison swung the flamingo through the air like a baseball bat. In high school, Madison had played softball, and she'd been damn good at it.

Uh-oh. Gia pitied the guy.

Lifting his butt up off the sand, he scurried

backward on his hands like a hermit crab, desperate to get away from flamingo-wielding Madison, but unable to scramble to his feet before she reached him.

Madison swatted at his crotch with the flamingo, but he rolled away before she made contact. "How dare you pee in the bushes! This is a family beach! There are children around! If you can't wait for the Porta Potty, have the decency to go in the ocean!"

Shelley and Gia flew down the beach toward them. Gia wasn't really sure whether they were there to back up Madison or save the jogger.

Maddie swung the flamingo again, but he was quicker and got out of the way.

Arm raised to protect his face, he cried, "I'm sorry, I'm sorry."

Maddie stood over him, breathing hard and straddling his legs, the flamingo cocked back on her shoulder, sweat beading her brow.

The jogger cupped his crotch. "Please don't hit me."

"Madison," Shelley said, her voice soft, but firm. "Put down the flamingo. He's not the one you're really mad at."

"He was peeing in our bushes." Madison held tightly to the flamingo, but Gia saw all the fight go out of her. "It's the third time this week, and I'm sick of it. Just because he has a penis doesn't mean the world is his toilet."

"You're crazy, lady." The jogger chuffed.

"I suggest you hush up," Shelley said. "Before we go back to the house and let her have at you."

"Don't go," the jogger said in a high, scared voice.

"For the record"—Maddie sniffed—"I didn't hit you."

"It wasn't from lack of trying." The jogger kept his hands firmly resting over his junk. "I was too quick for you."

"I could smack you right now." Madison raised the flamingo again.

The jogger squealed and curled into a ball.

"Maddie," Gia coaxed. "Please put down the yard ornament."

"Should I call the police?" Darynda asked from across the lawn, raising her voice to be heard.

Gia shook her head at Darynda, waved a hand. "We've got this."

Breathing heavily, Madison handed the flamingo to Gia.

Shelley snapped her fingers at the jogger. "Stop peeing in people's bushes. If you do it again, we're calling Beach Patrol and reporting you for indecent exposure."

"Don't get your panties in a bunch. It's no big deal. I was just taking a whiz." His eyes went flat.

"Gia." Shelley made *gimme* motions with her fingers. "Hand me that flamingo . . ."

The jogger clambered to his feet. “You’re all crazy.”

“Scram,” Shelley said from the corner of her mouth. “And if I were you, I’d find another place to jog.”

The jogger took off at a dead sprint, kicking sand all over them.

“What is going on with you?” Gia asked Maddie, concerned for her sister’s mental health. Was it the stress of Grammy’s illness? Or were there more wounds seething inside Maddie that Gia knew nothing about?

“I’m tired of men feeling free to whip it out whenever they want.” Madison crossed her arms over her chest. “Without consequences.”

“You need a hug.” Shelley held her arms wide.

Madison rolled her eyes, but she let Shelley hug her.

“See.” Gia counted the hug as a win. “That wasn’t so terrible, was it?”

“Group hug.” Shelley freed one arm and waved Gia over.

Together, arms around one another, they turned and walked back to the house. On the porch, they discovered that Darynda had closed and raised the quilting frame, poured four glasses of wine and set them on the table, and opened a second bottle.

Quilting was over for the evening.

They might not have made much headway on

the quilt, but they *had* shared a group hug and that was something. Gia would take any forward motion she could get.

For two hours, the four of them drank and talked and remembered.

Fun stuff. Silly stuff. Adventures they'd had. People they'd met. Stories of running the inn. Nothing heavy. Nothing sad. Nothing that stirred tension. As if they'd silently agreed upon a truce, and while the cease-fire might be tentative, for the first time since her sisters had come home, Gia saw genuine hope.

At eleven, Darynda called it a night. Because she'd had too much to drink, she took one of the guest bedrooms to sleep in.

Madison followed shortly afterward, leaving Shelley and Gia on the porch, both a little tipsy and riding the glow of what turned out to be a nice evening.

"I get the feeling something is going on with Madison. Something more than just Grammy," Gia said, finishing off the last of the wine.

"There is."

Gia sat up straighter, wished her head wasn't so fuzzy. "What is it?"

"She's been carrying around a big secret and she's too proud to tell us about it," Shelley said.

"What secret?"

Silently, Shelley got up, went to her tote bag,

took something out. She came back and slipped a framed picture into Gia's hands.

Confused, Gia stared at the dark grainy photograph that had been torn in pieces and then taped back together, trying through the haze of wine and the lull of the ocean to figure out what she was seeing.

When she finally realized what the picture was, Gia's heart broke right in two.

CHAPTER THIRTEEN

Madison

MIRROR IMAGE: The reverse of an image or how it might appear if held up to a mirror.

Standing at the open window of the blue room, the ocean breeze ruffling the material of her silk pajamas, Madison could see the corner of the back porch. She heard her sisters murmuring in the darkness below and thought, *They know.*

Thanks to May June, who liked to dig in trash cans.

It was a relief actually, that her sisters had found out and she hadn't had to tell them herself. Hadn't had to say the words *I was pregnant, but lost the baby*. Hadn't had to listen to the useless condolences, the sorrowful expressions, the too-tight hugs.

Still, it felt lonely here, by herself.

Disconnected.

Cut off.

Severed.

Not just from her sisters, but from herself. From the bright, industrious girl she used to be. The girl with such big dreams.

What a naïve child she'd been. Thinking she knew all the answers.

Madison put a hand to her belly, closed her eyes, and fell back onto the bed. The springs creaked softly underneath her weight. She thought of the pink bedroom in her apartment. Not a gauche color like bubble gum or Barbie DreamHouse, but a demure dusty rose that could grow with the child.

She'd given away the bassinet, the crib, the changing table. Donated the toys. Sold the clothes on Letgo. All the things she'd bought prematurely, optimistically. But she'd lost the momentum of her salty grief by the time the room was emptied, and she hadn't dredged up the energy to paint over those pink walls.

Besides, what color would she paint them? Certainly not blue. She'd been staying in this blue bedroom for only a few days and already a slow, steady indigo mood dragged at her, pulling her back toward the dark depression that had engulfed her after . . . well . . . everything.

A fan of old-fashioned names, she'd already had one picked out for the baby. Claire Estelle. Bright Star. After *it* happened, she'd named a star for her daughter through the Star Registry, paying extra for a bright, easily locatable star. Received a certificate with the coordinates to the Claire Estelle Clark star and a Swarovski crystal star to commemorate it. The crystal she'd turned into the necklace that she never took off.

Madison fingered the crystal at her throat. She'd thought naming a star would help her feel closer to the baby when she looked up into the night sky. But she lived in Manhattan, where you couldn't see the stars for the lights.

You're at the beach now, Madison. Go outside and look for your baby.

Not yet. Not while her sisters were still out there. She lay in bed, staring up at the ceiling, not the least bit sleepy. She thought of her mother. Wondered if she had loved her daughters as much as Madison had loved Claire Estelle.

Restlessly, she got out of bed, slipped into the hallway. Heard Darynda's gentle snoring from the room she was sleeping in.

Padding into the bedroom where the Moonglow sisters had once slept in the three black wrought-iron twin beds lined up in a row, Madison paused. Shelley had taken her old bed in the middle. Her sister's backpack sat at the foot of the mattress, as if waiting for her to pack up and take off at a moment's notice.

That morning, while Shelley had been at the hospital painting Grammy's toes, and learning secrets from Madison's number one fan, Gia had driven Madison all over town to run errands.

They'd gone to the bank and paid enough to prevent the foreclosure from going forward.

They'd contacted the police and learned they couldn't even file a police report against the contractor who'd absconded with Grammy's money because they weren't the victims. They'd consulted Grammy's attorney and learned she had a will leaving the Moonglow Inn to all three of them. They visited some of the Quilting Divas and collected quilts the ladies were donating to the Fourth of July pop-up store. Then they went by the AT&T store where Madison bought Shelley a cell phone.

All in all, a productive day, even though she'd forgotten to give Shelley the phone. Fixing things, ticking off items on a checklist, boosted Madison's spirits, but the organizational high didn't last for long. Soon, she turned bored and edgy, looking for more things that needed her intervention.

At the end of the twin beds sat three identical hope chests. Madison hadn't looked inside hers in years. She sank down on her knees in front of it, ears tuned for sounds of her sisters coming inside the house.

She didn't want Shelley to catch her in here. Not because she was snooping—it was her hope chest after all—she just didn't want to deal with her sister. They might have made some inroads toward civility, but Madison didn't trust the tentative cease-fire.

Shelley could test the patience of Job. And patience was not Madison's long suit.

The hope chest hinge creaked loudly. “Shh, shh.” Madison lifted a finger to her lips.

Look at you, trying to control an inanimate object.

Yeah, okay, she had control issues. Said everyone who took it upon themselves to point out Madison’s flaws.

She paused, ears cocked, wondering if the noise had alerted her sisters. She didn’t know why she was being furtive. She only knew she didn’t feel like talking to them about the baby. It was her pain and she didn’t want to share.

Her mind drifted from her sisters, to her lost child, and finally to her mother. In her head, she was eight again, remembering the time she’d found Mom sobbing in the kitchen one winter day. She’d rushed to her, wrapped her arms around her.

Hugged her tight.

Mom hugged her back. She remembered that clearly because Mom hardly ever hugged her back, so she did not forget the times when it happened.

“Sonny Bono’s dead,” wailed Mom. “Sonny was skiing in Tahoe and ran into a tree. It could just as easily have been me or your dad.”

Fear gripped her. What if Mom ran into a tree when she and Dad went skiing? What if Mom died? What if Dad died? That would leave just Madison to take care of her sisters.

"Maybe he's just hurt," Madison had said, trying to comfort her mother and herself. Not that she had any idea who Sonny Bono was. Someone Mom and Dad skied with? But if he wasn't dead, that meant you couldn't die while skiing. Right? "Maybe he's not *really* dead."

"He's dead. It was all over the news." A fat tear slid down Mom's cheek. "So sad."

"Are you going to the funeral?"

"Silly." Mom frowned and made fart noises with her mouth. "I can't go to Sonny Bono's funeral. He's a big celebrity."

"Oh."

Mom went back to crying, sobbing as if her heart would break over a man that Madison had never heard of. Would Mom cry that much if she died?

Dread took Madison's hand, and to this day she could still recall the stark fear that had driven through her. The fear was why the bizarre memory stuck. Goose bumps raised on her arms and she shivered hard as if she'd had a premonition.

Flash forward one year later. A babysitter was staying with them at their house in Denver while Mom and Dad skied Vail. It was early afternoon and they'd just trooped in from building a snowman on the lawn. Two policemen came up on the front porch. They looked grim and sad, as if they were truly sorry for something bad. The words the tallest cop had spoken were forever branded in Madison's mind.

Avalanche on the ski slope. Five lives lost.

Her mother and father were among them.

In a flash, Madison's greatest fear, that she'd be left alone to raise her younger sisters, came to pass.

Later, when they found out they *did* have a grammy, the burden lifted from her young shoulders. But Madison had never forgotten—and had never let go of her need for a family.

Even after Shelley blew it all up.

Kneeling in front of the hope chest, Madison reached inside and found the photo album she'd gone searching for, tucked it under her arm, and slipped out the front door, just as she heard her sisters coming in the back.

She settled into the front porch rocking chair. Moonglow Boulevard glimmered empty in the moonlight at this time of night. The blooming honeysuckle on the fence scented the air sweet.

Pulling in a deep breath, Madison opened the album.

In the first picture she saw her mother sitting in a waist-high snowbank with a red tasseled ski cap perched atop her shiny blond hair. A true snow bunny who'd been born on a Texas coast when she should have been born in the mountains. His little Snow Bunny, that's what Dad called Mom. On the next page she saw her mother in her wedding dress—not frilly and fancy, no lace or tulle—simple satin, a bluish white. Her hair pinned up in a French twist Bridget Bardot–style. She wore too-thick false eyelashes, and her lips were painted a deep scarlet as she winked coyly over her shoulder at the photographer. She saw Mom in her Target uniform, red polo shirt and khaki pants, headed out the front door, a spiteful expression on her face as Dad snapped the photo. Mom had hated having her picture taken in that uniform.

Hated that job.

Sometimes, her mother hated the world.

Madison had no idea where the bitterness came from, but from time to time she felt it brewing up inside herself. Whenever things didn't go according to plan, when her expectations went unmet, when people didn't dance to the tune of her drumming. It was an unattractive trait. She knew it, tried to harness her anger and rein it in, but she wasn't always successful.

Particularly around her sisters.

Once upon a time they'd been so close. Could they ever be the way they were before? Or would they, one day, end up completely cut off from each other like Grammy and Mom, because they could no longer find common ground?

Madison closed the album, curled her fingers around the binding. She'd never found out why Mom had left Moonglow Cove and the sunny beaches of the Gulf of Mexico to end up a snow bunny in the mountains of Colorado.

From her grandmother, Madison learned her mother left home at eighteen, after a big rift with Grammy, but she knew nothing about the fight or the circumstances. When, as an inquisitive teen, she'd asked Grammy what happened between them, Grammy had said with deep sadness in her eyes, "Some things hurt too much to talk about."

At the time the answer angered Madison. She felt she deserved to know *why* she'd been kept in the dark about having a loving grandmother for so many years.

But now, she understood. Some things just couldn't be fixed, so it was better not to talk about them. Putting a hand to her flat belly, Madison left the album on the rocking chair and wandered out into the yard in her nightgown.

Looking up into the night sky until she found the star Claire Estelle, she whispered, "Shine on, my little darling, shine on," while hot tears rolled down her cheeks.

Not having a car bothered Madison. It meant waiting for Gia or Darynda to haul her somewhere or using a ride-share service. She needed a rental car.

Even though it was long after midnight before she'd fallen asleep, she was up before six, and since the kitchen was in upheaval from the renovations, she popped over to the Moonglow Bakery for a box of pastries.

By the time she walked back across the street to the inn, Darynda was up and dressed. Stepping gingerly around the demolished floor, her grandmother's friend slipped a coffee pod into the single-serving coffee machine. She and Madison took their breakfast to the back porch where the wine bottles and glasses still sat on the table.

Madison snorted. Her sisters could have cleaned up at least.

Okay, that right there? It was Finn's voice in her head. *It's the kind of attitude that widens divides. You expect too much out of people, Madison. We can't all be saints.*

Feeling like a jerk, Madison forced a smile and pushed away her expectations that her sisters should have done what she would have. She threw away the wine bottles, picked up the glasses, and took them inside to wash. When she finished, she went back outside to find Darynda deadheading Grammy's rosebushes.

"Can you give me a ride? Gia is moving out of her apartment today and can't—"

Darynda pulled her car keys from her pocket, dangled them from her thumb. "I read minds."

"Thanks."

Darynda put the pruning shears back in the garden box and dusted her hands together. "You ready?"

"Just let me grab my purse and leave the cell phone I bought for Shelley."

"I wonder how she was living without a phone all this time," Darynda mused, following her inside and waiting while Madison grabbed her purse, scribbled a note for her sister, and left the note on the kitchen table with the new cell phone.

Madison shrugged. "My guess is they didn't have cell service where she was in Costa Rica."

"What is *that* story, do you suppose?" Darynda asked, leading the way to her Mini Cooper.

"Who knows? I'm not prying. It's Shelley's secret to keep."

"Don't you think there have been enough secrets around here?"

Madison narrowed her eyes, screwed her mouth up to one side. "What secrets are you referring to?"

Darynda shook her head and got behind the wheel. "Never mind me. It's none of my business how you Moonglow sisters interact."

"Seriously, Darynda, don't pretend like you're not part of the family. You're as important to Grammy as we are." Madison climbed into the passenger side and buckled up.

Darynda smiled at that and her face lit up.

"Besides, we're not really the Moonglow sisters anymore. I live in Manhattan. And Shelley lives . . . well, who knows where she'll eventually land."

"Life is a puzzle." Darynda backed out of the driveway. "Seems like by the time you've got it all together, it's time to die."

"Well, hello, Little Miss Sunshine."

"I don't mean to be gloomy." Darynda looked peaceful and her tone was even as she headed up Moonglow Boulevard toward the hospital. "It's just facts. But I really do wish you girls would mend fences. It would mean so much to your grandmother to wake up and see you getting along."

Madison's throat felt dry and scratchy. "We're working on it."

"Time isn't your friend."

"I'm sorry, but healing takes time."

"But forgiveness doesn't. It can happen in a twinkling. Besides," Darynda said in her no-nonsense voice, "you've had five years."

Right. Everyone wanted her to forget what Shelley had done. As if it were all Madison's fault the family had fallen apart. "I'm trying, Darynda, I'm trying."

"That's all anyone can ask." Darynda's smile softened and she reached over to pat Madison's hand.

Like an embattled knight after a bloody fight to the death, Madison felt dents in her armor. She'd taken a lot of hits and was still standing. That was saying something.

"Wouldn't it be nice," Darynda murmured, "to

let go of perfect? It's okay to be human, Maddie. More than okay. Your mistakes make the rest of us feel better for not living up to your lofty standards."

Madison blinked and stared out the window. Darynda was right. She had a hard time showing her vulnerability. Terrified she'd be taken advantage of if she dared let down her guard.

At the hospital, they found Erma Kelton, the feistiest Quilting Diva, asleep in the chair beside Grammy's bed. Darynda woke her gently and helped Erma gather her things.

"I'll walk Erma to her car," Darynda said. "And be right back."

"You don't have to stay. I've got this."

"I *want* to be here." Her tone said she had every right to be there and Madison supposed she did. Darynda was the one who'd been here for Grammy when the sisters had all gone their separate ways.

"Good morning, Grammy." Madison took the chair Erma had vacated. "No need to worry. We're getting things straightened out at the Moonglow Inn. Doing renovations. Paying the back payments on that mortgage." She reached for her grandmother's hand lying so white and still against the covers.

Grandmother's skin felt hot. Too hot.

She was burning up.

Fear blazed a path up Madison's spine. She

leaned over to press the call button to alert the nurses and tell them her grandmother had a fever, when suddenly a loud, obnoxious beeping blasted from the monitor and the squiggly heartbeat pattern on the screen went crazy.

What was happening?

Madison froze. Every bone in her body seemed made of rubber.

You're the oldest, Madison, the taskmaster voice in her head countered. The voice that sounded a lot like her late mother. *You're in charge. You're responsible.* The same voice that had whipped her throughout her life. Chiding her when she messed up or took a wrong step. Castigating her whenever she did not measure up.

Instantly, medical personnel flooded into the room. Men and women in scrubs, bustling and barking orders.

One stern-faced nurse grabbed hold of Madison, tugged her to her feet, and shoved her out the door. No apology. All business. She grunted, "Go."

Over the intercom, a woman's voice repeated, *Code Blue ICU stat, Code Blue ICU stat, Code Blue ICU stat.*

Anger crawled up to sit next to the fear inside Madison's chest. She would not allow them to shunt her off. Not when her grandmother's life hung in the balance.

Madison pushed back into the room.

The medical staff surrounded the bed. There were so many of them she couldn't see Grammy.

"Push a bolus of lidocaine," said the man in a lab coat with a badge identifying him as Dr. Pullman.

Madison took a pen from her purse and wrote that down in the spiral notebook she carried. "What's going on?"

"Ms. Clark"—the charge nurse took her by the elbow and propelled her from the room—"I know this is difficult, but please let us do our jobs. We'll come talk to you as soon as we can."

With that, she shut the door in Madison's face.

"But—" Madison was ready to shove the door open again. She had medical power of attorney over Grammy's care. She had every right to be in that room.

"Madison."

She turned to see Darynda standing there, eyes wide, hands trembling. "What's happened to Helen?" The poor woman looked as if she were about to collapse.

Madison wrapped her arm around her. "Come on. Let's go sit in the waiting room. They'll come tell us something soon."

Darynda barely nodded, shuffling along as if her feet were too heavy to lift.

"I know it's scary," Madison murmured. "I'm scared to pieces too."

"Is she going to die?"

"Not if I can help it."

Darynda leaned against Madison's shoulder. "I'm glad I talked her out of signing a Do Not Resuscitate. If she dies before—"

"She's not going to die today," Madison vowed as if she actually had control over it.

"But if she dies and we're just sitting out here in the waiting room, I'll never forgive myself."

"Do you want to go into the room and be with her?"

Darynda nodded.

"All right," Madison said, not caring who she had to fight. They were going in. She hooked her arm through Darynda's and escorted her back to the room.

Madison cracked open the door. The staff didn't notice her. They were too busy with Grammy. Darynda tightened her grip on Madison's arm.

Feeling fiercely protective of her grandmother's oldest friend, Madison held on tight.

Her gaze flew to the monitors over the bed. Instead of the haywire readout that had set off the alarm, there was now a steady, recognizable heart rhythm.

Grammy was back.

"What happened?" Darynda asked. "Is she going to make it?"

The nurse who had thrown Madison out of the

room left what she was doing at the crash cart, and another nurse took her place.

She came over to Madison and in hushed tones said, "Your grandmother suffered a heart attack because she's septic."

Septic.

That sounded bad. Really bad. Fear turned to terror. Madison thought she could handle this, thought she was prepared to lose Grammy. She was not.

"What does this mean?" Madison rubbed her crystal necklace as if it could save her somehow.

"She has developed an infection and she is in grave condition. If there are family members you need to notify"—the nurse paused—"now is the time."

"She's going to die!" Darynda wailed and she clasped both hands to her mouth.

The dread that had been sitting on Madison's shoulder swooped in like a vulture to feed.

"We'll do everything in our power to make sure that doesn't happen," the nurse said. "But you and your family do need to prepare yourselves."

Although the news was alarming, having knowledge calmed Madison. Ambiguity bothered her, but once she had facts, she could act. Facts she could work with. Not knowing? Well, she'd never been much good with open-ended scenarios.

"Now could you please stay outside?" The nurse's voice was kind, understanding.

Nodding, Madison took Darynda back to the waiting room. The elderly lady burst into tears.

Devastated, Madison knew she couldn't break down as well. She was in charge now. It was up to her. Putting on a brave face, she said to Darynda, "Grammy is a fighter. She's strong. She'll survive."

"I love her so much." Darynda sobbed.

Madison sat beside her, enfolded Darynda in her arms. "I know."

"She means the world to me." She buried her face against Madison's shoulder.

Darynda's tears battered Madison. She felt hollow, spent. She had no friends like Darynda and the rest of the Quilting Divas. No neighbors like Mike. No one who would turn up at *her* hospital bed with hugs and prayers and casseroles and well wishes. There was no cadre of people willing to put their own lives on pause while they helped her through a crisis.

Her friends were coworkers and nothing more. She had no life outside her job. No boyfriend. No baby. All she had were her sisters, and she wasn't even so sure about that.

When had she gotten so isolated? When had her world shrunk so small? She'd achieved everything she'd ever dreamed of—a hit TV show, wild financial success, a fine apartment in the most vibrant city in the world.

And yet, it felt so empty.

What was all that success worth without a family to come home to and friends to support you? A job couldn't hold you tight at night. All the money in the world couldn't cure loneliness.

When and where had her life gone so wrong?

It's you. You're the problem. All this time, she'd been blaming Shelley because she didn't have the courage to face the truth.

Madison knew she was the architect of her own life. She was the one who'd built and designed a frosty landscape. Only she could thaw it.

But dear God, that was a lot of ice to melt.

CHAPTER FOURTEEN

Gia

EASING: The process of working in extra fabric where two pieces do not align precisely, especially when sewing curves.

For a week, Grammy's condition was touch and go.

They threw away Madison's carefully constructed schedule. Let go of the house renovations and the quilting and the pop-up store. With Mike's help, Gia moved out of her apartment, and officially moved back into her old room with Shelley. Madison stayed in the blue room.

Memorial Day passed without acknowledgment or commemoration. It felt weird not to celebrate because holidays had always been a big deal at the Moonglow Inn. But for now, only one thing mattered.

Seeing Grammy through this crisis.

Terrified their grandmother might pass away without one of them at her side, the sisters thanked the Quilting Divas for their help but took over the shifts, sectioning them out in eight-hour stints that matched the nurses' shifts. Gia sat from seven A.M. to three P.M. Shelley from three P.M. to eleven P.M. Madison volunteered for nights.

They only saw one another during their shift changes. Darynda came as often as she could, but the experience took a toll on her and the three sisters insisted she take care of herself. They promised to call her if anything happened.

Grammy remained in a coma. The nosocomial infection had originated in her lungs and curing it took heavy-duty antibiotics. One bit of optimistic news was that her brain was healing from the surgery.

Gia would take whatever she could get. Hope was hope.

But along with the hope came a dark radical thought. Was it right to hold on? Should they be prolonging Grammy's suffering? When was it time to stop fighting and let go?

Not yet, Gia told herself. *Not yet.* Not until her sisters had fully mended fences. Not until they renovated the inn. Not until they finished the quilt.

The need to finish the quilt ate at her, but until Grammy's infection was gone, the sisters couldn't afford to do anything but sit vigil.

When the Chamber of Commerce heard about the latest news, they swooped in to help—neighbors, friends, shopkeepers. The community came together. With Mike acting as general contractor, the town's residents volunteered their time and resources to repair the inn—painting, patching, plastering.

Each afternoon when Gia came home from the hospital to find another chore completed she felt as if she must be dreaming. To find tile laid and fixtures replaced, and hardwood floors refinished. Where else but a place like Moonglow Cove did people come together to unselfishly give to one of their own?

The Moonglow sisters owed the town so much they could never repay the debt. The price was too precious; the rescue, too intense; the rehabilitation, too intimate.

Without the townsfolk, they simply wouldn't have made it.

Every day, Gia expected to wake up and realize it had all been a sweet, impossible fantasy. Before she opened her eyes in the morning, she'd take a deep breath and feel the soft corners of her sleep and test reality. Wriggled her toes. Heard the steady cadence of ocean waves. Smelled fresh paint and sawdust. Visceral and true. She lifted her eyelids by millimeters, searching for the first whisper of light, then slowly accepting that it was a new day, a new reality.

The inn was changing around her, while at the same time, nothing at the hospital changed. The contrast between past and future stood out glaring and stark.

Gia controlled none of it. She felt like a princess

trapped in her ivory tower, twiddling her thumbs and waiting for the spell to break. Fearing the freedom yet knowing in her heart that's where salvation lay.

Like the cracking of an egg, you had to fracture the shell to let the goodness out.

On the last day of May, she sat mindlessly playing Candy Crush at Grammy's bedside, when a soft knock sounded at the door.

Looking up, Gia glanced over her shoulder to see Mike and Anna standing in the doorway. The nursing staff had long given up holding the Clark family and friends to the visiting hours and the no-more-than-two-visitors-at-a-time rule. As long as they were quiet, respectful, and stayed out of the way, the staff allowed them unrestricted access to their grandmother.

"Morning, Short Stack," Mike murmured.

"How is she today?" Anna nodded at Grammy.

"The same." Gia turned off her cell phone and slipped it into her purse.

Mike inclined his head at Anna, who stepped forward and rested a hand on Gia's shoulder.

"I've come to sit with your grandmother until Shelley gets here to give you a break," Anna said.

"That's okay. I'm good."

"You and your sisters have been doing this around-the-clock shift for over a week," Mike said. "You've got to take care of yourself. You have no idea how long this will draw out."

He was right, but leaving her grandmother felt wrong.

"Let us help, we're family, too," Mike said.

"Or will be soon," Anna added.

Gia glanced down at his ring on her finger. The simple, round-cut diamond in a platinum setting. Traditional, but high quality. Just like Mike. She smiled and turned the ring around and around on her finger. *Too bad the engagement isn't real.*

Anna's voice lowered. "Please? I need to do this, Gia. Helen has been so good to me over the years. I want to repay her kindness."

"That's so sweet of you, Anna, but you've got a bakery to run and two little kids who keep you hopping."

Anna tucked a strand of hair behind her ear. "Penny's manning the bakery," she said, referring to her pastry chef. "And Kevin is home this week, so he's watching the kids."

"Besides," Mike said. "I've come to whisk you off for an afternoon of kiteflying."

Anna pulled an e-reader from her purse. "It'll be great. I can sit and catch up on my reading. Looking forward to diving into the new Kristan Higgins novel. She makes me laugh so hard."

"Are you two ganging up on me?" Gia asked.

"Yep," Mike said. "You have to stay healthy to take care of Grammy when she comes home." He sounded so sure it was true, as if it were a foregone conclusion that Grammy *would* come home.

Helpless in the face of his optimism, she nodded.

Now, twenty minutes later, here she was on the beach, wind in her hair, sand between her toes, and so happy she'd agreed to the outing, even if guilt was riding right along with her.

"This kite is amazing." Mike's grin lit up his face as the blue fish kite that Gia had mailed him from Japan for his September birthday swooped and soared in the wind. "I've been waiting for you to come home to fly it with me."

This was why she made kites. That look in his eyes. Giddy glee. His pleasure was hers.

"Style, grace, color. This kite has it all. It's not just beautiful, it flies high." Mike eyed her. "Just like the gorgeous person who built it."

"Oh you." She laughed and shook her head. She stood still, allowing the wind to take her kite higher. She was flying her favorite, a pink dragon with a long tail. It was a two-string kite she affectionately called Puff.

"I'm not kidding. This is the easiest kite I've ever flown."

"The wind speed is perfect today."

"Don't sell yourself short. It's not the wind. This kite is not just well crafted. It's art."

"That's why I went to Japan." Gia laughed again, happy to be on Moonglow Beach, flying kites with her best friend as they had so many times as children.

Mike's blue fish kite chased after Puff. "Your skills just keep getting better and better." He raised his voice so that she could hear him over the sounds of the wind whipping around the kites. "I'm amazed at how much you've learned."

"My mentor taught me that kitemaking forms a triad of scale, weight, and symmetry. If one aspect is off, the kite will not fly. It's all about balance," she said. "Just like with life."

"You've nailed all three." He stared up at the kite.

"That's because my teacher made me carve the bamboo over and over until I perfected the thickness and form. Sometimes, it would be off by barely a millimeter, and he'd shake his head and give me that look like he'd sucked on a lemon and say, 'Start again.' "

"Your attention to detail paid off big-time."

"He also had me study Eastern imagery to learn how to paint traditional designs. The fish kite has a very old history. It swims in a sea of sky."

Mike shook his head. "I'm so damned proud of you, Gia. You've carved out your niche in the world."

His words gave wings to her heart, and her hopes flew as high as their kites. "Just as you have with your woodworking."

"Who would have thought that day I took you

out to fly your first kite you'd end up making them for a living?"

"It's not a career they encourage you to pursue for career day in school." Gia chuckled. "Let me tell you, everyone but you tried to talk me out of it."

"When you love something as much as you love kites, you gotta go for it."

"I confess to plenty of doubts. To spend so much time and effort pursuing a dying art? I asked my mentor whether it was smart to work so hard for something that might never be anything more than a hobby."

"What did he say?"

"In the softest voice, he said, 'As long as there are people who care about kindness, beauty, and authenticity, people will make kites.'

"In my Americanness, I said, 'Yes, but will they be making money making kites?' "

"What was his answer?"

"He rubbed his bald noggin the way he does, like it's a magic lamp and if he just rubs it long enough, a genie will pop out and grant him three wishes. Then he said, 'Kiteflying is lucky; kitemaking even luckier. Make your own luck, Minarai. Build more kites.' "

"Why does he call you that?" Mike asked. "Minarai?"

"It means 'apprentice,' " she said.

"It's weird," Mike said. "You've had this whole life I hardly know anything about."

Gia winked at him. "I like to keep you guessing. Besides, who's the one who runs off to Caribbean islands to build homes for hurricane victims? You're a hero."

"Nah, just helping out where I can." His strong, capable hands played out the line, sending his fish sailing over her pink dragon's head. They'd flown kites together on Moonglow Beach since they were in grade school. It felt so comfortable being here with him. Familiar and safe. "God gave me a talent. It would be a shame not to share it with people in need."

"See? That attitude right there is why I love you."

I love you.

Startled, Gia hitched in her breath. Had she really said that? What would he think about it? And damn, but she did love him. He'd been a fixture in her life for as long as she could remember. But now? She was feeling a whole different kind of love for Mike.

Tentatively, she shot a glance over at him.

He was studying her, but she couldn't read his thoughts. Her pulse skipped. "How are you doing?" he asked.

"I'm g-good."

"Really?"

"Well . . . you know." She shrugged as if she were all chill and casual. "Under the circumstances."

"It feels like a month since I've seen you." Mike's eyes were on the kite, his hands expertly maneuvering the line of the jaunty blue fish kite he'd sent soaring, but his voice, that sexy masculine voice, was full of yearning.

For her?

Gia gulped, and her pulse quickened. "You see me every day."

"While I'm running a construction crew in your house. That doesn't count. I've missed spending time with you."

"We're here together now," she said.

"So we are." His smile was the sun, bright and cheerful, and she felt like a hungry sunflower, soaking it all up.

She was so busy watching him smile that she didn't notice her kite had lost momentum until the string slackened in her hand. Pulling back, she tightened up on the line and her pink dragon kite bobbled before catching an updraft and taking off again.

They flew kites side by side, and for a moment, it felt like they were kids again—carefree and easy. A peaceful camaraderie. Their connection growing deeper through silence and a shared activity they both loved. Being with Mike was a breeze. A respite from regular life.

"You didn't have to come rescue me from the hospital," she said after several minutes.

"I'm aware of that."

"How come you showed up?"

"You do so much for the people you love, it's time someone did something nice for you. Besides, your family expects us to spend time together. If we didn't, it'd be weird. I'm your fiancé, remember?"

As if she could forget that. Gia rubbed her thumb along the band of the ring he'd given her. The string fluttered in response to her movement, sending the pink dragon gyrating.

"I've been thinking . . ." she said, rescuing the dragon from the dive, pulling back, stepping away from Mike.

"About?"

"How long we should drag out this fake engagement?"

"You're not holding out for finishing the quilt?"

"That goal seems further and further away," she said. "Plus, my sisters are getting along much better. Do we really even need to finish the quilt?"

"It *was* your grandmother's last request."

"True, and my sisters' truce is probably because they barely see each other since the three of us started the shift rotation."

"I'll leave it up to you when to tell them."

"Sooner seems better than later."

"But is now really a good time?" he asked. "With your grandmother so sick?"

"You're right. It's just that . . ."

"What?" He met her gaze and his blue eyes took her hostage.

"You're in limbo. You can't date anyone else while we're pretending."

"Cuts both ways. Neither can you."

"I don't want to date."

"Me either."

"It's not fair to you."

"Don't I get to decide what's fair for me?" he asked.

"Yes, sure."

"Ultimately, Gia, this is your family. It's up to you. Just know that whatever you decide, I'll support you." His gaze refused to let her go. "I'm here for you . . . know that. Always."

"How did I get so lucky to have a friend like you?" she murmured.

"Gia." His intense stare was disconcerting. If he didn't keep his eye on his kite, it was going to crash.

Overwhelmed, she gulped. "Yes?"

She was staring at Mike's lips and he was studying hers and she had a feeling they were both thinking about the kiss they'd shared last week, and a hard, hot shiver shot down her spine.

"Gia," he repeated.

What was going on here? This was the man she had known for most of her life. They'd been to family celebrations together, swum in the ocean together, and he'd been the first man she'd ever danced with.

Was it just her imagination? Was he feeling something building high and fast, just as she was? Or was she fooling herself?

The wind calmed.

She felt her string go slack and before she could compensate for the dropping wind speed, the pink dragon slammed hard into the blue fish. Their kite lines tangled and simultaneously the two kites fell from the sky, enmeshed.

"Bravo!" Someone on the beach clapped loudly.

Together, they turned to see a slender woman in rhinestone sunglasses, a wide floppy hat, and a teeny string bikini. Behind her stood a tall beefy man, who looked like a security detail. Black shorts and a black polo shirt, thick arms folded across his chest. He wore dark sunglasses and an even darker scowl.

"A stunning display of kiteflying," the young woman enthused in a brown-sugar voice.

Something about the woman looked very familiar. Did Gia know her?

"Ar-are you Pippa Grandon?" A starstruck Mike's eyes bugged.

Pippa Grandon was an up-and-coming starlet from Houston. She'd made a big splash as the wide-eyed ingenue in last summer's blockbuster superhero movie and the media had dubbed her the new Jennifer Lawrence.

"I am." Pippa held out a delicate hand loaded

with bling on every finger, cocked her head, and sent Mike a coy glance through lowered lashes.

Petty to be sure, but Gia felt a jab of jealousy. Tightness gathered in her chest, and her pulse spiked. It was all she could do not to tell the woman to put on a cover-up.

"Might I see the kite?" Pippa said, affecting a slightly British accent. Gia had heard Pippa had just finished wrapping up a rom-com in Great Britain. "I've been watching you, and I don't think I've ever seen kites quite like these. Where did you get them?"

"She's the kitemaker." Mike slung his arm over Gia's shoulder and puffed his chest out as he grinned with pride.

For *her.*

A corkscrew of happiness twisted through Gia's middle.

"No kidding?" Pippa took off her sunglasses and examined the pink dragon kite more closely. Her bodyguard came nearer. "What do you think, Bruno?"

Bruno grunted.

"I agree." Pippa nodded.

"I'm Gia Clark." Gia held out her hand and added, "Mike's fiancée."

"I'm Pippa Grandon." She shook Gia's hand. "And congrats on your engagement."

"Thanks." Gia nodded, pretending she didn't know who Pippa was.

"Gia studied in Japan for a year under a master kitemaker," Mike bragged.

Pippa eyed Gia up and down. "Impressive."

Gia's cheeks warmed. Unlike Madison, she wasn't comfortable with the spotlight.

"Are you from Moonglow Cove?" Pippa asked.

"I live right there." Gia pointed at the Victorian on the incline rising up above the beach where they were standing.

"Oh my gosh, the house is adorbs. This is your place?"

"My grandmother's," Gia explained. "The Moonglow Inn."

Pippa shook her head. "I wish I'd known about your B&B when I booked this getaway to Moonglow Cove. Do you have any vacancies?"

Gia shook her head. "My grandmother is in the hospital; we're not taking guests at the moment."

"Bummer, why didn't I know about this place?" Pippa pulled out her phone. She opened the browser and searched for the Moonglow Inn. "It says here that the inn is closed, and you got a couple of tacky Yelp reviews. No wonder I didn't notice the place."

"Those Yelp reviews happened when my grammy was running the place by herself, but my sisters and I are back home and we'll be running it after the renovations." This wasn't entirely true, but she wanted to cast the inn in the best light. Pippa had a huge following on social media; one positive tweet from her could fill the Moonglow Inn with guests.

"A family business? Love!" Pippa turned to Bruno. "Next time I come to Moonglow Cove, remind me of this place."

Bruno gave a silent nod.

"Do you have more kites?" Pippa asked. "Are you selling them?"

"I did have a kiosk on the boardwalk, but I had to temporarily close the store while helping take care of my grandmother."

"Downer." Pippa shook her head. "Things been piling up, huh?" The British accent had melted as she slipped into her wrong-side-of-Houston pronunciation.

"It's been a challenge," Gia said, still not fully believing she was standing here with Pippa Grandon chatting like they were college roommates.

Pippa got a text and she held up one finger, indicating Gia should hang on.

Gia shot Mike a look, mouthed, *Pippa Grandon loves my kites!*

He smiled, his eyes warm and gentle.

Her heart swooped, dove, just like one of her kites.

"Excuse me." Pippa raised her head, waggled her cell phone. "I have to be somewhere in an hour, so if you can't show me the kites right now—"

"Yes, sorry, of course I can show you the kites. Please, come inside." Heart thumping as if she'd just run a race, Gia led Pippa inside the house, taking her around to the front entrance.

"Wow." Pippa ran her hand along the scrolled woodworking of the grand staircase. "They don't make 'em like this anymore."

"No, they don't," Mike agreed.

"He's a woodworker," Gia explained, leading Pippa toward the parlor where they'd stashed the kites the day that Mike helped her move out of the kiosk. "He specializes in furniture."

"Look at you two, all power-coupley and everything. You make kites, he makes furniture." Pippa chuckled. "Love! What do people call you?"

"Call us?" Gia scratched her head, confused.

"What's your couple name? For instance, me and my fiancé, Jackson Sledge, are Jippa," Pippa said.

Gia had no idea Pippa was engaged. She'd done a good job of keeping a lid on it.

"So are you Gike or Mia?"

"Mia," Mike said at the same time Gia said, "Gike."

They looked at each other and laughed.

"You two are so cute!" Pippa said.

Gia opened the door to the parlor. Kites were leaned against the wall, laid out on the sofa and coffee table. They rested against the stereo cabinet and fireplace mantel. Pippa gasped and grinned. She stepped inside and circled the room, examining each kite in turn while her dour bodyguard stood sentry in the doorway.

"These kites are absolutely amazeballs," Pippa gushed. "How much are they?"

Gia named the price and waited for the inevitable pushback. Most people didn't understand why artisan kites cost so much. They didn't know all the work and care that went into creating each one.

But Pippa didn't blink. Instead her eyes lit with passionate fire as if she'd been struck by lightning. "You know what, Mia?"

Gia's pulse quickened. Was she about to buy them all?

"I just had a *brilliant* idea." Pippa pirouetted around the room.

"What's that?" Gia asked, fingers crossed. If Pippa bought her whole collection she could add it to the fund to pay off the mortgage Grammy took out against the inn. *Don't count your chickens.*

"Before I say anything, can I take pictures?" Pippa asked. "I want to send pics to Jackson."

"Of course."

Pippa snapped photographs of each kite, then texted them to her fiancé. A few seconds later, her phone pinged.

"Oh!" Pippa grinned. "He agrees your kites slay. He's in."

"In for what?" Gia asked.

"Our beach wedding in Barbados."

"I'm not following."

"We want your kites in our wedding!" Pippa applauded her idea.

"How do you plan on using kites in a wedding?"

"That's the really brilliant part. Throwing rice is too traditional and there's the whole exploding bird thing, although I heard that was a myth. Releasing butterflies is apparently not great for the poor creatures. Doves are so 1990, and there's the poop issue. But what if . . ." She paused for dramatic effect, made a frame with her hands. "The guests fly kites while we leave the ceremony, creating a tunnel of kites for us to walk under. Then they get to keep the kites as party favors. You design the kites with our wedding colors, names, and wedding date. Whataya say?"

"Unique idea." Gia nodded. "But in reality, it could be a bit problematic for the actual ceremony. If the winds don't cooperate and the guests don't know how to—"

"It's a weekend event. We could fly you in early—first class, of course, and you can teach the guests how to fly the kites ahead of time and if the weather doesn't cooperate, then we'll have some funny outtakes on film." Pippa clapped her hands again. "Ooh, ooh, the more I think about it, the more I *love* the idea."

This wasn't what Gia was expecting. She had

never considered designing kites for weddings, but what a novel idea. Excitement lit her up. She could have a whole new career path. "I . . . I don't know."

"Don't be wishy-washy. Just say *yes!*" Pippa's enthusiasm was infectious.

"How many kites would you need?"

"It's an intimate wedding. Guest list of a hundred."

Pippa considered a hundred guests intimate? Each kite took around twenty hours to hand make. A hundred kites would take approximately two thousand hours. *If* she worked ten hours a day, it would take two hundred days. But who could work ten hours a day for two hundred days nonstop? She'd be exhausted.

And there was Grammy to think about and her sisters and the inn.

But if she did this, her career would be set. If Pippa Grandon used Gia's kites in her wedding, it would shoot her to the stars.

"When is the wedding?"

"Not until next June."

A year away. Gia's mind churned, trying to find a way to make it happen, but she couldn't see it and she wasn't about to promise something she wasn't sure she could deliver. "Miss Grandon, while the offer is flattering, and I'm so tempted to say yes, it would take me a *minimum* of eight months to hand make a hundred kites."

"Honey, delegate. Hire people to help."

Were there parts of the process she could delegate? Gia paused to consider it, saw her disappointed mentor shake his bald head in her mind's eye.

"Don't say no." Pippa's voice took on a cajoling tone and she shook her head. "This is your opportunity of a lifetime."

"I appreciate the offer so much, but my grandmother is in the hospital and I promised my sisters I'd help them get the inn back on its feet—"

"Please, please, please say yes." Pippa bounced on her toes and pressed her palms together in front of her heart. "You can hire someone to help them with the house on the deposit money I give you. You could hire nurses for your grandmother."

Gia wanted to shout, *Yes, yes, I'll do it!* and then figure out how to make it happen later. Just the idea of creating wedding kites stirred her creativity and she itched to do it. "I'll need to think about it."

"What's to think about? You'll make a boatload of money and get massive publicity for your kites. You'll become the kitemaker to the stars!"

But Gia had never been about status or lots of money. That was Madison's thing. Gia cared about quality and craftsmanship. She wanted to put out only the best products whether she made tons of money or not.

Pippa turned to her bodyguard. "What do you think, Bruno?"

Bruno grunted.

"See? Even Bruno thinks you should do it. Please, please, please with sugar on top." Pippa hopped around the room. "If you say yes, I'll buy all these other kites and gift them to my friends."

Her bank account was so close to empty it was scary, and they did need money to get the inn out of debt. To have ready cash from the sale of her inventory, well, Gia just couldn't dismiss that out of hand.

"Can I think about it?"

Pippa pooched out her bottom lip in a pout. "All right, but *only* because I really like you and this is a supercute house. But I don't get tripped up in go-nowhere projects. Let me know by six P.M. tonight or the deal's off."

The woman might come off as a flibbertigibbet, but she was a tough negotiator.

"All right." Gia nodded. "I'll let you know by six."

"Just understand me, I *really* want this and I'm accustomed to getting what I want."

"I hear you."

"Okay then, hugs." Pippa held out her arms.

Gia hugged the young woman, but it was like hugging air. Pippa floated away just as quickly as she'd rushed into Gia's embrace.

Pippa held out her hand. “Give me your phone so I can put my number in it.”

Gia complied, and Pippa punched in her cell number and gave the phone back to her.

“Ciao.” She bounced out of the room humming “Let’s Go Fly a Kite.”

Bruno followed close at her heels, leaving them with one last parting grunt.

CHAPTER FIFTEEN

Gia

ROCK THE NEEDLE: The process of bringing the needle back to the surface of all the quilt layers by using a rocking motion.

Gia stared at her phone. She had the cell number of one of the hottest young celebrities in the country. How had that happened?

Mike shook his head and let out a long audible exhale.

She shot him a glance. "What?"

"You're seriously thinking of *not* doing this?"

"You think I should?"

"It's not my place to tell you what to do."

"But you'd do it?"

"I would. But you have to figure out what *you* really want."

"I want to finish the wedding quilt."

"No, your grandmother wanted you to finish the wedding quilt."

"Same thing." She lifted and dropped her shoulder hard. The tone in his voice and the look in his eyes stirred weird feelings inside her.

"Is it?"

She cocked her head and studied him, her

pretend fiancé. He seemed angry with her. She nibbled a thumbnail and folded the rest of her fingers into a loose, anxious fist.

"Yes," she said. "*I* want to finish the quilt."

"Over making kites for Pippa Grandon?" He sounded disappointed.

Her stomach sloshed, and she felt like she was riding on a tiny boat rocked by vast ocean swells. "What do you want me to do?"

"I want you to stop trying to please me."

"Why are you in such a strange mood?"

"It bothers you when just being yourself upsets people."

True. Gia shuffled aside the kites and sat down. "Why is that so bad?"

"Because when you're busy trying to keep the peace, you don't get to do what *you* want." He stayed standing, arms folded Bruno-style, studying her with the saddest eyes.

Her heart lurched. "Maybe I want nothing. Maybe I'm plenty happy riding in the passenger seat."

"Are you?"

She was going to say yes, but then images filled her head, a mind map of shortchanged moments and missed opportunities. Agreeing with Grammy that piano lessons were fine because that's what Madison and Shelley were doing, and they already owned a piano. Never mind that she really wanted to play the flute. Or the times she left the decision making to others, so no one could blame her for the outcome. Or not even bothering to have a preference in the first place because she got lost in the sprawl of her older sisters' big personalities, always drifting along on a dream.

Maybe that's why she loved to fly kites—the loft, the drift, the glide. Easy and soft focused. She'd fallen in love at five years old, when Mike first put a kite into her hands.

"I wanted to go to Japan and study kitemaking and I did it. *That* was my choice. I wasn't trying to please anyone."

"Weren't you?"

"No."

"I was the one who encouraged you to go. You didn't want to leave home. You weren't going to go. Remember?"

Gia stroked her chin, recalling the conversation she'd had with Mike after kite master Mikio Tetsuya picked Gia and her award-winning design in art school as being worthy of his mentorship.

Grammy had wanted her to come home to Moonglow Cove after college, especially since Maddie and Shelley had left.

But Mike urged her to go to Japan, promising that he and Darynda would look after Grammy. She'd been like a fledging bird, too comfortable in the nest to attempt flying. It was only when

Mike said she was letting fear run her that Gia had packed her bags.

"I wanted to go," she insisted.

"But did you go to please me or yourself?"

"Maybe a little of both."

"Fair enough. I have another question."

"Okay."

"Why does everyone get their way except you? Why are your family's wants and needs more important than your own?"

"They're not."

"Then why don't you speak up? Make *your* wants and needs known?"

"I want to connect with people."

"Is that true? Or is it that you don't want anyone to get angry with you?"

"That too," she admitted, ducking her head so he couldn't see her eyes.

"And you believe that if you stopped sacrificing your wants and needs for them they wouldn't love you anymore?"

Yes. "Well," she said. "It sounds silly when you put it like that."

"That's because it is silly, Gia. Being connected to people is good. But living *for* other people is not. That's why I came to get you today. Sitting by your grandmother's side for eight hours a day won't change the outcome. It's as if you believe sacrificing *your* health and well-being will save her."

"Maybe it will."

"Gia . . ." The look in his eyes was so tender, his voice so light, but his words shot through her sharp as an arrow. "You simply don't have that much power."

"I know."

Mike moved the remaining kites off the sofa, stacked them on the floor, and plunked down beside her. He took her hand and his skin felt so warm.

"Do you"—he tapped his knuckles against her chest just above her heart—"want to make those kites for Pippa? Don't think. Just feel. What does your heart say?"

"Yes," she said. "I want to make the kites. But I also need to finish the quilt and help my grandmother heal and mend my relationship with my sisters. That's three things I must do weighing against the one thing I *want* to do."

"Why can't you just tell your sisters what you want?"

"*We're* supposed to be getting married," she said. "They'll want to know why I'm catering to Pippa's wedding and not my own."

"You can tell them the truth. Or tell them it's none of their business."

"C'mon, you know I'd never say that last part. Besides, there's one more reason I don't have time for Pippa Grandon."

"Why is that?" He studied her face so intensely, she had to look away.

"If I did this project for Pippa, I'd be putting in long hours every day for months and months until it's finished. There'd be no time for . . ." She couldn't bring herself to say *us* because she had no idea if he was having the kinds of feelings for her that she was having for him.

He leaned closer. "No time for what?"

She moistened her lips with the tip of her tongue, braved it. "You."

"Me?" His face lit up.

"You," she confirmed, feeling dizzy at her courage.

"Gia." His voice was husky. "Do you have any idea how long I've been waiting to hear you say that?"

"Really?" Her voice was squeaky.

"I've always thought you were amazing." He scooted closer.

She caught her breath.

"I missed you so much while you were in Japan that I signed up for the Habitat for Humanity Disaster Response program. Then you came home just after I left. Bad timing, *again*. First, you were too young for me and then when you were old enough, I had a girlfriend and you had a boyfriend. Then you went off to college. We've never been in sync."

"Until now," she whispered.

"Until now," he confirmed.

"When I saw you again . . ." He sounded

breathless now. "I didn't realize just how much I missed you. The sound of your voice. The sparkle in your eyes. I've missed hanging out with you and flying kites, watching movies, and having long talks on your back porch."

"I've missed you, too, Mike."

It was true. He was such a good family friend, but the way he was looking at her, the way her insides quivered, told her things were changing between them.

Rapidly.

Mike, the good ol' boy next door, was now the hottie she didn't want to keep her hands off of.

"Gia," he murmured and reached out to cup her cheek with his palm.

"Mike."

He hooked her chin between his finger and thumb, tilted her face up, and pinned her with his gaze, then her pretend fiancé lowered his head and kissed her.

And rocked Gia's world completely off its axis.

His previous kiss had been hot, but this kiss was so much more. His lips were sweet, sweeter than before. He tasted like the richest chocolate ever created. Wow, what a ride. All this time she could have been kissing him like this. The things they had missed out on!

It was wild. It was beautiful. It was overwhelming.

Gia sank against him and opened her mouth wider.

Mike kissed her as if there were no future, no past. As if he'd been waiting his whole life to kiss her. As if she were the only woman in the whole wide world.

Mike suddenly pulled back. "I don't . . . This is too fast." Mike hopped up off the couch, jammed his hands in his pockets, and stepped back. He did not meet her gaze.

"We are engaged," she said lightly.

"It's not real."

"The engagement isn't real, but my feelings sure are."

"This complicates things," he said.

"Only if we let it."

"I just wanted . . . Aww, hell." He shoved both hands through his thick, wavy hair, temporarily plowing down that cowlick.

"What is it?" she asked, alarmed that she'd upset him.

"I didn't want you to throw away the opportunity of working with Pippa Grandon simply because you think you have to be the peacekeeper between your sisters."

Wow. She fingered her lips.

"I kissed you as a wake-up call for you to stop pleasing other people and start pleasing yourself but . . . now . . ."

"Now?"

"*I'm* the one who woke up."

"What does that mean?" She sank her top teeth into her bottom lip.

"My head is spinning, Short Stack."

"Mine too."

"It's not my place to tell you what to do. I don't get to weigh in. This is your decision, your life."

"No, no, I want to hear what you have to say."

"Gia, remember when you were about five and I taught you how to fly a kite and you said I was magical and you wanted to marry me?"

"Oh, my gosh." She pressed her palm over her mouth, giggled. "I'd forgotten all about that."

Mike's eyes glittered. "I didn't."

Whew. Okay. The kiss was over-the-top magnificent, but this was disorienting. Seeing her friend and neighbor through a different lens. Her body was heating up in ways it had never heated before.

He was not the boy next door. He was a full-grown man. Tall, good looking, and bone-deep kind. How had she not seen before that they could be so much more than friends? It was as if she'd been wearing a blindfold and his kiss had slipped it off and let the light in.

Gia backed up. She needed time to absorb all this. "Mike?"

"Haven't you figured out by now, Gia, that I want way more than just friendship from you?"

"I . . . I . . ." She was speechless, rocked by the

paradigm-shifting idea of her friend becoming her lover.

They knew almost everything there was to know about each other, but still there was this mystery of seeing him in an entirely new light. She wondered what he'd be like in bed. How fun and comfortable sex would be with her best friend. He'd been there for all the big moments in her life. Was still here, looking at her as if she was the most precious thing on earth. Her heart filled hot and bright as the sun.

"But this is too soon. I can see you're not ready to absorb it all. The depth of my feelings took me by surprise, too, but kissing you . . . Gia, I want to find out where this could go. I hope you do too."

"Oh, Mike."

"If you don't feel the same way, I get it. I understand. It's too much to expect that you've been harboring feelings for me as well. I'm gonna back off now. I'm gonna go." And with that, he pivoted and almost ran out the door.

Gia sank down on the couch, the air leaking from her lungs in a long, slow exhale. She had not seen this coming. But it made perfect sense. They knew each other so well.

Mike.

Dear sweet Mike.

She thought of all the things she loved about him. There were so many. How he couldn't carry a tune in a paper bag and yet he loved to belt out karaoke. His love of roller coasters and B movies with sappy happy endings. How excited he got about the simplest things—flowers in bloom and butterflies in the yard, sea turtles and their nesting habits, taking long walks on the beach and flying kites. How he looked after her grandmother and fixed things around the house when the three sisters were gone.

His readiness to help anyone in need. His steadfastness. His honorable nature.

Maybe that's why she'd never gotten serious about anyone she'd dated. At the back of her mind, had she always secretly yearned for Mike?

Her heart thumped crazily. Hope was a dangerous thing, but she clung to it with all her might.

He was right.

She had to stop trying to please everyone else and do what made her happy. But now wasn't the time. Grammy came first. No matter what. Time was running out for her grandmother. Even if she made it out of the hospital, the cancer was inevitable.

Pippa's offer stroked her ego, but it wasn't her only opportunity. The kites could wait. If Pippa was this impressed over her kites, other people would be too. She was young. She had time. She could build her career slowly.

Her family came first. That's what pleased her.

Mike might argue, but Gia knew it was true. She couldn't be fully happy until she knew her sisters and her grandmother were going to be okay.

And in all honesty, she wasn't ready for the quick blowup of her career. If Pippa had kites at her wedding, other celebrities would want them at their weddings too. Not just celebrities, but regular people. And, while it might make for a fat bank account, it also meant giving up her goal of mending her family.

For a moment, she'd let the allure of stardom dazzle her head.

She didn't need Pippa Grandon. She was happy. She had a good life. She loved making her kites and taking her time in doing it. A rush order would lead to shortcuts and the quality would suffer . . .

No, her family came first. Because if she and her sisters didn't fix things now, she feared they never would. Madison would return to New York and Shelley, well, who knew what Shelley would do.

And Gia?

What about her?

There was only one right choice. Gia picked up her phone and called Pippa, thanked her for her generous offer, but bowed out of making kites for her wedding.

"If you change your mind," Pippa said, "you've got a job. The more I think about those kites, the more I have to have them. I want *you* to supply them, but if it doesn't work out, I can find someone else."

"I appreciate your interest," Gia said. "But family comes first. Thank you for the offer. It gave me a thrill."

"Let me check back with you in a month." Pippa sounded undaunted. "Maybe things will look clearer to you then."

"Okay," Gia agreed. No harm in that, but she knew she wouldn't change her mind and the second she hung up, it felt as if a fresh breeze had rolled in off the ocean and chased off the heavy fog.

Pyewacket jumped into Gia's lap as if she heartily approved of her decision. She flicked her tail and purred happily.

Back on track.

She was back on track and she couldn't wait to tell Mike that she had indeed pleased herself. Just as she hopped up to go see him, her cell phone rang again.

It was Shelley.

Instant dread filled her heart, and her mind jumped to the darkest place. She hit accept, brought the phone to her ear, and in a trembly voice said, "What is it?"

"Grammy." Shelley was sobbing, a soft little sound accompanied by hiccups.

A flood of fear coursed through Gia's body

and she sat rigid on the edge of the sofa, knees clenched together, bracing herself for the awful words she just knew were coming. Grammy had left them.

"Gia," Shelley gasped. "Grammy."

"Is she—"

"Just woke up."

CHAPTER SIXTEEN

Shelley

POUNCE: A chalk bag patted over a stencil to transfer a pattern to fabric.

On June 3, three days after Grammy came out of her coma, the Moonglow sisters planned an old-fashioned quilting bee.

The purpose was twofold: one, celebrate Grammy's fighting spirit; and, two, produce as many quilts as possible over a long weekend. Quilts that they would sell in the pop-up store to pay off the mortgage on the Moonglow Inn.

Madison had obtained permission from the city to set up a pop-up store on the beach in front of the inn during the Fourth of July holiday weekend. They had four weeks left to generate inventory, and it didn't seem like enough time to do anything.

Mike and the volunteer crew from the Moonglow Chamber of Commerce had finished renovations in the kitchen and moved on to painting the inn's six guest bedrooms and en suite baths. Drop cloths were everywhere. Five-gallon buckets of gray-beige paint named *Rumbling Thunder* lined the upstairs hallway; the rooms they'd freshly painted scented the air with the odd, damp aroma of dill pickles.

On Madison's decree, they'd stepped back from the themed rooms—per Victorian tradition—painted in different colors, to one solid unifying hue throughout the house. Shelley and Gia let her have her way. Madison was the design expert, plus, who wanted to argue when Grammy was out of her coma?

At the hospital, while Grammy had regained consciousness, she had not yet spoken. She was off the ventilator and while she could nod or blink when asked questions, she could not hold a conversation.

Not yet.

Dr. Hollingway said time would tell if Grammy would ever be able to speak again. The tumor had encroached upon the Broca area of her brain that controlled speech. In the meantime, the doctor encouraged them to keep talking to her.

Grammy was still in ICU, but they had hopes of moving her into the telemetry stepdown unit within the week. Fingers crossed.

Since she'd awakened, the nurses had become stricter about visitors. "No more around-the-clock vigils," the head nurse decreed. "Mrs. Chapman needs her rest and she can't get enough sleep if people are popping in and out all hours of the day and night."

That was encouraging news. It meant the staff

had shifted from a deathwatch to a hopeful recovery mode.

Grammy did best when it was Darynda sitting at her side, holding her hand. Her blood pressure lowered, and her breathing lengthened, and her pulse slowed. A quiet peace seemed to come over her the minute Darynda's footsteps sounded in the hallway.

Shelley tried not to take it personally that whenever she came into the room Grammy got restless. Her grandmother's eyes would go wide, and she'd struggle to sit up. Tried to speak, her mouth dropping open but no words coming out. Once when Shelley showed up, the pattern on Grammy's heart monitor quickened and set off a panicky electronic beeping that brought a nurse rushing into the room to shoo Shelley away.

Darynda had kindly said, "It's just because she's so excited to see that you've come home."

But Shelley feared otherwise.

Five years ago, Grammy had been pretty upset with her for ruining Madison's wedding. She'd kept repeating, *Why, Shelley, why?*

Of course, Shelley couldn't, wouldn't tell her. She'd take the reason to her grave and if it meant she had to put on the coat of scapegoat to keep the secret, then that was her life's sacrifice.

Although she really did want to believe Darynda's version.

Except for Darynda, who'd become a fixture

at the hospital, all the other members of the Quilting Divas were attending the quilting party scheduled to run from eight A.M. on Friday morning, through eight P.M. on Sunday night.

People would cycle in and out as their schedules permitted. Anna Drury would provide breakfast and lunch for the three-day event. Dinners would be a group affair, with everyone pitching in to help cook and clean. And meals extended to the volunteer workers renovating the inn.

The weekend was shaping up to be a crowded affair as the community came together for Helen Chapman. The outpouring overwhelmed Shelley, touching tender nerves. How would they ever repay the townspeople for their generosity and kindness?

On the Thursday afternoon before the quilting bee, while Gia spelled Darynda at the hospital so that she could go check on her dogs, Madison and Shelley swung by the liquor store for provisions. Madison had rented a car so that she wouldn't have to depend on Gia and Darynda for rides. Inside the liquor store, they had to stop so Maddie could sign autographs for the clerks. It was starting to sink in that her sister really was fairly famous.

"Is getting little old ladies liquored up while they quilt such a good idea?" Shelley asked as they stood in the vodka aisle boggling at the sheer volume of flavored alcohol.

"Gia and Mike have volunteered to be designated drivers."

"I was talking about their quilting abilities."

"Please," Madison said, picking up a bottle of coconut vodka and putting it in the cart. "These gals have been quilting longer than we've been alive. They could quilt blitzed out of their minds."

Shelley clicked her tongue. "This'll be interesting."

Madison picked up another bottle of vodka, pulled a sour face. "Seriously? Smoked salmon–flavored vodka? You gotta be kidding me."

"For the secret Norwegian in you?"

Madison shuddered.

"C'mon, can't you just imagine that cocktail? The Lox, Bagel, and Cream Cheese." Shelley giggled. "Smoked salmon vodka, capers, tomato juice, add a splash of heavy cream and a slice of bagel for garnish and— Dude, look!" Shelley exclaimed. "Bacon vodka."

"You know, that one might not be so bad. I have a chef friend who uses bacon in desserts and it's pretty scrumptious."

Shelley blinked. "Bacon desserts scrumptious? Are we even remotely related? I'm thinking one of us must have been adopted."

"We look too similar for that, but I'm serious. Bacon and chocolate is *good* together."

"What would that drink taste like?" Shelley crinkled her nose.

"Bacon vodka, chocolate liqueur, Irish cream, and a splash of half-and-half. Sugar-rim the martini glass . . ."

"No, just no."

"How about this one?" Maddie turned a vodka bottle on the shelf, so Shelley could read the label. "Glazed donut vodka."

"Ooh, I've got it. How about a Cop Martini? Glazed donut vodka, espresso, and Kahlúa."

"Your years of misspent youth as a mixologist should come in quite handy for this shindig." Madison chuckled.

Shelley shook her head and squatted, so she could peruse the bottom shelf. "This is just beyond. What have those wacky vodka makers been up to since I left the country?"

"Nefarious stuff, apparently, but hey, I live in hip Manhattan and I never saw this coming." She held a bottle of PB&J vodka to Shelley's eye level.

"Do people actually buy these flavors? I mean for real? Oh no! Worst yet!"

"What, what?" Madison bent down to check it out.

"Wasabi vodka."

"Yikes."

"I see it now. A sushi-tini. Mix the wasabi vodka with the smoked salmon vodka, toast and muddle seaweed, and—"

Madison waved her hands frantically as if

trying to scare off a hornet. “Hush, hush, no kidding, I’m gonna hurl.” She made gagging noises.

The door to the liquor store opened, and the bell over the door chimed a friendly two-toned ding-dong, but Shelley was having too much fun to notice who walked in. It had been a long time since she and Madison had laughed like this together.

“How about regular lemon vodka and make Lemon Drops?” Shelley stood up, holding the bottle of lemon vodka in her hand. “Remember when we got drunk on Lemon Drops and—”

A stocky man dressed all in white rounded the aisle and stalked straight toward her, followed by an entourage of skinny women flitting around him, each also dressed in white. Shelley recognized him instantly.

Once upon a time, she’d been one of those women.

She froze, terror gripping her. The lemon vodka slipped out of her hand and shattered against the polished concrete floor.

“Oh, Shelley,” Madison said, staring at the vodka mess and not noticing what was really going on. “Are you okay? Be careful, don’t move, you don’t want to step on glass. Hang on. I’ll go get a broom and dustpan to clean this up.”

Shelley heard her sister’s voice as if she were very far away . . . underwater. A muffled, slo-mo, burbling sound. She felt rather than saw her sister take off to find something to clean up the mess with. *Don't go, Maddie. Don't leave me when I need you most.*

It couldn't be *him*. It couldn't be *them*. Not here. Not in Moonglow Cove. Oh, but it was.

Guru Meyer had come for her and Shelley hadn't even had the good sense to anticipate this move. She should have known. He was all about his image and control. To take the time and effort to come after her, Guru Meyer must perceive her as some kind of threat.

But why?

It occurred to her that he'd somehow learned that Madison was famous, and he was worried Shelley might spill the beans to her powerful sister about his compound. Fear of being exposed must have motivated him. Plus, he considered it a personal affront whenever anyone left and would often pursue them with a fresh round of love bombing to lure them in again. She'd seen him sweet-talk more than one cult escapee back into the fold. Preserving his power and reputation had to be behind his appearance in Moonglow Cove if it meant leaving someone else in charge of Cobalt Soul and getting on a plane to come after her.

He stood at the end of the aisle, sucking all the oxygen out of the room with his bulky shoulders, intimidating Sanskrit tattoos, and smoldering ice-blue eyes. He pinned her to the spot, quiet intensity oozing from every pore.

Shelley's mouth dropped open and her body ached clean through her bones. She reeled and stumbled backward, heard glass crunch underneath her flip-flops, felt pain shoot through the bottom of her foot.

"My beloved," he said in that voice that had entranced her five years earlier. "We have found you at last."

Her heart slammed against her chest, pumping adrenaline through her, urging her to run, but she couldn't twitch a muscle.

But she could feel hot blood warming her heel. The glass shard had poked through her flip-flop, cutting her.

"There you are, Sanpreet," he said, reaching over to take her elbow. "I'm saddened to find you in a liquor store, but it's all right. We love you just as you are."

"We love you," chorused the four young women, all fairly recent recruits. Yoga tourists, Shelley knew. She'd helped recruit them.

This now was the reccurring nightmare she'd had since escaping Cobalt Soul. Guru Meyer coming after her, tracking her down, mesmerizing and love bombing her into coming back. She looked into his intense gaze and thought of all the things she'd left behind. Friends. Tranquility. The magnetic beauty of Costa Rica.

The meals of mung bean soup and fermented bread, the ice-cold showers, the four A.M. awakenings to sit cross-legged chanting for two and a half hours in a windowless, pitch-black room. The eighteen hours of hard physical labor and/or long, boring lectures with minuscule breaks espousing Guru Meyer's doctrine.

Guru Meyer had presented these practices as "chakra cleansing" and "spirit strengthening" but Shelley now saw them for what they were, the building blocks of mind control—deprivation, isolation, manipulation.

Five years ago, hurting so badly from Maddie's anger, and trapped in a shame spiral, she'd run straight into Guru Meyer's devious arms—ignoring red flags, checking her brain at the door, and surrendering her personal power to this man who offered what seemed on the surface unconditional love.

Enticing, heady stuff for a wounded, guilt-filled young woman desperate for salvation.

But why had he come after her?

It occurred to her then, while she stood transfixed and terrified, heel throbbing, blood pooling at her feet, that maybe, because she'd once been such a hard-core devotee of Guru Meyer and his group, when she'd left, others had woken up and jumped ship as well. For instance, where were Sach and Prem, the two older women who never left his side? They might have stayed back at Cobalt Soul, but wouldn't he have at least brought one of the faithful with him to ride herd on the four wide-eyed acolytes protectively surrounding him like bodyguards?

She saw the truth in his eyes, just for a flicker-second, his expression hot and needy. He *had* to get her back. His carefully constructed world was on the verge of collapse. If he could bring Shelley back into the fold, he would regain the upper hand with his flock.

"We've come to bring you home." He tightened his grip on her elbow, his tone firm.

Shelley's knees weakened. Once upon a time she'd been slavishly dedicated to this man. Had thought she'd loved him in a cosmic way.

"We've missed you so much."

"Come home!" exclaimed the youngest disciple with short, curly hair so red she reminded Shelley of Little Orphan Annie. She'd run away from her upper-crust New England family to eat gruel in a Costa Rican hut. Guru Meyer had bestowed the name Japji upon her. Japji's real name was Frieda and she was just seventeen.

"It's not the same without you, Sanpreet," said a sleek, blond, empty-eyed yogi named Sumran. She'd once appeared on the cover of *Yoga Journal* in some impossibly complicated pose, back when her name was Diane, before she'd left her husband and children to join Guru Meyer at Cobalt Soul. "Please come home with us."

Guru Meyer wrapped his arms around her, pulled her close in a tight embrace. As he held her, she closed her eyes, searching for that feeling of acceptance and forgiveness she'd once felt in his hugs.

Nope. Nothing. It all felt false and forced. The magic spell broken. Stiffly, her hands fisted, and arms locked to her sides, she did not hug him back.

"You smell of meat." He sniffed.

She stepped away, tilted her chin up, met his gaze fortified with steel. "Bacon does make the world go 'round."

"The *illusionary* world," he said. "I can see they've lured you back into the false dimension."

"The *real* world," she insisted through gritted teeth.

"You are deeply troubled, my child." His voice was soft, kind. "But there is nothing to fear. We are here. We have your back. You are loved. Always."

Such seductive promises. Everything she wanted to hear. *You are loved.* Who wouldn't want to hear that?

Maybe she'd been wrong about Guru Meyer and his group.

It wasn't as if she'd been harmed or sexually pressured, which she knew happened in other such groups. He'd offered her sanctuary when she'd had none. She *had* felt loved and accepted when she was there.

It was how she'd given them five years of her life. Working for a grass roof over her head and mung bean soup.

At Cobalt Soul, she never ate dinner alone and when disagreements did pop up, they were handled swiftly by a council. No punishment was ever meted out, unless you considered additional chanting and meditation assignments punishment, which she had not.

The only major drawback was that she conformed to the groupthink. If she stepped out of line, she was gently encouraged to readjust her thinking. Any attempts to stand out and individuate were tenderly quashed, until she believed it was her own idea to eat the foods they ate, dress like they dressed, spend her free time doing community service, and give Guru Meyer all her money and earthly possessions.

Was that really so bad? Her basic needs had been met and her rebellious ways curbed.

No, no it had not been that bad. Which is why it had been so easy to deny what had happened to her.

She'd lost her identity.

Which Guru Meyer told her was the point. To erase "Shelley" and become "Sanpreet," an enlightened spirit and part of the collective whole whose mission it was to save the planet with love and devotion to their cause.

Erase your ego. Dissolve the self. Eradicate your identity.

Once upon a time, it sounded so good. She'd been desperate to expunge the old Shelley and become someone else. Which, in retrospect, she'd done to great effect.

But suddenly, like a lightning bolt, she saw the flip side. No ego meant no self. Which she'd thought was a good thing. Then again, how many times had Guru Meyer pounded into her head that things were neither good nor bad, they just were?

Here was the head-scratcher that even cognitive dissonance couldn't quite sweep under the rug. If you eradicated your identity, just who in the jackfruit were you?

Reality was a kick in the teeth, truth the red neon signs she'd ignored. For five freaking years she'd been mumbling malarkey. Sacrificing two hours and forty minutes every morning at 4:30 A.M. and her soul was as grungy as ever.

She had never thought about exposing the group, because it was her word against theirs and he was so adept at gaslighting, projecting, and denial, she would come off looking like the crazy one. Plus, he knew all her dirty secrets from the confession sessions he imposed on acolytes. He could expose her just as much as she could expose him.

Fear kept her quiet.

Plus, this was all new to her. The notion that Cobalt Soul was rotten underneath the surface talk of peace, love, and acceptance. She'd only started to realize how much he controlled the group once she was out of it. He had a way of making you think that his ideas came from your own mind. He was a true puppet master. People who had never been in a cult didn't understand the psychological power such manipulators wielded.

And how sticky were the emotional webs they wove.

Shelley shivered, realizing just how much of her life she'd given away to this man.

"We have a van waiting," Guru Meyer said, keeping his tone even, his face smiling. His piercing, uncanny ice-blue eyes could stare straight through her as if he could see through all the muck and masks straight clean to the center of her soul.

At one time, his ability to truly "see" her intoxicated Shelley. In this moment, it was downright creepy.

"I can't go with you," she said.

"Why not?" he asked in that lullaby voice that had once lured her to sleep, but now rubbed every nerve ending raw.

His hug was tender and nonsexual. The loving way a father hugged a daughter. Not once had she ever gotten any sinister sexual vibes from him.

Guru Meyer wasn't a pervert taking advantage of the women in his group, at least as far as she knew. She hesitated. Maybe she was wrong after all. Maybe she'd just gotten confused. It had been so easy at Cobalt Soul. Nothing to think about. No angry sisters challenging her.

When he wrapped his arm around her waist again, she buried her face against Guru Meyer's shoulder and, to her horrified surprise, started to sob.

"Yes, yes, my beloved," he murmured. "You've had your little adventure, but now it is time to come home."

Where was Maddie? What was taking her so long with that broom? Her big sister would chase him off.

The others bowed and bobbed their heads, pressing their palms together in prayer pose. Sumran fingered her mala, twisting the beads. Japji smiled a moony smile of ecstasy and whispered, "Our sister is coming home."

Shelley suddenly shook her head, stepping back from the guru and wiping her eyes. She would stand her ground. She didn't need Maddie. She could save herself. "I can't go with you. My family needs me. My grandmother—"

"*We're* your family," Guru Meyer said, his voice changing, growing firmer. The way a loving father might guide his daughter.

"I'm talking about my blood family."

"How has it been for you since coming home?" He'd always had the power to see through her and get right to the heart of what was bothering her. He had amazing instincts.

She'd watched him use those same skills on other group members. Assuring them they were loved, convincing them he cared about them in a way no one else did.

"I—"

"Please." His hand was at her shoulders and his eyes, those piercing blue eyes, drilled into her as if he were trying to hypnotize her. "Come with us."

Go with him, whispered the part of her that had found salvation in Costa Rica. *Surrender. Give in. Let go. Go back to sleep.*

The thought was so appealing. Despite the rules and regulations, Cobalt Soul had been such a serene place. Yes, she'd surrendered her power. Yes, it had been rather surreal, but wasn't that part of the appeal?

"I—"

"Beat it, *buster*. Leave Shelley alone." Madison's voice from behind her was strong and commanding.

"There's no Shelley here," Guru Meyer murmured, never taking his gaze off Shelley's face. "Only our beloved *Sanpreet*."

Madison, bless her assertive heart, dropped the broom and dustpan she carried and got between Shelley and Guru Meyer, breaking his grip on her elbow.

Fists drawn, body cocked and ready for a fight, Maddie said, "She's *my* sister and I say step off, big guy, if you don't want me to call law enforcement and have you arrested for attempted kidnapping."

The acolyte bodyguards surged forward, linking arms around Guru Meyer.

"I've already called the cops, Madison," the checkout clerk hollered.

Guru Meyer's mask slipped then and for a split second Shelley saw fierce hatred directed toward Madison flare in his eyes. Her sister was keeping him from getting his way and Guru Meyer was accustomed to being obeyed.

"It's not kidnapping if she comes of her own free will," he said, haughtiness icing his voice. "Sanpreet, let's go."

Feeling as if she were standing a long distance away watching herself respond, she stepped away from his outstretched hand. Felt the glass shard dig deeper into her heel.

Heard Madison exclaim, "Shelley, you're bleeding!"

"I'm okay," she whispered.

"No, you're not. You have glass in your foot and you look like a *zombie*."

Shelley blinked and repeated, "I'm okay."

"What did this asshole do to you?" Madison wrapped her arm around Shelley's shoulder and dagger-glared at Guru Meyer. "Put your weight on me. I'll help you get to a chair and we'll tend to your foot."

Police sirens wailed up Moonglow Boulevard.

"If you don't come with us now, Sanpreet," Guru Meyer hissed, "you are no longer welcome in our group. We'll have no further contact with you. You can never return to Cobalt Soul. Think about it. You'll be losing your spiritual family. The ones who took you in when your blood sisters turned their backs on you. You'll have no support—"

"She'll have me." Madison tightened her grip around Shelley and said to her, "You'll have Gia and Mike and Darynda and the Quilting Divas."

"And me," said the shop clerk. "And everyone at AM-A-Zing Liquors."

"Shelley . . ." Madison said.

"Sanpreet." Guru Meyer reached for her hand.

"Come home, come home," the four young women in white chanted. "Come home, come home, come home."

Shelley looked first at Guru Meyer, then at Madison. Standing on one leg, hovering her injured foot off the ground, she slipped her arm around Madison's waist, met Guru Meyer's eyes that had turned from peaceful to stormy.

"Guru Meyer," she said, "I want to thank you for everything you did for me. You helped me when I was at my lowest point, but the truth is, I'm already home. I don't need you anymore."

"Don't throw away your salvation," he said.

"Mister, leave my sister alone. I have a TV

show and we can do a program on cults if you catch my drift." Madison growled.

"We are not a cult."

"Then if I did a show on breaking free from a cult you wouldn't be alarmed?"

His jaw clenched, and his eyes clouded. "And if I go quietly?"

"My show never mentions you," Madison said.

"I could sue if you do."

"I could countersue."

"I could destroy you."

"Ditto, buddy. We could go down in flames together."

He dropped the wise sage act and Shelley saw him for who he really was, like the wimpy Wizard of Oz behind the scary curtain. His lip curled in a scornful snarl and his face darkened. "So be it," he said. "You are dead to us, Sanpreet."

Then just as two police walked into the liquor store, their hands resting on the butts of their holstered weapons, Guru Meyer motioned for his disciples to follow him and they swept out the side exit.

"C'mon," Madison said, squeezing Shelley's hand. "Let's get you patched up, little sister."

CHAPTER SEVENTEEN

Madison

KALEIDOSCOPE: A quilt block pattern in which fabric is pieced so that it resembles the variegated image seen through a kaleidoscope.

The clerk at AM-A-Zing Liquors had a first aid kit she let Madison use to tend Shelley's foot. The police officers discussed the disturbance with them and left the store, issuing parting instructions to call them again if the big bald guy in white—who one kept calling Mr. Clean—returned to cause trouble.

A moment later, that same officer, wearing a sheepish grin, asked Madison for her autograph for his wife.

With a flourish of her pen, she sent him on his way and turned back to Shelley. The purple-haired clerk, Velma, according to her name tag, had parked Shelley on a stool behind the counter, with Shelley's bleeding right foot resting on her left knee. The first aid kit lay open on the counter beside a bottle of salted caramel Crown Royal.

Efficiently, Madison cleaned and dressed Shelley's wound while Velma swept up the shattered bottle of lemon vodka and cleaned the blood off Shelley's flip-flops. Madison left enough money to cover the mess, plus a little extra, thanked Velma for the use of the first aid kit, and offered Shelley her arm as she hobbled from the store.

"We forgot the liquor for the party," Shelley said.

"So we did." Leaving Shelley buckled in with the windows down to catch the ocean breeze, Madison buzzed back inside and bought several flavors of vodka, plus the salted caramel whiskey since Shelley was a fan of salted caramel.

Velma smiled shyly and asked for an autograph. Madison readily complied and bustled back outside to find the car empty.

Good grief, where had Shelley gotten off to on an injured foot?

She swept her gaze around, spied Shelley across the street, limping down the wooden staircase that led to the beach. *Not the sand! You'll get sand in your cut.*

Tossing the vodka into the back of the car, and the whiskey into her purse, she put up the windows, locked the doors, and took off after Shelley.

Madison caught up with her on the beach. Shelley parked herself near the water, but on a dry patch of sand and in full lotus position with both feet resting against the opposite thigh, the soles of her feet turned upward.

Man alive, her sister really was a limber pretzel.

Shelley stretched her arms out over her knees, touched the tips of her index finger and thumb together to form a circle, closed her eyes, and began a breathing pattern that consisted of a quick inhale followed by a forceful exhale that caused her flat belly to undulate on each out breath.

Madison sank down on the sand beside her, settled her purse next to her, and drew her knees to her chest. She wasn't even going to attempt that crazy cross-legged position. She hugged her knees and studied her sister.

Shelley's face softened and a small smile turned up the corners of her lips. The wind blew her scraggly hair over her shoulders as she tilted her chin up to the sun.

"What are you doing?" Madison whispered.

"Centering myself," Shelley murmured without opening her eyes.

Uh, okay. Madison had taken a few yoga classes in her life, but the meditations had always irritated her. She preferred moving to sitting. When she'd complained to the instructor that her mind was too active for meditation, the teacher had smiled knowingly and said, "That's like saying you're too dirty for a shower."

After that, Madison left the studio and never went back.

"I—"

"Shh," Shelley said.

Madison wriggled in the sand. Did her best to stay quiet. Failed miserably. "How long is—"

Shelley cracked open one eye. "Just be quiet for a moment, okay? Feel the sand beneath your body."

"Yeah, about that. It's really uncomfortable."

"So what?"

"So what?"

"You're not going to die from it. Just experience the discomfort."

"Mr. Clean teach you this?"

"He did."

"But you didn't go back with him."

Shelley sighed, unfurled from the lotus position, stretching her legs in front of her, and opened both eyes. "No."

"Why not?"

"I learned everything he had to teach me."

Madison stabbed a quick glance over at her sister. "So," she said. "You were in a yoga cult?"

"Yep."

"How did *that* happen?"

"I didn't know it was a cult." Shelley had her wounded foot on her knee again in that flexible, yoga-instructor way of hers, ironing the edges of the bandage completely flat with her fingers. "Please don't bag on me. I feel stupid enough as it is."

"I wasn't going to bag on you."

"Weren't you?"

"No. I feel like I drove you into his clutches."

"Everything isn't about you, Maddie."

"Touché." *Ouch, that smarts a bit.* "Still, I can't help feeling if I hadn't shunned you, you wouldn't have ended up in a cult."

"It wasn't like that. Guru Meyer—"

"Aka Mr. Clean?"

"Yes."

"He thinks he's all that." Madison snorted.

Shelley let out a bone-deep sigh and Madison realized she needed to shut up and listen if she wanted to fix the damage they'd done to each other five years ago.

"Once upon a time, he was the most important person in my life." Shelley brushed sand from her bandage.

"*That* guy?"

"He helped me so much."

"You were searching for something."

"And he had the answer," Shelley said. "Too bad the answer was a cult."

Madison dropped her face into her palms. "I'm still trying to wrap my head around this. You, the nonconformist, ending up in a place that requires complete conformity. How? Why?"

"It felt nice belonging to something bigger than myself."

"Nicer than our family?" Madison whispered.

"After what happened? Yeah." Shelley paused, and Madison felt like utter crap for causing

Shelley to feel so abandoned and alone that she'd preferred a cult to her sisters.

That explained why Shelley was broke.

"You gave him all your money, didn't you?"

Shelley raised her shoulders in a controlled shrug. "I had no use for money. Guru Meyer made sure all my needs were met."

"Except for a hair and nail salon."

Fingering her brittle, frizzy hair, Shelley burst out laughing. "You make a good point, my sister."

Madison took the salted caramel whiskey from her purse and twisted off the lid.

"There's no glass containers allowed on the beach," Shelley said mildly.

"Are you gonna tell on me?"

"No open alcohol containers, either."

"I'll take my chances. I just found out my sister's been in a yoga cult for five years and I did nothing to try to rescue her." Madison took a hit off the salted caramel whiskey and it slid down smooth. She held the bottle out to Shelley. "You want some of this?"

Shelley looked at the label, raised an eyebrow. "You don't like salted caramel."

"No, but you do." She waggled the bottle at her.

"I really don't need alcohol anymore," Shelley said. "I've learned how to regulate my emotions without it."

"I'm trying here, Shelley. Could you meet me halfway?"

Shelley grinned and reached for the bottle, took a quick sip, and passed it back to Madison. "Dang, that is good. But stick it in your purse in case Beach Patrol shows up."

Madison hooted. "Since when did *you* ever worry about Beach Patrol?"

"I've changed."

Resting her head on her knees and turning her cheek in Shelley's direction, Madison eyed her sister for a long moment. "So you have. Tell me everything."

"After . . . well, you know . . . I applied for a job as a barista at Cobalt Soul. I'd always wanted to go to Costa Rica and it seemed like a great place to lie low until you forgave me for Raoul. They were so good to me there. Guru Meyer said, 'It's like we've been waiting for you to walk in the door.' "

"Love bombing."

"I know that now. At the time? It just felt good to have people accept me."

"They changed your name. Sanpreet, was it?"

"Everyone had cool nicknames. I didn't think of it as altering my identity. I was honored. I was part of the pack. I felt loved."

Madison reached out to squeeze Shelley's hand. "I'm so sorry I made you feel unloved."

Shelley's eyes misted. She blinked and looked away from Madison. "He told me I was a natural healer and enrolled me in their yoga teacher training program. I loved yoga. It helped me so much."

A pang of regret intertwined with sadness jabbed Madison's heart. Leaning over, she wrapped her arm around Shelley's shoulder and held her tight. "I was selfish. I thought only of myself and my hurt. Can you forgive me, Shelley?"

"You're not the only one with regrets. The way I handled things with Raoul . . . I was inept. Stupid. I just didn't want you to marry him and when I tried to tell you how I felt about him, you told me I was jealous."

"I was terrible. I should never have said that to you."

"No, you were right. I've been jealous of you my whole life. You're prettier, smarter, more accomplished. You're sharp and on the ball. You're—"

"Completely obsessive with an anxiety disorder," Madison said. "I've been in therapy for six months. My life came crashing down around me. My job was the only thing holding me together, so you can bet I held on with both hands."

"The sonogram . . ." Shelley whispered. "The baby."

It was Madison's turn to look away. She simply couldn't bear the pity in Shelley's eyes. "She was the love of my life and I never even saw her face."

"Oh, Maddie."

Madison toyed with her crystal necklace, then told Shelley about the baby and naming a star after her. Her voice cracked as she spoke, but she managed not to cry.

"Can I have some more salted caramel?" Shelley reached out a hand.

"You betcha." They both took a swig before putting the alcohol back in Madison's purse.

"Who was Claire Estelle's father?"

"One of the producers on my show."

"You still have to work with him?" Shelley asked.

"No." She shook her head. "Finn left me and the show. I was a wreck. He wasn't ready to have a baby and I guess I blamed him for that. I wanted her so badly and he was ambivalent." She dug her foot in the sand. "I hurt him by pushing him away. I know that. Even though he wasn't wild about the idea of having kids yet, he was heartbroken when we lost her. He tried to comfort me, but I couldn't be comforted." She paused, thought of Finn, who deep down was a good man. "He wanted to love me, and I wouldn't let him."

"Can I say something?" Shelley asked. "I don't mean this in a judgmental way, I promise."

"Go ahead. It's not as if I don't judge you." Madison shuddered. "I've got so much to work on myself."

"We all do. No one is perfect."

"What was it you wanted to say?"

"Once in a while, Madison, you've got to let someone else take the reins. You don't always have to be in control. The world won't fall apart if you let go a little."

"More of Mr. Clean's wisdom?"

"No, this one is all Sanpreet." She giggled, her voice lightened by salted caramel whiskey.

"So, *Sanpreet,*" Madison said, dusting the sand from her hands. She wasn't one for pity parties and this was tuning up to be one. "How did you come to realize you were in a cult?"

"It was pretty abrupt, really, but when I look back on it, I can see the red flags now. Red flags I ignored and blew right past because I was so desperate for love."

"Desperate is not a pretty color."

"Nope."

"Been there, but where you ran *to* people, I ran away from them. I put up walls, built barriers. Finn complained that I would never let him in."

"At least you had boundaries. I was an open door." Shelley made come-on-in motions with her arms. "I accepted anyone and everyone who walked over the threshold."

"We're polar opposites."

"Always have been," Shelley said.

"But hey, don't opposites attract?" Madison rested her head on Shelley's shoulder.

Shelley stroked her head. It felt so good. "How big a swig did you take of that salted caramel?"

"Not big enough."

"You know," Shelley said. "I've never seen you drunk."

"That control thing. Can't stand the thought of losing it. But we're talking about you. What were the red flags you ignored?"

"For one thing, I thought the way he isolated us was a good thing. At Cobalt Soul there were no TVs, no internet, no cell phones, no animal products, no alcohol, no arguing or dissenting allowed, and oh yes, no sex."

"No sex? You gotta be kidding."

"We were purifying ourselves."

"He's a dude, though. He was having sex with someone."

"Not me."

"And you haven't *done it* in five years?"

"No. Making up for all the years I overdid it when I was younger, I guess."

"I get the feeling that Mr. Clean has an instinct for what people need and he caters to it to control them. You needed to feel safe and loved, so he kept sex off the table for you."

"Maybe. There was a shit-ton of magical unicorn thinking going on," Shelley said.

"Such as?"

"Got a headache?" Shelley grew animated as if she were narrating a TV commercial. "Buddha forbid that you take aspirin. Try chewing organic, all-natural feverfew leaves. Give it a few days and voilà, headache gone."

"You sound like the old Shelley now." Madison applauded. "Snarkalicious."

Shelley was just getting warmed up. "Or if that doesn't do the trick, then your sixth chakra must be blocked. Swing a crystal pendulum counterclockwise over your forehead and it'll fix you right up."

"Seriously?"

"Got anxiety? Flush those benzos and release the issues from your tissues with primal screaming and an ice-cold shower first thing in the morning. It will shock your system and make room for calm."

Madison startled. Did Shelley know she had a Xanax prescription? Was that a dig at her?

But no, Shelley rolled right along without a manipulative bone in her body. Madison had long admired her guilelessness.

"Got doubts?" Shelley's voice lowered as she pretended to sound like a man. "That's just your inner resistance. Your ego wants to hold you back. Numb that pesky *thang* with a five-day juice fast, and ten hours of kneeling meditation."

"Then again . . ." Madison opened her purse. "There's always salted caramel Crown Royal."

They each took a third swig of the whiskey, both getting giggly and loose.

"Or here . . . Let's scribble cray-cray hieroglyphics into your palms and make you an open channel for chi to flood your soul." Shelley demonstrated by taking Madison's hand and tracing squiggly symbols over her skin.

"That tickles." Madison hiccuped. Laughed.

"See!" Shelley pointed a finger. "There's your chi!"

"A miracle. I feel chi-ed all over."

"Oh, and don't forget to tithe eleven percent of your income to Cobalt Soul to ensure more feel-good karma."

"Gosh, Shell, you were in a weird place."

"Tell me about it. Still, I couldn't see the weirdness." Shelley frowned. "No, that's not true. I saw and embraced it anyway."

"Let's give credit where credit is due." Madison hiccuped again. "You *are* more open-minded and less reactionary." She paused, lowered her voice, and in a loud whisper said, "Maybe I should go to Cobalt Soul."

"No! You are fine just the way you are."

"So are you." Madison's words slurred slightly. She could count on the fingers of one hand the times she'd had more than two drinks in one day. "Am I drunk?"

"Maybe. Can you say the alphabet backward?"

"Z, Y . . . Oh, forget it." Madison waved a hand. "It's official. I'm drunk."

"Don't worry, I've got your back, but maybe you should let me hang on to your purse."

"Here you go." Madison plopped her purse in Shelley's lap, and then spun around on her butt and laid her head on top of her purse and stared up at her sister.

"Oh, okay, we're doing that."

"Hey, how come you're not hammered?"

"After the first sip, I pretended to drink."

"No fair!"

"Someone has to drive us home."

"Not you. Your driving foot is wonky."

"I'll figure it out."

Madison felt mellow and floaty. Above Shelley's head the clouds danced. "You never did tell me when you snapped to the fact you were in a cult."

"It's not been that long," Shelley said. "It happened the day Gia called and left a message that Grammy was having surgery for cancer. I was in a treatment room, undergoing one of Guru Meyer's healing sessions, when I—"

"What's that like?"

"The hieroglyphics stuff I showed. Rattles, drumming, circle breathing. Things that blast you into an altered state of consciousness."

"Like salted caramel whiskey."

"Like salted caramel whiskey without the hangover."

"Sounds nice." Madison felt like Pyewacket. Lithe and warm and feline.

"Ahh, but like salted caramel whiskey, altering your consciousness has a dark side," Shelley said.

"Ye*sss*. The loss of control."

"It's all a balance," Shelley said. "Between having boundaries to protect yourself and being open and kindhearted."

"We both went off the deep end in opposite directions."

"But, look, we're back together in the middle."

"Back to the realizing you were in a cult thing. I'm sorry, I keep butting in. Please go on. Tell me what happened."

"During the healing session, the receptionist knocked on the door and Guru Meyer, who was pretty peeved about being interrupted, went out into the hall. I was lying on the treatment table, floating in this warm cocoon of bliss, and I heard them whispering about Grammy. And then he said, 'She's not to be told, we can't risk letting her go home.' Just like a lightning bolt, it hit me, and I understood that everything he'd been doing was mind control. And yes, maybe I did need to control my mind. But *I* needed to be the one doing it, not some narcissistic cult leader."

"Wow, that must have been mind-blowing."

"It was." Shelley leaned back on her elbows and looked down at Madison, who still had her head in Shelley's lap. "I kept trying to talk myself out of it, but I couldn't get past the fact that he was keeping me from Grammy."

"I can't even imagine."

"So I packed my meager clothes in my backpack, stole my passport out of the office where he kept all our passports locked up—duh, another red flag, Shelley—and I took off. I didn't have money for airfare, but I went to the American consulate, told them what had happened. They'd heard about Guru Meyer's cult. They'd had people come in before in the same shape I was in, but the authorities considered him fairly benign and left him alone. They put me in touch with an ex-pat group who paid for my ticket home."

"Shelley, things could have gone wrong in so many ways." Madison sat up abruptly. "You do impulsive like no one else, but somehow you come out of it smelling like roses."

"I'm here, none the worse for wear."

"Well, except for your hair and nails," Madison teased.

"Yeah." Shelley grabbed a hunk of her hair and stared at her split ends. "But I haven't paid you back for the taxi and the phone and I don't even have money for a haircut."

"No, no. The haircut is on me. The taxi and the phone, too. We're taking you for a spa day, right now."

"Maddie . . ."

"I'm serious. We're going, but something's missing."

"What's that?"

"Gia."

"She's the only one of us who's been balanced all along."

"She had to be to even us out." Madison snapped her fingers. "Quick, hand me my purse."

"You don't need any more salted caramel hooch."

"I don't want whiskey, I want my phone. Let's call Gia. The Moonglow sisters are getting makeovers! My treat."

CHAPTER EIGHTEEN

Gia

ON POINT: The orientation of a quilt when its corners are placed up, down, and to the sides.

Things changed between the three sisters after their spa day together. For the first time since coming back home they relaxed around one another. They laughed and teased Shelley about being in a cult and told stories and passed around the bottle of salted caramel whiskey and for a few hours it felt like old times.

Gia lightened her hair for the summer and Madison rocked a watermelon-themed mani-pedi, but it was Shelley who emerged from the spa looking truly transformed. Gone was the long, frizzy hair and in its place, she sported fashionable, layered, shoulder-length beach waves. The stylist had also streaked chunky golden highlights through her hair. Her fingernails and toenails were trimmed, buffed, and polished, and she had a facial that brought out her natural glow.

"Wow," Madison said. "You look so much like Mom it's freaky."

"I do, huh?" Shelley checked herself out in the mirror and fluffed her hair, getting used to it.

"I don't remember Mom at all," Gia said. "I try, but I simply can't. If it weren't for the photographs . . ."

"She was a beautiful woman." A wistful tone crept into Madison's voice. "But she really didn't spend all that much time with us. She was obsessed with skiing."

"I wonder what happened between her and Grammy," Gia said. "We might never find out."

"Maybe, after all this, Grammy'll be more inclined to talk about it," Madison mused.

"If she ever speaks again." Gia shook her head.

"I wish I could recall more about Mom." Shelley tossed her hair this way and that in front of the mirror.

"Well, I for one think she would be very proud of her daughters," Gia said. "Maddie's a TV personality. I make kites. Shelley escaped a cult. We Moonglow sisters are anything but dull."

"*I'm* proud of us." Madison paid for their services and gifted her sisters with a group hug right there in the spa and Gia left thinking, *Flying pigs! Miracles do happen.*

The next day, even with organized, whip-cracking Madison at the helm, dissolved into beautiful chaos as the Quilting Divas descended upon the Moonglow Inn en masse.

Enthusiastic women armed with fabric, needles, thread, rotary cutters, self-healing cutting mats, acrylic quilting rulers, basting safety pins, wonder clips, scissors, and portable sewing machines overflowed the house, the porches, the lawns.

Quilters were everywhere.

Pyewacket found sanctuary on top of the refrigerator, staring down at the collective with narrowed Siamese eyes and leonine disdain.

Directed by Madison, the quilters formed an assembly line to make as many quilts as they could possibly make in three days. No hand sewing for these projects, there simply wasn't time. The Divas called them stash-buster quilts, meaning they selected simple, efficient designs that used up fabrics from the quilters' personal stashes of material.

One group of quilters formed the cutting station, a second group did the backing, a third group handled the batting, and a final group did the ditch stitching. Gia volunteered to do all the ironing. She set up an ironing board in the kitchen, steaming block after block of quilt tops.

With all those people, the house came to life. Laughing, talking, music, the air buzzed with voices.

"Light! I need more light!" called out Erma Kelton from behind her thick-lensed glasses, squinting at the fabric pieces in the bright sun beaming in through the kitchen windows. The kitchen table had been transformed into the cutting station laid out with self-healing mats, rotary cutters, and rulers.

Gia had already raised the blinds, turned on every light in the kitchen, and cleaned the windows to let in more illumination, but Erma had cataracts and refused to admit she needed surgery.

"On it," Mike said, breezing through the kitchen.

He winked at Gia on his way past. He returned a few minutes later with a five-foot adjustable tripod graced with a two-headed, rotating LED light bar that lit the place up like a construction site.

"Now that's more like it." Erma nodded her head, satisfied.

"Good gravy, Erma," mumbled another elderly lady at the cutting table. "I feel like I'm being interrogated. Turn off the floodlights. I'll talk, I'll talk."

"Does that mean if I keep 'em on you'll stay quiet, Viv?" Erma shot back.

"Stuck my foot in my mouth with that one, didn't I?" Viv chuckled. "Keep it on, turn it off. I'll talk either way."

Mike readjusted the lights so that all the shine was on Erma. "How's that, ladies?"

Everyone at the table gave a thumbs-up.

"Help!" called wizened Mrs. Turner, who was ninety if she was a day, from the backing station in the dining room. "I need somewhere to plug in my power scissors."

Gia looked to Mike.

"Be right back." He trotted from the kitchen, returned momentarily with a multiplug adapter, and soon had Mrs. Turner and her scissors in business.

Gia clasped her hands, tucked them under her chin, tilted her head, and in a swoony, moony voice said, "My hero."

A collective "aww" went up from the group.

"He is a keeper," Erma said. "I'm glad you finally realized that, Gia."

"She sure took her sweet time, didn't she, Mike?" Viv asked.

"A man who's good with his hands and puts up with old ladies is a treasure," Mrs. Turner called from the dining room. "Hold on to him tight."

Looking inordinately pleased with himself, Mike strolled over to where Gia had set up the ironing board on the other side of the kitchen island. "Hear that? I have a fan club."

"Should I be worried you'll leave me for one of these quilting whizzes?"

"I'll take him off your hands," Erma chirped. "Just saying."

Mike chuckled and wrapped his arm around Gia's waist. Gia set the iron upright on the ironing board and smiled at him through a cloud of steam. "Sorry, Erma, I'm true blue. Gia's the one for me."

"Rats," Erma mumbled with a grin. "Fifty years too late. Story of my life."

Mike nuzzled Gia's neck, putting on a show for the ladies. "It's been a long time since the place has been this much fun," he murmured.

"Thanks to you."

"No, I'm not the special ingredient. It's because the Moonglow sisters all came home."

"You're pretty special to me," she said. "And all this"—she flapped her hand at the group—"happened because of you. Without you, I couldn't have gotten my sisters on the same page."

"Okay." He kissed the top of her head. "We're the dream team."

"Yes," she whispered, and in that moment, she wished with all her heart that their engagement was real.

The quilting bee was a stunning success. In three days, twenty-six quilting wizards made seventy-eight quilts. Adding that number to the quilts they'd already collected as donations, they had one hundred and ten quilts to sell in the pop-up store. The stash-buster quilts would sell for one hundred and fifty dollars apiece, while the more artistic and handsewn quilts would be priced accordingly.

The most prized? Darynda's masterpiece, a tumbling blocks quilt, designed as wall art, and estimated by the Quilting Divas as worth fifteen hundred dollars.

If they sold every quilt for its sticker price, they'd bring in over twenty-five thousand dollars. Minus the amount Maddie had already paid to keep the inn out of foreclosure, they were still left with a sixteen-thousand-dollar shortfall to pay off the mortgage. But then there were Gia's kites, Madison's wreaths, Shelley's yoga classes, and the furniture Mike had donated to fill in the gap.

For the first time, Gia felt optimistic that they could actually pull this off and save the Moonglow Inn.

On Monday morning, June 8, the three sisters headed for the hospital to check on Grammy and Darynda, whom they hadn't seen in four days.

Gia entered the room first.

Grammy was sitting up in bed. The bandage on her head had been removed, revealing her head shaved bald and the vivid surgical suture line. In her lap lay a photo album. Darynda had put the bed rail down on her side and was leaning over to look at the album with Grammy. The minute Grammy spied Gia, her eyes lit up.

"Morning, Grammy." Gia smiled and zoomed across the room to swallow her grandmother in a big hug. She felt so thin and frail in Gia's arms.

Darynda pulled back to let Gia get closer.

Grammy's hand fluttered up to touch Gia's

shoulder, but she was too weak to hold her hand aloft for long and it dropped to the photo album. Gia glanced down to see a photograph of their mother at eighteen on some ski slope somewhere with an intrepid smile on her face, and the bright sun shining on her golden hair flowing from underneath a blue toboggan cap. She looked like a coquettish angel full of daring innocence.

Gia ached for the woman she'd never known, wishing she'd had more time to find out who her mother was. She knew her only by pictures and other people's memories. Sassy, they said. Outspoken. Stubborn. Knew her own mind. Beth Chapman Clark sounded a whole lot like Madison.

Although Madison might have their mother's personality, Shelley was the one who most resembled her.

"Has she spoken?" Madison asked Darynda as she waited behind Gia to give Grammy a hug.

"No." Darynda's voice was strong. "But she nods or shakes her head in response to questions." Darynda reached over to squeeze Grammy's hand. "We're getting there."

Gia slipped out of the way to let Madison lean over and kiss Grammy's forehead. Shelley held back, hanging in the doorway. Gia motioned her in.

Glancing over her shoulder, Shelley shook her head. "The last time we had this many people in here, the nurses bawled us out."

"Since when did you start following rules?"

Madison asked. "Get in here and give Grammy a hug."

Shelley hesitated, then came on in, shutting the door behind her. She turned and headed over as Madison stepped to the foot of the bed with Gia.

Grammy's eyes widened at the sight of Shelley with her newly made-over hairstyle. Pure joy illuminated her face and she cried in a halting, scratchy voice, "Beth!"

All three sisters startled and exchanged stunned glances.

Grammy had spoken! But the name she'd called Shelley was the name of a woman who'd been dead for twenty years. Their mother.

Tears streamed down Grammy's face and her bottom lip quivered. "Y-you c-came . . . home."

Simultaneously, the three sisters swung their gazes to Darynda, who looked as surprised as they were. Tears brimmed in her eyes too.

Shelley blinked, and then shot a what-should-I-do glance at Madison.

"Helen," Darynda murmured. "That's not Beth. That's Shelley, Beth's middle daughter."

Grammy shook her head. "Beth," she said, her voice clearer, steadier now.

"Should I pretend to be Mom?" Shelley whispered to Madison and Gia.

"Give it a whirl," Gia said. "It seems to make her happy."

"Don't deceive her," Madison contradicted. "It's not fair."

"Okay." Shelley inhaled. "Not helpful at all."

"Beth." Grammy looked from the photo album in her lap to Shelley. "Beth?"

"I told you that makeover made you look like Mom," Madison said.

Shelley inched over and sank down on the thin ledge of mattress beside Grammy. Spoke the truth. "I'm so happy to be home."

"I-I—" Grammy's mouth twisted in upset as she struggled to find the words.

"Shh," Darynda soothed. "It's all right. It's okay. You don't have to talk."

Grammy darted a quick glare at Darynda, then gave her attention back to Shelley. "S-so-sorry."

"I'm sorry too." Shelley rubbed Grammy's forearm with her palm.

Gia watched her sister with her grandmother. Feeling both of their pain as they struggled to communicate, she wished she could make things easier. The moment seemed weighted, monumental. A long time coming.

A rift between mother and daughter. A rift between sisters. It seemed like her family was full of cracks and fractures, rips and schisms. Gia fingered the woven bracelet at her wrist.

"For . . . give . . . me." Grammy's voice was so hoarse that Gia could barely hear her. She worried Grammy was overdoing it. Saw the same fear on Darynda's face.

"You've done nothing to be forgiven for," Shelley said. "I'm the one who needs to be forgiven. Me. I caused all the trouble."

"No." Grammy's whisper was the only sound in the room. She reached up a hand to touch Shelley's cheek. "Beth."

Shelley looked to Madison and Gia again, her eyes asking if she should play along and pretend to be their mother or correct her.

Gia shrugged. Hey, she was trapped in the midst of a pretty big whopper, she had no advice. Madison frowned and shook her head.

"For . . . give . . . me."

"Shh," Madison said. "Save your strength. You can talk more later. This is a lot for one day."

Grammy gave her the same glare dart she'd shot at Darynda earlier. "*You* hush."

Gia giggled, glad to see her spunky grandmother was still in there somewhere.

Turning her attention back to Shelley, Grammy repeated, "For . . . give . . . me."

"I forgive you . . ." Shelley hesitated, then plunged ahead. *"Mama."*

Madison made a you-handled-that-wrong noise. Gia poked Madison in the ribs with her elbow. Sometimes a kind lie was better than the cruel truth.

Grammy was crying. Shelley was crying.

Gia felt warm tears on her cheeks. Even crusty Madison was sniffling. Darynda passed out Kleenex.

Their grandmother closed her eyes, a soft smile coming to her lips. She looked happy.

Shelley sat beside Grammy holding her hand and saying over and over like a mantra, *I forgive you, I forgive you, I forgive you*.

Ironic when all this time, Shelley was the one needing forgiveness.

Grammy's breathing slowed, and it seemed she'd fallen asleep. Shelley hung on to her hand.

Gently, Darynda took the photo album from Grammy's lap and settled it onto the bedside table next to the medical accoutrements.

"I need to know something." Gia surprised herself. She hadn't meant to speak her thoughts aloud.

Everyone, except Grammy, who was either asleep or so exhausted she couldn't respond, swung their gazes toward Gia. She'd backed herself into the far corner of the room, enjoying the security of having the wall at her back.

"Yes?" Darynda sat up straighter in her chair.

"What happened between our mother and Grammy?"

The uncomfortable expression on Darynda's face had Gia wishing she hadn't started down this road, but dammit, there had been too many secrets in this family. She flicked a glance at

Grammy, who looked both peaceful and worn out. Grammy's eyes opened, and she exhaled a sigh so deeply they all felt the shuddering effort of her breath.

Concerned, Darynda scooted forward in her chair, wedging her upper body in between Shelley, who was still sitting on the hospital bed mattress, and their grandmother resting heavily against the pillows.

"I mean . . ." Gia continued. Now that she *had* started it, she was determined to see it through. Grammy had begged her to convince her sisters to finish the quilt and mend the family rift. Surely, her goal had been to keep from replicating the family gulf in the younger generation. How could they keep from repeating the past if they didn't know the story of what went wrong? "What did Grammy do to make our mother so upset with her that she didn't even acknowledge she had a mother?"

Darynda and Grammy exchanged a long look.

Shelley got off the mattress and came to stand at the foot of the bed with Gia and Madison. The three of them waited. Madison had her arms folded over her chest. Shelley had her fingers interlaced, palms pressed together and clutched at the level of her throat. Gia's arms hung passively at her sides.

"Beth?" Grammy's eyebrows went up, asking the question more than her voice did, and motioned toward Shelley with her two fingers.

"Shelley."

"She . . . looks like Beth."

"But it's not Beth. Beth is gone."

Fresh tears sprang to Grammy's eyes and she nodded as if she understood.

"Should I?" Darynda asked.

"Tell . . ." Grammy moistened her lips with a dry flick of her tongue. "Them."

Darynda hooked Gia's gaze with her own. "Are you asking what your grandmother did that caused your mother to pack up her bags in the middle of the night, drive off to Colorado without saying a word of good-bye, and never contact Helen again, not even when she had three children of her own?"

"Y-yes."

Darynda pulled her spine up straight, looked each sister squarely in the eyes, first one and then the others. Her face was fierce. "She loved me."

"What?" Gia blinked.

"Your grandmother dared to love me, and Beth just couldn't accept that."

Stunned, Gia stared at Darynda as her meaning sank in. She'd known her grandmother and Darynda were very close. She'd accepted them as the best of friends. Had actually never thought twice about their relationship except to wonder why Darynda didn't already live with them since they had so much room. "You and Grammy are—"

Darynda notched up her proud chin and narrowed her eyes as if challenging them to judge her. "Life partners."

"And that bothered Mom?" Gia asked, confused. Why would her mother care if her grandmother loved a woman? Love was love, right?

Shelley slanted Gia a glance, looking at her as if she'd just dropped off a turnip truck from some greenhorn farm. "You didn't already know Grammy and Darynda are gay? Why do you think I painted rainbows on Grammy's toes?"

"To be cheerful?" Gia asked.

"I thought everyone knew." Madison shrugged and turned to Darynda. "What's the big deal?"

"Not much these days," Darynda said. "But twenty years ago, minds were just starting to open to the possibility that everyone deserved the same fundamental human rights no matter whom they loved. And you know, there are still people today who don't accept differences. Your mother was one of those people."

"I can see that," Madison said. "Mom could be very rigid in the way she viewed the world. She was a black-and-white thinker. There were friends she'd had, relationships she dropped when people didn't behave the way she thought they should. In Mom's eyes, when you were out, you were out."

"Guess I would have been in trouble with her," Shelley mumbled.

“Why didn’t you tell us about being life partners years ago?” Gia asked, honestly confused that they would keep their love a secret.

Darynda looked to their grandmother, who was watching them with heated eyes. “Your grandmother was afraid you might react the same way Beth did, and she couldn’t bear the thought of losing you.”

“You couldn’t be free to be yourself because of us.” Shelley shoved her fingers through her hair and blew out an exasperated breath. “What a shame.”

“Just as it was a shame you and your sisters had a falling-out,” Darynda said.

“How did Mom find out?” Madison asked.

Embarrassment colored Darynda’s cheeks. “She walked in on us during a private moment. I’m sure it was quite shocking to her, even though we were just in bed together snuggling, but with no clothes on—”

Shelley held up both palms. “You don’t owe us the details.”

“It wasn’t so much what your grandmother was doing, but who she was doing it with. Beth never cared for me. I called her out for sassing Helen. She thought it wasn’t my place and it probably wasn’t, but I can’t stand for anyone to mistreat the love of my life.” Darynda smiled at Grammy, both of their eyes shining with more tears.

“Is that why you’re rough on me sometimes?”

Madison asked. "When you see my mother's unattractive traits in me?"

"I can get pretty territorial when it comes to protecting Helen," Darynda said. "I apologize if I've ever made you feel harshly criticized, Maddie. I was coming from a place of insecurity."

"I appreciate you saying that, Darynda. It gives me courage." Madison turned and took Shelley's hand.

Shelley startled, eyes widening, then she said in a voice with a let's-not-get-too-serious tone, "What?"

"I've been just as rough on you, Shelley. If not more so."

"Pah." Shelley slipped out of Madison's grip. "Water. Bridge. I'm over it. Don't get mushy."

Grammy smiled a small wavy smile, her lips barely able to hold it up.

That sweet brief smile was both happy and heartbreaking.

Sadness moved through Gia, and she clenched her hands to keep from weeping at the pain they'd all suffered. Her body hurt over the past misunderstandings, the miscommunications, the missteps, the mistakes. They all loved one another and yet they'd caused each other so much heartache, and now they were losing Grammy, bit by bit.

But here was the beautiful thing. They'd finally come together.

Just in the nick of time.

In unison, without a word spoken, the three sisters moved closer, encircling the bed. Madison reached out and took Darynda's left hand with her right, and Shelley's right hand with her left. Shelley took Gia's hand and on one side, Gia slipped her fingers through Grammy's, while Darynda did the same on the other side.

They all looked from one to the other in their first moment of solidarity in five long years. Then Shelley, the cutup, who couldn't bear much seriousness, started singing "Who Let the Dogs Out."

Laughing, they sang and danced madly about the room until the stern head nurse burst in and threw them all out of the room.

CHAPTER NINETEEN

Gia

PAPER FOUNDATION: A thin piece of paper with a drawn, printed, or stitched pattern that becomes the base for a quilt block when fabric is sewn directly onto it.

From that day in Grammy's hospital room forward, the Moonglow sisters were once again inseparable, working in harmony for one unifying goal—to set up the pop-up store for the Fourth of July weekend and earn enough money to get the Moonglow Inn out of debt.

Grammy's condition improved dramatically—even Dr. Hollingway was impressed and surprised—and they moved her to the local rehab hospital. The sisters visited whenever they could and devoted Darynda stayed by Grammy's side, even bringing her own cot into the room so she could sleep there.

Mike took care of Darynda's dogs, bringing them to his house to stay until Grammy was released from the rehab hospital. The Moonglow sisters would have readily taken on her dignified German shepherds, but the dogs were terrified of Pyewacket. Mike and the volunteers from the

Chamber of Commerce finished the renovations and Madison updated the website just in time to book their first guests for the Fourth of July weekend, a middle-aged couple from Cleveland on their twentieth anniversary, returning to the beach where they'd first met.

The weeks leading up to the Fourth were frantic with activity and Gia had little time to hang out with Mike, but running the inn with her sisters felt like old times.

During the renovations, they'd all moved back into the single bedroom they'd shared as teenagers. They left it untouched to save money. Later, once the inn was on its feet again, they'd redo this room too.

Each night was like a slumber party as they dished about their lives while they'd been apart. Shelley regaled them with stories of cult life in Costa Rica with that irreverent hilarious way of hers. Madison glammed it up with tales from a TV reality-show host. Gia kept it exotic with her kitemaking adventure in Japan.

The healing had begun in earnest.

On the holiday weekend of the pop-up store opening, everything ran like a well-oiled machine, thanks to Madison's organizational chart. Shelley's assignment was to cater to their guests and give morning yoga classes on the beach. Mike and Madison, with help from the Chamber of Commerce and the Quilting Divas, ran the pop-up store. Gia gave kite lessons and flying demonstrations, while Darynda manned the kitchen, feeding the volunteers.

When the long weekend was over, their guests departed raving about the Moonglow Inn and promised a five-star Yelp review. Shelley had been offered a job teaching yoga at the local studio. Gia had sold every single kite she had in her inventory, leaving only Mike's blue fish and her pink dragon of the kites she'd spent a year amassing in Japan. It was gratifying to see her artwork flying the skies of Moonglow Cove.

Most important of all, they'd earned enough to not only pay off all Grammy's debt, but to also repay Madison for her investment in the back payments to keep the inn out of foreclosure.

They celebrated with champagne on the back porch at sunset on Sunday night. To top off the victorious event, the head nurse at the rehab hospital called to say that Grammy could come home in a week.

That glorious news spurred an impromptu party with Shelley cranking up the sound system and creating a playlist. She spun Madison around on the porch to "Sisters Are Doin' It for Themselves" by the Eurythmics and Aretha Franklin.

Mike held out his hand to Gia and they joined the dancing as the music shifted into "Ocean Eyes" by Billie Eilish.

He pulled her close to the slow song and

whispered, "I love falling into *your* ocean eyes."

Gia's pulse quickened. Her body was exhausted from the pace of the past four days, but her spirit, oh, it soared to the sky as surely as one of her kites.

He rested his forehead on hers and she went cross-eyed staring into him. His blue eyes transfixed her hazel ones. They'd stopped moving and were just standing there peering deeply at each other, Mike clasping her hands in his, his mouth so close, his breath warm and fruity with the smell of champagne.

"Hey, you two," Shelley hollered from where she'd collapsed into one of the rocking chairs. "Get a room."

Gia stepped back, heart pounding. This was it. The time she should tell her sisters they weren't really engaged. Things had been going so well. Everyone was working so hard on forgiving and letting go of the past. They'd forgive her. Of that she felt certain.

But there was still the wedding quilt to finish.

And then Mike cocked his head, smiled softly, and whispered, "Do you want to come home with me?"

Gia slipped her hand into the palm Mike extended toward her.

"We won't wait up," Madison said.

"Be here on the porch at nine tomorrow morning to finish Grammy's quilt," Gia called over her shoulder, not bothering to turn around to look at them as Mike led her down the steps and across the lawn toward his house. The hem of her dress swayed softly against her bare legs. "Both of you."

"Have fun!" Shelley called.

Gia grinned in the dark, her blood pumping hot and sticky through her veins. Maybe the champagne had gone straight to her head, but she was all in. She had no idea what she was getting herself into, only that she was mad excited about it.

Sweet, sweet, yes.

The moon was rising, a full and magnificent beach ball above the dark waters of the ocean. *Pay attention,* it seemed to say. *See . . . truly see . . . the ephemeral beauty of this glorious moment. Listen to the waves. Hear the seagulls call. Please yourself, Gia. Do what feels right.*

They climbed over the small stone wall, hand in hand. Mike led her to the cozy little bungalow cottage wreathed in vines and greenery. The house had a gabled roof straight out of a fairy tale. It was whimsical and inviting. A hand-carved bench sat on the front porch and the scent of hedge honeysuckles filled the air.

She hesitated at the steps.

Mike stopped. Said nothing, just waited for her. Patiently. As if he'd happily wait a lifetime for her if necessary.

The moment hung suspended, quivering like the moon glinting off the water.

Likewise, Gia quivered, dangled, caught in the moonglow.

It was a sudden utopia, unexpected and transient. A gingerbread house. A storybook idyll. Mythic and legendary, as if some gentle forest creature lived here. Holding, if just for an instant, the snapshot of utter peace and tranquility.

Her first time with Mike.

She didn't know where their relationship was headed. If there would be more times or this was one special moment. Right now, it didn't matter. All that mattered was the way he drew her to him, kissed her softly, opened the door and welcomed her inside.

A few minutes later, after they fed Darynda's German shepherds and let them outside into the fenced backyard, she curled up on his couch while Mike drifted into the kitchen to fetch them two beers.

She glanced around as if seeing his house for the first time, through a lover's eyes. Inside, it was just as cute as the outside. Tidy, organized, rustic but with a touch of whimsy, just like Mike. The color scheme was black, white, and gunmetal gray with pops of vibrant red accents. Leather furniture, industrial light fixtures, nubby rug over hand-scraped dark wood flooring. Framed artwork of seascapes. A saltwater fish tank filled with colorful fish. On the bottom of the tank was an open treasure chest with a skeleton pirate popping out, grinning, and waving.

Gia smiled when she saw that.

Beside the fish tank sat a hand-carved sailing ship on a stand. The work was intricate, delicate, and she knew before she asked that Mike had done it even though it was nothing like the comfortable design of his furniture pieces. She reached for it, stroked her fingers over the bow, admired the artistry.

"You carved this?" she asked as he walked back into the living room and handed her a cold beer.

He looked sheepish, like he'd been indulging in a guilty pleasure. "It's something I've been working on in my spare time. It's not finished."

"I didn't know you did this kind of woodworking. It takes a fine hand."

"Coming from a kite artisan like yourself, I consider that high praise." He settled onto the couch beside her, his body heat seeping warmth into her. "I've missed you, G," he murmured, setting his beer on the coffee table and giving her his full attention. "We've been so busy saving the inn we haven't had much time together."

She put the wooden ship back where she'd found it and took a sip of her beer, more out of nervousness than because she really wanted it.

She set down her beer and took his hand, traced

the hard calluses on his palm. "Tell me about the first thing you ever made."

"I've never told you this story?"

Gia shook her head.

"See this?" He held up his thumb to reveal a faint silvered scar at the base. "My first cut on my first project. My granddad gave me a pocketknife for my sixth birthday and showed me how to make my own slingshot."

"I think your knife skills were pretty rudimentary."

"Yep. I still have the slingshot, though. The nurse in the emergency room cleaned the blood off for me. My first woodworking mishap and my first stitches."

"Oh, poor baby." She brought his thumb to her mouth and kissed it.

Mike shivered. "You do dangerous things to me, woman."

"Oh?"

"Don't play coy, Gia Jasmine Clark." He rested his arms across the back of the couch and his right ankle over his left knee. Spreading out.

"You remembered my middle name?"

"I heard Madison call it out enough when she was ticked off at you."

"You know everything about me," she said. "Where's the mystery?"

"Not everything." He lowered his voice and his eyelids and leaned in to kiss her. "There's the whole Japan thing. I have no idea what went on there."

"I ate a lot of fish and seaweed."

"And wasabi, too, apparently."

"I've gotten a little spicier as I've gotten older."

"Hmm." He kissed her again. "Wasabi at twenty-three? What's left for your thirties? Habanero?"

"You'll have to stick around and find out."

"I'm a Moonglow Cove man. I'm not going anywhere."

"Plan on spending your life beachcombing and making furniture?"

"I do."

She peered into his eyes. "Sounds like heaven to me."

"You're easy to please."

"You say that now." She grinned. "Just wait."

"Now you've got my hopes up." His hot lips branded her with a long, deep, dizzying kiss.

"What are you hoping for?"

"To please you."

"Hey, wait, aren't you the one who's always preaching please yourself?"

"That advice is exclusively for you. Most people please themselves too much without regard for others. You, on the other hand, take other people's opinions too much to heart."

"I'm working on it."

"I can tell. That's why my aim is to please

you. To help you learn exactly what it is that you like." His voice turned deep and throaty.

"Oh my."

"Oh yeah."

"So, *you're* going to make me happy?" She gave him a sly grin.

"I'm gonna give it my best shot, Short Stack."

"Where do we start?"

"Where all good woodworking starts. By taking inventory."

"Oh, so we're working wood now?"

He angled her a sultry stare. "Did you ever doubt it?"

"What do you mean by 'taking inventory'?"

"What kind of wood do you have? What kind of tools?" He ran the tip of his finger along her collarbone.

"That's similar to kitemaking." She canted her head, enjoying the way her body was heating up at his touch. "Especially when you're a poor student and can't afford the fancy kite cloth."

"What's the first thing you remember that made you truly happy?" Mike toyed with her hair.

"Honestly?"

"Yeah."

"You're gonna think I'm just buttering you up. But it was that moment on the beach when you helped me get my first kite in the sky. I was four or five, but what I remember most is wriggling with joy at the sight of it taking off. I laughed at that bright red kite in the sky and you were so encouraging. Clapping and laughing right along with me. You made me feel like I could do *anything*."

"You can. You do." His smile widened, and he stroked her cheek with his knuckle. "You were cute as a shiny penny."

"What about you?" she said. "What's the first thing that made you truly happy?"

"Puppy," he said. "Lassie. A collie. Yes, I wasn't very creative with names at three."

"I do remember Lassie. You'd taught her a bunch of tricks. Aww, that's so sweet. How come you don't have a dog now?"

"I've got two in the backyard."

"Darynda's dogs."

"She's given them to me," he said.

"What? Why?" Gia curled her legs up underneath her on the couch. "Those dogs are like her children."

"Don't say anything to your sisters, it's their business to tell, but she and your grandmother want to live together. Helen plans to move into Darynda's place and leave the Moonglow Inn to you girls."

"And they told you this, but not us?"

"Are you feeling hurt?" he asked.

"A little."

"C'mon, sweetheart." He kissed her forehead. "Sometimes it's easier to talk to a friend or a neighbor than family. And it just came out because I was looking after the dogs."

Gia didn't know how she felt about that. She'd resolved in her mind how she'd be the one to nurse her grandmother through everything.

"Don't look so stricken." He cupped her cheek. "It's what they want. They're pleasing themselves. Finally. You should do the same."

"It's not easy." She played with the button on his shirt. "Letting go of a lifetime habit."

"That's where I come in." One corner of his mouth quirked up and his eyes softened.

"How is that?"

"Helping you find out just what you want."

God, he was saying all the right things. It felt so good being here with him. It felt inevitable. As if they'd been building toward this moment for years.

"In bed?" she asked.

"That's a start."

"What if we're not good together like that?"

He reached out and rubbed her forehead with the pad of his thumb. "You worry too much."

"Mike," she said. "This is important. If things don't work out in the bedroom, what will it do to our friendship?"

"Gia." His thumb continued the rhythmic rubbing. "Stop worrying and just let yourself *feel*. Pay attention to what your body is telling you."

Easy to say, really hard to do when her mind

was spinning with all the ways this could go so wrong.

"Close your eyes," he murmured.

Slowly, she let her eyelids flutter shut.

"Check your body. What are you feeling?"

"My heart is racing," she admitted.

"Keep your eyes closed." He took her hand and kissed her wrist, his mouth soft and damp against the throb of her pulse. "How about now?"

"My blood feels like liquid fire."

"Is it uncomfortable?"

"Yes, but in the best way possible."

"Can you sit with that feeling without analyzing it? Just feel it and accept it for what it is?"

Lust? Yeah, she could accept that, embrace it even.

"So now," he said, tugging her into his arms again. "Talk kitemaking to me."

She partially opened one eye and peeked at him.

He was smiling at her.

"Why?"

"Do you have any idea how sexy you are when you talk about kites?"

"Sexy? What do you mean?"

"I watched you all day from the pop-up store. Teaching those kids how to fly kites, you lit up like a Christmas morning. Your passion is exciting. Tell me about kiteflying."

"Another kiss first," Gia negotiated and puckered up. "And make it a good one."

He kissed her, pressing a quick light brushing of his lips against Gia that left her wanting more. So much more if she played her cards right. She tried to deepen the kiss, but he said, "Not yet. Tell me about kitemaking."

"I'm guessing you don't use this line of seduction with your regular dates."

"Nope, just you." He lightly flicked her nipple with his thumb and it got hard all the way through her bra.

She wriggled, desperate for him. "What do you want me to say?"

"What's your favorite material to use? Not the most practical, but the one that feels the best beneath your fingers?"

"Is this getting you hard?" She touched the waistband of his jeans.

"No, *you* get me hard. Which is why I want you to talk about the things that please you. So what is your favorite material to make kites out of?"

"Silk," she said, hissing the *S* sound against the back of her teeth. "Pippa wanted me to use silk."

"You'd like to do it, wouldn't you? Make those one hundred kites for Pippa Grandon's wedding."

"There's nothing I'd like to do more . . . oops . . . except you, right now."

He laughed. "So why don't you?"

"Grammy." Gia shook her head. "There's no telling how long she has left. I can't afford to lose time with her."

"That's a tough one."

"Yeah."

"I knew it was the silk," he said.

"You're Mr. Know-It-All?"

"Nah. I just remember one time when you wanted to make a silk quilt."

"Grammy said silk was too hard to work with."

"And you came storming over here to complain about it."

"I did?"

"You used to talk to me a lot," he said. "You were a cool kid."

"So were you. Putting up with a little tagalong."

"I wish I had silk sheets for you."

"No, you don't. You slide right off them."

"Slipping and sliding is part of the fun."

"You're weird . . ." She paused, grinned. "But I like it."

He dropped fresh kisses on her mouth, a rapid-fire tease. She wrapped her arms around his neck and wriggled around on the couch until his back was against the cushions and she was straddling him.

Passion mounted. Blood strummed. Bodies heated. *Yum.*

Fingers dealt with belts, zippers, and buttons. Their clothes fell away, and she got to see his rock-hard muscles again. *Yum, yum.*

"So what is the favorite kite you ever made?"

"Your fish kite." Gia licked her lips. Sent her gaze over his body.

"Why is that?"

"The whole time I was working on it, I thought of you. How you gave me my love of kiteflying. My career."

"You give me too much credit."

"You underestimate yourself."

"Tell me how to fly a kite," he said. "The way you were telling the people on the beach."

"You know how to fly a kite."

"But I want to hear it from you."

"Ahh," she said. "You want my spiel."

"Yeah, now we're getting somewhere." He was rubbing her in all the right places and all the right ways.

"There are four forces of flight," she said breathlessly as he did amazing things to her with his fingers. "Lift . . ."

"Lift?" He stroked her cheek with his knuckle and stole another kiss.

"Lift is the upward force that pushes the kite into the air."

"Like this?" He lifted his hips, pushing himself deep inside of her. He tugged her head down and sucked her bottom lip up between his teeth.

She gasped, closed her eyes, gripped his shoulders. He tasted so damn good.

"Don't stop." He ran his tongue over her lip. "More."

"Differences in air pressure generate lift created by air as it flows over the body of the kite."

"Pressure." He groaned.

"Kitemakers angle and shape the kites so that the air moving over the top goes faster than the air moving over the bottom." She quickened her speed, outpacing him. "And ta-da, you have lift."

He shuddered beneath her. "Do. Not. Stop. What else is important besides lift?"

"Weight."

"How does that work?" His mouth was in all kinds of places, exploring. He was an inquisitive sort. She'd give him that.

"Weight is the force created by the attraction of gravity pulling on the kite."

"Attraction, huh?"

"The downward force tugs the kite toward the center of the earth."

"I see. So, lift is taking it up, while weight drags it down."

"Yes," she whispered. "Tension. That's what causes the thrust."

"Hmm, thrust is my favorite part."

"Mine too."

He flipped her over onto her back and showed her what thrust was really all about. Their eyes locked as they stared into each other's eyes, their bodies moving in union. Feelings assaulted Gia from every direction—pleasure, delight, joy, excitement, ecstasy. Here she was making love to her lifelong friend. The friend who'd always had her back like a steady prevailing wind, lifting her up to lofty heights.

Here, now, with Mike she felt completely at peace. No conflict or problems. She was tuned in. To him. To her own body. To their joined movements. It seemed so natural, as if they'd just been waiting all this time to slide into each other.

She was so glad for him, her hopes sweetly grateful. She had fallen in love before, and things had not worked out the way she'd foreseen, but she believed in the foundation she was building with Mike. The growing tenderness, the compatibility of their bodies, the certainty of her fate.

"There's lift." He panted. "Weight and thrust. What's left?"

Her gaze cemented to his, and she gasped at the sensations rippling through her center.

"Gia?"

"Drag," she managed.

"Tell me about drag." His hand trailed over her waist as he pinned her in place against the leather of his couch.

"Drag originates . . ." Gosh, she was having so much trouble talking.

"Uh-huh?"

"Drag . . ." She was panting now too. "Is the backward force in opposition to the forward motion."

"Mmm."

"T-to launch a kite . . ." Her body shivered from head to toe, consumed with pleasure. "The force of lift must be greater than the force of weight."

"Like this?" He did a miraculous move with her body, which quickened and deepened the quivers quaking her.

"Exactly like that."

"I see."

"To keep the kite in the air, all four forces must stay in balance. Lift equal to weight and thrust equal to drag."

"Everything smooth and fluid."

"Yes," she murmured.

"Flying higher and higher until—"

"You reach the end of your string."

"What happens then?"

"Then you've *come* to the highest moment of tension." She lowered her voice, injected extra husk into it. "And . . ."

"Yes? Yes?" He was panting.

"You linger at the apex for as long as you can. As long as the lift, weight, thrust, and drag are in perfect balance."

"And, and, and?" He was barely breathing now. Every part of his body tensed rigid against her.

So was Gia.

"You move your fingers to see how the kite will respond . . ." She tickled him in a spot that had him wriggling hard.

"Oh, God." He groaned.

"Then before you lose control . . ." Just like when she was out on the beach flying a kite, Gia was dazzled and dazed and delighted. Her eyes always on the prize.

"And the kite is ready to, ready to, ready to . . ." He closed his eyes, his body moving faster, throwing the forces out of balance. Thrust without lift and weight and drag led to an inevitable fall.

"Come . . ." She meant to add *crashing to the earth,* but she couldn't get any more words out. One syllable was all she could manage.

"Down?" He palmed her breasts.

"Oh yeah." She writhed underneath him. "You betcha."

"Drag it right down." He exhaled long and slow.

"You got it."

"It's falling?"

"Tumbling. Spiraling." She strapped her legs around his waist and pulled him more deeply into her.

"Diving."

"Oooh," she whispered.

"Aah." He moaned.

She wriggled.

He thrashed.

They gasped.

And right there on Mike's couch, they flew their own special kite all the way to the stars.

CHAPTER TWENTY

Madison

REPEAT: Repetitions of a pattern or design in a fabric, or repetition of a quilting design or motif.

Madison had accomplished what she'd come home to Moonglow Cove to do. She'd fixed things. Her grandmother was on the mend. She'd saved the inn—okay, credit where credit was due, *they'd* saved the inn—and things between her and Shelley, while not tension-free, were certainly much better.

They were communicating. A huge improvement.

On the beach that morning following the Fourth of July weekend pop-up event, Madison watched the sunrise proud, happy, and warmly nostalgic. She'd treated herself to a raspberry Danish and espresso from the Moonglow Bakery and experienced a blissful caffeine and sugar rush as she strolled the sand.

The only thing holding her back from returning to New York was the wedding quilt she'd promised Gia she'd finish.

A week.

They had a week to finish the quilt. A week until

Grammy was released from the hospital. A week to get the business side of the inn straightened out so she could turn the reins over to Shelley and Gia and return to her life in Manhattan.

A week didn't seem like nearly long enough.

Overcome by inexplicable loneliness, she slipped off her sandals, carried them hooked between the fingers of one hand, dug her warm toes in the wet sand, and took a deep breath.

Madison felt so different now than when she'd arrived six weeks ago. Then she'd been harried and hurried, battling frequent migraines and near-constant anxiety.

But with the slower pace of life in Moonglow Cove, the rhythm of the ocean, and the nearness of family, her frantic symptoms had slowly dissipated, and along with them the wounded anger she'd once clung to so tightly.

For the first time in five years, she felt as if she could fully breathe.

She took a deep inhale, filling her lungs with the smell of home, and hugged herself. She was starting to heal, too, from losing Claire Estelle, although that was a bone-deep pain only time could fully ease.

Soon, she'd be back in New York and the days would whiz by in a flurry of activity.

She paused, realizing for the first time why she pushed herself so hard to achieve, her primary driver—she was afraid to be alone with herself and her thoughts. Staying busy kept the demons at bay.

The demons had dogged her since her parents' death, when she'd taken on adult responsibilities. Even though Grammy had been there for them, Madison had never been able to shake the role of dutiful oldest daughter, the one who took care of everything whether anyone wanted her to or not.

"Face it. You like playing the hero," she mumbled to herself.

Okay, she did. Was that so terrible?

If you get too bossy, it is.

Madison bent down to pick up a seashell, raised her head, and spied a handsome man striding across the sand toward her.

She knew him.

Madison froze in place, unable to breathe.

The man was her ex-fiancé, Raoul Chalifour.

"Madison," Raoul called out to her in that French accent of his that once upon a time melted her like butter in the hot sun. She'd heard he moved to Houston after their breakup and thought she was safe from seeing him here. What was he doing back in Moonglow Cove?

She jammed on her sandals and started trotting toward the Moonglow Inn as fast as she could without breaking into a full-on sprint.

"Please don't run away," he called.

Ignoring every instinct in her body to get away

from him, Madison forced herself to stop and turn around.

If he was determined to speak to her, he'd just follow her anyway. Better to do this on an empty beach than at the Moonglow Inn.

"What do you want, Raoul?" She kept her voice cool, detached, and ignored the hard thumping of her pulse in the hollow of her throat. Not because she wanted him—she most certainly did not—but because she was still angry.

And here she thought she'd been making progress.

Unclenching her jaw at the things she could not control, Madison studied her ex.

He wore chinos and a crisp, white long-sleeved shirt, like some guy from a cologne commercial. Swarthy skin, straight white teeth, a thatch of thick black hair, a devastating dimple in his right cheek. Ocean waves rolled in behind him. He pushed up his shirtsleeves, jammed his hands in his pockets in that boyish way of his, and gave her a lopsided smile that begged *Don't be mad at me*.

Once upon a time, she'd been unable to resist that smile. "What are you doing here? I thought you moved to Houston."

"I did."

He still owned the car dealership in Moonglow Cove, she'd noticed when she drove past the car lot on her way to the hospital. But it seemed a bit early in the morning for him to be checking in on the dealership.

"Can we talk?"

Madison held up both hands. "Look, I gotta go."

"I came to see you."

"I have nothing to say to you, Raoul." She turned away again.

"Wait." He hopped across the sand, snagged her wrist.

She shot him her best quelling stare, the one Shelley said could dry oil paint in under sixty seconds. "Do *not* touch me."

He dropped his hands. "You are right. I should not touch you."

"What is it, Raoul?" she asked, feeling off-kilter. "What do you want from me?"

"You look beautiful, Madison," he murmured.

"What do you *want?*"

"I heard about your grandmother. That you were back in Moonglow Cove, and I came looking for you—"

"Why?" she asked, hearing the desperation in her own voice. Did he not understand he was an ugly reminder of the past she wanted to forget?

"I'm sorry about your grandmother. She was a great woman."

"*Is* a great woman."

"I always liked her."

"What. Do. You. Want?" She gritted her teeth.

"To ask for your forgiveness."

"Why?"

"I treated you badly."

"Yes, you did."

"I shouldn't have done what I did."

"Forget it." She waved a hand. "I'm so over it . . . over you."

"I'm in SAA." His tone was light.

"SAA? What's that?"

He ran a palm over his nape, looked sheepish. "Sex Addicts Anonymous."

"Ahh." She leveled him a hard glance, trying to decide if he was serious or not. A sex addiction explained a lot.

"It's a twelve-step program. I'm on step nine."

"Which is?"

Raoul's eyes seared into hers. "Make direct amends to the people you've hurt except where doing so would injure them."

This was an unexpected turn of events. She paused, ready to hear him out. "Don't try to charm me, please. Just say what you need to say." She folded her arms over her chest, feeling suddenly claustrophobic in the wide-open space.

The sky seemed too blue, the beach too sandy. She could hardly catch her breath and she had a bizarre sensation of falling. She rooted her feet into the ground and took a deep breath.

Do not pass out.

"I have a sexual addiction," he explained.

"So I gathered." Her tone came out drier than she'd intended. "That's *your* problem, not mine."

"I know, I know, but you need to understand that what I did to you was never personal. My cheating was not your fault. Nor was it an intentional slight on you. I simply couldn't control myself. Cheating is not something I willingly choose. I'm an addict."

"I'm sorry you have a problem, Raoul." She softened her voice, understanding him now. "And I'm sorry that you're struggling, but I'm not feeling sorry *for* you."

"No," he said. "I do not want your pity. I screwed up my own life. I get that."

"Then what do you want?"

"To make amends for the way I treated you."

"It's not necessary. That was five years ago. I've moved on. I have a great life in New York—"

"I heard," he said. "*Madison's Mark.* Congratulations."

"Thank you." She bobbed her head. "I'm going to go now." *If I can move.* She'd anchored her feet so firmly into the sand her legs felt heavy as barbells.

"Please, don't go." He started to reach for her. "Not yet."

She jerked back.

He tucked his hands into his armpits, looked sheepish. "I need to make amends to you, Madison. For my own healing." He paused. "And yours."

"Since when did you ever care about how your actions affected me?"

"Always. Forever."

"You had a funny way of showing it."

"As I said, my cheating was never about you."

"Oh, well, that makes it okay then."

"I know it does not make it okay." He tugged at his collar with casual fingers, looking devastatingly insouciant.

The man was still drop-dead gorgeous, but Madison had learned to see past the handsome and she'd vowed never to be lured in by looks again.

Still, while Raoul was shallow and self-absorbed, he *was* trying. He was getting help. Attending meetings. That did mean something. Didn't she owe him a chance to explain?

"Okay," she said. "Go ahead. I'm listening."

"Thank you." He pressed his palms together in front of his heart, bowed his head. "First, I *am* very sorry I hurt you."

"I accept your apology."

"Really?" A hopeful smile plucked at his lips.

"Yes."

"I never thought you would forgive me."

"I didn't say I forgave you. I said I accepted your apology."

"*Can* you forgive me?"

"I don't know. You humiliated me with my sister on our wedding day. That's a pretty big sin."

"I was wrong, so wrong." He did look contrite, but he'd always been pretty good at presenting what he knew she needed to see and hear.

"Yes, you were."

"You were the best thing that ever happened to me." Still clutching his hands to his heart beseechingly, he dropped to his knees in the sand at her feet. "And I threw it all away."

"Look," Madison said, backing away, "you figure out your life. Do the twelve steps, or whatever. I've got problems of my own."

She headed toward the inn.

"Madison," Raoul called. "Just know this one thing."

She stopped, inhaled sharply, turned back around. "What is it?"

"I'll do whatever it takes to earn your full forgiveness. I messed up and I lost the best thing that ever happened to me."

"Just do better with the next woman, Raoul," she said. "That's all I ask."

"Yes, yes, but, Madison, do know that I am truly, deeply sorry, to the bottom of my heart, that I had sex with your sister."

CHAPTER TWENTY-ONE

Gia

BLEEDING: When colors or dyes from one fabric transfer to another during washing.

While Madison was walking the beach, Gia lay sated and drowsy in Mike's arms as the rays of dawn pushed through the curtains.

Mike reached over to brush the hair from her face, grinned. "Hey, you."

He looked so happy, so warm and comfy, and his tone was so loving that Gia got scared. They were moving too fast. Yes, they'd known each other for twenty years, but not in *this* way. Was she ready for this?

He was treating her as if their engagement was real, and while she had deep feelings for Mike, so much had happened in such a short time she didn't know if she could trust her emotions.

Mike tightened his arms around her, holding her close, their legs entangled willy-nilly.

Oh, but he made her feel good, better than she'd felt in ages. Being with him was easy and fun, relaxed and breezy. A man who was at peace with himself and his world.

She rested her head on his chest. She lay

listening to his heart beating, strong and solid. Contentment stole over her, and she realized she wasn't thinking about anything. She smiled. It felt like recess. A time-out from the craziness her life had become.

"Are you hungry?" Mike asked. "I have all the makings for breakfast burritos."

"Oh yum. I'll go wash up and then come help you in the kitchen."

He kissed her forehead and untangled himself from her. "You can use my bathroom. I'll take the guest bath. Meet you in the kitchen in ten."

Smiling, Gia padded into his bathroom and caught sight of herself in the mirror. Her hair was all over the place, messy and tangled. Bedhead. Her eyes seemed wider and her cheeks hollower.

She took a quick shower and dressed in the clothes she'd worn the night before. She started to apply the makeup she kept tucked into her purse, then decided, *Screw it*. Mike thought she was beautiful no matter what. She had no one to impress. She could be herself with him.

That felt good.

How many times had she tried too hard to please guys in the past? After a late-night tryst, she'd sneak out of bed before her dates awoke, slipping into the bathroom to brush her teeth, scrub her face, and apply fresh makeup and then slip back under the covers, to act as if she naturally woke up like that.

Looking at her reflection in the mirror, she realized how silly she'd been. Thinking she couldn't be herself in order to find love. That she was responsible for everyone else getting along. That it was her job to keep the peace at all costs.

Her family had put her in that role. Not intentionally, to be sure. But they'd done it nonetheless; and Gia, because she was naturally empathetic and easygoing, had been unaware it was happening.

And when she'd had flashes of awareness, she'd brushed them aside, buried the effects that people-pleasing had on her down deep, numbed out, and rolled with the flow.

The need to stay comfortable had kept her from growing as a person.

Laziness.

She wasn't lazy about working a job. In fact, she used kitemaking as a method of zoning out. To her way of thinking, anger and conflict should be avoided at all costs and creativity gave her that escape.

Rather, she used people-pleasing as a way of going unconscious to her own needs. Instead of expressing her wants and desires and tolerating conflict, she sank into sleepwalking through life.

Laziness.

It had closed her off.

Oof!

She did not know what jostled this realization

loose. Success with the pop-up store? The invitation from Pippa to make wedding kites? Working on the quilt that held so many memories in the fabric? Faking an engagement to get her sisters to sew the quilt in an underhanded bid for control? Learning that Madison had lost a baby, and Shelley had joined a cult? Finding out how Grammy and Darynda had hidden their love to please society? Sex with Mike?

All of the above?

This then was her wake-up call. Her invitation to move through life with increased attentiveness and to stop hiding her own wants and needs in favor of catering to the needs of others.

But first, she had one last task to finish before she could turn her attention to fully healing herself. One last person to please.

Grammy.

She had to make sure she and her sisters finished the wedding quilt before Grammy came home next week. Honor her grandmother's last request while they still had time.

Suddenly overwhelmed, she felt tears pushing at the back of her eyes as emotions swelled. Emotions she'd been tamping down and avoiding for a very long time.

Don't cry, don't cry.

But the dam had broken.

Great wrenching sobs rolled through her and Gia sank to the bathroom floor. She hugged herself. Told herself to snap out of it. Sobbed some more. Reached for big gobs of toilet paper. Sopped at her face.

Stop it, stop it, stop it.

Nothing doing. Her body shook. Her mouth filled with salty tears.

A gentle knock sounded at the door.

"Honeysuckle? You okay?"

Honeysuckle.

A fake term of endearment for a fake engagement. She felt sad. Sad and angry and filled with grief she had not processed for twenty years because she hadn't wanted to burden her family with her sorrow.

She couldn't answer him. Her throat was too constricted.

"Gia?"

"Pl-please . . ." She gulped back the knot of tears blocking her throat.

The next thing she knew he was in the bathroom with her. Darn it. Why hadn't she locked the door?

He took one look at her and shook his head.

From her past relationships with men, she expected him to either panic over the tears, and get the hell out of there, or ask her a million questions as he went into caveman mode to solve her problems for her.

But Mike did neither of those things.

Instead, he sank down on the floor beside her

and hauled her into his lap. He did not say a word. Just held her and let her sob it out against his shoulder.

When she was done, he handed her a fresh batch of toilet paper.

She dabbed her face and apologized. "I'm an ugly crier."

"Don't put labels on yourself like that, Short Stack. No one looks good swamped in tears. You're not supposed to look good when you're crying, but damn if you don't. Even red-eyed and runny-nosed, you look beautiful to me."

Her body shuddered as she shook off the rest of the tears.

They sat for a good long time on the floor until Gia's butt got numb. "I hope you didn't start those eggs for the breakfast burritos yet. Otherwise they're burned."

"They're ready to assemble. I was waiting for you."

Gia swiped at her eyes. "You're amazing."

"Nah," he said. "Just a guy who finally learned how to give women the space they need to feel what they're feeling."

"You should teach classes," she said. "I know a few guys who could use your brand of sensitivity training."

"Ah, Short Stack, you're not calling me sensitive, are you? I'll have to surrender my man card."

"I'm just stunned to have a friend like you."

His eyes darkened, and his voice lowered. "After last night, I hope you're looking at me as a whole lot more than that."

There was that panic again that she'd felt earlier. The squeeze that said, slow down, Gia, things are moving too fast.

But this was Mike and he was so great. Why was she afraid of progressing?

"Thanks for putting up with me, but I'm going to have to skip breakfast. Madison and Shelley promised they'd get back to work on the wedding quilt and I need to be there to make sure they don't flake."

"Okay." He looked confused but didn't push her. "Just know I'm right here if you should need me."

"Thanks," Gia said, but instead of making her feel safe and secure, that only caused her to feel more pressured than ever.

Gia escaped Mike's house as fast as her legs would carry her. Heart pounding, confounded by her desire to run, she rushed up the back steps of the Moonglow Inn to find Shelley waiting on the porch.

Her sister had put the quilt in the wooden frame and arranged three chairs around it, and set out the sewing notions, but there was no sign of Maddie.

"Are you all right?" Shelley asked.

"Yes, sure, why wouldn't I be?" *You slept with Mike. Everything's changed. You can't handle it. You're anything but all right.*

"O-*kay*." Shelley held up both palms. "Forget I asked."

"I'm sorry. I didn't mean to be snappy. Was I snappy?"

"You were channeling Madison a bit, but that's not always a bad thing. The woman does know how to stand up for herself."

"And I don't." Sighing, Gia sank down in the chair across from Shelley.

"Are you sure you're—"

"I'm fine."

"Gotcha."

Just then Madison came into view, storming up from the beach, and headed toward the porch, a thundercloud frown on her face.

"Uh-oh," Shelley said. "She makes your mood look like a smile convention."

Simultaneously, they stood.

Her face twisted into a mask of rage, Madison stalked up the steps on wooden legs, her fisted hands clutched at her sides, her rage directed squarely at Shelley.

"You *slept* with Raoul?" she howled.

Shelley shrunk back and raised her arms over her face as if to protect herself from physical blows. "N-no. Why are you saying that?"

"I met Raoul on the beach," Maddie said. "He's in a twelve-step program for sexual addiction and one of the steps is to make amends. Maybe Raoul isn't the one who needs to be in recovery. Maybe it's *you*." Madison threw words like stones.

Shelley flinched, shot a desperate gaze at Gia.

"*Did* you sleep with Raoul, Shelley?" Gia asked in a small, tight voice.

"No, no." Shelley looked and sounded desperate. "Madison, Gia, you've got to understand. Anything I did, I did it to protect our family. I thought—"

"Liar!" Madison exploded. "You didn't think at all. You had an impulse and you followed it. Just like you always do. It wasn't so much that you crushed my soul on my wedding day. It was the fact that you're claiming you did it for *my* good. That you wanted to help *me*."

"I-I . . ." Shelley's knees bobbled.

"Let's explore the *real* reason you slept with my fiancé, Shelley. You wanted attention. Yes, maybe Raoul was a cheating jerk. Maybe I was blind and stubborn, and you felt like it was your place to force me to see Raoul for what he was. But don't pretend it was for me. It was for *you,* Shelley. You wanted to rub my face in my mistake."

"No, no, Maddie, no."

Madison was wound up and taking no prisoners. "You wanted to look like my savior while you were having sex with my fiancé behind my back. You wanted the spotlight on *my* wedding day. For once in your life, just admit the truth of it."

Shelley shook her head, and a strangled cry of pain and shame escaped her throat. "No, no. You don't understand. I—"

"You wanted me to praise you for being such a wonderful sister. You wanted to cast me in the role of villain again. Poor misunderstood Shelley. Her mean old sister Madison doesn't get what she's trying to do. Shelley means well, and Madison is just so hard and unforgiving." Madison knotted her hands into fists and jumped across the porch to toe off with Shelley nose to nose.

Shelley gaped like a landed fish, her mouth moving but no words coming out. Her face flushed. "Me? *I'm* the one looking for attention? I'm not the one desperate to be on TV. I'm not the perfectionist who spends a ridiculous amount of time creating fancy-schmancy art, food, flowers, and design. *You're* the selfish one. Thinking only your feelings and opinions matter."

"Stop it!" Gia yelled. "Stop it right now. Both of you."

Pyewacket, who'd been curled on the porch when this started, yowled at them and took off. The Siamese made a strong point.

For her entire life, Gia had been the mediator between these two fiery women, who were so different on the surface, but underneath both of them so similar. Both headstrong and defiant, each in her own way.

"I won't tolerate this. If you can't be civil to each other, you have to leave."

"You?" Madison turned on Gia. "You're no golden child either. You wouldn't even take my side when Shelley ruined everything."

"Madison," Shelley insisted, "I'm telling you that I did not sleep with Raoul! There are circumstances you know nothing—"

"You want me to take sides?" Gia rolled up the sleeves of her shirt and stalked over to Madison. "Well, I'm taking sides now, Maddie. It doesn't matter whether Shelley actually slept with him or not. You've got to forgive her and let it go, or you'll go to your grave a bitter old woman."

Madison blanched. "You're siding with her?"

"Shelley might have been misguided, but she has a good heart and she's been trying so hard since she came home. Give her a chance to explain."

Madison folded her arms over her chest, and her face hardened to slate.

"Shelley is *trying,* dammit," Gia roared. "But I can't say the same for you."

Madison's face went completely blank. "That's it then."

"No! It's not it. For twenty-three years, I've been between the two of you. I'm tired of being pulled apart. I'm tired of trying to smooth things over and make this family work. If you two want to destroy what's left of us, then fine. I give up." Gia threw her hands in the air. "Have at it."

"When did you try to put us back together?" Shelley asked, turning on Gia, who'd just stood up for her. "You never once tried to contact me in Costa Rica."

"I had no idea where you were."

"I got sucked into a cult, dammit, and not one of you people tried to get me out. Do you know how abandoned that makes me feel? If I tried to get attention, well, no wonder. Everyone thinks the sun shines out of Maddie's butt because she's so accomplished. And of course, the youngest, sweet one got all the petting from everyone. There was nothing left for me. So yeah, I took love where I could find it, in a damn cult. But neither one of you cared."

"Oh, Shelley," Gia said. "Maybe we could have tried harder to follow you, but Grammy knew where you were, and we thought if you wanted to be contacted, you would let us know. We didn't realize you were in a cult! We thought you could come home whenever you wanted!"

"Easy to say now." Shelley's chin hardened.

"I don't like the way this family communicates," Gia said. "It's gotten so toxic. Maybe we're all better off apart than together."

"You don't really mean that." Madison gasped.

Gia was breathing hard. Twenty-three years of walking the tightrope between these two and it had come to this. The truth will out. She'd let the chips fall. "Guess what? Mike and I aren't really engaged. Yep, it's a bald-faced lie. If you guys can have secrets, so can I."

"What?" Shelley and Madison said in unison.

"The fake engagement was a ploy to get you two to stay here and talk to each other. Yes, I'm a big fat liar! I compromised my values for you two and you don't appreciate what I've done. Grammy wrote that letter to me begging me to get you two back together and finish this stupid quilt and the only way I could think to make that happen was to come up with a fake engagement. That is the craziness I've sunk to and it's not worth it. You know what? I'm done. D. O. N. E!"

Her sisters were standing side by side now. Finally, they were united by their stark disbelief. Too damn little, too damn late.

Gia was finished talking. She would show them exactly just *how* done she was. Gritting her teeth, she grabbed the cordless power scissors sitting next to the quilting frame and sliced the triple wedding ring quilt straight down the middle.

"Gia!" Madison cried. "What are you doing?"

"Putting an end to this nonsense! If you are done being sisters, that's fine with me."

Never in her life had Gia felt such anger. She didn't stop with cutting the quilt in half; she attacked each square, hacking it into pieces. Cotton batting floated in the air.

"You've lost your mind." Madison came toward her.

Gia spun, pulled the trigger on the scissors, and wielded them at Madison. They buzzed in the air, chewing nothing. "Back off!"

"This isn't like you." Madison cowered against the porch railing.

Shelley was already in the corner eyeing her as if she were a madwoman. Well, she was. Mad and crazy and fed up with their feuding. Gia tore into that quilt, butchering it until the only things that remained were the thin scraps of their lives.

Panting, she stopped, chest heaving as she stared daggers at her sisters.

Shelley and Maddie had their hands over their mouths, studying the cloth carnage with stunned silence.

"You can clean it up," Gia announced, blood surging through her veins, the spent anger leaving her jittery and shell-shocked over what she'd done.

She looked around at the tufts of material blowing across the porch. What *had* she done? With the triple wedding ring quilt annihilated, there was no hope of keeping her promise to Grammy.

Hot tears pushed at the back of Gia's eyes. She had to get out of there. The last thing she wanted was to let her sisters see her cry. Finished with her carnage, she dropped the scissors to the porch floor, pivoted on her heel, and stalked off.

CHAPTER TWENTY-TWO

Gia

STAB STITCHING: Process where the needle is pushed to back side of the quilt sandwich with one hand and returned to top side with the other hand, pushing needle from back to front.

Gia's vision was so blurry with unshed tears that she couldn't see where she was going. She swiped at her eyes with the back of her hands. Remorse, guilt, and shame washed away the anger.

Oh damn, oh damn, oh damn. What had she done?

With nowhere else to go, and no one else to turn to, she fled the house, leaving the Moonglow Inn behind her as she padded over the wall, back to Mike's place, barefoot and hotheaded. Was this what it felt like to be Shelley? A loose cannon? Going off script without any filter?

Gia shivered.

Had Shelley really slept with Raoul? But why? Shelley wasn't a cruel person. No, but she followed her impulses, did as she pleased.

Just as Gia had when she'd cut up the quilt.

Guilt overwhelmed her.

She plodded up the steps to Mike's house to tell him that he no longer had to pretend to be her fiancé.

The day was warm and bright, a sweet happy sunshine Monday. Except she was anything but happy. It should have been a fabulous day, but she'd lost control.

Lost her mind.

Her grammy was coming home in a week, expecting to find the quilt finished. Her sisters were still at each other's throats and the one thing that had a chance of reuniting them was obliterated into a thousand little pieces.

Because of her.

She'd done it.

Fine. Okay. Enough. She'd been the peacemaker far too long. Now, she was the warmonger, bringing fights and destruction where she'd once brought peace.

The tears were impossible to stanch. They flowed from her eyes like a faucet. Despite what Grammy had said, it *wasn't* up to Gia to fix things. This issue between her sisters went too far back. Before Raoul. It had nothing to do with Gia. She couldn't change who they were. She couldn't control them.

Hell, she couldn't control herself.

By the time Mike answered the door, she was trembling all over. "Reconsider that breakfast burrito, did y—" He took her hand and pulled her over the threshold. “What is it? What’s wrong?”

“Madison. Shelley. I’m done.” It was all she could get out, she was breathing so hard.

He tugged her into the crook of his arm, kicked the door closed behind her, and guided her into the living room.

“Sit, sit.” He eased her onto the couch. “I’ll get you a glass of water.”

“I don’t, I need—” *Oof,* she still couldn’t find her voice.

“Shh, shh,” he soothed. “No rush to talk.”

She nodded, blurted, “It’s over. Done.”

Mike’s eyebrows shot up. “What is?”

“My relationship with my sisters. The quilt.” She lifted her head and met his eyes. “Me. You. Our fake engagement.”

“Wait, what?” He sank down beside her, not bothering to go for that glass of water.

“I told them the truth. That we aren’t really engaged.”

Mike’s face was unreadable. “I see.”

“Come on, Mike. Have some emotion. Tell me what you really think.”

“I think you have enough emotion for both of us right now.”

“I destroyed the quilt.”

“What do you mean by ‘destroyed’?”

“I chopped it up with power scissors. Madison and Shelley were like two pit bulls fighting over a bone, and I'd had it. I've spent my whole life moderating those two and I'm finished. *Kaput.*"

Mike snorted.

Was he mad at her?

Anxious, she looked over to see his eyes twinkling as he struggled not to burst out laughing. That irked her. "What's so damn funny?"

"Nothing." He held up both hands in surrender. "I would have paid to see the expressions on your sisters' faces while you cut up that quilt."

"They looked terrified. As if they thought I'd go after them next." Gia rubbed her chin.

"Well, they should be terrified," he said. "For what it's worth, I'm on your side, Gia." He paused for a long beat and held her gaze, adding, *"Always."*

"It was pretty satisfying for half a minute," she said. "The look on their faces, that miserable quilt that was the symbol of everything wrong with our family, hacked to pieces, but now . . ."

"What?" he prodded.

"I feel like a jerk."

"You're not a jerk."

"I lost it. That is so not cool."

"It might not be cool, but maybe it was necessary."

"Necessary for what? To break me down?"

"Or to free you."

"From what?"

"To be *you* outside the confines of your relationship with your family."

Gia plastered both hands to the top of her head. "There has to be a middle ground between doormat and bully."

"You're neither a doormat nor a bully."

"Right now, I feel like both."

"You've done nothing wrong. Okay, maybe cutting up the quilt was a bit excessive, but it got your point across, didn't it?"

She remembered the horrified expression on her sisters' faces, grinned briefly. "Oh yeah."

"Well then." He shrugged.

"It's not good to lose your cool."

"Says who?"

That gave her pause. "Hmm, everyone."

"Meaning Madison?"

Gia shrugged. "Maybe."

"From my way of thinking, when you finally expressed your anger and cut up that quilt, you killed off the part of yourself that's been holding you back and keeping you from realizing your full potential."

"You think?"

"I do. Look at the ways keeping the peace and not speaking your mind has held you back."

She paused a moment, considering that. He had a good point. How many times had she held her tongue and not rocked the boat? How many times had she been overlooked and dismissed out of hand because she didn't express her wants and needs? Her entire life had been spent keeping the peace.

She'd suppressed her own wants and needs to avoid conflict, but the reality was, conflict could not be avoided. You had to deal with it or it just festered inside you until one day you snapped and scissored a quilt to scraps. Maybe it was time to just start doing what *she* needed to do.

"Feeling better?" he asked.

"I don't know."

"That's okay that you don't know."

"I bet you're relieved," she said.

"Why is that?"

"You don't have to pretend to be my fiancé anymore."

"Actually," he said. "I kind of liked being your intended."

"Even now?"

His eyes lit up. "Now even more than ever."

"You're warped, Straus."

"Nah, I'm human, just like you."

Gia chuffed out her breath. "What now?"

"Between you and your sisters?" His voice lowered along with his eyelashes. "Or between you and me?"

She meant between her and her sisters, but the way he was looking at her jumbled her head. "We're still friends, right?"

"Gia," he said. "No matter what happens, I will always be your friend."

"Even if you marry someone else?"

He touched her wrist. "Are you okay?"

"No, no, I'm not." She hauled in a deep, shuddering breath. "I've ruined it all."

"Have you really?" he asked in a calm, steady voice. Mike's voice normally soothed her, but right now his composure irritated Gia. He wasn't taking her seriously.

"Yes."

"Or did you just free yourself from everyone else's expectations?"

Had she? Letting go of pleasing people felt as terrible as she feared it would. "I don't like it."

"Why not?"

"I don't like being angry."

"It's normal. Human. Are you saying you don't like being human?"

"When you put it that way . . ." She interlaced her fingers and stared down at her palms. Saw the engagement ring on the third finger of her left hand.

"It's not your job to keep everyone happy, Gia. It's an impossible task you've set for yourself."

"I know," she mumbled, twisting the ring back and forth, working it up the length of her finger. It was time to do what she'd come here to do. Give him back his ring. End this. Set him free from the sham.

He put his hand over hers.

She looked up into his intense gaze.

"About last night . . ."

"Yes?" Gia moistened her lips.

He looked so sexy, with that adorable cowlick sticking up in the back. He wore cargo shorts and a thin cotton T-shirt that showed off his muscular biceps and layered eight-pack abs beneath. The shirt read: HAPPINESS IS HANDMADE.

She remembered exactly what his body felt like beneath her palms, and instantly sweat popped out on her brow.

He smiled at her, warm and sincere. "It changed me. *You* changed me."

His words churned something inside of her. Her chest tightened, and she couldn't draw in a full breath. "Mike."

"Gia, please don't tell me that you aren't feeling some pretty powerful things too. That we aren't working on something that has nothing to do with your sisters and that quilt or our pretend engagement."

"I am feeling some things. Too many things. That's the problem. It's too much, too soon."

"There's no rush, Gia. I'm not going anywhere."

"Maybe I am," she said, sounding a bit hysterical to her own ears. "I might be going somewhere. You said yourself you were a Moonglow Cove man and wouldn't leave, not even for the woman you loved."

"No, what I said was, that's how I knew Cassandra wasn't the One. If I wasn't willing to leave Moonglow Cove for her, then there was a problem."

"You'd leave Moonglow Cove for me?"

"I would."

She sucked in her breath, and her entire body shook, processing what he'd said. Felt fear gnaw down into her bones. But along with the fear, she felt another emotion. Something she didn't want to admit.

Every time he looked at her with those kind, patient blue eyes, she felt comforted by him the way she'd been comforted by that blanket she'd brought with her to Grammy's house all those years ago.

He represented stability at a time she'd long ago stopped believing in it.

Mike sat beside her, holding her hand, her dear family friend, but now he was so much more than that. Or could be if she didn't run away, terrified.

He stared deeply into her eyes, fusing his gaze to hers. "Gia," he said. "There's something I've been needing to tell you."

Oh no, what was he going to say? Her heart thundered. "Yes?"

"I lied."

She cocked her head, asked leerily, "About what?"

"That engagement ring."

She took it off, handed it to him. Weird that her hand suddenly felt so bare.

Mike closed his fingers around the ring, making a fist. "I didn't buy the ring for Cassandra."

"No?"

He shook his head.

"Who did you buy it for?"

He stared at her. No, not *at* her, into her. He stared at her as if she was the most incredible thing he had ever seen.

Gia's jaw dropped, and a sweet, hopeful shiver ran up her spine. *"Me?"*

Mike nodded. "I was going to ask you to marry me. I had this idea where I would tie the ring to a kite and ask you to reel it in for me."

Gia plastered a palm over her mouth and stared at him, gobsmacked. "What? When?"

"A year ago. The day you came home from college. The day you told me you were moving to Japan to study under master kitemaker Mikio Tetsuya."

Stunned, she could only stare at him.

"Say something," he pleaded.

"Omigosh, I had no idea." Gia twirled her hair around her index fingers, freaked out by what Mike had just revealed. "Why didn't you tell me?"

"How could I stand in the way of you studying with one of the world's greatest kitemakers?"

"But you've had this ring for over a *year* and

never said a word about how you felt? When did you know you wanted to marry me?"

"When you were off to college and you weren't around anymore. I tried to forget you. I dated. But no one ever compared to you."

"Mike, that's so heartbreaking. I don't even know what to say. To put your life on hold for *me?*"

"I love you that much, Gia. All I want is what's best for you."

"Why didn't you say something before? You never even tried to kiss me."

"I didn't want to screw up the good thing we had. Or risk losing my best friend." He shrugged. "And our timing always seemed off. You were either dating someone or I was."

"I-I'm speechless."

He smiled again and dipped his head, sending her a whiff of his cologne. Her emotions were all kinds of crazy and she didn't have a clue how to unpack them.

"I love you, Gia. I have for years and I'm hoping after last night that maybe you love me, too, in the same way I love you."

She gulped. Mike Straus, the man who'd been her friend for twenty years, *loved* her. *He* loved *her* and not just in a best-friend kind of way.

In all her twenty-three years, no man—although granted she didn't remember her father—had ever said those three words to her.

Gia hopped off the couch and backed up. "I need to go home."

"Short Stack." His voice was steady, but she could hear the layer of hurt running through it. "Don't run away from your feelings. Stay here and talk to me."

"This is too much. You're too much." She felt as if she couldn't breathe. She had to get out of here, get some air before she passed out. He'd bought her a ring last year. He'd been loving her for years.

"You're right. I shouldn't have sprung my feelings on you like that. It *was* too much, too soon."

"Mike," she said. "You're not at fault. It's not you, it's me. *I'm* the one who's gone off the rails."

"You haven't gone off the rails. You've been through a lot in a short amount of time. And I think you're holding it together beautifully. But I do want a real engagement and you need to know I'm serious about that."

Everything they'd gone through and done together over the course of the past six weeks had come from a place of heightened emotion. Emotions she wasn't sure she could trust. She needed to take a deep breath and regroup. Once upon a time, she would have automatically flung herself into his arms over his proclamation of love.

But right now, after the mess with her sisters, she just wasn't ready for it.

"Mike," she said. "I hear you and appreciate your feelings, but right now, I can't tell you what you want to hear."

"Are you saying you don't love me, too, Gia? Because that's not how it felt last night." His Adam's apple worked as he gulped, and he set his mouth in a grim line.

"Look, you're the one who told me to give up my people-pleasing ways. You're the one who encouraged me to stand up for myself. And now that I'm doing it, you're upset with me?"

"I'm not upset with you."

"Aren't you? Be honest."

"All right," he said. "I'd gotten my hopes up that maybe for once our timing wasn't off. That you and I had—" He broke off. "Never mind. Go do what you need to do."

Tears burned her eyes and she swallowed them back. "Mike."

"Please go." His voice cracked.

"I—"

"Not now, Gia." He clenched his jaw and went to open the front door.

Heartbroken over her feuding sisters and Mike's lack of understanding, she walked past him and out the door. On the steps, she turned to tell him how disappointed she was with his response.

He stood there, fist unfurled, staring at the engagement ring he'd bought her lying in his open palm.

"Mike?"

He raised his head, met her gaze with tears in his blue eyes, and then quietly but firmly shut the door in her face.

CHAPTER TWENTY-THREE

Madison

SQUARE UP: After quilting, square up by trimming the edges of the quilt so that the measurements are even.

Madison couldn't believe Gia had cut the wedding quilt right in two. Seeing the quilt sliced and scattered around the porch in little pieces hit her hard.

The shock of it blasted her with hurricane force, knocking her breath from her body. It wasn't so much the destroyed quilt, although that was damn symbolic of her destroyed relationships with her sisters, but rather the fact that sweet, kind, gentle Gia had been the one to do it.

She stared after Gia's retreating back. She didn't dare look at Shelley. Her own emotions were too raw, too volatile.

A dozen different feelings flooded her at once. Hurt, pain, betrayal, shock. But there were more feelings underneath. Sadness, nostalgia, longing. And beneath that, she hit a wellspring of bad moods—agitation, irritability, frustration. Building and growing.

All the feelings she had run from. All the

feelings she fought to control. All the feelings she'd hidden behind her climb up the ladder of success. She thought achievement would bring her the happiness she longed for. The peace of mind she'd lost in childhood after her parents' death. She had achieved much in her life, things many people envied.

Success, in and of itself, did not bring happiness. It wasn't the *things* that mattered. Not the house, the cars, the designer clothes and expensive haircuts. Not the honors or awards, promotions or titles. It was the journey and the people you met along the way. It was the experiences that mattered and the relationships you built.

And she'd done a damn shabby job on both accounts.

Her experiences centered around her goal—sewing, entertaining, cooking, decorating, making a home look pretty. And there was absolutely nothing wrong with that. Unless you made a single-minded goal the whole center of your life and neglected the people who loved you.

Ahh, new feelings. New pain.

But this time, the feelings weren't directed outward. She wasn't angry at Gia or Shelley or Raoul. Rather, Madison was mad at herself.

Wow, oh wow. She was angry at herself for not knowing how to make peace with her sisters.

Something else hit her.

She'd ended up with Raoul not because she was, as she feared, a loser magnet, but because somewhere deep inside, she'd been seeking to punish herself.

Finally, Madison shattered the shell of her anger with a stark laugh and sucked in salty sea air. She was so thankful to see that stupid quilt destroyed that she took several heartier gulps to steady herself before she noticed, *Something's wrong with Shelley*.

Her sister seemed wrecked—even more so than when she first showed up, bedraggled and woebegone after escaping her cult. She wasn't just upset. She was . . . *vaporized.*

Shelley crawled on her hands and knees, picking up scraps of severed quilt pieces and tucking them in the front of her shirt that she had fashioned as a sling. Tears streamed down her face, dripping off her chin as she mumbled, over and over, "I'm sorry, I'm sorry, I'm sorry."

Watching her, Madison felt her heart break and she realized that it didn't matter if Shelley had slept with Raoul or not. That was the past. It was over. What mattered was this precise moment and her sister's fragility.

Madison dropped to her knees in front of her. Touched her shoulder. "Shell?"

Shelley's eyes met hers and she looked utterly grief-stricken. "Gia," she choked out. "Rampage."

"She finally had enough of our crap." Madison laughed.

Shelley stared at her as if she'd lost her marbles, but Madison was done being angry. She'd been angry for twenty years and it hadn't gotten her anywhere. "She showed me how reckless I've been."

"Who?"

"Gia. I've never seen her like this." Shelley rocked back and planted her butt on the porch, brought her knees to her chest, and wrapped her arms around her legs as if she were six years old. She was still in her pajamas. They both were.

"She acted out of grief and rebellion. So did you."

"No excuse."

"It's understandable. Don't beat yourself up for being impulsive. Spontaneity is one of your strengths. When you were a kid and we turned gloomy after Mom and Dad died, you were the one to burst into song or do a magic trick or crack a joke or race around the house turning cartwheels to cheer us up."

"I rely on it too much."

"Maybe," Madison reassured her. "But we all depend on our defense mechanisms too much. Trying to control life is my defense mechanism but it makes me bossy and hard to live with."

"But I'm not a kid anymore, and I've had

plenty of time to reflect on where I went wrong. My downfall was my own fault. It wasn't my place to decide who you should marry." Shelley crossed her legs, yogi-style. "I shouldn't have kissed Raoul and I can never make up for how I hurt you."

Madison went in the house, got a broom and dustpan, and came back out to the porch.

Shelley sat with her palms pressed against her eyes.

Pyewacket swatted a ball of cotton batting across the porch.

"Here, kitty." Madison bent and wriggled her fingers. She'd missed the ornery cat.

Pyewacket moseyed over to sniff Madison's fingers, and she stroked the cat's furry little head. Sighing, she straightened and went to sweep the floor.

Shelley raised her head, looking slightly unhinged with her windblown hair and tear-streaked face. She was barefoot and braless. "Do you want me to do that?"

"There's another broom in the kitchen closet," Madison said. "We can do this together."

Silently, they did what they couldn't do before—work well together—cleaning up the mess their little sister had made.

"Gia shocked me." Shelley shook her head. "Making like Edward Scissorhands on the quilt. She was so amped up about us finishing it."

"I did not expect that at all." Maddie swept up a big pile of fabric slivers and cotton batting. "It's something more like you would have done."

"Yes, I'm the queen at destroying things."

"No more so than I."

"Can you believe she lied about being engaged to Mike?"

"Not our good girl Gia." Madison shook her head. "And you know, deep down, I've always thought the two of them would get together. They're just so perfect for each other. And I suspected Mike's had a crush on her for years. I kept waiting for them to realize how deep their feelings for each other ran. I'm kind of sad that their engagement was a lie."

"I'm sad because she thought the only way to get me and you to work together was to lie about being engaged."

"It worked, though, didn't it?"

"I guess it did."

"Listen," Maddie said. "I've been a complete witch since I've been back home."

"You had your reasons and I didn't make things easy on you."

"Shelley?"

"Uh-huh?"

Madison looked at her sister and her heart skipped a beat. "You've got some cotton . . ." She leaned over to pluck a wad of cotton from Shelley's hair.

"My best intentions always seem to go off the rails." Shelley sighed. "Everything backfires."

"Yeah, well, I'm so uptight no one wants to be around me."

"That's not true."

"You don't have to lie."

"*I* want to be around you." Shelley stopped sweeping.

Madison stopped too. "Since when?"

"Since now."

"Because I lost a baby?"

"Because I've always admired that no matter how bad things get, you dust yourself off, pick yourself up, and move forward."

"Always?" Madison was having trouble believing that one.

"Yes. You were so accomplished. You had everything together. Why do you think I acted like such a goofball? It was the only way I could get the spotlight off you for half a second."

"Shelley, it's not easy being me and I'm not saying that for you to feel sorry for me. It's the truth. I'm hamstrung. You? You're free. You're *you*. Me? I'm all the time trying to live up to this perfect standard that people have of me. It's a nonstop job."

"Hmm, could you relax about that a little?"

"Honestly, I don't know how. If Mom and Dad hadn't died . . ."

"You put too much on yourself. You thought

you had to make up for us not having a mother and father. It wasn't your responsibility to parent us, Maddie. You didn't even let yourself have a childhood."

"That's why I tried so hard to make things nice for you and Gia. With Mom and Dad gone . . ."

"I remember how you dyed Easter eggs with us and put on plays for us and read us bedtime stories. We appreciated it."

"I loved doing it for you guys."

"You turned homemaking into your career."

Madison nodded as she swept the material remnants into a pile. "Could you hold the dustpan?"

Shelley squatted to hold it while Madison swept up the massacred quilt.

"What about you now? Are you going back to New York when your summer hiatus is over?" Shelley stood up and dumped the dustpan in the trash bin.

Madison shook her head. "I don't know. Depends on how things go with Grammy."

"Do you *want* to go back?"

"I'm not sure what I want."

"Do you think you'll ever get married?"

Madison thought about Finn. Felt a strange tremor of hope. She had loved him so much, but her hidebound pride had gotten in the way. "Maybe not. I'm too high maintenance."

"Says who?"

"Everyone I've ever dated. Apparently, my standards are too high."

"Hmph. I say their standards are too low."

"I expect too much from people," Madison admitted.

"Hey, your kooky, clueless sister joined a cult and didn't even know she was in one for five freaking years. I can't judge anyone."

"I drove you into a cult."

"Nah." Shelley waved a hand. "I'd been searching for something for years. And when I found the love and acceptance that I was looking for, I didn't ask questions. I just went for it. Which, surprise, surprise, was really stupid on my part."

"You did it because you weren't getting what you needed from our family. I'm ashamed of that."

"I don't blame you guys. After that thing with Raoul, I took a wrong turn and I just kept going. You got rewarded by stepping up to the plate and mothering us and Gia got rewarded for going along to get along. Me? I never learned how to play the game."

"No," Maddie said. "You were the only one of us who was true to yourself. You didn't try to be something you weren't."

Shelley laughed. "You never saw me at Cobalt Soul, wearing drapey white clothes and chanting like a loon for two and a half hours every morning at four A.M. They convinced me *that* was my true self, but now I know it was a false identity they invented for me. They even changed my name and I embraced it, because I didn't want to see the truth."

"What was the truth?"

"The love they offered and claimed was unconditional wasn't unconditional at all. It was based on me fitting in and doing what they told me and giving them all my money. It was great at first because I'd had no direction and I wanted so badly to belong. It was easy to lead me astray."

"You were hurting because your very own sister accused you of terrible things," Madison said, humble and contrite. "You were right. Raoul is a total douche."

"I handled that whole situation poorly."

"So did I."

"I can't believe we went five years without speaking to each other over a guy like that."

"My fault. Not yours."

"What did you ever see in him?" Shelley asked.

"I've been trying to answer that question. I think it's similar to why you ended up in a cult. I was looking for attention and he gave it to me. He was full of flattery and praise."

"But it was false flattery just to snag you," Shelley said. "Not real compliments."

"I see that now."

They stared at each other across the porch swing.

"I'm sorry, Shelley," Madison said.

"Not more than me."

"I think we both really blew it with Gia," Maddie said.

"Don't worry, she'll forgive us. It's her nature."

"I don't know about that. She was pretty furious when she left here."

"She was the one pushing us to finish that quilt and here she's the one who destroyed it."

"I'm glad she destroyed it," Maddie said. "I feel freed of Raoul at last. From all the crap in my life that's kept me stymied. Like not being able to forgive you."

"Hey, I *did* kiss your fiancé. I'm lucky you didn't deck me." Shelley chuckled.

"But you *didn't* sleep with him?" Madison looked at Shelley closely.

"I did not."

"Why would he say that you did?" Madison asked, wanting to believe Shelley, but a part of her unable to fully release her five-year grudge.

Shelley hauled in an audible breath. "I think I know why, but—"

"Look," Madison interrupted, pointing. "There's Puff."

Bobbing in the sky down the beach was Gia's pink dragon kite.

"Uh-oh," Shelley said. "If she's out flying a

kite after this . . ." She swept a hand at the quilt mess in the trash bin. "She must be super upset."

Shelley was right. Kiteflying was Gia's happy place, but it was also what she did when she was troubled.

"Do you think something happened between her and—" Madison didn't get any further because Mike came bounding over the stone wall looking like a thundercloud.

"Super-duper upset," Shelley muttered.

Mike growled at them as he trod up the steps. "I don't know what you two did to Gia, but you better go make it right." His eyes snapped fire. *"Now."*

"What bee got into your bonnet?" Shelley asked.

"Gia broke up with me because of you two." He put his hands on his hips.

Madison had never seen Mike look so fierce or protective. "I thought your engagement was fake."

"Maybe to her it was, but it was never fake to me." The tips of his ears flushed with anger. "I was going to ask her to marry me for real when this silliness was over, but she says there's too much emotional turmoil in her life right now to figure out if her feelings for me are real or not."

"Did you tell her that your feelings were real?" Madison asked.

"That's why she gave me this back." Mike held

up his hand with Gia's engagement ring on his pinkie finger. "When you see her, tell her I'll be at the kiosk on the boardwalk if she wants to talk."

"I'll fix it." Shelley jumped up and grabbed Madison's hand. "*We'll* fix it."

"We will?" Madison blinked.

"We will," Shelley confirmed, dragging Madison down the stairs after her.

"How?"

"I'll explain when we get there."

"Explain about what?"

"Go with the flow for once, will you?" Shelley released Madison's hand and started walking backward toward the beach, the wind whipping her hair around her face like a golden mane.

"I—" Madison started to protest but realized, one, Shelley couldn't hear in the wind since she'd turned back around and, two, her sister was right. If Madison was working on her tendency to control things, she had to get comfortable with letting others take the lead sometimes.

Okay, maybe *comfortable* was a strong word. Rephrase. She had to tolerate others taking the lead sometimes.

That already felt more doable.

Besides, it was beautiful watching Shelley be her old self again. Infused with joy and the richness of being imperfectly human.

Could she try that? Not only accept, but

embrace her flaws as part and parcel of Madison Clark?

The thought was terrifying.

And yet, wildly exhilarating.

She longed for that girl she used to be. For that innocence she had to leave behind in order to be strong for her younger sisters.

In abandoning her innocent heart, she'd donned a me-against-the-world attitude that had kept her strong but entrenched her in her ways. That attitude no longer served her.

By coming home, she'd learned that true strength, *real* strength, came from being a part of a community. Her willfulness had hindered her growth.

It had pushed Finn away when she'd needed him most. Had kept her sisters at arm's length because she was afraid of getting hurt. She had clung to her righteousness and kept punishing Shelley for something that was over and done with. By clinging to her anger, she'd intensified her own pain and kept her family at a distance, when they were the very thing she'd needed in order to heal.

She thought she was the one who'd been wronged, when in reality it was she who'd wronged the people in her life with her rigid, unbending opinions and judgments. She'd denied her own culpability in alienating her family, friends, and lovers.

Uncomfortable with her guilt, she'd projected the blame onto others. Then she'd stuffed down her feelings, closed off her emotions because she considered them a sign of weakness and she hated to show vulnerability.

But inside, she was that tenderhearted, sweet, frightened little girl who'd been forced to don warrior armor to keep herself and her sisters safe twenty long years ago.

Up ahead on the beach, Gia flew her kite.

The pink dragon undulated high in the sky. In her solitary silhouette, Madison saw her youngest sister's raw pain and thought, *I caused this.*

Because she'd been so unyielding, so dug into her ways, Gia—the most honest person Madison knew—had been forced to lie.

A lie that affected her relationship with Mike, the man who loved her.

Fix this.

The words rose in Madison's mind as ironclad as they had the day she'd swept back to Moonglow Cove.

Fix this.

And then another, clearer thought stamped out that one. Guidelines for how to live her life from this day forward.

Don't fix. Listen.

Then leaving Shelley behind, Madison kicked into a run and caught up with her kiteflying sister.

CHAPTER TWENTY-FOUR

Shelley & Gia

DRUNKARD'S PATH: A quilt block created from sewing a concave curve to a convex curve.

Shelley studied her sisters deep in conversation and felt her gut wrench. What she must do would not be easy.

She'd avoided this moment for as long as possible, but it was time to reveal her deepest secret. The one she'd kept hidden for five long years. The secret that had sent her seeking refuge in a cult. There was no way to avoid telling this truth. Not if she wanted a permanent mending to her family.

Unfortunately, what she had to say would emotionally destroy kindhearted Gia.

Hitching in a breath, Shelley gathered her courage and joined her sisters.

Madison was calm. Not speaking for once. Listening as Gia spoke a mile a minute, rattling about her fake engagement and her jumbled feelings for Mike. She loved him, but could she trust it? Was a relationship born in a lie really something she could count on?

"That's something you need to discuss with

Mike," Madison said. "He's manning the boardwalk kiosk if you want to go talk to him."

As Shelley drew closer, she saw Gia's body tense. The muscles in her sister's jaw clenched. She turned her back to Shelley and started reeling in the pink dragon kite.

That hurt.

Even though Gia had refused to take sides after *The Incident with Raoul,* Shelley had known Gia agreed with her that Raoul was the wrong guy for Madison. And although she'd been hurt by Gia's lack of support at the time, this seething anger directed toward her was new and hurt like hell.

Gia didn't get mad. She zoned out.

Ahem, apparently not anymore.

Nervously, Shelley darted a glance at Madison. Her older sister shrugged, lifted her palms as if to say, *Out of my hands.*

How to start this conversation?

Gia busied herself with folding up the kite, assiduously avoiding Shelley's gaze. Okay, she was not making this easy.

She reached to touch Gia's shoulder, but her sister shied away, leaving Shelley patting air. *Oh boy.*

"Do you need any help?" Shelley ventured.

Gia folded the kite with practiced precision. "I've got it."

"No, really, let me help." Shelley grabbed for the dragon's tail spilling onto the sand.

“Back off!” Gia said, high and shrill, as she jerked the kite from Shelley’s grasp. Then came a ripping sound that froze Shelley’s heart. She held Puff the Magic Dragon’s pink tail in her hand.

Gia stood in front of her, the body of the dragon tucked against her chest, her mouth agape.

Shelley surged forward, stricken. She had torn the first kite her sister had ever made. “Oh my gosh, Gia, I am so sorry—”

“Stay back.” Gia held up a palm. She was shaking all over. “Haven’t you done enough damage?”

That was a knife straight through her heart. “I am sorry about Puff and I’m sorry if I drove you to cut up the quilt.”

“Give me that.” Gia snatched Puff’s tail from her hand.

Shelley’s chin quivered as she fought hard not to cry. There had been too many damn tears today.

“Why did you do it, Shelley?” Gia rasped.

“I didn’t mean to tear Puff—”

“I’m not talking about Puff!”

Shelley stepped back at the anger in Gia’s voice. Felt the salt water lap against her ankles.

Madison stood to one side, not getting involved, which was pretty stunning, considering she usually had to be right in the big middle of any conflict.

"Why did you sleep with Raoul? Why did you do that to Maddie? Why, Shelley? Why?"

Oh, here they were. Knocking on the door of the secret she'd kicked into her mental basement and locked the door closed on half a decade ago. It killed Shelley to say what she said next, to watch Gia's sweet face crumble with shame and remorse.

"Gia, I didn't sleep with Raoul . . . *you* did."

"Excuse me?" Gia blinked. Had Shelley just said what she thought she'd said? "That never happened."

"Gia, I *saw* you."

"You saw me having sex with Raoul?" Why was Shelley saying this? Gia shot a glance over at Madison, who stood with her arms crossed and eyes bugging.

"Well, I didn't actually *see* you doing the deed, but I put two and two together."

"What on earth are you talking about?" Gia tucked the torn kite under her arm, her heart slamming into her chest. She could sew Puff's tail back on. The kite would be all right. Too bad she couldn't say the same for the quilt she'd destroyed.

Gia turned to address Madison. "I swear to you, I never slept with Raoul."

"You don't remember it," Shelley murmured. "Because you were drunk off your gourd."

Drunk? Gia hadn't been drunk in years and years. Not since . . . oh wait . . . "When did this happen?"

"The Mardi Gras party two months before Madison's wedding."

Gia frowned, her world cocked topsy-turvy. She honestly had no idea what Shelley was talking about.

"The masquerade party we threw at the Moonglow Inn," Shelley went on. "You'd been flirting with that cute guest who'd come with his parents on vacation."

Gia's cheeks burned as the memories slowly unfolded in a mental snapshot of blurry images. That guy had been really cute. His name was Todd, or had it been Tad? Either way, dressed as Captain Jack Sparrow from *Pirates of the Caribbean*, he'd lured her to the beach to share a bottle of his homemade dandelion wine. They had both been eighteen, way underage, but he'd been cute and charming, and she'd always had a hard time saying no . . .

One thing led to another and they'd gotten pretty looped and were making out on a blanket stretched across the sand when Beach Patrol rousted them off the beach.

They mapped a plan to hook up later, returning to the party to mingle before reconnecting. Then Gia would give him a sign and slip off to her room and Todd or Tad or whatever his name was would follow her when he could.

The main problem? She shared a room with her sisters, so they'd have to be quick. Second problem? There were three Captain Jack Sparrows at the party and through the haze of dandelion wine, she wasn't totally sure which one he was when she crooked her finger and disappeared upstairs.

It was exciting. Thrilling. Gia had never done anything like this and she felt so adult. Getting drunk and having a wild Mardi Gras fling in costume. She could be anyone. *He* could be anyone.

She slunk up the stairs, darting glances over her shoulder to see if anyone was watching, and slipped into her bedroom, plunked down on the mattress to wait, and . . .

Promptly passed out.

Sometime later, she awoke still in her costume. She could still hear the party going on downstairs. She fumbled for her phone to see what time it was and to text Tad for his whereabouts. And found a text from him already waiting on her phone saying his parents had taken away his dandelion wine and grounded him.

So much for feeling like an adult.

She was about to flop back on the bed and go back to sleep when there was a short, soft knock and her door swung open to reveal Captain Jack Sparrow lounging insouciantly against the doorframe.

"You got away?" She breathed heavily and hopped to her feet.

He didn't speak, just sauntered in and closed the door behind him.

The second she'd kissed him Gia had known it was Raoul, even in her inebriated state, and she'd cried out and spun away from him, asked him what did he think he was doing?

So drunk that he was unable to answer, he'd stumbled to the floor and passed right out. Gia assumed he'd come looking for Maddie, and not knowing what else to do, Gia crawled back into bed, leaving Madison's soused fiancé for her to deal with.

When she'd awakened the next morning, with a vicious pounding headache, the bedroom was empty of her sisters and Raoul. She convinced herself it hadn't been Raoul after all, but Tad (or Todd) who had come to her room in his Captain Jack costume. Downstairs at brunch, she learned he and his family had already checked out and so she never got to ask if it *had* been him in her room. She'd stuffed the incident into the back of her mind and that was the end of that memory.

Until now.

Madison was staring at her with an icy coldness that chilled Gia to her bones. "Come clean, Gia," Maddie said in that same stony voice she used with Shelley but had never turned on her. "Time for the truth to come out. Did you sleep with Raoul?"

"No!"

"Then why would Raoul and Shelley say you did?"

"Please, you have to believe me," Gia begged, then turned to Shelley. "I never slept with Raoul. Why don't you tell us what you remember about that night?"

"I saw you on the beach with your date," Shelley said. "And I saw Raoul watching the two of you."

"Why were you keeping tabs on Raoul?" Gia scowled. "Were you obsessed with him?"

"I wasn't." Shelley shook her head. "I was keeping tabs on *you*. Where do you think Tad got the dandelion wine?"

"He said he made it."

Shelley rolled her eyes. "He was showing off. *I* made the wine in the cellar."

"As I recall, it had one helluva kick."

"I wanted you to have fun," Shelley said. "But not get into too much trouble. Boy, did that backfire."

"Seriously?" Madison glared at her. "You set Gia up to get drunk?"

The old shame nibbled at Shelley, gnawing away at the emotional gains she'd made since coming home. She paused before continuing, studying her older sister's face for a moment, the small pearl studs nestled in her earlobes, her proud chin tilted up, her eyelids lowered to cloak her vulnerability.

"I just wanted her to have fun. It was stupid, and I feel guilty as hell. That's why I never told a soul about what happened." Shelley sucked in a deep breath. "Not even when it would have saved me from your rage."

Tears formed in Madison's eyes. Blinking, she turned her head and pressed a knuckle against her eyelid.

Gia twisted the woven bracelet at her wrist, the torn dragon kite still clutched underneath her armpit. "Go on."

"I monitored you throughout the party, watching, but out of the way so you couldn't see me," Shelley explained.

"Where were you spying on me from?" Gia asked.

"*Spying* is a strong word—"

"*Spying,*" Gia said through clenched teeth.

Okay, that was the mood. She accepted it. Still in the weeds with her sisters. "On the back stairs landing."

From that third-floor vantage point Shelley had been able to look down at the party below and see the bedrooms on the second floor. But the spot had been dark, her viewpoint murky in the shadows.

"I watched you go up to your room and then

sometime later, I saw who I thought was Tad, dressed as Captain Jack Sparrow—geez, why does everyone think that costume is sexy—go up to your room. I saw you let him in and I saw you kiss him."

"It wasn't Tad," Gia said. "It was Raoul."

"Yeah, I found that out later. I stayed on the landing because I wasn't going into our room while you were having a romantic tryst and Madison was downstairs, ramrodding the party. I fell asleep and when I woke up, I saw your lover leaving your room. Except he'd taken off the Jack Sparrow wig and I saw it wasn't Tad you'd been with, but Raoul."

Shelley and Gia both darted glances at Madison, who stood like a stone, hugging herself.

"Here's what happened, Madison," Gia said, and she told the story of how Raoul had come into her room while she was expecting Tad. How he'd passed out on the floor and she'd left him there because she thought he'd come to find Madison.

"Why didn't you tell us when it happened?" Shelley asked.

"Because I wasn't sure it was Raoul. I was blitzed, and Tad was supposed to be coming to my room. When I woke up and there was no one there, I started to think I dreamt the whole thing."

Madison's face paled and she looked as if she might throw up. Her gaze moved from Gia to

Shelley and back again. "He was planning it all along."

"What?" Gia asked.

"Raoul. To take advantage of you. He planned it. We were supposed to attend the party in couple's costumes as French mimes. When he went to pick up his costume at the rental place he said they didn't have his size, so he'd gone with the Captain Jack outfit. But that was after he learned you were attending the party as Tad's date and Tad was wearing the same costume. I remember because I mentioned that Tad was already going as Captain Jack and Raoul should pick another costume. He said it was too much trouble to go back to the rental place." Madison was trembling all over. "Dear Lord, I was such an idiot."

"Not an idiot," Shelley soothed. "You were in love and you thought he loved you too. Raoul could be very charming."

"Why did Raoul say he had sex with me when he didn't?" Gia asked.

"Maybe he thought he did," Shelley said. "And was too drunk to remember. Or maybe it was a roundabout way of hurting Madison all over again."

"How blind was I?" Maddie put a hand to her mouth.

"Don't beat yourself up." Shelley moved to touch Madison's arm and when her sister didn't pull away, her heart filled with hope.

"I was so mean to you when he was the problem all along. You were trying to protect me when you kissed him."

"It's over, it's done." Shelley slid her arm around Madison's waist.

"You could have thrown Gia under the bus. You could have told the truth about why you kissed Raoul. Even though it wasn't true, you believed Gia had slept with him. Why didn't you tell me then?" Madison asked.

"I couldn't hurt Gia. She was an innocent in all this. She thought she was with Tad. Besides, I felt responsible. It was my wine." Shelley pressed her lips together to keep them from quivering.

"So you took all the blame." Madison's eyes were shiny with tears. "Oh, Shelley, I am so deeply sorry for the way I acted."

"And you didn't sleep with Raoul," Shelley said to Gia. "You don't know how happy that makes me. All these years I kept thinking I caused you to sleep with him."

"You protected me at your own peril." Gia's eyes misted.

Finally, after five long years Shelley saw that her sisters realized the sacrifices she'd made for them. Yes, she'd acted impulsively and gone about it all wrong, but she had always had their best interest at heart.

Madison slipped her arm around Gia. Gia dropped the kite to the sand to wrap her arm about Shelley's waist and the three of them stood there in a connected circle.

Shelley inhaled, taking in the moment of her redemption, fully appreciating how far they'd all come.

Cobalt Soul and Guru Meyer had taught her how to center herself through contemplation and reflection, but it was only by coming home and facing her past that she had found herself.

She didn't need to go beyond her interior borders to find freedom. Didn't need restless action or relentless distractions to escape from her emotions. Now, she felt free to be herself inside of her family and she found so much richness to feast on.

Accepting herself had in the long run translated into accepting her sisters, because when she was fully and unreservedly Shelley, her inner joy transcended her outer exploits and spilled out in glorious technicolor, tinting her entire world.

When she allowed her joy to bubble up and didn't try to contain her essence, life was a delight, and she found that she didn't need to do a lot except accept that her life was already brimming full to the top with love.

Completely engulfed in this beautiful moment of honest reunion, Shelley realized, on a level most profound, that life was a precious gift and she wasn't going to waste another second on hurt, anger, guilt, or fear.

Overcome with awe and gratitude, she brought her sisters in closer for a tight group hug.

And there she had it.

Her life lesson in a nutshell. The real source of her joy sprang from constant gratitude. Gratitude for her home, for Moonglow Cove, for her family, for the fierce, abiding love of her sisters.

Two passersby on the beach stopped to watch them, and Shelley recognized the elderly ladies as members of the Quilting Divas, Erma and Viv.

Viv turned to her friend. "Get a load of that, Erm. The Moonglow sisters are back together again, and by George, I can't help feeling that all is finally right with the world."

CHAPTER TWENTY-FIVE

Gia

CHAIN STITCHING: Chain stitching refers to the practice of stitching squares or blocks with one continuous length of thread rather than breaking between pieces.

The boardwalk was packed, families everywhere, summer in full swing. Colorful flags flapped in the breeze. Kids ran, giggling, playing hide-and-seek behind the benches and planter boxes. Beach music issued from outdoor speakers on the pier. The smell of cooking food wafted on the air—hot dogs, street tacos, funnel cakes. Gia could almost taste the fried dough dusted with cinnamon and powdered sugar.

Warm sun beat down, but goose bumps carpeted Gia's arms as she drew closer to the kiosk she'd once rented, now hallmarked with the sign STRAUS HAND-CARVED ART.

Her heart skipped a beat.

Mike saw her at the same time she saw him. He stood in the doorway of the kiosk, his gaze latched on to hers.

Breathlessly, she ran to him.

He gathered her in his arms and hugged her for a long minute.

They didn't speak. He locked up, hooked a Closed sign to the door of the kiosk, took her elbow, and guided her from the hustle and bustle of the boardwalk to a small park near the pier.

He led her to a picnic table in the shelter of the Moonglow pear trees. Sat her down on one side, took the bench opposite her. Stared into her eyes without a word.

Gia's heart started pounding.

Today, she had felt a dozen different things at once. Things had piled higher and higher. Her rage, her shame, her regret, her remorse, her embarrassment. And something else, a brave little flower of hope sending up a shoot through the toxic sludge, reaching for the sun.

She and her sisters had come together. They'd talked things out. Cleared the air. Now it was time to do the same with Mike.

He'd seen her at her absolute worst and he was still looking at her with that sultry gleam in his eyes.

She gulped and told him what had happened with her sisters. About the big misunderstanding that had dismantled their family. About how Shelley had taken the blame for Raoul's misdeeds.

"I'm glad things are on good footing with your sisters."

"Me too."

Their eyes locked.

"What about us?" she whispered. "Did I ruin things with you?"

He stuck out his hand. "C'mon."

"Where are we going?"

"Where we always go when we need to sort things out."

"But what about the kiosk? You're losing sales."

"I don't care about that. *You're* what matters."

He led her to his vehicle parked in the boardwalk parking lot. Opened up the sliding cover of his pickup bed, took out two kites. One was the blue fish kite she'd made him. The other was a store-bought unicorn kite.

"Allie's," he said by way of explanation as he handed Gia his niece's unicorn kite.

She thought about Puff, who'd sacrificed his tail to reunite the Moonglow sisters. "I need to make Allie a proper unicorn kite."

"She'd love that," he said.

He was whistling the song from Mary Poppins. "Let's Go Fly a Kite." How upset with her could he be if he was humming? Smiling, Gia joined in, singing along.

In his left hand he carried both kites. With his free hand, he took her hand and guided her back to the park. It wasn't particularly breezy, but there was enough wind that with a little effort they could achieve lift.

There, in the afternoon sunlight, they flew their kites.

As they flew, three children joined them with kites of their own. Three little girls carrying matching red kites.

Gia watched as the oldest helped the two younger ones get their kites in the air.

Aww, how sweet. But then, once all the kites were aloft, the oldest girl used her kite to smash into her sisters' kites. The younger sister fought back, tugging on the string to strangle the oldest sister's kite. Soon it was an all-out kite war among the siblings as they battled for control of their part of the sky. But they were laughing and smiling the entire time.

Gia reeled in her own kite, getting out of their way. Mike followed suit, and they returned the kites to his pickup.

She glanced around, looking for a parent, but the girls seemed to be on their own. It struck her then, how much responsibility had truly been on Maddie's shoulders. No wonder she'd been a prickly perfectionist. At only nine years old, Madison had thought it was up to her to make sure their home life ran smoothly.

Maddie hadn't had a childhood. Not from the time their parents died, and while Grammy had tried her best to give them love and structure, Madison still felt responsible.

It was why Gia had never questioned her.

Maddie was in charge and Maddie had been there. Her one solid constant.

Gia gulped. And this time the tears she cried weren't for herself, but for her sister and all Madison had lost. She understood Maddie in a way she'd not understood her before. Why success and achievement meant so much to her. Why she pushed and pushed and pushed. Because if she didn't, Madison feared everything would fall apart.

But now that Gia's own world had fallen apart, she was discovering that until things fell apart, the new couldn't come through. She realized that things falling apart was a natural part of the process and that as the old fell away, the bright and fresh could flourish and bloom.

"Are you okay?" Mike asked.

"I'm fine." She smiled. "We're all going to be fine. And I have *you* to thank for it."

"What did I do?" he asked, smiling.

"You were there," she said. "You were willing to lie for me to make my life easier. Only a true friend would do that."

"I love you, Gia. I know it makes you uncomfortable to hear me say that, but it's the truth. I can't change the way I feel about you."

"I don't want you to."

"What do you mean?"

She could see the pulse in the hollow of his throat throbbing, could feel a corresponding throb in her own chest. "I mean . . ." She took his hand in hers. "I'm sorry for being skittish. It threw me when you told me you'd bought that engagement ring for me. I wasn't ready to hear it."

"I get it," he said. "I was disappointed at your reaction, but I did spring it on you."

"I just need some time."

"I understand."

"It's not that I don't want you. I do. Want you."

"I understand," he repeated.

"You do?"

"Haven't you learned by now, Short Stack, that I mean what I say? I think it's smart to take your time. I was the one rushing things. I was just so happy to make our engagement real I didn't think about what a bind I was putting you in."

"Not a bind—"

"You do need to please yourself and if that means taking a year, I'll be here. If it means five years, I'll be here. If it means ten years. Ditto."

"You'd put your life on hold for me?"

"Gia, don't you get it? I *love* you. I would do anything for you. I admire that you had the ability to put on the brakes when you felt rushed and not get caught up in the excitement. It's the adult thing to do. Nothing will be lost by us taking our time. I want you to be one hundred percent certain that I am what you want."

"I'm already certain about that," she said. "I want to marry you, Mike. I love you with all my heart and soul. Have loved you from the time you took that five-year-old girl out on the beach and taught her how to fly a kite."

He put his hands on her shoulders, stared deeply into her eyes. "What's different since this morning?"

She smiled at him, honest and true. "I patched things up with my sisters. I see things differently now. I'm less scared."

"What were you scared of?"

"Things falling apart. I love my sisters more than anything in the world and yet, I thought I'd lost them forever. I lost my parents and now Grammy is so ill, we're going to lose her, too, eventually. I know that."

"So why the change of heart?"

"I experienced a paradigm shift when I learned Shelley sacrificed herself to spare my feelings, and to save Madison from a huge mistake. I thought all this time she was being selfish, when she was the exact opposite."

"But how did Shelley's sacrifice adjust the way you look at the world . . . at me . . . at *us?*"

"She was so brave. She's always been brave. She calls it recklessness. Others have called her impetuous, but Shelley is just brave. She follows her heart. She takes chances. Sure, she gets hurt, but she lives. Fully lives with abandon. I want to be brave like that. I want to take chances. I can't do that if I'm busy trying to please everyone else."

"I agree, so don't say you want to marry me just to please me."

"This isn't about you, Straus." She laughed at his confusion. "It's about me. I want *you*. But there is one small catch."

"What's that?" he asked, looking a bit nervous.

"I got a call from Pippa Grandon. Remember she told me she'd give me a month to think about her job offer?"

"Did you say yes?"

"I did." Gia grinned. "But that means I can't start planning my wedding until I get those kites done."

"Fair enough," he said.

"Do you still have that ring?"

He reached in his front pocket and pulled out the ring. "Do you really like it? Should I buy a better one?"

"Don't you dare. You bought this ring for me and it's the one I want."

"I want you to be pleased with it."

"I'm thrilled."

"Honestly?"

"Are we doing this or not?"

He laughed, took her left hand in his, and sank down on one knee.

Her whole body shook, and her heart sang, and

the sun was shining, and there were three red kites bobbing in the sky behind him.

"Gia Jasmine Clark, will you do me the honor of becoming my wife? For real this time?"

"Oh, Mike." She laughed. The day that had started out as one of the crappiest days of her life was turning out to be the best. "I only have one thing to say."

"Yes?"

"What took you so damn long?"

"Is that a yes?"

"Yes, yes, yes!"

He slipped the ring on her finger, stood up, enveloped her in his arms, and as those three red kites flew over their heads, they kissed with the passion that only lifelong friends who'd recently become lovers could feel.

In the sweetness of sunset, in the circle of Mike's arms, Gia felt her true self emerge, whole and complete. She was fully present to the moment and aware of the unity of existence while at the same time holding on to the sense of self she'd found by letting go of pleasing others.

She and Mike were part of something larger than themselves. As were she and her sisters. They were connected, not only to each other, but to Moonglow Cove, and the big wide world beyond. They were part of the ebb and flow of life. Their love for each other had helped them to transform and break down barriers.

As enduring as the ocean waves, unconditional love was the cornerstone of transformation.

Gia's heart was wide open, and she was no longer afraid. She let go of suffering, let go of the pain of the past. She was here now, with the man she loved, and everything was absolutely perfect.

With undying gratitude, she looked up at the sky, at the three red kites bobbing in the dying light, and whispered the truest words she knew. "Thank you."

CHAPTER TWENTY-SIX

Moonglow Cove

FUSIBLE WEB: A material that has been treated with an adhesive that fuses fabric pieces together when pressed with a warm iron.

Word spread from one side of Moonglow Cove to the other. The Moonglow sisters were back together again, twenty years after they first came to live in the stately old Victorian at the end of Moonglow Boulevard, and the townsfolk rejoiced.

But there was more to the reunion than simple homecoming.

The sisters bore the scars of five years spent apart; they had become warriors through trials and tribulations. Their union was stronger now than ever, their suffering forging them into the steel of courage, truth, and right action.

They were sisters in every sense of the word, banding together to make their grandmother's final days extraordinary. They expanded their world to include their loving community of Quilting Divas, the Chamber of Commerce, and the hospital employees. They threw galas and fundraisers for those in need, hosting quilting bees and beach events.

With their blond hair blowing in the Gulf breezes as their smiles pumped everyone around them with enthusiasm, the sisters conducted yoga classes and wreath-making workshops and kiteflying lessons. Every night that endless summer, they linked arms and walked along the beach, before returning home to Grammy and Darynda.

When summer turned to fall, and Grammy's health improved, she moved in with Darynda closer to the city center. Fun-loving Shelley transformed the Moonglow Inn into a vibrant B&B with a gourmet chef, a six-month waiting list, and stellar Yelp reviews. She and the chef hit it off and food was not the only thing cooking in that sizzling kitchen.

Responsible Madison went back to Manhattan to her homemaking show and reconnected with her ex-fiancé, Finn. They worked through their issues and the grief over losing their baby that had torn them apart and were rebuilding their love and trust with each other. Madison stayed in contact with her sisters every day and flew home once a month to see them.

Gia moved in with Mike and she worked hard to fill Pippa Grandon's wedding kite order. Mike helped in the evenings when he'd finished his woodworking. Together they got the job done in half the time and were able to move on to planning their wedding.

The sisters *looked* like moonglow—shimmering, golden-haired, luminous. There was magic to them. A softness. A shining. A warm, gentle light.

Once again, the sisters brought smiles to faces and the entire town embraced them. Loved them. Rejoiced when they all came together for Gia and Mike's wedding day.

It was a joyous family reunion. Things had shifted and changed, but one thing stayed constant and enduring, their deep abiding love for one another.

People whispered, "If the Moonglow sisters can make it through the worst of times, so can we."

Indeed, they were the shining example of a family transmuted by overwhelming grief into open acceptance of the sweet mystery of life. They had all come full circle back to wholeness.

EPILOGUE

Helen

GRANDMOTHER'S FLOWER GARDEN: Grandmother's Flower Garden is a popular and traditional quilt pattern made using clusters of hexagons to create flowers.

Gia's Wedding Day, One Year Later

My Dearest Darling Granddaughters,

As I write this, I sit on the back veranda in my favorite Adirondack chair, watching as Gia and Mike take their wedding vows in front of the altar he built for her with his own hands. Beyond them the Gulf of Mexico stretches out true and blue, a timeless reminder that love is enduring.

Draped across my lap is the Grandmother's Flower Garden quilt that Madison, Shelley, Darynda, and I sewed for Gia's wedding present, created from the remnants of the quilt Gia destroyed when she stopped trying to please everyone, including me. She passed her challenge with flying colors. The quilt now stands as the perfect symbol of what you girls have learned. That the old must fall away to make room for the new.

Holding on to the past is what hamstrung us all. Letting go of the hurt and embracing the love and the people we have in the present moment is the key to happiness. Never forget this, my loves.

Quilting holds the key.

I hope you continue to use the skills I've taught you. Use your memories to create something that keeps you warm at night, instead of clinging to worn-out emotions that tie you to past mistakes. We are all flawed, but we are also all perfect in our humanity.

Forgive one another. Love one another.

That is the lesson of the quilt.

Pyewacket, the scamp, is hiding in the flowers atop the altar, and I pray she does not decide to jump down onto them when the minister tells Mike he may kiss his bride. Although I suppose it might make for a lively ceremony and what a future quilt that memory will make.

Looking at the layer cake set on the table awaiting the beach reception, I feel so much joy. Three layers of flavor. A beautiful compromise thought up by our dear friend Anna Drury, now your sister-in-law, as each layer represents each of your personalities. White cake on the bottom for our traditionalist, Madison, devil's food cake in the middle for our rule-breaking Shelley, and strawberry cake at the top for our peacemaking Gia.

The three of you unified again, as it should be.

So many symbols today and if you see tearstains on this letter, it is only because I am so very happy.

My heart overflows to see Madison with her Finn, who keeps his hand so softly on her pregnant belly. This little one will thrive and survive and be the first one to bring forth the new generations in Moonglow Cove. And Shelley grinning at her sous chef, Sebastian, who kneads the back of her neck as they sit together. I sense another wedding in the offing.

I watch as Mike takes Gia's hand and puts his ring on her finger and vows to love, honor, and cherish her to the end of his days. I know with certainty that he will. Never have I seen such devotion, except in the eyes of my own partner. I recall, in the misty way of newlyweds, our sweet Christmas wedding, one month after I finished chemo, when I was blessed to marry the woman I have loved for over fifty years. It was thrilling to publicly declare my love for her and to have all of you there as witnesses.

These things I will remember until I draw my dying breath. Love. Devotion. Selflessness. How all you girls came together to save the inn, to save me, and in turn, to save each other.

Bliss fills me now as I look back on what we've regained. Our sense of family. Our closeness. Our unconditional acceptance of one another's strengths and flaws.

I am prouder of you than I have ever been, and I'm filled with the knowledge that you girls are strong and resilient and can weather life's storms without me.

—With all my abiding love, Grammy

Helen Chapman finished writing the love letter to her granddaughters, set down her pen, and turned to the white-haired woman sitting beside her. "I'm ready to go. They don't need me anymore."

Tears streamed down Darynda's face as she leaned in to kiss Helen. "When the time comes . . ."

"You know what to do." Then Helen closed her eyes, sank back against the Adirondack chair, clung tight to Darynda's hand, and with a smile on her face, listened to the loving sounds of her family around her.

And it was the happiest moment of her life.

About the Author

Lori Wilde is the *New York Times*, *USA Today*, and *Publishers Weekly* bestselling author of eighty-seven works of romantic fiction. She's a three-time Romance Writers of America RITA Award finalist and a four-time nominee of the Romantic Times Reviewers' Choice Award. She has won numerous other awards as well. Her books have been translated into twenty-six languages with more than four million copies sold worldwide. Her breakout novel, *The First Love Cookie Club*, has been optioned for a TV movie.

Lori is a registered nurse with a BSN from Texas Christian University. She holds a certificate in forensics and is also a certified yoga instructor.

A fifth-generation Texan, Lori lives with her husband, Bill, in the Cutting Horse Capital of the World, where they run Epiphany Orchards, a writing/creativity retreat for the care and enrichment of the artistic soul.

Letter from the Author

Unlike the Moonglow sisters, I did not grow up in a bucolic coastal area, but rather, my childhood more closely resembled Darynda's. I was a sand hill tacky sprouted in the arid wilds of West Texas, complete with grass burrs, rattlesnakes, sandstorms, coyotes, and cowboys. By the time I was twelve, I'd learned to ride horses, shoot rifles, raise cattle, and make mesquite bean jelly.

I have vivid memories of my maternal grandmother and her friends gathering to quilt on the back porch. Just like in the book, my grandfather suspended eyebolts to the porch ceiling for the quilting frame so that my Gammie could sew outdoors in the cool of the evenings.

Gammie was a staunch believer in hand quilting. She was a precise, hardworking woman, and you could see her personality in her tightly controlled stitches; she created the most beautiful quilts. She was also a conscientious hostess, making sure her guests had freshly squeezed lemonade and homemade baked goods to nibble on as they quilted.

I'd lounge in the shade of the crepe myrtle hedges, sipping nectar from honeysuckle blossoms and eavesdropping on their stories. If I was really quiet, they wouldn't notice me and send me on my way when they started in on the juicy gossip. That's where I learned who was mad at whom, who was doing things they weren't supposed to do, and who was keeping secrets. Their talks stoked my imagination and helped form me as a writer.

My passion for the coast came later, when I took my first trip to Galveston at age twenty-one and fell in love at first sight. The southern beaches were so different from the desert west where I grew up (well, except for the sand; there was that unifying factor), and I couldn't get enough of the water.

I vacationed in Galveston every summer for thirteen years, soaking up the fascinating history. I borrowed heavily from those experiences while creating Moonglow Cove, adding in dashes of other Texas coastal towns I visited—Port Aransas, Corpus Christi, and South Padre Island among them.

In writing *The Moonglow Sisters*, my intention was to marry memories of my homespun childhood with my love for the coast. This book was a true labor of love and I do so hope you enjoyed reading it.

Reading Group Guide

1. Gia has spent her life suppressing her own needs in favor of keeping the peace. Have there been times in your life where you put the needs of others ahead of your own? Did your identity get buried in the process? How did you find yourself again?
2. During a vulnerable time in her life, Shelley got sucked into a yoga cult. Do you have trouble understanding how people get lured into group thinking? Or have you ever found yourself in an environment that looked good on the surface but turned out to have a darker underbelly you didn't see at first?
3. The Moonglow sisters were so close until they weren't. In what ways have your familial relationships changed as you've aged? Are you closer to your loved ones now or have time and circumstances impacted your closeness? In what ways?
4. What do you think of the way Helen's daughter, Beth, turned her back on her mother for who she loved? What do you think motivated Beth's behavior? Fear? Shame? Or something else?
5. Do you think Helen ever regretted her

decision to take in her three orphaned granddaughters? Why or why not?

6. What do you think about Mike having bought an engagement ring for Gia long before they had a romantic relationship? Have you ever loved someone from afar without letting them know?
7. The town of Moonglow Cove is a tight-knit community. Have you ever been part of a group that you could count on when you needed them?
8. In her letter to Gia, Helen writes that Shelley is the kite, Madison is the anchor, and Gia is the string. What popped into your head when you read that line?
9. Everyone in the book had some kind of secret. Do you believe most people have secrets they've never shared with anyone? Do you have secrets? If so, how has keeping secrets affected you?
10. What do you think of Pyewacket? How do you imagine she got her name?

Center Point Large Print
600 Brooks Road / PO Box 1
Thorndike, ME 04986-0001 USA

(207) 568-3717

US & Canada:
1 800 929-9108
www.centerpointlargeprint.com